C000226650

About the Author

In 1978 Peter Whalley abandoned teaching to write full-time. Since then he has written eight crime novels and written extensively for television and radio, including over two hundred episodes of Coronation Street.

Also by Peter Whalley

The Baby War

PETER WHALLEY

Ringpull

First published by Ringpull Press in 1993

Ringpull Press Ltd, 86A Church Street, Littleborough OL15 8AU

A CIP catalogue record for this book
is available from the British Library

ISBN 1 898051 00 3

Typeset by Datix International Ltd, Bungay, Suffolk
Printed in England by Clays Ltd, St Ives plc

1

Lauren took in the room at a glance: battered chairs arranged around a knee-height, Formica coffee-table, a carpet of faded, indistinct pattern, and pale green walls on which a number of posters were Sellotaped. A threadbare attempt at comfort and intimacy which failed to convince.

She held out a hand experimentally and watched it tremble. Calm down, she told herself. Deep breaths.

'You all right?' asked James. She saw he had flopped into one of the chairs, looking relaxed, indifferent to his surroundings.

'Nervous,' she said, but it came out in a near-whisper so that she had to clear her throat and repeat: 'I feel nervous.'

'I don't see why. They only want to have a look at us, see what we're like.'

She resented his detached, easy manner but was determined not to be irritated by it. 'I feel like we're doing some sort of audition,' she said. She had once been a dancer, ballet to start with and then modern dance, though early hopes of a career had come to nothing and she had gone to University to read Chemistry.

'Well, all right,' said James. 'Think of it as an audition if it makes you any happier.'

'It doesn't. I always used to throw up before auditions.' She saw his smile turn to a look of alarm when she added, 'Might throw up now.'

'You're not serious . . . ?'

'Oh, don't worry. I didn't eat any breakfast.'

One of the posters was an appeal for blood donors; another for Ethiopian famine relief. She couldn't settle but went from one to the other and then back again. A third explained how to claim social security benefits. 'Come and sit down,' said James gently, patting the chair beside him.

She did so and found there was a mirror opposite, part of the room's random furnishings. Its silvering had decayed but it still gave a view of James in his herring-bone sports jacket and knitted tie, sitting with his arms folded. Something about him – the tie probably – made him seem unfamiliar, a stranger she had brought with her only because having a husband was a prerequisite for the application.

She shifted slightly to obtain a view of herself, then winced. She had begun the morning in her 'Save The Whale' t-shirt and a pair of loose, cotton trousers, then, thinking it smarter and so safer, had changed into the high-shouldered suit she sometimes wore for working at the garage, then had had misgivings about that too and had rejected it in favour of a burnt-orange dress with broad butterfly belt and matching high-heels. She pulled her coat closed, hiding the worst of it.

'Wish I hadn't worn this dress.'

'Why? You look nice.'

'Bit obvious though. Looks like I've dressed for the occasion.'

She wanted to get to her feet and do some stretch exercises, limber up to absorb some of the tension. But, of course, it was out of the question,

2

lest she be caught in the act and pronounced eccentric.

'You don't think they're watching us?'

'Watching . . . ?'

'Yes. Got a spy-hole somewhere. Or a camera even.'

She knew she was talking wildly. It was the pressure of being in the room with a stranger.

She heard footsteps approaching from outside the door. 'Shhh,' she warned, though James hadn't spoken. Then the door opened and a young woman appeared. First impression was of someone younger than Lauren had expected, with frizzy, auburn hair and a wide, generous mouth.

'Mr and Mrs Eaglesham . . . ? said the young woman, approaching.

'Yes,' said Lauren, and lurched forward out of her chair, aware she was smiling inanely. Beside her, James had also stood, so that there was an awkward hiatus of hand-shaking before they subsided again into their seats and the young woman placed the file she was carrying on the coffee-table. She was perhaps in her late twenties, registered Lauren, anyway no more than thirty. And was wearing faded jeans and a red-and-green striped sweatshirt, with thin, gold bangles and a wedding-band on her finger.

'My name's Stella,' she said. 'Stella Priestley. And I'm a social worker, and I work for the agency here.' She took a sheet of paper from her file – inside which Lauren caught an unnerving glimpse of her own handwriting. 'And you're James Eaglesham . . . ? And you're Lauren Eaglesham . . . ?' Lauren nodded and smiled. Couldn't stop herself smiling.

Till what Stella Priestley said next made her hold her breath. The room seemed to tilt beneath her and she gripped the arms of her chair.

3

'And you've come to us because you want to adopt a child.'

It was as though a secret nourished between herself and James and never publicly confessed had been wrenched into the open. They had told no-one, superstitiously fearing that to do so might damage their chances. To hear it now declared aloud was such a shock that Lauren had to fight the impulse to deny it.

'Yes,' she said.

'Well, good,' said Stella. 'That's what we're here for.' Another smile then, 'Of course I've read your letter and the form you filled in but perhaps, if we ignore them for the moment, you could just tell me in your own words what led you to apply.'

Lauren caught James' sideways glance, cueing her to answer.

'Well,' she said, and cleared her throat. 'We've been married for eight years, nearly nine in fact. And we've been trying for a child for most of that time, only it hasn't happened. We even had fertility tests. That was, what, three . . . ?' She turned to James, knowing it was almost exactly three years ago to the day but wanting to include him, to show this Stella that they were in it together.

'About three,' he nodded.

'Three years ago. But they didn't reveal anything out of the ordinary. And I'm sure we're doing it right,' she said, risking the small joke, then immediately regretting it. 'But, well, the longer it's gone on, the more we've had to face the fact that I'm probably never going to get pregnant.'

'And would that be such a terrible thing?'

She thought for a moment it was a bad-taste joke, but no – Stella was waiting for an answer.

'Yes,' she said defiantly. 'Yes, it would. We both want children. Always have.'

She felt her voice wavering, finding it difficult to speak calmly about such a thing to this woman who had the power – or anyway a share in the power – to give her what she wanted so desperately. It wouldn't do to become over-emotional and out-of-control.

'Suppose . . . ' asked Stella, 'suppose you were to adopt a child and then found you became pregnant after all?'

This was all right, one of the questions they had anticipated and rehearsed.

'Oh, well, that would be wonderful. Because then they'd be company for one another. And we've always thought we'd like to have more than one child eventually so . . . wonderful.'

'And have you thought how old you would like this child to be?'

They had discussed this too. Had agonized over the dilemma: would it improve their chances to say any age or would that merely give the impression they hadn't given it sufficient thought?

'Well, ideally we'd like a baby. But if not, well, then a toddler or – '

'But not an older child? Not a teenager?'

'Well, I suppose – '

'No,' said James firmly.

'Probably not,' she admitted, pressed into reluctant agreement. Though it irked her that this should be his first real contribution, sure only of what he *didn't* want.

'So ideally a baby,' said Stella. 'Well, I've got to tell you that most people say that, and obviously we're not able to satisfy everybody.' Lauren was gripped by a small panic, feeling their answer had

5

lost them points. Was it too late to retract, to say they would take a child of any age? But there was another, tougher question to be faced. 'And would you want the child to be white, like yourselves?'

'Not, er, not necessarily.' It was an aspect she and James had edged around, not expecting they would be called upon so soon to declare themselves.

'So you'd be happy to consider a mixed-race child for example?'

'Yes.' Then, because this was, after all, the truth – she would be happy, more than happy, to consider any child – she repeated it more firmly. 'Yes.' And was encouraged to hear James muttering his agreement beside her.

'And suppose the child were handicapped in some way?'

This time, as she hesitated, it was James who spoke. 'I suppose we'd prefer it not to be.'

She made a sound, not knowing what she wished to say but feeling she must qualify the bald rejection. They both turned to her.

'Prefer it, yes,' she said. 'But not . . . I mean . . . ' She saw herself in the mirror, making a gesture of helplessness. Beggars can't be choosers – was that what she was saying? She hadn't intended it to be like this, picking and choosing, laying down conditions. She had come wanting only to tell them she would love and care for any child, any child in the world.

'But you're not exactly looking for a handicapped child,' said Stella, who seemed to understand. 'Well, few people are, at least not as a first choice.'

The questions now seemed to be over and Stella was talking, telling them of the problems adoption brought with it, in addition to the normal stresses and strains of child-rearing. Processes of binding were different and accelerated; expectations were sometimes unrealistic. And there remained always the element of the unknown, the child's inheritance of genes and characteristics, which might at any time assert itself.

Well, yes, thought Lauren, these might be problems for many people, but not for her. There was nothing she couldn't overcome. How could she let Stella know this, impress on her that this wasn't your average sort of applicant but one desperate enough to overcome any odds?

Stella was now talking about the law and the safeguards it imposed. Lauren realized she wasn't listening and tried to make herself concentrate. It wouldn't do to appear inattentive – to give the impression she was someone who, if handed a child, might one day forget where she had left it.

An adopted child – this was the gist of it – had to be told it was adopted. If, after the age of eighteen, it wished to trace its natural parents, then it had that right. The adoptive parents, for their part, would be given a full medical and social history of the child's natural parents, though not their names or anything that might help identify them. The natural parents would remain cyphers, always slightly out of the picture.

Does this mean we're going to be accepted, wondered Lauren. Would Stella be bothering to tell us all this if she saw us as no-hopers?

'Now,' said Stella, 'do you want to continue with your application?'

'Oh, yes. Definitely.' James was nodding beside her. Well, say something then, Lauren silently urged.

But Stella seemed satisfied and continued, 'Well, what I'd like you to do is write me a letter. I know you've already done that once, but this time a less formal one. Setting out your reasons for wanting to adopt and what you think you can offer a child and ... well, anything else that seems relevant. Something about your own backgrounds, that kind of thing.'

'Fine, yes,' said Lauren, suddenly wanting to be out of there. They had crossed the first hurdle; now she needed to re-group her emotional defences before coming to a second.

But James, silent for so long, delayed them with a question: 'And what will happen after that?'

'Well, assuming we consider your application to be for good reasons – which I'm sure we will – then we'll have a series of four or five longish interviews. These will be at your home. Basically we're trying to find out as much as we can about you. Oh, and we'll need some references, but I'll tell you about those later. Then we draw up a report and submit it to the Panel – they're the sort of governing body of the agency – and they'll decide whether to accept your application or not.'

'I see,' said Lauren. 'Thank you.' And began to stand, but then had to stay where she was as James followed up with a supplementary: 'And do we have to appear before this . . . this Panel?'

Stella smiled and shook her head. 'They don't meet you. They just have our report and, whatever they decide, well . . . '

'That's it.'

'It is. But don't worry about it. You're still on square one. There's an awfully long way to go yet.'

'Yes, but . . . have I got this right?' Lauren saw he had switched into his pernickity mode – where everything had to be spelt out meticulously before he would leave it alone. It annoyed her at the best of times. 'This Panel who we never meet and who never meet us – they decide whether we can adopt or not . . . ?'

'Yes.'

'And if they say no . . . ?'

Which they won't, insisted Lauren to herself, not in a million years. So you needn't answer that. Just let's get out please.

But Stella did answer: 'If the Panel say no, then there's no appeal, no second chance. If they say no, then you would get a letter and that would be the end of it.'

Outside at last, they walked through the city centre to where they had parked their car. Lauren's overriding feeling was of relief that at least they had avoided disasters and were still in the running. They might have done better – she hadn't really communicated with this Stella Priestley, not really got through to her – but there would be other opportunities, first in this letter they had to write, meaning she had to write, and then in the interviews to follow.

'Well, what do you think?' she said, when they had passed the grey stones of the library and post office and still he had offered no opinion.

'Much as I'd expected.'

'Wasn't she young? I'd expected somebody . . . well, older.'

And hadn't she smiled a lot. Beguilingly, putting them at their ease where the improvised surroundings had failed to do so. Perhaps she was one of those permanent smilers so that what you at first took as warmth and approval in fact meant nothing, was no more than a nervous tic.

All around them, Lauren saw mothers pushing

9

babies in prams or toddlers in push-chairs. They passed a babywear shop, bright with outfits, and her step faltered.

'It's a bit early for that,' said James, sounding amused.

'I know.' She fell back into step beside him. The clouds were gathering, typical of the miserable summer, and there was a faint dampness on the air. The babies in their prams would need to be covered, she thought.

'They will accept us, won't they?' she asked him, wanting reassurance. 'Don't you think?'

'I'm sure they'll accept you. Not so sure about me.'

It may have been intended light-heartedly, but she couldn't contradict him, knowing all too well she had been the one making the running, during the interview and in everything that had led to it. She who had found out about the agency and had written to them. Not that James had ever objected. He had merely pointed out the difficulties – her having to give up her job for example – with the air of one seeking to anticipate pitfalls. When what she had wanted had been somebody up there alongside her, hammering on the agency door, not a nitpicking, legal type, monitoring progress with a critical eye.

It was a dangerous course they had embarked upon, this application, changing things irrevocably. If James let her down, if his lukewarm approach should sabotage their application, it would be the end between them. Even if they failed and she never knew the reason for certain, there would remain that residue of suspicion – that it had been *his* fault – to eat away at their marriage and bring it down.

Don't think about it, she cautioned herself, and

took his hand as they walked along. Surely somewhere in the whole wide world, among those millions
of infants, there was one she might be allowed to
love and cherish. Then she would guard it with her
life and would love and cherish James too for being
its father.

2

Marcus knew he had only himself to blame. Where lunch with one beautiful woman might have been a delightful adventure, lunch with two was threatening disaster.

From the moment he had introduced them and each had raked the other with a critical gaze, the omens had not been good. Claire was in halter top and shorts which called attention to her pert figure and revealed the small butterfly tattooed on her left shoulder. Her blonde hair was in baby-doll ringlets. Her mouth was vivid with lipstick but pulled into an expression of boredom and topped off by impenetrable sun-glasses, which might have been excusable had not Marcus taken pains to ensure their table was well within the shade of the canopy.

Ragula, the older of the two women, was positively demure in a white cotton dress. Her jet-black hair was pulled back and tied in a scarf of white-and-gold. It was a display of elegance and restraint, beside which Claire was a spoiled cherub, delightful and unruly and, Marcus noted with alarm, already gulping down her third glass of Chardonnay.

'Why, you look charming,' Ragula had exclaimed when he introduced them.

'Thanks. You look very nice too,' said Claire,

then had shot Marcus a warning look, decipherable even through the sun-glasses.

And I deserve it too, thought Marcus ruefully. To have made the offer of lunch to Ragula while Claire was still in his house and in his bed smacked of someone who either didn't know his own mind or who had an insatiable and dangerous curiosity. 'So have you a new girl-friend to tell us about?' Marie-Louise, his sister-in-law, would ask whenever they met. What would he tell her now? That he was in the middle of a sea-change, yet again about to bestow his emotions elsewhere?

It made him wonder about himself, this urge for fresh conquests. Was it simply – as Marie-Louise had often attempted to reassure him – that he had yet to find the right woman, or was there something in his make-up that condemned him to be forever seeking the comfort of strangers?

They were all three of them speaking English for Claire's benefit, though Ragula had twice slipped into French as though forgetting, then apologised – 'Of course, you don't speak French, my dear, do you?'

'No. Believe it or not, there are lots of languages I don't speak,' said Claire, whose gaze was either on the distant Alps or on her own immaculately mani-cured nails.

Improvising hastily, Marcus asked her about her recent trip to Salzburg, but she responded with a sulky indifference, saying only that the shops were expensive and there seemed to be a lot of churches. It was left to Ragula to enthuse on the baroque architecture of that city, while Claire helped herself to more Chardonnay.

'Claire is a cabaret artiste, a singer,' Marcus of-fered, hoping this might prove a subject on which they might dwell for a while in peace.

13

'Really,' said Ragula brightly.

But he saw that Claire was concentrating on her lasagne and refusing to be drawn. 'That was how we met,' he continued. 'Claire was performing at the Dorchester, in London.'

'How interesting,' said Ragula, and turned to the other woman. 'And are you over here for your work?'

'No,' said Claire, and continued eating.

Marcus took it upon himself to elaborate: 'She is visiting me. Having a small holiday.'

She had been with him three weeks, after surprising him with her phone-call taking up his long-standing offer. He saw her as a gypsy, making her home wherever fortune landed her, and wondered whether this was why he felt so at ease with her – because her demands on him were so light and because she spoke so seldom of the future?

He saw with a feeling of relief that she did at last wish to speak. She had put down her fork and was smiling.

'Let me ask you something.' She was addressing Ragula. 'Something I don't understand about this place.'

'About Geneva?'

'Yes.'

'And what don't you understand, my dear?'

'Why do all the women act so, you know, so smug?'

Marcus winced. He had been present before when Claire had cut up rough and knew her to be no respecter of persons or places.

'I really don't think – ' he attempted to interpose, but she was still speaking, ignoring him and addressing Ragula.

'Got their noses in the air and their hands sort of

14

clasped in front of their fannies all the time. I mean am I the only one who fucks around here?'

Normally Marcus enjoyed Geneva, with its patrician atmosphere and operatic setting between flat lake and towering mountains. Above all else, it was a sanctuary. His trade as arms-dealer had taught him that civilisation was the exception, not the rule, and so was to be cherished. To watch the sober Swiss citizens walk their dogs through well-tended gardens was always a welcome respite on his return from a business trip spent haggling with tribal war-lords, messianic generals and lunatics of all persuasions.

It had not been his intention to spend this particular lunchtime acting as peace-keeper over a terrain of crystal and white table-cloth. He had known Ragula Veuillet for some time, but vaguely, as someone to chat to as he browsed her small art gallery, which was off the Rue de l'Athénée and specialised in contemporary, mainly American, artists. On his last visit, two days ago, he had browsed for longer than his interest in art – though genuine – could excuse. She had brought him coffee and entertained him with her account of her two failed marriages, both to artists she still exhibited. He had bought a small Weidmann, she congratulated him on his good taste and he invited her to lunch.

Was this because he believed he might at last have found the 'right woman' of Marie-Louise's imagination or was he merely addicted to the chase and couldn't help himself?

The one thing he hadn't counted on was that Claire would return early from her sight-seeing jaunt to Salzburg and so join them on the terrace of the Grappe d'Or restaurant.

At least her observations on Swiss womanhood didn't seem to have shaken Ragula, who was now questioning Marcus about his own armaments business. Well, he was happy to talk about that. There at least his life had purpose and direction. It was a relief, too, to see that Claire seemed to have lost interest and was gazing inquisitively around her at their fellow diners.

'And so when you've got all these guns,' asked Ragula, 'who do you sell them to?'

'Anybody. Depends who wants to buy.'

Her smile suggested she didn't believe him. 'Anybody at all?'

'Providing they have the money, yes.' He detected her disapproval and prompted: 'You think that's terrible?'

'No. Because I don't think you really mean it.'

'Why not? I'm in business. I'm not a politician or a moral philosopher. I'll sell to anybody who has the money to buy.'

'You may not be a moral philosopher, but you are still a human being.'

'Oh, I hope I'm that, yes.' Risking a smile. And then a sideways glance at Claire, but she was still paying no attention.

'Well, then how can you sit there and tell me you would sell to any murderer or terrorist, just so long as you can make your profit?'

'I don't think I put it quite like that,' said Marcus, raising his hands in a gesture of self-defence. Though, in truth, he found her accusations familiar and easily parried. They were the same that had once tormented his own conscience and with which he was still taxed by acquaintances whenever they discovered that the source of his wealth wasn't banking or pharmaceuticals.

'I don't care how you put it,' said Ragula. 'It sounds like a pretty shitty business to me.'

16

Her sudden vehemence surprised him but he didn't object. In fact, he admired her boldness, the way she had come out with it to his face.

Claire said, 'Sounds a pretty shitty business to me too,' and giggled. So perhaps she was at last beginning to enjoy herself.

'OK,' he said, addressing himself to Ragula. 'I can understand that anybody who sells guns to murderers and terrorists doesn't rate very highly in your book.'

'Too damn right they don't.'

'But then, you see, these people I sell to, they don't see themselves as murderers and terrorists. They see themselves as . . . well, you name it . . . as freedom-fighters or as martyrs in a holy war or as down-trodden people taking up arms in self-defence.'

He saw that Claire had closed her eyes and was holding her face to the sun. Expressing her boredom or, hopefully, about to fall asleep?

'That might be how they see themselves,' said Ragula doggedly. 'I'm sure it is. Doesn't mean that you can't tell the difference.'

'Between martyrs and murderers?'

'Yes.'

'I can't.' She began to protest but he insisted. This was something he believed in. He wanted her to see that he wasn't being flippant or arguing for the sake of it. 'I'm serious. Take who you want . . . the Jews in Palestine . . . Biafrans . . . the A.N.C. in South Africa . . . the Afghan Mujahadeen . . . Are these murderers?'

She said nothing. He pressed on, paying her the compliment of not pulling his punches.

'Or are you saying it's only governments that should be armed? Governments that should have a monopoly on guns?'

17

She hesitated, then said, 'No, but – '

'I hope not. Because that would only stand up if they also had a monopoly on justice and compassion. Whereas most governments . . . well, I don't have to tell you about most governments. In fact, it might be better if it were the people who were armed and governments who weren't allowed to be.'

He saw that now it was she who was surprised, taken aback by the force of his response. She raised an eyebrow and said, 'You'll have to give me time to think about that one.'

Before he could reply, his attention was claimed by a waiter appearing beside him. 'Excuse me, monsieur, but your car is blocking another one that wishes to leave – '

Was it? Well, yes, they had arrived a touch late for the booking, made so by Claire's unexpected appearance. The marked off spaces had been taken and he had left the car by the entrance.

'Yes, I'm sorry – ' he said, but the waiter was gesturing for him to remain at the table.

'There's no need for you to disturb yourself, monsieur. If you would just be so good as to let me have the keys . . . ?'

'Certainly.' Marcus fished them from his pocket and handed them over. 'And I think we'd like some coffee if you could organize that.' The waiter nodded and went away.

He heard Claire give a small but expressive cough and saw that Ragula was lighting a cigarette. Claire coughed again and wafted a hand before her face. Ragula ignored her and said, 'But I still think it's a pretty shitty business,' but now didn't sound so concerned about it. He sensed that she had said her piece and he had said his and that neither was going

18

to let it alter what might or might not be about to happen between them.

'I must take you to visit my warehouse,' he said. 'Let you see for yourself.'

'A warehouse full of guns . . . ?' She shuddered. 'I'm not sure I'd find that very attractive.'

'You might surprise yourself.'

He knew that few could resist the lure of weaponry once they were close to it. She would want to hold the guns, gingerly at first, then with relish, sliding the bolts and mimicking the gestures of firing.

'I've been,' said Claire, rejoining the conversation. 'And it's pretty boring. Unless you're nutty about guns I suppose.'

'I'm not.'

'No, well, I shouldn't bother going then.'

Oh, please, please, don't let's start the roughhouse again, Marcus silently pleaded.

'Would you like anything else to eat?' he asked Claire.

'No. In fact, I think I'd like to go pretty soon.'

Ragula eased her chair back from the table so as to be more comfortable and asked, 'So how did you come to be involved in this business of yours anyway?'

'I said I'd like to go,' insisted Claire.

'I'll ask for the bill,' he said to her, hoping to soothe. Then he turned back to Ragula: 'How did I get into it? Well, I did an apprenticeship in electronics. This was in Marseilles. I was born there . . . '

'Ah, so you're French . . . ?'

'By birth, yes. I am now Swiss. Naturalised Swiss. I fell in love with your banking system.'

'That I can understand.'

Claire gave a small, contemptuous laugh.

19

Marcus ploughed on. 'Anyway, after my national service, I ended up working for Dessault. Dessault Industries.'

Ragula looked blank.

'They're a French armaments manufacturer,' said Claire, with a patronising smile.

'Really.'

'But then, of course, you wouldn't know anything about that. You only know about artists.'

He wondered suddenly how much had she must have had to drink. An aperitif, then the wine . . . plenty of wine. Perhaps he should cut his losses and rush the meal to a close.

'I beg your pardon . . . ?' said Ragula icily. Sounding like she, too, was about to mix it.

There was a sudden, muffled retort, like a single clap of thunder, but closer than any thunder, coming from below, somewhere beneath their feet. The terrace shuddered, sending cutlery and glasses skidding from the tables. Claire screamed as all around people stared at one another with bemused and frightened faces.

Outside the restaurant he saw that traffic was still passing and people walking in the sunlight, though their heads were turned and their hands pointing. Whatever had erupted then, it was within the restaurant, or close by.

'What's happened?' said Ragula.

'I don't know,' said Marcus, standing. 'No idea.' Perhaps he should get them out. There might be a fire or further explosions.

'I'm going to have a look,' said Claire, and, before he could remonstrate, she had left the table and gone to where others were already peering over the edge of the balcony.

20

'Let me see if I can find out what's happened,' said Marcus, looking around. But the waiters seemed to have disappeared, sent fluttering away by the retort. Ragula was lighting another cigarette, though he saw that her hand was trembling.

'Does this often happen?' she said.

'I don't think so, no.' He saw that other people were leaving, though there was no panic, no pushing or calling out. This was still Switzerland. Ragula was speaking again. 'So, you were telling me what happened to you after you worked for these Dessault people . . . ?'

Either she was intent on demonstrating her sang-froid or, more likely, on not following Claire's example.

'I, er . . . I ended up as a salesman, stationed in Beirut,' he said, still gazing round, trying to weigh things up. 'Then we had the civil war and, er . . . and I left Dessault and set up a partnership of my own.' Now there was an acrid smell, as though of burning. Reminiscent of Beirut. 'Look, I really think we should get out of here,' he said, looking round for Claire. 'Come on,' he called to her. 'We're going.'

'We haven't had our coffee yet,' said Ragula, though she was standing as she spoke, evidently not willing to make an issue out of it.

'Monsieur Revachier . . . ?'

Marcus looked and saw it was the restaurant manager, wide-eyed and out-of-breath, hurrying up to them. His expression filled Marcus with a sudden, new alarm – that they weren't simply on the out-skirts of somebody else's catastrophe but that what-ever had happened had happened because of them.

'What?'

'Your car . . . there's been an explosion . . . your car has been blown up . . . !'

21

His car . . . Even as it registered, his mind leapt forward, considering the possibilities.

'*My* car . . . ? What, you mean a bomb . . . ?'

'I think so, yes,' said the manager. 'A bomb, yes.'

So who would have . . . ? Well, yes, he knew that. Or, anyway, he could make a pretty good guess.

Yet he couldn't admit to knowing, not here, perhaps not anywhere. And so reacted as though stunned and understanding nothing. 'But I mean why – '

The manager shook his head, meaning he didn't know either. 'Come with me please,' he said.

Marcus looked round and saw that Claire had returned to the table and was standing beside Ragula. They were both staring at him.

'But will the ladies be all right . . . ?'

'Yes, yes. But you must come with me please.'

Ragula said, 'You'd better go. We'll stay here.'

Marcus nodded and allowed the manager to lead him across the terrace, past a line of curious diners, through the foyer and down the steps which led to the small parking area to the rear of the building. Here there were billows of black smoke that caught in his throat. Then he saw the car – or the wreckage where the car had been. The manager gestured unnecessarily. 'There, monsieur.' It was a blaze of dense orange flames from which the smoke was pouring. He saw that fragments of metal had been hurled across the parking-lot, some embedding themselves in other cars.

'But the waiter,' shouted Marcus over the noise of the fire, 'the one who – '

The manager was shaking his head and pointing at the burning wreck. Marcus peered but could see nothing through the flames. 'He's in there . . . ?' The manager nodded. 'Christ,' said Marcus, feeling sick.

A man had been roasted alive, and in his place. It was his body that should have been in there melting. Well, and the bodies of Claire and Ragula too, had they all three left together.

May the man who has done this rot in hell, he cursed silently, hating his enemy not just because this had been an attempt on his own life but for the sheer callousness and savagery of it. He would give thanks to God that his own life had been spared and would pray for the soul of the dead man who had suffered the dreadful fate that should have been his own. To die in such an inferno . . . The thought of it left him numbed and breathless.

He put out a hand to the wall, needing to steady himself, and breathed deeply, taking in the acrid-tasting air. He was alive. It was a realization that for the moment blotted out everything else.

By a sheer fluke he had survived and was alive, able to feel the heat from the burning car and to hear the wailing of distant sirens.

3

Marcus forced himself not to look away as the charred body of the waiter was prised from the foam-covered wreck and carried away on a stretcher. It seemed the least he could do, an act of respect towards the man who had died in his place.

It felt a strange and even shameful thing to owe his life to a stranger in this way. He was haunted by the notion that he might have taken steps to save him. But what? How on earth could he have known?

The on-lookers had been pushed back and the car park draped in red-and-white tape. What seemed like a whole fleet of emergency vehicles had arrived, disgorging police and firemen. Before his eyes, the scene had become one made familiar by television – the scene of a terrorist outrage, just another among so many. The restaurant manager had already identified Marcus to one of the senior police-officers, who had taken his name and instructed him to stay.

'I have some companions still inside the restaurant,' Marcus had tried to tell him. But either the policeman didn't understand or he was too preoccupied to concern himself.

Having stood and watched as the pathetic remains of the waiter were recovered, Marcus now turned and walked swiftly away, defying anyone to stop him. But no-one did. No-one called out or came after him, and so he kept going until he was back on the open, terraced area of the restaurant, which at first appeared deserted.

Then he saw them, Ragula and Claire, sitting close together and holding hands, not at the table where they had eaten but in a corner close to the bar. Around them, tables were littered with stained glasses and crockery and chairs askew.

They, too, were alive when they might not have been. The waiter had been their saviour also.

Ragula stood up as he hurried towards them.

'It's your car . . . ?' she questioned. When he nodded, she gave a little gasp, then said, 'Oh, my God.'

'Are you two all right?'

'Claire is a little shocked. But she's being very brave.' And switched to English, in order to ask her: 'How are you feeling now? You're feeling better, yes?'

Marcus saw that Claire had removed her sun-glasses and that her face was streaked with tears. 'My dear,' he said, 'I'm sorry.' Bending and kissing her cheek.

Claire sniffed and said, 'They're saying a waiter has been killed. That he was blown up . . . ?'

Marcus hesitated but there could be no point in denying it. 'Yes.'

Claire shook her head and closed her eyes as if she would not accept such a thing. Ragula put an arm round her and held her. 'It's probably best if we get her out of here,' she said.

'They won't let me go,' said Marcus. 'They want to talk to me. But if you wouldn't mind taking a taxi –'

'Of course not.'

25

'And probably the quicker the better. Or they might decide they want to keep you here too.'

Ragula needed no further urging. 'Come on,' she said, helping Claire to her feet. 'We're going to get you home.'

But Claire clutched at the arm of his jacket. 'But what were they trying to do?' she said tearfully. 'I mean were they trying to kill you, or kill all of us, or what?'

Ragula, too, was observing him, waiting for his answer.

'Nobody knows,' said Marcus, choosing his words. 'It might have just been a mistake. Perhaps they picked the wrong car. Or perhaps they're the kind of bastards who simply don't care whose car it was.'

He caught Ragula's glance and wondered whether she saw through him. Though, if she did, she said nothing.

Between them they got Claire out of the restaurant. Marcus hailed a taxi, then waited while he saw them into it. For a moment he was tempted to make his own escape with them. What would the police do but waste hours questioning him and all to no avail? (To no avail because he was going to tell them nothing – he already knew this. They could not help him and, anyway, he did not wish them to. He intended to see this through on his own.) Nevertheless, he would have to endure their questioning.

Walking back towards the scene of the explosion, he thought again of the waiter who had died in his place. Even more awful was the realization that he would not have had it otherwise. Sincerely as he might mourn the man and the tragedy of his death, he had no wish to change places with him. If God

26

had offered to reel back those few moments of receding history, so that Marcus might this time move the car himself and die as he had been meant to die . . . he would have had to decline.

Was it cowardice or merely human, this clinging on to life at all costs? It was a fearful thing to be the target of a resourceful and powerful enemy; worse still to know that that enemy would indulge in the casual slaughter of anyone around him.

It made him a pariah, a leper. He should have a bell around his neck to warn others of the risk of associating with him. Perhaps, after all, it was better that he was not married and had no children.

The back of the police-car was fusty and hot. He tried to lower one of the windows but found it sealed. Beyond the glass, Geneva was going about its business, as it had for centuries while the rest of the world quarrelled and went to war. It was why he had moved to live there, believing himself safe.

They arrived at police headquarters on the Boulevard de Saint Georges in the old town. He came out of the car into the sunlight, then into the cool of the building. He was led through a warren of corridors, passing rooms where ceiling fans creaked as they turned and men sat in shirt-sleeves. There was a murmur of voices and the occasional shout of laughter. Marcus sensed a never-ending and patient routine that would absorb and reduce to paperwork even the most dreadful and cataclysmic of events.

Though not in his case. What secrets he had brought with him he was resolved to take away.

The room into which he was shown was small and starkly furnished with no fan to move the still air. 'The Inspector will be with you in a moment,' said his guide, and left him alone. He sat down and

27

found that the chair, and table too, were screwed to the floor.

It was an opportunity to take stock, to contemplate the miracle of his survival. Perhaps it was the element of random chance he found so disturbing. He had neither fought for his life nor guarded it with caution and foresight. All he had done was park in a way that blocked in someone else who was dining at the restaurant and who had happened to want to leave before him.

But for that bizarre intervention of fate, he would have been dead and the waiter would be living, enjoying his time off between lunch and dinner. ('Somebody up there loves us,' his mother would say whenever anything fortunate had happened in the family. Perhaps this time he might have been inclined to agree.)

The Inspector arrived as promised, a tall man in grey, pin-striped suit. An accountant, Marcus might have guessed in different circumstances.

'Inspector Marti,' he announced himself, holding out a thin hand. 'I believe you were the owner of the car that – '

'Yes.'

'Marcus Philippe Revachier . . . ?'

'Yes.'

'Very well, Monsieur Revachier.' Sitting down and unscrewing the top from a fountain-pen. 'You are how old?'

'Forty-four.'

'Single or married?'

'Single.'

'Since it was your car, we might assume that you, and not the unfortunate waiter, were the intended victim of the outrage.'

But Marcus was now on his guard, determined to

allow the Inspector not even that simple assumption.

'I really don't know.'

Inspector Marti looked at him and raised his eyebrows. 'Well, what else?'

'I don't know that either.'

This time the Inspector gave a tolerant smile.

'Well, let us assume you were the intended victim. Can you think of anyone with a motive for wanting to kill you?'

Marcus answered abruptly, not even pretending to search his memory. 'No.'

'No-one at all? You have no enemies, no rivals . . . ?'

'Oh, I'm not saying that. I probably have as many as most people.'

'I would have thought more. Considering the line of business you are in.'

So Inspector Marti had done his homework. Well, that was hardly surprising. It might also explain the cold, unsympathetic approach. Not even the offer of a glass of water. Clearly they saw him less as the intended victim of the outrage than as someone who, in an obscure way, had contributed to it.

'My line of business . . . ?' he countered.

'You are an importer and exporter of armaments.'

'I am, yes.' No denying that.

'On quite a large scale.'

Marcus permitted himself a modest nod of agreement. 'I wish it were larger.'

'And you're still telling me that you have no enemies?'

'I'm telling you I don't know who fixed a bomb to my car.'

The Inspector sighed, as though disappointed with

him. 'Monsieur Revachier, I hope you're going to cooperate with this investigation.'

'Of course. What possible reason would I have for not doing?

'I don't know,' said the Inspector. 'I was wondering that too.'

Marcus shrugged and said nothing. He could hardly blame the Inspector for becoming impatient with him but nor was he going to cooperate and it might not do any harm for the Inspector to realize that. Get the whole thing over with.

'OK,' said the Inspector briskly, as though he, too, had decided there was no point in delay. 'We'll want a complete list of all your customers and details of your dealings with them.'

'Certainly,' said Marcus, though privately resolving that he would do no such thing. His dealings with his customers were based on a confidentiality as sacred as that offered by any priest in the confessional-box. It was unthinkable he should betray it, especially since, when this investigation was over, whatever he told Inspector Marti would no doubt find its way onto computers across Europe.

There were more questions, in answer to which Marcus patiently recited his movements of that day and explained when he had made the table booking – the previous day – and who else had known of it – his secretary, Claire, Ragula, no-one else he could remember. And then, suddenly, the Inspector was screwing the top back onto his fountain-pen.

'I may, of course, want to talk to you again,' said Inspector Marti.

'Of course.'

'In the meantime I would advise a degree of caution. If, indeed, you were the intended victim – '

'He might try again,' Marcus completed.

It seemed to give the Inspector a moment of renewed hope. 'You have somebody in particular in mind . . . ?'

But Marcus stone-walled to the last. 'No. Just he, she . . . whoever it was.'

Emerging into the fresh air was a physical relief. He had refused the offer of a car to take him home, deciding to walk, though now, as he strolled through the cobbled streets of the old town, past windows shuttered against the afternoon sun, he found himself glancing about him, uneasy about these open and near-deserted spaces.

He had become a target. A man who needed to watch his back.

So he hadn't escaped unscathed after all. His life might have been saved but it had also been changed. He was not, he believed, a physical coward and would have faced his enemy there and then, had he appeared. It was this feeling of being stalked by death, the thought that any one of the tourists at the pavement cafes might turn out to be his assassin, that was unnerving. He walked for no more than a few minutes before he forsook his earlier resolution, hailed a taxi and directed it to take him home.

His house was off the Rue de Fernay, on a discreet cul-de-sac which branched off from the main highway connecting the city to the airport. It was one of four large villas constructed in the 1870s as summer palaces for the nouveaux riches of the industrial revolution. Following the First World War, it had been bought by a wine merchant from Luxembourg, who had brought with him five daughters and his country's love of privacy and had promptly enclosed the entire property – garden, stables and all – in a twelve-foot-high stone wall topped with metal spikes.

It was this fortress-like aspect that had attracted Marcus to it. He had no daughters but shared the wine merchant's desire for privacy. So he had bought it and modernized its defences with the addition of electronic surveillance and flood-lighting.

Returning to it now, he felt more than ever the comfort of those protecting walls. Though additional measures of defence would have to be taken, and taken quickly.

As he went in through the hallway, with its display of German water-colours and bronzes, Claire came rushing to him, still wide-eyed and panicky. 'What's happening?' she demanded. 'Who do they think did it?'

He took her in his arms. 'They don't know. But don't worry. Whoever did it failed. That's the important thing.'

'It was meant to kill you, wasn't it?'

'Well, nobody knows. They probably got the wrong car. Don't even think about it.'

He sensed that she wasn't totally convinced but wanted to believe him. 'Is that what the police say?'

'Yes. They're enquiring into who else was dining there. Perhaps there was somebody political or . . . well, they don't know, not yet.' However, it wouldn't be fair to disarm her completely. He was responsible for her safety while she remained at the house. 'But, look, I am going to take one or two little precautions just in case, all right? So for the moment can I ask you not to go out without letting me know. Just as a precaution.'

The look of panic came back into her eyes. 'You mean, if it was you they were after, they might try again . . . ?'

32

'I mean we've just got to be a little careful, that's all.'

He felt an increased tenderness towards her, remembering the look of the frightened child she had given him when he had found her on the terrace being comforted by Ragula. Should he urge her to leave? Warn her that he was someone best avoided? Yet he wanted her there with him. It surprised him and made him wonder, this sudden need in himself not to be alone.

Later, he saw her in her usual spot in the garden, armed with her thick paperbacks and suncream. So the trauma had been short-lived. Well, he was glad of that. He was fond of her and must see she came to no harm.

He rang Ragula Veuillet and they commiserated over what had happened. Certainly she didn't sound at all deterred by the explosive finale to their lunch. To her, too, he repeated the lie that the police believed the bomb had been intended for someone else and attached to his car by mistake. She seemed to accept this; anyway, she didn't contradict him. They agreed to meet again soon but neither offered a suggestion as to when this might be.

There was one person, and one person only, to whom Marcus could bare his soul and speak the truth. He rang the office of Jacques Martin-Achard and was told sorry but Monsieur Martin-Achard was in court for the whole of the afternoon. Marcus left a message asking if he could see him that evening on a matter of the utmost importance.

Jacques Martin-Achard was a Swiss lawyer, a short, balding man whose genial good humour masked a crafty intelligence. It was some ten years since Marcus had first consulted him, since when they had become firm friends. For one thing, Jacques was a formidable exponent of the game of chess, testing Marcus' prowess to its limits. In summer they would sometime stroll as far as the Park des Plainpalais and play on the giant, outdoor sets in front of a critical audience of passers-by.

Tonight they were seated in Marcus' office, with the door closed and the shutters pulled to against the late evening sunlight. Jacques reacted with astonishment and concern at Marcus' account of the explosion.

'And this waiter, the one who was moving the car . . . ?'

'Oh, he was killed. Killed outright.'

It still took an effort to say: as though he were admitting to some act of gross negligence on his part.

'God rest his soul,' Jacques said and made a small sign-of-the-cross on the front of his silk tie.

'I believe he had a family,' said Marcus. 'I want to pay some money to them. If I give it to you, could you see to it?'

It was something he had decided upon that evening. If he couldn't restore the man to life, at least he could offer some compensation to his defendants. A phone-call to the restaurant had told him that the waiter had a son aged three and a daughter no more than a baby.

'Certainly.'

'I thought fifty thousand francs. Or should it be more? Should it be a hundred?'

'It's your money.'

'Yes, and it was his life. Let's make it a hundred. Here, I'll make out a cheque to you, then you can locate the family and transfer it to them.'

While he was writing, Jacques asked, 'And the

police have no idea who was responsible for this outrage?'

'No.' He handed the cheque to Jacques, then
said, 'But I have. In fact, I *know* who was responsible
for it.'

Jacques stared, taken aback as Marcus knew he
would be. 'Who?'

'Jarman.'

Jacques frowned. 'How do you know?'

'Oh, I haven't got proof. Not what you would
call proof. And I'm not saying that he planted the
bomb with his own hands – '

'So why claim it was him? Why couldn't it have
been . . . well, political? I mean some terrorist group
out to commit an outrage for the sake of it?'

Marcus made no reply but moved to his desk and
opened one of its drawers.

'Or someone wanting to strike not at you but at
the restaurant,' said Jacques, sounding as if he were
warming to his theme. 'Or, if it were you they were
after, then it could have been for personal reasons
or business reasons or simply because you are an
extremely wealthy man. Some people don't like
wealthy men. Or it may have been because you were
taking two ladies to lunch. Some people don't like
that either.'

Marcus took a brown manila envelope from the
desk drawer where he had placed it three weeks ago
for safe-keeping. He opened it and extracted two
Polaroid photographs. 'It was Noel Jarman,' he
repeated quietly.

'Marcus, you must not become obsessional – '

'I'm not becoming obsessional. I know the man.
And, if we're talking about becoming obsessional,
I've known him cross half the world to collect a bad
debt, a small debt, a few dollars.'

'Oh, I'm not denying – '

'And now he's obsessed with killing me. With taking what he sees as his rightful vengeance.'

'Vengeance . . . ? What, because you dissolved the partnership . . . ? I don't see that – '

'No. Because of this.' And he handed him the two photographs.

Jacques fumbled for his glasses, put them on, then stared hard at each picture in turn. Then held them one in each hand so that he could see the two together.

'That is Peter Jarman,' said Marcus. 'Noel Jarman's son. Or rather it was.'

Both pictures showed the same young man, aged about twenty, hair and clothes fashionably cut. One picture showed his body lying by the side of a rough dirt road. His right leg was drawn up beneath him and his arms flung wide as though embracing the death that had come to him.

The second picture was a closer shot of the young man's face, or more particularly of his neck, showing the gash across it that must have ended his life. Blood seeping from it had formed a pool almost the size of the head itself. The head was turned sideways, the eyes open and fixed as if mesmerized by the congealed mass.

'Look on the back,' said Marcus.

He watched as Jacques turned over both photos and then read aloud from the back of the close-up one. 'Vengeance is mine. I will repay, saith the Lord.' He looked up and asked, 'These were sent to you?'

'Yes.'

'Anything else with them?

'No.'

'So how do you know – '

'I recognized the young man. I used to see him quite often before we ended the partnership.'

'And Jarman thinks . . . he thinks you killed his son?'

'Evidently.' Marcus moved to freshen his scotch-and-water, though without offering any to the other man. Jacques had forsworn alcohol since his wife's death some years ago in a drink-driving accident. 'The way I see it, he thinks I did this because he was poaching my clients. You know the agreement we made when we split the partnership – '

'I should do. Worse than any divorce I've ever handled.'

'We agreed that certain areas of the business should be exclusively his, other areas exclusively mine. Neither would trespass on the other's.'

'An agreement which I told you then was as full of holes as a sieve.'

'Yes, well – '

'I also told you that Noel Jarman was one of nature's wolves. A South African wolf at that, which makes him a particularly dangerous breed.'

Marcus held up a hand. 'Jacques, you're very wise and you can see into the future. I know that. Only I couldn't and so I ignored your advice. And for a year or two things weren't too bad. We kept in touch, even exchanged information, traded stock. Then I heard that he'd been trying to move in on clients that we'd agreed were mine. Particularly in the Middle East, since that was where we'd set up the business and so had a lot of contacts in common. I tried to talk to him about this but – '

'He wouldn't.'

'He wouldn't, no. As you, no doubt, could have told me.'

'As I did tell you.'

'Right. So now we were rivals, competing in the same markets. End of last year, he made a big break-through when he grabbed an order that should have come to me. A consignment of Belgian FAL rifles and Dushka machine-guns going to the Christian Falangists. Which I, again, protested about.'

'And he, again, wouldn't listen.'

'No. Anyway, I gather the consignment was being unloaded at Aquamarina and taken to Junieh. And Peter went along to supervise.'

Jacques handed him back the photographs. 'And he never came back.'

'No, he didn't.' Marcus replaced the photographs in the envelope and then in the drawer. 'Since I received these, I've talked with one or two people – Israeli friends of mine who're in touch with this Falangist group – and they tell me the word is that Peter was pulling some clever deal of his own. Possibly drugs, they're not sure, but anyway one that his father certainly didn't know about.'

'And it was that that got him killed?'

'So it seems.'

'Then you must tell Jarman this.'

'I've tried. Through intermediaries. I have tried. But, as you know, he's not a very good listener.'

'Then you must tell the police.'

Marcus shook his head. 'No.'

'Marcus – '

'What can they do? They'll be lucky even to find him. No, this is something . . . something I have to find an answer to myself.'

As he had expected, Jacques would accept none of that, urging him to go to the authorities. 'For one thing, you can't be sure. It still might have been somebody else behind the bomb.'

'Jacques, there are some coincidences I might believe in, but this isn't one of them.' He moved to the window and pushed back the shutters. The evening was darkening, though still warm. Music was playing in the distance and he thought about the open-air concerts in the Bernix park. 'A man as good as threatens to kill me, a man I know has the will to carry out such a threat, and a couple of weeks later my car turns into a blazing inferno. No, it was Jarman. Has to be.'

'I agree there's a probability.'

Marcus smiled. 'For you that's a bold statement.'

'I know. I'm regretting it already. And, as your lawyer and as your friend, I'm still saying you must go to the police with this.'

'Why? They'll never get within a million miles of Jarman. They'll only investigate me, make things harder for me. No, I'll handle this my own way.' He regretted he couldn't take his friend's advice, knowing it was sincerely offered, by someone who had only his welfare at heart. He understood, too, how Jacques, a citizen of Geneva, had a deeply-felt commitment to propriety and order, believing that everything could be solved through the proper use of legitimate authority. Noel Jarman might have been his opposite. A bull-headed Afrikaner, whose buccaneering style had always put a strain on their business relationship and had led to its eventual collapse. He was a gun-freak, too, liking to be surrounded by them, decorating the walls of his office with an ugly array of rifles, machine-guns and grenade-launchers.

Marcus explained to Jacques the steps he had already taken to step up security around his home, hiring guards from an agency he had used before and trusted. 'There'll always be two men on duty, to

39

patrol the grounds and man the main gate. I won't pretend I like it. It's not the way I want to live, but . . . ' And a gesture which meant he had bowed before the inevitable.

'I'm glad to hear that. But then what happens when you go out?'

'I'm going to employ a driver. And vary my routes . . . all the usual sorts of precautions.'

'It will cost money.'

'Yes,' he said, ' the business will have to stand it. And, anyway, it won't be forever. It will only be until . . . ' He stopped, unable to predict how long the measures might have to be continued, not knowing what it would take to make him feel safe again.

'Until what?' prompted Jacques.

'I don't know,' snapped Marcus, finding himself suddenly out of patience. 'How the hell can I?'

'I'm only asking – '

'I know what you're asking and I can't answer.' He knew his friend didn't deserve this outburst but couldn't stop himself as the pent-up fury and frustration took over. 'It'll probably go on till one of us is dead. So what're you going to say – that I should let him kill me? Because I'm not going to. What I'm going to do – I'm going to kill him.' He hadn't thought this out; in fact, only knew he had decided it when he heard himself saying it. 'Yes, I am. And don't tell me about your precious laws. I don't care about them. All I care about is stopping that maniac from killing me, and there's only one way to do that. Oh, yes, there is, Jacques. Only one way, and that's to make sure the next bomb is under his car and not mine!'

Later, of course, he apologised. It shocked him that he should have turned like this on his one sure

friend. Jacques was understanding and forgiving –
insisting, indeed, that there was nothing to forgive.

When Jacques had gone – repeating his warnings
and his advice that Marcus should go to the police –
Marcus joined Claire in the small sitting-room. She
had bathed and struck him as young and
vulnerable-looking without her make-up. She had
been writing postcards but put them aside and began
chatting to him about her plans for tomorrow. She
had planned a small excursion for herself, a drive to
Chamonix, then the cable-car to the summit of
Aiguille du Midi. Marcus encouraged her, thinking
it safer she should be away from him and away
from the house till he had his new security arrangements in position.

They neither of them mentioned the explosion, or
anything relating to the lunch with Ragula, but he
thought he detected a nervousness about her, an
uncharacteristic edginess.

He left her briefly to tour the house, checking
doors and windows and setting alarms. And moved
his pistol, a Spanish-made Astra, from the drawer
of his desk to the cabinet beside his bed. He had
barely done so, just closing the drawer in time,
when Claire followed him into the bedroom. Even
before he could undress, she had thrown off her
wrap and was presenting herself to him, wanting
him to hold her. He put his arms around her naked
body and felt her trembling.

'They could have killed us all,' she said, sounding
near to tears.

It dismayed him to realize how upset she still was.
He held her tightly and caressed her, whispering
that she mustn't worry and that it was all over.
Their embraces had aroused him but he held back
from letting her know this, assuming she would be

41

in no mood for love-making. She moved away from his embrace and climbed into bed while he completed undressing.

The surprise came when he joined her in bed and found her pulling him to her, thrusting her mouth down on his and then taking him into her. It was a frantic coupling, quite unlike their normal, leisurely love-play. He climaxed quickly, unable to resist.

Perhaps then the brush with death had affected them both, leaving them greedy for the pleasures of life.

Claire fell asleep in his arms, her breathing light and regular as a child's. He couldn't join her but lay awake, still on edge after the events of the day. As the minutes passed, he became aware as never before of the empty house around him. Was this all it had been for, his striving and his achievement – a few moments of snatched passion while he hid from his enemy inside a house that must now become his prison?

It was becoming morning, a faint light showing beyond the curtains, before he finally escaped from consciousness into an uneasy sleep.

4

'Sorry,' Lauren sang out, approaching James' raised newspaper. 'Me again.'

'It's all right,' he said, quickly lowering it and taking the letter she was holding out. It was the fifth draft she had attempted and given him to read. He had professed himself happy enough with each of the other four but she had had qualms, had torn them up and started again.

'I'm not sure they're getting any better,' she said, gazing regretfully into the waste-paper basket. 'I wish I'd kept the first one. I think it's all starting to sound a bit polished.'

She had always been the letter-writer of the two, scribbling postcards from abroad and thank-you letters after parties, but this asking for a child was harder, painful even.

'Good,' he said, as he finished reading it and handed it back.

It was what she wanted to hear but still she couldn't accept it. 'Yes, but what do you really think?'

'What I say. I think it's good. You've told them everything they wanted to know, about us and why we want to adopt. I don't see what more you can do.'

She was almost swayed by him and read it again.

'Dear Stella Priestley . . . ' Even that had gone from 'Ms Priestley' to 'Stella', then back again, and now back to the original. 'I am writing this letter to explain something about my husband and myself and our reasons for wanting to adopt a child.' No harm there surely. Then came the factual stuff, which had been relatively easy – dates of birth, details of education, the fact that James ran the garden centre in partnership with his brother and that she worked as a salesperson in the local Toyota garage. Though that had caused her to hesitate. Might they not find it peculiar that, with a degree in chemistry, she sold hatchbacks and sports-cars for a living? Would she strike them as someone who had failed in one career and jumped sideways to an unlikely alternative? Someone not to be relied upon to carry things through?

'Do you think I ought to explain why I gave up teaching?'

'Why? I thought everybody wanted to give up teaching.'

Well, yes, certainly the ones she had worked alongside had often talked of it. Besides, her own reasons for quitting were straightforward enough – simply that she preferred selling cars to struggling to control unruly classes. And she was good at selling cars. Very good at it. It was her secret belief that being a woman gave her a head start on her two male colleagues, exempting her from the suspicions most people bore towards car salesmen.

It was the final part of the letter that had caused her the greatest problems, after she had recounted all the factual stuff and explained again her own failure to get pregnant and so reached the concluding appeal/declaration. ' . . . Both James and I feel very strongly the lack of a child in our lives and are

44

confident we could offer a loving and secure home to a child in need of one. It is something to which we have given much thought before making this application and so hope you will look upon it favourably. Yours sincerely . . . '

'You're sure it's OK?' she said, still wanting his reassurance.

'It's better than OK. It's perfect.'

Well, no, she knew it wasn't that, but it would have to do. Otherwise she would be writing all night. She quickly folded the two sheets of writing-paper, slipped them inside the envelope and sealed it.

'There is one thing you haven't mentioned,' said James.

She sighed. 'What?'

'Well, how many cousins this child would have. There's Rachel with her two and Sarah with four. So he wouldn't be short of company.'

'I know.' In fact, she had made reference to it in the second draft – or had it been the third? – but had then dropped it. Rachel and Sarah were James' sisters; Rachel was now pregnant again. She tried to explain: 'I was worried they might think I only want a child because I feel inadequate alongside everybody else in your family. They all reproduce at the drop of a hat.'

James shrugged. 'Just a thought.'

She was grateful to him for his attempts to help her and for his never complaining though she could talk about little else since their return from the agency. She knew she was railroading him into all this and that he was going along with it because he loved her. He might not have been as bubbling over as she was, but she knew he would stand by her and so felt the letter on behalf of both of them to be an honest one.

'No, I think I'll settle for this,' she said, addressing the envelope. 'And I'm going to post it now then I can't change my mind.'

They walked out together to the post-box and even, at Lauren's urging, held the letter together before letting it fall. Instead of returning home, they called for a drink at the Ring O'Bells, the pub that served as their local. Lauren was conscious, as she was with everything now, how a child would change their lives. Instead of being able to leave their tidy house to pop to the pub whenever they felt like it, there would be all the clutter she saw at her sister-in-law's, with every minor outing having to be arranged in advance. How she longed for it.

'How soon do you think they'll reply?' she asked, when they had bought their drinks.

'No idea.' He smiled. 'But not tomorrow, so don't start worrying when it doesn't come by first post.'

She saw that a group of their friends had entered the pub. 'Don't let's tell anybody yet,' she begged James quickly as they approached. 'Not till we know what's happening.'

Perhaps being pregnant felt a little like this. The excitement of having a secret and being torn between wanting to share it with everyone yet reluctant to do so till the promise had been confirmed and you felt the first stirrings of new life.

In fact, it was no more than a week before Lauren went to collect the post and found among it an envelope which bore the agency's logo – a baby being enclosed in protecting arms. 'Oh, please, please, please,' she muttered as she tore it open.

She took in the letter in one glance. It said yes, that the agency would be happy to consider Lauren

46

and James as prospective adoptive parents and would be in touch soon to arrange the necessary interviews. She gave a shriek of delight, then re-read the letter, just to be sure she wasn't mistaken – no, she wasn't – then gave a happy, little jig there in the hallway.

When she stop jigging, she noticed James standing in the doorway, looking anxious. 'What's the matter?'

She thrust the letter into his hands. 'They've said yes. The agency have said yes!'

'They have?'

She saw his smile grow as he read the letter and knew that he was pleased, genuinely pleased, and that this wasn't some reaction being put on to keep her happy. Her heart warmed to him.

'Well, that's marvellous,' he said. 'I told you that letter you wrote would do the job.'

'I can't believe it. I really can't. Mind, we've got to remember they've only said yes to us applying. It doesn't mean they've said yes, we can have one. They might still say no to that, even though they're saying yes, we're OK for now.'

She knew she was talking near-gibberish but James was nodding and seemed to understand. He said something about crossing bridges when they came to them, then was giving her a kiss on the cheek and had left for the garden centre almost before she realized so that she had to run to the door to call goodbye. Her own stint in the garage didn't begin until ten: nobody wanted to buy cars first thing in the morning. She took her cup of coffee and walked about the house, envisaging the changes a child would bring, which of the bedrooms would be his/hers and where they would store the pram and all the other paraphernalia babies seemed

47

to need. It was self-indulgent, this day-dreaming, of course it was. So she allowed herself till nine-thirty, not a moment longer, then sat down to do her hair and put her eye-liner on.

She parked her Corolla in its usual spot, around the back of the garage, away from the rows of for-sale cars, and stopped to say hello to old Joe who came in mornings only to give the cars their wash-and-brush-up. He told her about his grand-children, what they'd been getting up to.

She went into the office, to find Greg already there. He was one of her colleagues on the sales team, a year or so younger than herself.

'Morning,' she said, trying to sound like this was just another day.

He look her up and down and shook his head. 'Why do you do this to me?'

'Do what?' Opening her diary and pinning on her name badge.

'Come in here every morning looking like a mil-lion dollars. I'm only human, you know that.'

'Oh, Greg, come on please,' she responded sharply, reprovingly.

He stared at her in surprise. 'Hey. You get out of the wrong bed or what?'

'Sorry,' she said, taken aback by her own manner. 'I suppose I must have.'

God knew she ought to have been used to his flirtatious banter by now. It was the kind of thing they exchanged every morning and which meant nothing, an alternative to discussing the weather or congestion on the roads.

She went out into the showroom, with its smell of polish, hoping Greg wouldn't pursue her since she liked him and didn't want to fall out. It was the letter that had placed her on her guard and made

48

her suddenly wary of their easy-going, jokey relationship. Stupid. As if the agency would ever know how she addressed her colleagues at work. All the same, the letter had made her feel she needed to put a brake on her behaviour. Watch herself.

It even cost her a sale that afternoon. The customer was a Mr Rotsinger, who had bought cars from them before, a middle-aged man who had already been back twice to look at a silver-grey Celica GTX. All he needed now was a little reassurance and gentle encouragement and he would be signing on the dotted line. She stood beside the open door of the car while he sat in the driver's seat, feeling the padded steering-wheel and manoeuvring the gear-stick.

'Why don't you just come and sit next to me,' he said, patting the seat beside him. 'See how it feels then.'

She spoke before she had time to think. 'I'm all right standing here, thank you.' Then could have kicked herself, seeing his embarrassment.

'Yes, I, er, I wasn't serious,' he muttered. He fiddled with the controls for another moment or two as she tried to redeem the situation with some bright sales patter but it was no good. She could see that his interest in the car had evaporated. He got out, saying that he would have to think about it some more but avoiding looking her in the eye so that Lauren knew she wouldn't be seeing him again.

'Shit,' she said, going back into the office.

Greg held his hands before his face, as if to protect himself. 'Don't hit me,' he pleaded. 'Or, if you do, make it somewhere that won't show.'

'I just screwed up a sale.'

'How did you manage that?' he asked, now sounding genuinely interested.

49

'Oh, I don't know,' she said dismissively. 'Just lost contact when it mattered.'

She didn't want to have to tell him of their adoption plans. No doubt she would soon get over these strange inhibitions. In the meantime Mr Rotsinger would go and buy his car elsewhere and she would have lost out on commission but that was hardly a major tragedy.

The phone rang ten minutes after she got home that evening. As she answered, she told herself it would be Suzie Brandon, wanting to confirm that she and James would be at her party that evening. It was some sort of belated house-warming: Suzie's excuses for giving parties became ever more esoteric. But no, it wasn't Suzie at all; it was Stella Priestley from the agency, her voice somehow softer over the telephone so that it took Lauren a moment to identify it.

'Hope you don't mind me ringing at tea-time?'

'No, not at all.' Lauren suffered a small rush of panic: was this bad news, that Stella should be ringing so hard on the heels of the letter?

'Only I know you're both out working through the day. Did you get the letter from us?'

'Yes, this morning. I was . . . we were both delighted.'

'Good.'

'And I mean thanks for replying so quickly.'

'Well, we don't like to waste time. Ideally – and I mean it doesn't often work out like this, but ideally – we aim to complete everything, from application to actual adoption, within nine months.'

'Oh, so that –'

'Same length as a normal pregnancy.'

'Yes,' said Lauren, liking the notion.

'Anyway, what I'm really ringing for is to arrange a time I can come and see you.'

'To see me? I mean just me?'

'Well, both of you together if possible.'

At which James walked in bang on cue, so that she was able to call him to the phone and get him to agree to an afternoon when she could make herself free – which meant any afternoon because she wasn't going to let the garage stand in the way of this, no sir – and he could take time off from the garden centre.

'No problem,' he said. 'You arrange it and I'll fit in.' Which pleased her again that he should be showing this more positive attitude towards the whole business in place of his earlier begrudging acceptance of it.

'One thing you might like to be thinking about in the meantime,' said Stella, when they had arranged the meeting. 'I'm going to need the names of three people who can act as referees for you. If possible, people you've known for some time. Oh, and not relatives. More-or-less anybody else but not relatives.'

Lauren told this to James in the car on their way to Suzie Brandon's party and they debated the possible candidates. 'What about Jane?' suggested Lauren. 'I'm sure she wouldn't mind.' Jane was one of their neighbours, living next-door with a husband who was in sportswear and two teenage sons.

'You think you can rely on her to say the right things?'

Lauren looked at him, perturbed by the suggestion that the whole thing might be somehow fixed, then saw his smile and realized he was teasing.

'She'd better or there'll be no more feeding the cat when they go on holiday,' she said, to show that she could joke about it too. 'But seriously, I think she'll be all right, don't you?'

51

So they agreed on Jane, then on Simon Pilkington, who had known James since school-days and been best man at their wedding. Also he was younger than Jane, which helped give the feel of a balanced ticket.

'And then who's going to be third?' said Lauren, wondering aloud.

'Well, one of your friends,' said James. 'Any one. It's up to you.'

'OK, let's see. Who do I know who's respectable? Well, look, what about Suzie since we're seeing her tonight anyway?'

'Suzie Brandon?' He sounded doubtful.

'Why not?'

'I don't know, I just don't think she's ... reliable.'

'That's ridiculous!' she protested on behalf of her friend. It struck her as odd that James should be talking like this about Suzie when the two of them had always seemed to get on well. 'She's known me a long time. We worked together when I was teaching. She'll be perfect.'

He said, 'Well, if you think ... ' in a way that suggested he still wasn't happy. She waited a moment, giving him the chance to raise a further objection but he said no more, concentrating on his driving.

'I'm going to ask her tonight,' said Lauren, deciding to ignore his strange behaviour and excited at the prospect of having a legitimate reason for sharing her secret with someone.

When they got there, the party seemed to be still at its awkward stage, with people conversing quietly with their own partners. 'Am I glad to see you,' said Suzie, greeting her at the door. 'It's as dead as a dodo in here.'

'Not for long,' said Lauren, who felt that tonight she was capable of single-handedly resurrecting any party going. 'I've something I want to tell you. And then, I promise, we're going to have a ball.'

5

His attempts to discover the whereabouts of Jarman had proved fruitless. The business was still based in Johannesburg, no doubt about that, but none of Marcus' contacts could tell him where he might find the man himself. And his enquiries had to be cautious, made through intermediaries. After all, it was likely that the police were tapping his phone. He didn't want them to learn of his sudden interest in his ex-partner and put two and two together.

In fact, they seemed to be putting very little together. Inspector Marti, ringing to keep Marcus informed – this was what he claimed – reported that the explosive used was Semtex-based, with a mercury priming-device, which classified it as relatively sophisticated but common enough and difficult to trace. Otherwise, the police struck Marcus as having no leads, nothing to go on, but to be waiting around for whatever might happen next.

He even wondered grimly whether they were hoping for another attempt on his life, one that would this time furnish them with more clues.

The hired guards had moved into his home, working in pairs and stationing themselves in the garden, just inside the wrought-iron gate. They seemed the open-air type, lolling about in cut-down jeans and t-shirts. Their brief was to patrol the grounds, check the identity of visitors and go through his mail for any suspicious-looking packages. It was what he had asked for and was paying for; still, he found it eerie and unnerving. His home, planned as a haven and retreat, had been turned into a fortress. Wasn't there even something cowardly about hiding away like this?

And what did it solve? Was he hoping Jarman would lose interest and go away? Hardly likely, knowing the Afrikaner's obsession for pursuing matters to the limit and then beyond. No, all this hiding away could be no more than a temporary measure, that he would sooner or later have to abandon and come out fighting.

Then either he would have to persuade Jarman that he had had no hand in his son's death or he would have to kill Jarman before Jarman could succeed in killing him.

It was as stark and simple as that, and there were moments when he accepted it; then others when he would try and push the dreadful decision away. Hoping, without any real hope, for some other release from the dilemma.

And always hating his enemy for what he had done, not only for the useless murder of the waiter but for the way the explosion had all but taken away the life that he, Marcus, had known, turning him into a hunted animal, living with his own fear and beginning to hate himself for it.

Claire had already gone, another loss. She had sought him out, the day after the explosion. He knew immediately from her over-eager smile what it was she had come to tell him.

'I've just been on the phone to my agent,' she said.

'Yes?' He would let her break the news her own way.

'Apparently I'm back in demand. There's a hotel chain offering some cabaret work. It's not wonderful but, well, it's better than nothing . . . '

She was avoiding his eye. Perhaps it wasn't even true. Perhaps there was no work; perhaps there hadn't even been a phone-call. Still, he didn't want to embarrass her or to make her departure difficult.

'Then you must go,' he said, managing a smile. 'Perhaps I'll be able to come and see you.'

He saw the relief in her face. 'The trouble is, it's all a bit short-notice,' she went on, a shade too quickly. 'I've really got to let them know today and be back tomorrow.'

'There's no problem,' he said, taking her hand. He felt suddenly sorry for her, that she should have to dissemble like this. 'We can get you on a plane.'

'Well, yes, I've already enquired. There's a flight to London in the morning that has seats going and so I've made a reservation.'

She extracted her hand from his, moved away from him and began messing with her hair in the mirror as if becoming aware of how transparent her excuse was. Not that he could blame her for wanting to be away from him and so be safe. He would have made his escape, too, if only escape were allowed him.

The following morning she was on her way, laden with souvenirs and promising she would ring the moment she landed and that they would meet again soon. He wanted to tell her that the lies weren't necessary, saying he knew how busy she would be, making her excuses for her.

After all, she had only come to him for a holiday, they had both known that. He told himself, almost

56

believing it, that there had never been any possibility of anything lasting, even before Jarman's attempt on his life.

Two weeks later he was in Paris, walking the left bank of the Seine. Around him, coaches were disgorging tourists into the heat of the afternoon and boats were plying for hire.

Born in Marseilles, Marcus had grown up with a view of Paris as the fabulous city of the north, wealthy and sophisticated, a city of politicians and tarts. Now, of course, he knew it better and knew it also had endless suburbs and chronic congestion. Still, he never failed to enjoy it, as well as finding it a useful centre for conducting business.

And now it also offered him anonymity and so freedom of a sort. He had been careful – switching his flight booking at the eleventh hour and then ignoring his reservation at the Georges Cinq and booking into another, less conspicuous hotel. Even while strolling in the sunshine, he kept his wits about him, noticing not only the attractive women and the familiar landmarks but stopping from time to time to allow those walking behind him to pass, making sure he wasn't being followed.

There was a difference, he told himself, between becoming neurotic about his safety and taking sensible precautions.

Jacques, of course, had been against the whole idea. 'But why do you have to go?' he urged. 'You say that it's business, but what business could be so important as to risk your life?'

'I'm not risking it,' countered Marcus patiently. 'And, anyway, if I have to stay hiding away here for much longer, I'm going to go crazy.'

'Then take someone with you. Don't go alone.'

But no, he wasn't having that either. 'I have only a couple of appointments. I'll be careful and I won't stay more than two or three nights. Now please, Jacques, don't try and turn me into a frightened, old woman.'

'I'd rather do that than have to attend your funeral.'

'You won't be attending my funeral for a long time yet. And, if I have to sit here for the rest of my life, I won't be able to afford a funeral.'

While in his mood of bravado, he phoned Ragula Veuillet, something he had been intending since the day of the explosion but had been putting off. She sounded pleased to hear from him and, after an exchange of pleasantries, he asked if he might take her out for dinner.

There was a moment's silence – was she unsure? was she checking her diary? – then she said, 'No. No, I don't think so.' He had just time to feel the beginnings of his disappointment, and bewilderment that he should so have misjudged her, before she went on: 'You took me out to lunch. I think this time I should give you dinner. Why don't you come here and I'll see what I can manage to throw together?'

Yes, wonderful. He was only too happy to agree. (Even thinking that it might be *safer*, to be alone with her in her flat rather than a public place. Then wondering if she, too, had thought of that.)

They settled on a date, the evening when he was due to return from Paris, and he rang off, his spirits lifted. He felt he had regained something of his self-respect by these modest acts of defiance. He would live as he wished to live, out in the open, and not stay huddled away like some hermit, terrified of his own shadow.

'I'm talking about Eldorado,' said the little man with the gold-capped teeth. 'Weapons that have never been used, never taken from their boxes. Thousands of them, Marcus. Tens of thousands.'

'Tell me more,' said Marcus warily. He had known Francois Lucchi for many years, long enough to take such claims with a pinch of salt. The little Algerian, a near-dwarf, with coarse, bulbous features and an ill-fitting, sandy-coloured toupee, was one of those who enjoyed the conspiratorial side of the arms business, the secret rendezvous and coded telexes. Yet Marcus had done business with him in the past and had kept up the acquaintance for old times' sake and because you could never tell when he might just come up with the goods.

Besides, he enjoyed the man's company, his fund of stories and gossip. They had met today in Lucchi's scruffy office close to the Gare Du Nord, then walked down the Avenue Lafayette. Following some instinct of his own, Lucchi had steered them past a variety of restaurants and cafes and into a bistro of bare, wooden tables where they had ordered pastis and two helpings of bouillabaise.

'And let me promise you, my friend,' said Lucchi, gripping his sleeve with stubby fingers, 'you are the first to hear this. I said to myself – who do I want to deal with? Bandits and robbers or a man of honour? So you are the first.'

'I'm flattered,' said Marcus, wondering how many other people had been told the same. 'But you still haven't said – '

Lucchi glanced round, then spoke in a hoarse stage-whisper. 'Vietnam.' He nodded at Marcus and grinned, a conjuror who has performed his greatest, breath-taking trick and was waiting for the applause. 'Vietnam.'

'Really,' said Marcus. 'Yes, well, that would be El-dorado.'

He was intrigued though still dubious. There had long been tales of the fabulous arsenals abandoned by the Yanks in their helter-skelter evacuation from that country and speculation about when and where these arms might finally appear on the international market. Though, coming from Francois Lucchi, this might still be no more than a re-cycling of rumour and hearsay.

'Tell me more.'

'America M16 rifles,' said the little man, his gold caps twinkling. 'Other things too, but I know it's the M16s that will most interest you. I can get you any amount, all in factory condition.'

Marcus pressed for details of how he had come by this information and how such a deal might be handled. But Lucchi was playing his cards, if he had any, close to his tiny chest. They ordered another round of drinks and haggled genially about what Lucchi's own commission might be if and when such treasure really was forthcoming and if the Hanoi government were willing to play ball. It might still all be in the realm of fantasy, based on inaccurate, fifth-hand information. Marcus was happy to agree to Lucchi's suggestion that he should arrange for a sample to be delivered for inspection and, only if that proved satisfactory, would they then meet again and attempt to close a deal.

'By the way,' said Lucchi, 'guess who I am meeting tomorrow, right here in Paris?'

'Who?'

'Or perhaps you are meeting him too. So it is not such a coincidence.'

Marcus was gripped by a sudden fear. Telling himself no, it couldn't be what he was thinking.

But, if not, then who else could Lucchi be hinting at behind his arch manner?

'Who?' he insisted.

'You don't know? Then it is a coincidence.' It was all Marcus could do not to grab him by the throat and force the name out of him. Lucchi gave a chuckle, took a long pull of his cigar, and finally announced: 'I am seeing Mr Jarman. Your old partner, Mr Noel Jarman.'

His first instinct was to feel himself in some kind of trap, to suspect that Lucchi had lured him there and that Jarman was about to appear before them. He gripped the arms of his chair, poised for flight yet unable to move.

Lucchi chuckled again, then said, 'But I will tell him nothing about the Vietnam business. That is between you and me only.'

Marcus stared, then managed to nod. 'Excuse me,' he said. Feeling clumsy, he left the table and went out to the toilets at the back of the premises. He found himself in a foul-smelling cubicle but at least he was alone and had time to calm himself away from the gaze of the other man.

So it really was coincidence, no more and no less? He wanted to belive so. He had schemed almost nightly of how he might confront Jarman and so end this thing between them – and had dreamt of doing so, in endless, blood-soaked nightmares – but he was not ready for it, not yet prepared to test his own resolve. It was only in the past two hours spent with Lucchi that he had truly relaxed and managed to forget the threat hanging over him. And now to learn that his enemy might even at this very moment be in the same city . . . !

He washed his face and wiped it with a rough,

61

paper towel. Returning to their table, he glanced about him but saw only old men playing cards and a young couple, their heads together in earnest conversation. Surely there was nothing here to be frightened of.

'Do you know where Jarman is staying?' he asked, trying to sound casual. (And not knowing why he wanted to know – except that he might avoid it.)

But Lucchi was shaking his head. 'I have no idea. You know your Mr Jarman. Not one for the social graces. We have done a little business since the two of you split up . . . ' Said with an apologetic shrug, as though such business had been a distasteful necessity. 'Now he tells me he is going to be in Paris and might well call at my office.'

'What time?'

'He doesn't say. Why? Would you also like to see him?'

'No, no,' said Marcus. Then, added, lest that might seem too forceful, 'Not particularly.'

They parted without Marcus learning any more about his adversary's plans. Lucchi had doubtless been right to call it a coincidence. He couldn't, of course, have been expected to anticipate the effect of such a coincidence on Marcus, for whom the allure of Paris had been banished at a stroke.

He walked to his hotel, to dispel the effects of the liquor, wanting a clear head. He had intended calling on his brother, who ran a restaurant in Monmartre on the Boule Poissonière. It was a working-man's restaurant, without frills or pretensions but always busy and full of appetizing smells. A place where Marcus knew he would be made welcome and feted. He would be given pride-of-place at the well-scrubbed family table in the back room, with the jugs of wine set on it, and the three children – Jean-

Paul, 10, Nicole, 9 and Natalie, 5 – holding their breath while they waited to see if he had brought them presents.

But how could he go there tonight, with things as they were? How could he go into the home of his own brother and sit down with him and his wife and children, all unsuspecting, when he carried with him everywhere the possibility of violence and danger? It was unthinkable.

The explosion in his car below the Grappe d'Or restaurant had cut him off from the world around him in ways he had not foreseen and was only now beginning to understand. Not only had he been forced to retreat behind the high walls of his home; now here he was avoiding family and friends lest he bring disaster on their heads too. He thought of the solitary evening ahead of him and cursed Jarman afresh. Would he really have to kill the man as the only way of bringing this business to a close?

He had one remaining business appointment the following morning – with a Mr Choi from Hong Kong. They met in the lobby of the Georges Cinq, where Marcus was supposedly staying. (Suppose Jarman was, in fact, staying there?) Marcus hurried things along with the briefest of formalities. Mr Choi was interested in having Marcus tender to supply small arms to a government agency in Indonesia. That, anyway, would be the destination on the end-used certificate; only Mr Choi would ever be certain of their true destination.

They talked solemnly about notes of credit and dates of delivery, Marcus forcing himself to pay attention. This, after all, was his livelihood and important. They eventually shook hands on a provisional agreement and he was at last free to leave.

Free to do some shopping. He called in at the Galleries Lafayette and, with the help of a sympathetic saleswoman, chose a silk scarf of black-and-gold for Ragula. A small gift to take with him that evening.

At two forty-five his plane left the runway at Charles de Gaulle, banked wide over Paris and headed south-east towards Geneva. He gave a sigh of heart-felt relief as it did so and thought of Jarman somewhere in the city below him, perhaps at that very moment meeting Francois Lucchi and learning how close their paths had been to crossing.

He thought again about killing him. Not that it would be a simple matter, even if he could square it with his own conscience. He was a businessman – how often had he assured others of that! – not a medieval chieftain with hit-men awaiting his command. He had contacts. Of course he had contacts and no doubt they had their own contacts and so it might be possible . . . Well, yes, one thing he had learned long ago was that, given the money and the will, anything was possible.

Hiring someone to kill Jarman on his behalf – that was possible.

But then what new dangers might he be bringing onto his own head? Exposing himself to possible blackmail at the very least. No, it was a solution for when all else had failed and for which he would have to prepare with infinite care.

By five o'clock he was home and ringing Jacques at his office.

'I thought I'd better let you know I survived Paris.'

'You're lucky. Few men can claim to have survived Paris.'

64

Marcus laughed. He had already decided that he wasn't going to tell Jacques about his near-miss with Jarman. If he were ever going to take steps to have him killed, then he must make sure Jacques knew nothing of it. Better that they should speak of him as little as possible.

'I have to talk to you about a contract. You ever dealt with the Idonesian government before?'

'Never. Are you sure you want to?'

'Well, I'm not committed to anything at this stage. I'll talk to you about it tomorrow.' And they arranged a time when Jacques would come to the house.

Marcus went and showered, then shaved, using the same cut-throat razor he had been given by an American 'uncle', a friend of his mother's, when he was fourteen in Marseilles.

It was six-fifteen. With time to kill, he sat in the drawing-room and skipped through the mail he secretary had left for him. Then sent for the house-keeper and spent some minutes talking to her, not because he doubted the woman's competence, which was formidable, but because he knew she would be all the more conscientious if he made a show of keeping tabs on her work. For the same reason he walked down to the gate where the two guards from the agency were in deck-chairs, enjoying the last of the afternoon sun. They were wearing shoulder-holsters and one had a pump-action shotgun resting across his lap. They got to their feet when he approached but he invited them to sit down again and chatted about the job. He learned that one had been in the Foreign Legion and the other was an ex-police-man.

What he didn't ask was what they thought about risking their own necks to protect him. Did they

65

realize the danger they might be in? Perhaps they were the kind of men who would revel in it. He had spoken to the agency only about his need to increase security following a police tip-off.

At five-past-seven he sent for Eduardo, the young Italian he had taken on as chauffeur. He was aged twenty-one, thin-faced, with long, wavy hair he tucked up beneath his chauffeur's cap. He had polished the new Mercedes – the replacement for the one demolished by Jarman's bomb – to a high shine and held the passenger door open for Marcus to climb in.

'I'm going to the Old Town,' Marcus instructed him. 'You can drop me off at the Rue Madeleine, then come back here. I'll ring if I want you later.'

They were there in twelve minutes. Marcus left the car and ascended the stepped, cobbled street that went up by the side of the cathedral. It was a pleasant evening for walking. He checked that he had the wrapped silk scarf in his pocket.

The Rue de l'Athénée was a long, narrow street of shops and galleries, all of which were now closed so that Marcus was presented with line of shutters and doors on both sides. Deserted. His footsteps echoed before him as he headed for the far end where Ragula had her gallery and the flat above in which she lived.

He looked at his watch and saw it was seven twenty-eight. He would be on time almost to the second.

Then he saw that he wasn't alone: there was someone else ahead of him, at the far end of the street. A young man, swarthy-looking, possibly an Arab, leaning against the wall. He was wearing a jacket, which might have been leather. He was looking in Marcus' direction.

66

Marcus' heart began to thud inside his chest and his mouth went dry. Oh, God, no, he prayed. Oh, no. Not here, not now.

His step had slowed but was still taking him closer to the youth. Who had now stopped leaning on the wall and had straightened up – looking at him.

Then suddenly, miraculously, Marcus came to an alleyway, a break between the buildings which had been invisible until he was upon it. He turned abruptly and without hesitation into it, as though that had been his destination all along.

But it proved a cruel sham, taking him nowhere save to a high wall. It was a place where refuse bins were stored and perhaps in the day-time vehicles parked there, nothing more. He had to turn and face the street again, now sweating with the terror of it. And still telling himself he might be wrong. The youth might be there for any of a hundred reasons. It was a public street – he had a *right* to be there.

He would step out into the street and walk back the way he had come. Decisively and without looking back.

Doing so, he saw there was now another youth coming towards him even as he headed for the comparative safety of the Rue Madeleine. This one was also wearing a leather jacket and wasn't just standing waiting but was walking the narrow pavement towards him.

Before he could decide anything, they were almost face-to-face, for a moment about to collide, then the youth had stepped aside and Marcus had gone past him and was striding forward, trying to estimate the distance – thirty, forty yards? – to the end of the street.

67

He heard running footsteps behind him. Were they both after him? He didn't dare to look, couldn't bring himself to turn his head, but kept walking, his hands in his pockets, fingers clutching the silk scarf.

He heard the first shot even as he felt the blow of it, jarring and winding him, then a burning sensation. He tried to run but there were more shots and he was burning again, in different places. He began to tumble forward and tried to put out his arms to save himself, but his arms would no more obey him than his legs and he went sprawling.

His last thought, before he lost consciousness, was that it was a machine-gun – a Browning or an Erstal, he couldn't be sure which.

6

'So how would you see the responsibilities being divided where a child was concerned?' asked Stella.

'We'd share them,' said Lauren.

'Yes, absolutely. Share them,' said James, nodding beside her.

'So who would get up in the night to do the feeds, change the nappies?' asked Stella.

Lauren hesitated, then said, 'I suppose I'd probably do that. I mean if I wasn't working it wouldn't be fair to expect James. And, anyway, I'd want to.'

She would want to change nappies in the middle of the night? She could almost hear her sister-in-laws guffawing at the notion.

Stella also seemed to have her doubts. 'You might say that now,' she said. 'Wait till you've been doing it a month or two.'

'I'd still be saying it then,' insisted Lauren. 'If I had a child, then I'd want to care for it. I know it's a lot of hard work but I can do it and I would.' She felt herself losing control, suddenly at odds with these other two people in the room with her, not willing to play their game any longer. She needed to get out. 'Does anyone want another coffee?'

For this, their first interview, Lauren had taken the whole day off work and cleaned the house from top to bottom. Then wondered whether it wasn't just too clean, the kind of house you couldn't envisage a child living in, and so she had gone back and untidied a little of what she had just tidied.

James had been late returning from the garden centre, so that she had to begin by apologizing for him, something that irked her, though Stella didn't seem to mind. 'Why don't we use the time for you to show me round the house?' she suggested.

'Yes, of course,' said Lauren, and looked around. 'Well, this is the, er . . . this is the hall.'

Actually the guided tour turned out to be a good idea, giving them a more relaxed start than sitting down face-to-face would have done. Lauren felt herself warming to Stella by the time they came downstairs again.

James came hurrying in through the door, pulling off his anorak and offering his apologies. They collected coffees from the kitchen and then, at last, were settling in the lounge, she and James side-by-side on the sofa and Stella with her clip-board on her knees in the armchair to their right.

So this was it then, her audition – their audition – for the one part she yearned for above all others.

'Some questions I have to get out of the way first,' began Stella briskly. 'Does either of you have a history of ill-health?'

They exchanged a look, then assured her that no, apart from the usual childhood ailments, they had both managed clean bills of health. Nor did they smoke, and nor had they ever been treated for any kind of alcohol or drug dependency.

So we're ahead, thought Lauren. Off into an early lead.

They did, however, have to admit to drinking occasionally. No point in denying it with the loaded drinks cabinet only feet away. How often did they go out? It surprised Lauren to hear herself saying

70

most nights, yet that was the truth when you came to think about it.

So were they losing points now? Their early lead already being eroded?

Stella asked how they would manage if they lost one of their incomes yet had an extra mouth to feed. But they had already done their sums on this and Lauren was able to sit back as James explained how they would manage things.

'So you both work,' summarised Stella. 'And you have quite an active social life. How would you see this changing once there was a child in the house?'

'Oh, totally,' said Lauren quickly. 'I'd give up work and, well, it's obvious that we couldn't keep going out all the time. Or even go out at all, not to start with.'

'And would you mind giving up your job?'

'No. No, I enjoy it, but it's never been something I saw myself doing for the rest of my life. It's just . . . just a job.'

'You used to be a school-teacher . . . ?'

Oh-oh. So she was going to have to explain that after all. Why had she left the job that actually did involve caring for children – *children*, the one thing she was supposed to be so desperately seeking – in order to sell cars.

'Yes, but not for very long. About three years altogether and, well, I just don't think I was cut out for it. So I decided to try something else, something that was as different from teaching as I could find.'

It sounded feeble and defensive, even to her own ears, a poor reference for someone crying out for a child of her own. Yet Stella Priestley was smiling.

'I know the feeling,' she said. 'I started off in teaching, then couldn't wait to get out.'

Lauren's spirits soared. 'Really?'

71

This was an unlooked-for bonus. So she didn't have to explain; Stella knew from her own experience. They were gaining points where she had expected to be losing them.

'Let me ask you both,' said Stella. 'How do you see your marriage? I mean do you have very distinct roles when it comes to things like cooking and housework?'

'No, I don't think – ' said Lauren. Then heard James saying, 'Well, Lauren does most of it. In fact, to be honest – '

'But that's only because I have more free time,' she objected. 'I mean James can cook if he wants to. Can't you?'

Though, even as she spoke, she realized that she couldn't remember the last time he had done any cooking. The odd breakfast perhaps, but not real cooking. That fell on her side of the divide, as, come to think of it, did most other things relating to the house. She saw to them while he . . . well, he had his work, didn't he. The garden centre, that he had established with his brother, putting in all the hours God sent to build it up from scratch.

'I suppose we're fairly ordinary really . . . ' she heard James saying.

Were they really as corny as all that? The husband absorbed by his job while wifey did hers for pin-money and made sure he had a hot meal to come home to every evening? She had somehow thought they were different.

She went out into the kitchen, hearing Stella ask James what he considered to be the father's role in a family. She let the door swing closed on his reply. No doubt he would say supporting, providing. She thought of her own father – a bank official with a

72

passion for fly-fishing – who had supported and provided all right but had remained an outsider to herself and, she believed, to her mother till the day he died.

The kitchen was shining from the cleaning she had given it that morning. Stella had admired it when she first arrived. Though it had probably meant nothing: she must be used to walking into houses where everything was spick and span. No pulling the wool over her eyes.

Lauren poured the coffees. This time they were getting instant, not percolated. She saw her hand was trembling and wondered what it was that had upset her like this when on the whole the interview had been going so well.

Was it the sudden picture of herself and her marriage as so ordinary, so typical, when she had always secretly believed herself different, liberated? Post-feminist, if you wanted a label. She remembered the long, serious debates she had had with James about whether they should marry or whether it would be more adult simply to live together. And now here she was, nine years on, doing the shopping and the cooking and the housework. No different from her mother.

A child would only reinforce the pattern. She would be the one to care for it. Well, yes, she would. Let's be honest about it. Never mind the double act they were putting on for the agency. She would be the one. Doing the bottles and the nappies and dragging it around with her everywhere she went. Training it to wave James off in the morning and keeping her fingers crossed it would be clean and contented for when he came back at night.

Well, but so what? she told herself fiercely. It's what you want, not him. You want to do the things

73

your mother did. And, if it upsets you to realize that, then perhaps you're not half so clever as you thought you were.

She went back in to join them, feeling a new recklessness about her. Never mind the carefully considered answers, the super-clean house – all sucking up to Stella Priestley. Let her ask her questions and let her get some straight, honest answers.

Stella was still talking about *their relationship*, hers and James'. What sort of stresses did they think having a child would impose on it?

'Well, I suppose we'll have to learn to be less selfish,' said Lauren, taking over. 'I mean upto now there's only been the two of us and so we've been used to a pretty easy time of it – '

'And two incomes,' added Stella.

'Well, yes. Plenty of time . . . plenty of money. If we feel tired, we can stay in bed. If we feel randy, we can stay in bed.' She caught James' look of surprise. 'And we can go out when we want to. Well, a child is going to change all of that. I know it is. We both know it is, don't we?' Turning to him.

'Yes,' he said, still looking startled. 'But it's a question of . . . well, I suppose it's a question of what matters most.'

'And what does matter most to you?' said Stella, leaning towards him.

Lauren watched him struggle to answer but knew from Stella's manner that she was forbidden to help. So perhaps Stella did suspect him then. Perhaps she had recognized where all the drive for this adoption was coming from and saw how James was being towed along.

'What matters most . . . ' He cleared his throat. 'Well, the child would come first, of course. I mean we both want that, don't we?'

74

Well, he might have managed more conviction, more fire, but at least he'd said it, and Lauren felt she could now move in to help.

'We know it's going to change our lives,' she said, knowing she was haranguing them both but not caring. 'I suppose we'd even be disappointed if it didn't. Though, let's be honest, it doesn't mean we're never going to see any of our friends again or never go out for a drink again – '

'No,' said Stella, encouragingly.

'I can't see it being good for the child, or for us, if we turned into some sort of obsessives who based our whole lives around it.'

'I couldn't agree more. Though you'll probably find that at first – '

'Well, at first, yes – '

'Especially with it being your first child – '

'Well, yes – '

'Most people do find it an enormous shock. They think nothing's ever going to be the same again, and you've got to be prepared for that.'

'I think we are.'

Goodness knows she'd been lectured on this often enough by her sister-in-laws. And, anyway, things were already not the same. A month ago she would have sold Mr Potsinger his Celica GTX, no problem.

Stella was moving on, talking about their having both had higher education. They were, she said, both quite successful in their different ways and enjoyed a middle-class life-style. Lauren wondered about that 'middle-class' tag but let it go.

'So, if you were to adopt a child,' asked Stella, 'what expectations would you have for it?'

There was a pause, then Lauren said, 'Well, I wouldn't want it to be a teacher.' Stella laughed.

'But otherwise . . . otherwise I suppose we'd just want it to be happy.'

'Yes,' said James.

'Just that,' said Lauren, with nothing to add and so repeated: 'We'd just want it to be happy.'

Original it wasn't, she knew that. Prince or pauper, beautiful or plain, at least let my child be happy. The heart-felt prayer of a million women over a million kids. All that made her and James different was that their hopes were riding on somebody else's child.

Stella seemed to be running out of questions, scanning her clip-board while the silences lengthened. Lauren had a sense of the interview coming to its end. She glanced at her watch and saw it was two hours since Stella had arrived.

So how were they doing then? She had lost track of the points gained and points lost but had a sense that at least they hadn't done badly. They had skated round the more obvious pit-falls and had surely done enough at least to keep themselves in the running.

'Now, just one other thing,' said Stella. 'I did ask you if you could think of three people to act as referees for you . . . ?'

'Yes, we did that,' said Lauren. She went to where the piece of paper was lying on the mantelpiece, with the names and addresses written on it. She handed it to Stella and gave her a quick resumé on who everybody was. Jane the Neighbour, Simon the Best Man and Suzie the Friend.

'Have you warned them I'll be getting in touch?' asked Stella.

Lauren said that she had, yes. She had also sworn them to silence. She was still nervous about their adoption attempt becoming common knowledge, superstitious that it might in some way harm their chances.

Stella stood up. 'I'll leave it a couple of weeks before I bother you again. And then I'd like to talk to you, James. So can we agree on a date now, or would you rather leave it and give me a ring?'

James shrugged. 'We can fix a date now if you like.'

Well done, thought Lauren. Another small bonus point for that. Now don't spoil it by being pernickety about the date. Tell her you'll be available any time that suits her.

Which James came close to doing, preferring the second of two dates Stella was able to offer.

They went with her to the door and called their good-byes. Lauren could hardly wait for her car to pull away before she was asking him, 'Well? How do you think we've done?'

'Oh, I don't think we did ourselves any harm.'

'No,' she said, relieved to hear him say it, even though she knew he had no more real idea than she had. 'I thought that too. I mean I think we came across as . . . well, fairly normal.'

That was what they wanted, wasn't it? Normal people. And was that what they were?

But James was looking at his watch, clearly in no mood for post-mortems. 'Look, you don't mind, do you? Only I promised I'd get back to work as soon as I could. There's a bit of a rush on.'

'No, you go,' she reassured him. 'We can talk later.'

In truth, she preferred to be left alone and given time to think. She would go over the interview again, every line of it, in her head, and see if this time she couldn't work out where the points had been gained and lost and what sort of total they had amassed.

James was looking at her with concern. 'You are all right, aren't you?'

'Of course I am, yes. You go on.'

She just didn't want to have to be with anybody or to have to talk any more.

It was a dangerous thing, this adoption lark. You went into it with hands extended, as a supplicant, saying Give me a child, and they said Wait. We want to dissect you first, find out what sort of person you are and what your marriage is like. Which is where the dangers came in. Perhaps you didn't want to know too much about the kind of person you were or to stare too closely into the entrails of your marriage, which had been ticking along all right up to now but which might not withstand too close an inspection.

She cleared away the coffee cups. There was nothing else to do: the house was spotless, the garden immaculate. She had two or three hours of unaccustomed leisure before James would return and then she, the wife, would cook for him.

With a baby, each day would be like this. Minus the leisure, of course. The house would be a shambles and the garden running away with itself. She would have thrown in her job and the identity it gave her, to become a twenty-four-hour-a-day wife-and-mother.

If that was the price, then so be it. She couldn't wait for it to happen.

7

If he was in pain, then he must be alive. Being alive and being in pain were the only two things he was aware of. It was a dull, aching pain that blanked out everything else. He wanted only that it would end, even if it meant he wouldn't be alive any more.

Now, his eyes were beginning to work, though everything was blurred; nothing was clear or distinct. Just an impression of whiteness surrounding him. He blinked – the only movement he was capable of – and a white ceiling with fluorescent lights came into focus. The walls meeting the ceiling were also white and on one of them was a clock, though he couldn't focus to read it.

He was lying in a bed, with his arms out straight above the sheets. One of them was covered in bandages and had a thin, transparent tube snaking from beneath it. There was a steady bleeping sound coming from behind his head where he couldn't see.

He remembered being on the Rue de l'Athénée and his fear – he remembered that most of all – his fear as he had been pursued by the youths. He must have been shot and was now in hospital, wounded, or dying even.

There was another sound, a groaning, which filled the room. He didn't know where that noise was coming from. And the pain was excruciating, more than he could stand.

Now there was movement about him, figures in white, a face that he didn't recognize suddenly close to his own. Till at last the pain began to recede and he was able to ease himself away from the body on the bed, not by leaving it but by retreating more deeply within. The groaning noise had ceased.

He was in Beirut. No longer in hospital but in the Chichi Bar by the waterfront. Everything was restored to what it had been before the civil war. There were businessmen in their suits, the serving-boys in their white robes and the sweet smell of cannabis wafting on the sea air.

While he . . . he was swathed in bandages, with blood seeping from between them. But no-one seemed to mind. No-one seemed even to notice him. He tried to warn them of the horrors that were to come but couldn't get their attention.

So he lay back in the sunshine, feeling drowsy and indolent, no more concerned for his own fate than they were for theirs. Not even sure whether this was life or death, or whether he was in some kind of limbo precariously balanced between the two.

'And you won't be late again, will you,' said Lauren, though smiling, not wanting to antagonize him on this day of all days.

'I won't,' he said, pulling on his anorak and about to leave.

But she couldn't leave it at that; she had to be sure. 'Because I won't be here this time – '

'I know.'

He took her in his arms. She smelt that familiar combination of soap and gardening clothes. Should she tactfully suggest he got home in time to change . . . ?

'I'll be here and I'll have washed my hands and I'll be on my very best behaviour,' he said. 'For one thing . . . ' – as he let her go and moved towards the door – ' . . . she's a very attractive lady.'

Lauren laughed but thought wow, yes, that would be a sure way to screw up your application and no mistake – make a pass at the social worker even while you were trying to convince her you had the soundest of marriages.

It must happen, too. There was an intimacy about this process that some men might find a turn-on. Not James though. Her worries on how he might perform, what he might say in his interview with Stella, were of a different sort.

Would he take the opportunity to admit his misgivings? Would he confess to her that the application had been Lauren's idea and that he had gone along with it this far only for her sake? She was sure that this was the truth, even though he had never actually put it into words.

But there was nothing she could do. She wouldn't be there and she could hardly have rehearsed him in his answers. She must have faith in him. Well, she did have faith in him, yes: she had not the slightest doubt that he would always stand by her and that he would be a good father to their child. She could only hope and pray that Stella Priestley would see this too.

In the meantime, she would pretend it was just another working day and try and concentrate on selling cars. She even managed to flirt mildly with Greg so as to demonstrate to herself that her every waking moment didn't have to be an audition for Stella Priestley's benefit.

As the afternoon wore on, she wondered if James might ring her with news of how the interview had gone, but no. Five-thirty came and there had been no word. She flung herself into her car and raced home. His Land-Rover was standing in the drive, the name of the garden centre stencilled along its sides. She hurried into the house and found him in the lounge with his newspaper.

'Hello,' he said, and gave her a smile. Then, unbelievably, he lowered his head and continued reading.

'How did it go?' she cried. 'Come on. I want to know everything!'

'What about?'

She knew he was joking. Was that a good sign? Surely he wouldn't be in this playful mood if it had gone badly? Still, she wanted to have it spelled out and snatched the newspaper from him.

'The interview, what do you think? What did she ask you? And did she say anything about how we're doing?'

He was laughing and holding up his hands in mock-surrender. 'I'll tell you. I'll tell you everything. Do you want a drink?'

'No. Yes. I don't know. Just tell me please.'

He went and opened a can of beer, splitting it into two glasses. 'First, she wanted my life-story. Where I was born, family background, education . . . all that.'

'Yes,' she said, impatient, trying to hurry him on.

'And then she wanted to know all about us. How I met you, what sort of courtship we had – '

'And what did you tell her?'

'Well, the truth. What else?'

She needed to know more. 'Did you tell her your parents didn't like me because I was a jazz freak and had purple nails?'

'It wasn't that they didn't like you – ' he began,

82

but she stopped him. They had argued about this often enough; she didn't want to waste time on it now.

'Well, all right. But what else did you talk about?'

'Oh, about how we'd been when we were first married. How we are now. Our sex life, that sort of thing.'

But she wasn't going to let him get away with that so easily. 'Our sex life?'

'Yes.'

'And what did you tell her?'

'She wanted to know whether either of us had ever been unfaithful. And I said no, we hadn't.'

Well, yes, that was true. It must have been worth a few points in their favour, surely.

'And we talked about faithfulness in marriage and how important I thought it was –'

'And how important do you think it is?' she asked, surprised to realize she didn't know what his answer might have been.

'I said I thought it was important to us. But that I knew of marriages where husband and wife had the odd affairs and it didn't seem to do any real harm.'

'Like who?' she asked, unable to resist her curiosity.

'Oh, some of the people I deal with in the business. Nobody you know,' he said, smiling.

'OK, so anything else? About our sex-life I mean?'

'I told her that we made love about once or twice a week –'

'Once or twice . . . ?' she protested, wondering if he was joking again. Then, seeing him nodding, he exclaimed, 'Oh, it's more than that. It must be!'

'It might be for you. That's all it works out at for me.'

He spoke lightly but she felt her resentment growing. She couldn't accept that. 'No,' she said, shaking her head.

'Well, it's not far off that,' he insisted. 'Anyway, what does it matter?'

But it did matter. It mattered to her that the love-making side of their marriage shouldn't sound so conventional and half-hearted. She tried to think back over the past week, and the week before, wanting some facts with which to contradict him but she was able to recall only two occasions they had made love since her last period, which was, what, ten or eleven days ago.

So perhaps he was right and she wasn't as hot in bed as she had imagined.

'I'm sorry,' she said stiffly.

'Oh, please, love,' he said, taking her hand. He looked bewildered, as though unable to understand the way things had suddenly soured between them. 'I was probably wrong. I wasn't exactly consulting my diary or anything. I mean does it matter?'

She made an effort to overcome the feelings of resentment within her. 'No,' she muttered. 'It doesn't. And so what else did you talk about?'

'Oh, went over a lot of the stuff the three of us had talked about before. And then she asked me about my thoughts on children . . . all that.'

Now her feelings of resentment were forgotten, banished completely. For this, of course, was the gist of it. 'Oh, yes?' she said. 'And just what were your thoughts on children?'

He looked her in the eyes. She had the uneasy feeling that he could read her mind and knew the doubts she had been harbouring.

'I said I was as desperate as you that we should adopt one,' he said firmly. 'And that I knew we'd both make fabulous parents.'

She felt a rush of tenderness for him. Well, of course, he had said that! How stupid she had been to doubt him! She put her arms round him and kissed him.

'Was that the right thing?' he asked.

She saw that he was teasing. 'Yes, it was. And thank you,' she said, kissing him again.

She felt him growing excited against her. 'Come with me, little boy,' she said, taking him by the hand. He laughed, a little wildly, and allowed her to lead him up the stairs to their bed. 'How many times a week?' she said, and now she was teasing, pulling at the belt of his trousers, till he began hurriedly unfastening it himself and she pulled off her own clothes, letting them fall around her. 'I only said that because I knew it would get you going,' he said. Oh, no, you didn't, she thought, but now there were other, more urgent things to occupy her as their legs locked together and she felt his erection pushing into her.

After they had finished, they lay together still naked on top of the bedclothes. 'My love,' he said, and ran his fingers slowly over her face, as if trying to commit it to memory.

It pleased her that he hadn't moved away in his usual, abrupt fashion. It was a rare thing, this lying together in the early evening, hearing the sounds of the avenue outside the window.

'Did she say – Stella – did she say how we were doing?' she asked, speaking quietly so as not to break the spell.

'No.' Then he added: 'I didn't ask her. But I don't think there's anything to worry about. I think we're doing rather well, don't you?'

'Yes,' she said. 'And do you know what else I think?'

'What?'

'I think that our baby's already out there some-where. I think he's already out there, just waiting to be born.'

8

First the saline drip was taken down and the needle removed from his arm. He began drinking normally, though he still had to be propped up into a sitting position, buttressed by pillows. Then the drain which had been inserted into his abdomen to take the blood from his stomach wound was also removed.

He knew that these were steps to be welcomed; they were signs of progress and confirmation that he wasn't going to die. Yet he also found them disturbing, since they signalled that the hospital would not continue forever to take responsibility for him, feeding him and bathing him like a child, but that he would sooner or later have to return to the world he had left, the world in which Jarman was still roaming free and out for his blood.

He had been told about the police guard outside the door of his room. Occasionally, when the door was opened and he was in his propped-up position, he glimpsed a uniformed figure.

The consultant in charge of his treatment was an Italian of about his own age who introduced himself as Doctor Salvatore Garrone. Marcus had gazed up at him, feeling groggy and helpless, as Doctor Garrone smilingly explained how lucky he was, not only in having survived the attack and being able to look forward to a complete recovery, but also in being treated by someone who had dealt with many such gunshot wounds in his native city of Palermo and so knew what he was doing. He was a man who delighted in his own expertise, lecturing Marcus on exit and entry wounds and the different damage to tissue caused by smooth-bore and rifled weapons.

They were, of course, at different ends of the same trade, reflected Marcus. Professionals in the business of killing. The one distributing the means; the other patching up the bloody results.

Jacques Martin-Achard had been his most constant visitor, bringing him books and newspapers, as well as contracts and cheques to sign. He was another one who told Marcus how lucky he was.

'There have now been two attempts on your life. First they try to blow you up and then to machine-gun you to death. You are the luckiest man alive. Do you realize that? The luckiest!'

He spoke with such vehemence that it was almost an accusation. It was a vehemence, as Marcus recognized, that was fuelled by concern.

'I know,' he said. 'I'm so lucky that, when I get out of here, I'm going to start buying lottery tickets.'

But Jacques was not amused and only shook his head sadly.

There were other visitors too. He was told that Ragula Veuillet had been to see him, but he had been asleep and so she had left. He found a bunch of red roses on the bedside locker, together with a card that said, 'All my love and concern, Ragula.'

He was glad to have missed her. That was another thread from his past that he wasn't yet ready to take up, though he asked Jacques to contact her on his behalf and thank her for the flowers.

88

Of his three wounds, the one in his right leg hurt him the most, though Doctor Gerrone explained that the most serious threat had been from the bullet in his abdomen, which they had removed via a laparotomy. The other wound, to his fore-arm, was described as superficial but still felt blazingly painful if he attempted to move it. He was beginning to learn how each had its own time of day for asserting itself and demanding his attention. He was still on six-hourly injections of Pethidine, each of which he longed for with the desperation of an addict. The major preoccupation of each day remained avoiding pain.

Mercifully, his periods of wakefulness were still short. He never knew when he might slip back into sleep, even when in mid-sentence or while having his dressings changed. His dreams were of his childhood. A recurring one was of himself and his brother hiding beneath a table while, above them, his mother and an American 'uncle' were banging glasses on the table top and shouting. What they were shouting or why he had no idea. Then the American had gone and he and his brother, oddly unperturbed, were staring down at their mother, who was lying on the floor with blood trickling from her nose.

He awoke from one of these sleeps to see a dark-suited figure sitting by his bed. Not Jacques, no, but Inspector Marti, the policeman who had questioned him after the explosion. Marcus felt a sudden panic – he didn't want to speak to this man, not here, not now – and closed his eyes. But it was too late.

'I think you're well enough to talk, aren't you?' came the Inspector's voice, carrying a barely concealed impatience.

Marcus opened his eyes and gazed at him without speaking. Wondering if he could feign distress and call a nurse to have the Inspector ejected, while knowing that this wouldn't really be wise. He felt vulnerable, unprepared for the encounter.

The Inspector was speaking. 'Monsieur Revachier, I know you are still recovering, but it's important you tell us all you can about the identity of your attacker. First we had the car-bomb, now this. Somebody is trying to kill you, yes?'

Marcus nodded. Only please don't tell me I'm lucky. I know that already.

'I didn't think you were absolutely frank with us when we spoke before. If you had been, then perhaps you wouldn't have had to suffer this further attack.'

Marcus said nothing but put out his arm – his good arm – towards the water-jug.

The Inspector ignored the gesture and went on: 'So tell me please. Who is this who is trying to kill you?'

'I don't know,' said Marcus, sinking back onto his pillows.

'Well, I'm sorry, Monsieur, but I think you do. Only, if you won't help us, then there's very little we can do. We certainly can't provide you with an armed guard for the rest of your life. Once you are out of here, I assume you will once again be at the mercy of your enemy, whoever he is.'

Marcus gave a small shake of the head and closed his eyes, hoping for sleep. But it wouldn't come, not while the Inspector was sitting there beside him.

'I don't know,' he said again, not caring whether the Inspector believed him or not, wanting only that he should go away.

'You must realize,' said the Inspector, 'that, if you won't help us, there is a limit to the amount of help we can give you.'

Marcus nodded. Yes, he did realize that and he

was resigned to it. Though there was one thing he wanted to ask.

'The gun . . . the one that was used to shoot me?'

'Yes?'

'Was it a Browning or an Erstal?'

He saw the Inspector stare, trying to see the significance of the question. 'I'm told it was probably a Browning,' he said finally. 'Why do you want to know?'

'Just professional . . . professional interest.'

And that, he resolved, would be his last word. He lay staring at the ceiling as the Inspector continued to cajole and threaten him, before finally giving up with ill-disguised anger and walking out.

Though still dopey, and tired from the confrontation, Marcus felt he was seeing things with total clarity.

He wasn't trying to protect Jarman by his silence: that would have been absurd. No, his silence was to protect nobody but himself.

It was insurance against the time to come, when he would repay Jarman for the pain and the nightmares and for the death of the waiter. He would replay him by killing him.

How he would do it he didn't yet know. Or even whether it would be by his own hand or through an intermediary. But, lying there in the hospital ward on that afternoon of late autumn, he knew that he could evade the decision no longer.

Which was why he could tell the police nothing. Otherwise he would be pointing the finger of suspicion at himself for that time in the future when it would be Jarman's death they would be investigating.

The next day should have seen the removal of the

catheter so that he would at last be independent of the tubes and drains that had kept him alive. He would then be free, in theory anyway, to leave his bed and begin an independent life again. It would be welcome, of course, but also a challenge, to leave the Intensive Care room and face the world beyond.

The nurses arrived to prepare him for the moment. He lay back, accustomed now to letting them work on his body, then was surprised to see them hurrying from the room. When they returned, it was with Doctor Gerrone.

'A slight problem,' he said. 'I think we must postpone giving you your freedom, at least for a day or so.'

'Something wrong?' asked Marcus, feeling a spurt of anxiety.

The consultant waved his arms dismissively. 'Nothing we need worry about. We have taken tests and discovered traces of blood in your urine. This probably means nothing. We must wait for it to clear. Two days at the most.'

And he was gone, leaving the nurses to re-connect the catheter. Marcus felt annoyed: he had psyched himself up for the move. He was also concerned as to whether he was being told the truth about the unexpected set-back.

Suddenly getting out of that room struck him as the thing he wanted most in his whole life. To be outside in the fresh air . . . to be moving about again . . . he couldn't imagine that he would ever want anything more than those simple gifts, if only God would see His way to granting them.

Jacques Martin-Achard arrived that evening, bringing with him a small chess-set, so that they begun a game with it balanced on the bed-clothes.

Between moves they talked about Marcus' business. For the past couple of weeks Marcus had been attempting to keep in touch by phone, on top of which he had asked Jacques to talk to the manager of his warehouse and to form his own opinion on how the operation had survived Marcus's protracted absence. They agreed it had survived remarkably well. The manager seemed to have seized the opportunity to prove his worth.

'Perhaps I should retire,' said Marcus jokingly.

'Perhaps you should,' said Jacques, not joking. 'And go and live somewhere you will be safe.'

And just where would that be? thought Marcus. Nowhere on this earth, that was for sure. But he didn't rise to the bait; instead, he moved his queen's bishop and said, 'Check, I think.'

They talked about the house, where only the housekeeper and gardener remained, keeping things in trim for Marcus' return.

'What will you do?' asked Jacques. 'Will you want the guards back again?'

'I'm sure you'll tell me that I should.'

'Of course I'll tell you that you should. Let me know when you're coming out and I'll arrange it.'

Well, he wouldn't quarrel with that. He had already decided himself to re-employ the guards at the house; indeed, to increase their number.

'You're not concentrating,' said Jacques, as Marcus made a move which left his queen vulnerable. Jacques dispatched it with his knight and then placed Marcus' own king in check. Feeling suddenly tired, Marcus conceded the game.

It had been a day of decisions. A big day for somebody whose life had moved at a snail's pace for the past seven weeks. He had taken his own decision about Jarman. And then there had been the decision by Doctor Gerrone not to move him yet. He still wondered about that. Then he was aware of sleep overcoming him even as Jacques was still at his bedside, packing away the chess pieces.

The catheter was removed two days later, as Doctor Gerrone had promised. It was a relief to Marcus, dispelling his doubts. Then came the moment when he had to raise himself from the bed. Even with the nurses to help him, it caused him renewed agonies, making him cry out. He wanted to lie down again, but they wouldn't let him. They coaxed him to stand, then to take small, shuffling steps to the door and out of the room at last.

'Two weeks,' Doctor Gerrone told him. 'Three weeks at the most and then you'll be ready to leave.' Marcus was now installed in a new room, where there were no machines, just the basic fittings of a middle-class hotel. 'You are a very fortunate man. Very fortunate indeed.'

He could now manage to shower and so was able to observe his own body in the bathroom mirror. It was a surprise to see how healthy he looked. He still felt weak and couldn't stand for more than a minute or two, yet the body he observed in the mirror was tanned and fit-looking. He flattered himself he might still be taken for younger than his forty-five years. Though the damage was there to be seen; it could hardly be ignored. There were inflamed areas on the leg and arm and, most eye-catching, the long abdominal scar with its even stitching. He ran his finger along it, feeling where the puffy flesh was pulled tight.

They were his war wounds, inflicted in a conflict in which he had up to now been the innocent party, wanting only peace and reconciliation. Well, no longer. Once out of here, he was going onto the offensive.

9

It was Christmas. They had put up their usual tree and last year's decorations. In fact, come to think of it, decorations that went back several years. She had never taken that much interest in the so-called festive season, leaving it to those who had children.

She and James sat up late on Christmas Eve, keeping the radio on for the carols and sharing a bottle of good claret that had been on offer from Sainsbury's.

'We'll have our own child next year,' she said. 'And then we'll have a real Christmas.'

'Let's just take it one step at a time,' said James, cautious as ever, but she felt that he knew it too. She snuggled up to him, loving him and grateful for the way he had stood by her.

Her own one-to-one interview with Stella Priestley had been over a week ago. She had approached it with confidence, no longer seeing Stella as the annonymous, hostile interrogator but as an ally.

They sat in the lounge, as before. Though this time she had merely tidied the house as she might have done for any visitor, not scrubbed and polished it to mint condition.

'I know you've told me some of this already,' said

Stella, 'but I'd like it if you could give me some sort of life-story. Everything you can think of.'

It was a tall order, but Lauren did her best, beginning with home – modest, with everything in its place – then school – where she'd been a bit of a high-flyer, expected to do well. She told her about the Sunday-school classes, which she had jacked in as soon as possible, the ballet lessons, and the holidays at Weston-super-Mare, with its slot-machines and the chance for some cautious flirting with loud and dangerous-looking boys.

They talked about Lauren's life at University. She explained how her heart had been set on a career as a dancer, till she had had to face up to the fact that she was not quite good enough. Almost, but not quite and never would be. Why she had then opted for Chemistry she couldn't remember, except perhaps that it was as far away from dance as you could get.

'And did you involve yourself in many clubs or societies . . . ?'

'One or two, yes. In fact, I was co-founder of the Women's Solidarity Campaign.'

She said it with a smile, conscious of how pompous the title now sounded and, anyway, doubting whether it was the kind of thing the agency would favour. But Stella said, 'Good for you,' so that Lauren was encouraged to elaborate.

'Well, there was a lot of it about. I mean feminism was just taking off. It was like we'd discovered a new religion. We were all zealots.' God, they were too. Forever in huddles, calling one another sisters and hassling the University over the masculine tone of its publications. Amazing days. 'Any man who asked me out, I accepted, then turned on him and asked him why he thought he had the right to open

96

doors for me or buy me drinks.' She shook her head at the memory. 'Terrible time I gave some of them.'

'I'm sure it did them a world of good.'

'Oh, I don't know. Hasn't improved them much, has it.'

They laughed together over that. Stella had stopped taking notes and put aside her clipboard.

'And so what happened to the Women's Solidarity Campaign?' she asked.

'Ah, well. We did what zealots always do – started turning against one another for not being real feminists.' Their simple cause had splintered into political groupings, each barely speaking to the other, plotting and counter-plotting. Lauren sighed, remembering. 'In the end it was a relief to find a man to talk to. I mean they were just, well, they just seemed simpler.'

'They are, aren't they?' And they laughed again. 'And was that when you met James or did he come later?'

'A bit later. In fact, he was always a supporter of feminist causes. Till we went and got married.'

'And then he changed . . . ?'

'No,' Lauren said quickly. 'Not really.'

Stella had taken up her clipboard and was writing again. Lauren warned herself to be careful. It wouldn't do to forget the serious purpose behind all this jolly chat. It would be all too easy to kick off your shoes and embark on a real heart-to-heart, then regret it later, realizing how much you had unwittingly revealed.

'Do you regard your own marriage as a traditional one?' asked Stella.

'Well . . . ' Lauren hesitated, finding the question difficult. 'I'm not sure what traditional means – '

'Is it like your parents' marriage?'

'Not like my parents', no – '

'Why not? In what ways different?'

'Well, they . . . ' She stopped, then started again. 'I suppose we're aware that there are alternatives. I mean in a way that my parents never were. When they got married, that was forever, whereas . . . '

She stopped, feeling the quicksands beginning to shift beneath her feet. So her parents had regarded themselves as being married forever whereas she and James . . . what? She saw that Stella was waiting for her to complete her answer.

But she took her time, thought about it and then said, 'Whereas me and James, well, of course, we also believe we're married forever, but that's because we choose it. As two individuals, we choose it. Not because we have some church dictating to us.'

Had she been nimble-footed enough? Stella was smiling and nodding, so perhaps yes, she had managed to scrap home by the skin of her teeth. Perhaps now she could even afford a small admission.

'But I suppose it is a fairly traditional sort of marriage in terms of responsibilities. I mean he's the main bread-winner and I do most of the cooking and all that sort of stuff.'

'And what would the Women's Solidarity Campaign have to say about that?'

'Oh, I daresay they're mostly married themselves by now.'

Immediately she had spoken, Lauren regretted the flip response. It made Stella smile, as it had been intended to, but why was she doing this, betraying her old self in order to score easy points?

She knew she was losing control and becoming agitated but it didn't matter. She held up a hand to prevent Stella asking another question, then said, 'No, I don't really mean that. I think what we stood for was right at the time and I don't want to sound as though I'm making a joke about it now.' She didn't know what she was going to say next. Only that this was a statement about herself and about her life and so had to be true, and if the Adoption Board didn't like it then they could go hang. 'We all make compromises, don't we. Especially when you're in a marriage, when you're in a relationship with another person, well, you can't always base that on principles. A lot of it has to depend on the kind of individuals you are. So, all right, our marriage might not be an ideal one from the feminist point-of-view, but I don't think that matters so long as it works and so long as we're both happy with it.'

She stopped, feeling herself flushed and trembling. And she had been so determined to remain calm! Still, there it was. She had said her piece and she wasn't going to retract it.

'Fine,' said Stella.

'So I'm still a feminist. It's just that I'm married as well.'

'Right.'

She shrugged. 'That's it.' She felt suddenly exhausted. This process of answering questions about yourself was harder work than selling cars. Harder work than teaching even.

Christmas dinner was at Sarah's, as usual. A house so full of children you could only suppose they had been rearing them under greenhouse conditions. The living-room was already littered with discarded wrapping-paper when Lauren and James arrived. Their own presents were opened, adding to it.

Rachel was installed in an armchair, massively pregnant. The children were instructed not to climb onto her knee.

99

'Why don't we tell them about the adoption?' muttered James.

But no, she didn't want that, not until everything was confirmed. 'No, not yet,' she said quickly. 'Please.'

'All right,' he said, putting a reassuring arm round her. 'We'll keep it a secret for just as long as you like.'

Then she wondered whether she wasn't just being silly. After all, what was stopping her telling them but some vague superstition that to do so might be a sin of presumption and so provoke the gods into turning against them? Ridiculous really.

And perhaps it did matter more to James than she had realized. They were his family so it was understandable that he should want them to know, yet here she was frustrating him when she owed him so much.

She waited till after dinner, when the turkey had been picked clean and the crackers pulled and then said, 'Actually we've got something to tell you.'

James looked at her in surprise, and the others in expectation. She realized at once that they thought she was pregnant and so hurried on quickly: 'We've applied to adopt a child. And, well, everything seems to be going very well so . . . with a bit of luck we might need an even bigger turkey next Christmas.'

There was a chorus of congratulation and delight. All the adults came forward and kissed her and told her what a wonderful thing she was doing, and congratulated James too, while the children sat and stared, not understanding what was going on even when it was explained to them.

She felt proud, pleased that she had overcome her foolish misgivings and told them. One of James' brothers made a little speech and proposed a toast.

Then Rachel and Sarah delegated the men to clear away the table; they wanted to talk to Lauren, pestering her to tell them everything about the adoption process.

She even caught a note of envy in Rachel's questioning, as though Lauren's announcement had put her own pregnant condition into the shade. Well, she was sorry about that; it hadn't been her intention. All the same, it made her realize for the first time that adopting wasn't just equal to being pregnant. It was better . . . !

The phone rang on Boxing Day morning and Lauren answered it. 'Hello? Lauren Eaglesham speaking.'

'Lauren. It's Stella Priestley.'

On Boxing Day? It struck her as odd. Still, she was glad to hear from her if it was going to mean another step forward.

'Stella. How are you? Surviving Christmas all right?'

But Stella evidently wasn't in the mood for exchanging pleasantries. 'I wondered if we might come and see you,' she said, sounding official and distant. The alarm-bells began to sound in Lauren's head. 'That's myself and Marjorie Daniels. She's the agency's principal social worker – '

'Come and see us? But why?'

'Something's come up. With regard to the adoption.'

'What sort of something?' The alarm-bells were now loud and clear. Lauren felt herself panicking. If 'something had come up', then it had to mean something bad, something that was going to count against them.

'I'd rather not talk over the phone. Would it be

all right if we came this afternoon? Say about two o'clock?'

Lauren said yes. What else could she say? She left the phone, her mind whirring and told James what had happened.

'What could it be?' she demanded. 'Why do you think they're coming? And two of them. Why should she be bringing this other social worker with her?'

But he could only shake his head. 'I've no idea. None.'

'It must be serious. Something's happened!'

'Now, you don't know. Just let's wait until – '

'It must be! Why else should they be calling on Boxing Day?' she cried.

She should never have made the announcement. They should have kept their application a secret. She had known it was wrong but had persuaded herself it could do no harm and that she owed it to James. She should never have made that damned announcement!

He took her in his arms and tried to comfort her but she didn't want to be comforted. What she wanted, the only thing she wanted, was to know. She was angry with her own inept performance on the phone when she had been caught flat-footed, not thinking quickly enough. Why hadn't she suggested an earlier time? Or insisted that Stella had given her some clue, some indication, of what this was about?

They sat around the house, with nothing to do but wait. She tried to interest herself in a book on gardening, which had been one of her presents, but the words swam before her eyes on the page and, anyway, she could think of nothing else but Stella's phone-call and the impending visit. Finally James insisted they put their boots on and went out for a walk.

102

They trudged silently beside the canal, then crossed a foot-bridge and came back along the other side. It was ten-to-two when they turned into the avenue, just in time to see Stella Priestley's red Fiesta stopping in front of their house.

10

Marjorie Daniels, the agency's principal social worker, turned out to be a heavily-built, middle-aged woman. Lauren disliked her on sight, judging her to be a bully, someone who would pride herself on not pulling her punches.

Hardly surprising, of course. She mistrusted this Marjorie Daniels' reason for being there and was still fearful that something calamitous must have occurred. It didn't help that Stella avoided Lauren's eye when they met on the doorstep – Lauren was sure she didn't imagined this. Then, when they entered the lounge, Stella took the chair in the corner, where she had never sat before, as though seeking to distance herself as far as possible from the proceedings.

Marjorie Daniels settled herself in an armchair and asked if they minded her smoking. It was, she conceded cheerfully, a filthy and disgusting habit but it helped her stay sane. James said no, they didn't mind, and Lauren went to the kitchen to dig out their only ashtray.

But what was this all about? wondered Lauren desperately. For God's sake, get on with it and tell us.

Marjorie Daniels did get on with it. 'What's happened is this,' she said, wafting at the smoke from her cigarette. 'We got the last of your references in just before Christmas. It had been held up in the Christmas mail. It was the one from, er . . .'

'Mrs Brandon,' prompted Stella quietly, from the corner seat.

'Mrs Brandon. Well, anyway, most of what she said was very complimentary to you both. Very much the kind of things we like to hear. But then, at the end of her letter, she said that she felt herself honour-bound to tell us that she and Mr Eaglesham . . .' Here she paused to turn and look at James. Lauren tried to complete the sentence in her own mind but couldn't. She and Mr Eaglesham had what? She had to wait for Marjorie Daniels to complete it for her: 'Well, that she and Mr Eaglesham had had an illicit sexual relationship approximately two years ago.'

There was a silence. Lauren began to smile. It was all so absurd, a joke, a mental aberration, a fantasy. Of course it was disturbing and a mystery that Suzie should have written it; all the same, it was a relief to learn that there was nothing more serious behind their visit.

She turned to James. He was staring ahead, not looking directly at any of them. Why wasn't he smiling too? Come to that, why wasn't he protesting?

Oh, Christ, she thought, feeling a sudden dread. Oh, God, please no.

She heard Marjorie Daniels speaking again. 'Obviously this is not the kind of thing we can ignore. We invite these people to tell us what they know about you and we have to take what they say seriously. So the only fair thing we can do is come to you and ask you – is this true? Mr Eaglesham, did you have an affair with this Mrs Brandon?'

105

Lauren watched mesmerized. He passed a hand over his brow, then said quietly, 'Yes. I did, yes.'

She wanted to beat him with her fists. She also wanted to run from the room and find somewhere where she could be alone. But she did neither. She sat there, seeing the familiar room with its furniture and photographs and its tinselly Christmas decorations. She was aware that Stella was looking at her at last and James was still rigid and looking at no-one.

Only Marjorie Daniels moved, turning towards her. 'Right. So now, Mrs Eaglesham, I have to ask you. Did you know about this?'

'No,' Lauren heard herself say. 'Not a clue.'

Her voice seemed to come from far away. It surprised her she could speak at all. She had been betrayed. Dreadfully betrayed. Her husband, whom she had loved, and her friend, whom she had trusted, had done this to her. Betraying her not just in this affair of theirs, the sordid details of which she didn't want to know, but betraying her most in letting it come to light in these circumstances.

Now she would never have a baby.

Nor would she have a husband. Not after this. Her marriage was over. Everything was at an end.

Marjorie Daniels was speaking again. Lauren closed her eyes, willing her only to get it over with and leave. What more could there be to say?

'Well, I'm sorry I've had to tell you this. I know it must be painful for both of you. But now I'd better tell you how it affects the adoption.' No, don't, Lauren silently pleaded. I already know and don't need to be told. But she couldn't shut the voice out. 'Firstly, it doesn't mean that we automatically reject you or anything like that. We aren't necessarily

106

looking for people who don't have a stain on their character. We're looking for people who're going to provide a loving, secure home for a child in the future. What matters now is how you two feel about things. And I don't expect you to know that yet. I'm sure this must have come as a shock and you'll need time to think about it and talk about it.'

None of which Lauren believed for a second. One look at Suzie Brandon's letter and the Panel – the all-powerful Panel – would dismiss their application out-of-hand. If they paused at all it might be to wonder how a couple whose marriage was so clearly founded on sand could have had the temerity to make such an application in the first place.

She was struck by another thought following on that, one so awful that it almost made her cry aloud.

He had allowed her to put Suzie's name forward as a referee, knowing that all this would come out and that their application would be sabotaged. She now saw it all with a terrible clarity. How he had humoured her, letting her believe they were on the brink of success, even persuading her to boast of it to his family over Christmas dinner, while knowing all along that it would come to nothing.

'Mrs Eaglesham . . . ?'

She saw that Marjorie Daniels was speaking to her. Both she and Stella were on their feet, though Lauren hadn't been aware of their moving.

'I'm sorry. What?'

'I said I think it's best if we leave you two alone to sort this out between you. Decide what you want to do. Then, whenever you feel ready, you can ring Stella and we'll both come back and hear what you have to say.'

Lauren nodded. 'Thank you,' she said, not knowing what she was thanking her for. James had stood up, though not looking at her. No, he couldn't bring himself to do that! He went with the two women out into the hallway so that she was left alone. She heard them talking but couldn't make out what they were saying.

She looked around the room. This was the house they had moved into during their second year of marriage, the house where they were to have reared a family. There was their wedding photograph framed on the mantelpiece, evidence of what they had once been.

It was as if everything had been blitzed and she was sitting in the midst of ruins, her hopes and dreams lying in ashes around her.

She heard him coming back into the room and felt a need to move, not to remain the passive victim. She stood up and went to where the drinks – bottles of sherry, port, whisky – were on display as part of the Christmas festivities. She uncorked the sherry bottle, not really wanting it but needing the excuse for her movement, and poured herself rather more than she intended.

She was aware of him watching her and said without looking round, 'I'm going to have a drink. Do you want one?'

'Lauren – '

'I mean it's still Christmas, isn't it. We're still supposed to be celebrating.' She knew she was talking wildly. It was to delay the moment when she would have to say those things, those awful things, that were in her heart.

She went and sat down again.

'Will you listen if I try and explain?' he said.

She hated the meekness in his voice. 'So you had

an affair with Suzie Brandon,' she said, wanting to challenge him, to make sure he knew the enormity of what he had done, the crime with which he was being charged.

'I would have told you but ... well, it never seemed very important.'

'Never seemed very important ... ?' She couldn't prevent the sarcasm. 'Oh, really? And why was that? Have you had lots of affairs or was it just that this one didn't live up to expectations?'

She saw him sigh as if it were she who was being unreasonable. 'Will you please just listen – '

'Of course I'll listen.'

'It happened just after – '

But she couldn't listen, no, not if it meant remaining silent while he paraded his excuses and evasions. She wanted to accuse him, to hammer home to him just what it was he had done. 'Well, congratulations,' she said, interrupting him.

'What?'

'You've done it, haven't you. You've got what you wanted all along.'

'I have?'

'You've stopped us adopting.' He gave a groan. 'Because that's what you did want all along, wasn't it?' She was shouting now. 'Wasn't it?'

'No – '

'Oh, yes, it was, you bastard!' She sprang forward out of the armchair and hurled the sherry into his face. It splattered across his forehead. The glass slipped from her fingers and bounced on the carpet. 'Oh, shit,' she said, stooping to retrieve it. 'Oh, you bastard.'

She hadn't intended doing that. She hadn't known what she had intended or even what she was intending to do next. She went and poured herself some more sherry, then flopped back into the chair. He still hadn't moved but stood there with the rivulets of sherry running down his face and onto his collar.

'So go on then,' she said, finding herself breathless. 'Tell me if you're going to.'

Not that she had finished with him yet. Before they parted – as they now surely must; that went without saying – he was going to answer in full for what he had done. But now she was ready to hear his defence. In fact, she was suddenly desperate to hear what it might be, knowing that there could be no defence in the whole, wide world that would serve as apology for his betrayal of her. 'Go on,' she insisted.

'Well,' he said, and lowered himself into a chair facing her. 'It was that time just after we'd been for the fertility tests. You remember . . . ?'

Of course she remembered. She gave a brief nod. He pulled a handkerchief from his pocket and began to wipe his face as he talked.

'Well, I don't know how they made you feel but . . . well, I found the whole business left me feeling pretty depressed. I mean, even though the tests didn't show anything. Or perhaps it was because they didn't show anything – '

'So you turned to Suzie for comfort,' she mocked. 'Well, now I see, yes. That explains everything. Good, old Suzie. I suppose I ought to write and thank her.' She knew her sarcasm was only letting him off the hook, saving him the humiliation of trying to justify his terrible deception, but she couldn't stop herself. She wanted to hurt him, as he had hurt her, but this, her scorn, was the only inadequate weapon to hand.

'Well, and is that it?' she taunted, meeting his stare. 'That's all you've got to say, is it?'

'No.'

'What then?'

'Well ... when she called it an affair ... when Suzie, in her letter, called it an affair ... I mean it wasn't, not really.'

'So what would you call it?'

'I don't know. I'm just saying it only lasted, what, a few days. A few weeks at the most – '

'How many times did you sleep with her?' He slowly shook his head, as though to say no, you surely can't want to know that. But yes, she wanted him on the rack, forced to give a full account. 'How many?'

'I think ... I think it was three times.'

'I see.'

'I'm still not sure why. I mean apart from the fact that I was feeling pretty low after – '

'You said.'

'I didn't, you know ... enjoy it very much.'

'Oh, for Christ's sake – '

'What?'

'Why're you saying that? Is that supposed to make me feel better or what?'

He sighed. 'Not really.'

She found she had finished her sherry and went to pour herself another. After all, what did it matter now? What did anything matter now? She wasn't on trial anymore and could behave in any way she chose. Wonderful. She should welcome all this as a deliverance, the chance of a new freedom.

She felt a tickling sensation on her cheek and realized it was tears. She wiped them away quickly with her hand.

'Do you want me to go?' said James.

She turned. 'Go?' Then she realized what he meant and shrugged. 'Do what you like.'

111

She felt that she would probably be the one to go. What had she left here to stay for? Whereas he had his family and his business. His family who would no doubt forgive him and find some way of blaming her and his precious business to which she had always come second. Anyway, she *wanted* to go, to get away. She would go to London and live alone in a flat, never seeing him or communicating with him again.

'Lauren, what happened with Suzie, it was just stupid. It had nothing to do with us, nothing to do with our marriage – '

'It's stopped us having a child!' she cried, newly affronted by the nerve of the man, that he could still try and wriggle off the hook. 'How can you say it's got nothing to do with us when it's stopped us having a child?'

'I never dreamt she would tell the agency about it – '

'Ha.'

'I didn't. Please, believe that. I mean whatever else you want to think about me, well OK, I can't blame you. But I never in a million years dreamt that Suzie would have told the agency!'

She heard the passion in his voice, forcing her to recognize that this was probably true. Despite what she had felt, she couldn't continue to believe that he had deliberately stage-managed the whole thing in order to undermine their application. Not that it excused him. Not that it excused anything or ever would. It simply meant he had been stupid and feckless rather than machiavellian.

Strange how she had always believed herself the more complex of the two of them. It was she who had always been prey to uncontrollable impulses and emotions while he had been the steady one, reliable, predictable even. And now this.

112

'So why did you let me put her name forward?' she countered. 'Why the hell didn't you stop me doing that?'

He gave a small shrug. 'Because I thought it was all dead and buried. I thought she'd put it behind her just as I had.' Then, with a sudden bitterness of his own that startled Lauren: 'The nasty, vindictive bitch . . . !'

She looked at him, surprised. So perhaps he, too, felt betrayed. Well, good, if it helped him know anything of what she was suffering.

'You know what I think? I think she's done it to get back at me.' He seemed animated by this new idea. 'See, I was the one who stopped seeing her. Oh, you might think I'm lying and obviously I can't prove anything, but it's true. I was the one who stopped seeing her. She left messages at work for me but I didn't take any notice. And now this is her way of getting back at me!'

His anger seemed genuine but she resisted joining his condemnation of Suzie, however much it might be deserved. Siding with him in this would only suggest she was forgiving him, which she wasn't and never would.

'You could have stopped me using her as a referee,' she said.

'I tried to. I tried suggesting other people but you wouldn't listen. You were determined it had to be her!'

Was that true? She couldn't remember. 'So why didn't you tell me about the affair? That would have stopped me, wouldn't it!'

She had the satisfaction of seeing him bow his head, an admission that he had no answer. Seeing him like that, vulnerable and prostrate and without even the courage to stand up for himself, prompted her to a renewed attack.

113

'You're a coward, you know that? A pathetic coward. So you had an affair – or a fling, I suppose that's what you thought it was, did you? *A fling*! – with Suzie Brandon. You couldn't even go out and find somebody for yourself, could you. You couldn't even manage that. It had to be a friend of mine, didn't it.' She was standing now, above him, wishing she could strike him. But she couldn't bring herself to slap or hit. It wasn't in her. She was shaking, her body out of control, and her words too. 'Then when you'd had this pathetic, little affair, which you say wasn't an affair at all because you can't even face up to that either ... then you couldn't even end it properly, could you. You didn't even have the guts to face her and end it properly. No, you had to leave it festering away. And, when I said I wanted Suzie as a referee, you could have stopped me. Oh, yes, you could! You could have stopped me any time you wanted. All you had to do was tell me about your sordid little fling. That would have stopped me! But no. No, because you're too much of a coward for that, aren't you. So you don't say anything. You let me carry on. You let me put her name down. And now you want me to believe it's all her fault ... ? Well, I won't, because it's your fault. All your fault and I'll never forgive you. Not because you've gone and slept with some other woman – I don't give a damn about that – but because you're such a pathetic coward about everything!'

She stopped, her fury spent. Yet she couldn't leave it at that. There was something more she had to add to complete the indictment. 'But the real reason that I will never, ever forgive you as long as I live is because what you've done means that we can never have a baby.'

She saw him wince at that, turning his head away. Well, good. So she had hurt him at last then.

She moved to the window, still trembling, and put down her glass. Outside, the last of the light was fading from the winter skies. She realized with a small surprise how dark it was inside the room where the only lights were those of the Christmas tree.

James was a hunched silhouette in his chair, his attitude almost a parody of remorse. She wondered whether she should pack some clothes and go now or whether it would be enough to let him know that this was her intention. Then she wondered just where was she going to go to?

'She said it didn't necessarily rule us out.'

He spoke flatly, as though reciting a catechism in which he held little belief. She had to think for a moment before she realized what he was referring to. 'You mean the adoption?'

'Yes.'

It struck her as a sick joke. 'You really think they're going to let us adopt a child after this . . . ?'

'I'm just reminding you what they said. That it was up to us to tell them what we wanted to do.'

Well, yes, Marjorie Daniels had said that, along with a load of other platitudes designed to avoid the hard truth. No doubt she was being kind in her way, believing they had had enough bad news for one day. And yet . . . Despite everything, Lauren felt the faintest of hopes reviving within her. She despised herself for it, knowing it had to be futile.

'I don't care what they said. They'd never consider us now. Can't you bloody well see that? Or is this something else that you can't face up to?'

She couldn't make out his features clearly but he didn't seem to react. Anyway, what kind of farce

115

would it be to continue playing the ideal couple with things as they were between them, their marriage in tatters?

And yet . . .

'What do you want to do?' she said.

There was a pause, then he said quietly, 'Try again.'

She fought an impulse to scream at him, to tell him that he was being wilfully stupid. Still the coward seeking to avoid the full implications of what he had done. What stopped her was this new idea, one she didn't really believe in but couldn't shake off. The idea that things might be redeemable after all. They might repair their battered marriage and challenge Marjorie Daniels with her own words: that they could still be eligible no matter what had happened in the past.

'Do you think we can?' she said, to herself as much as to him.

'I think we have to,' he said. 'Otherwise what else is there?'

Well, yes, she could see the truth of that. Ironically, the adoption process was now probably the only thing that could save them.

She saw that he was moving towards her, not attempting to touch her but simply standing beside her in the half-light of the Christmas tree. She took a breath and forced herself to take his hand.

There remained a demon in her head urging her not to forgive him, not to let him off the hook. But now there was also another voice, more like her own, contending with it, telling her not to turn her back on him while there remained even the remotest possible chance that the child she had given up for dead might yet be delivered to her.

11

Francois Lucchi, dapper and diminutive as ever, was shown into Marcus' study by his house-keeper. 'Don't get up. Don't get up!' he cried, waving his arms and hurrying towards the desk.

But Marcus was already standing and held out his hand. 'I'm not such a total invalid. And how're you, my old friend?'

'I'm very well. But to hear of what happened to you . . . ! I was devastated.'

'I was in quite a state myself,' said Marcus drily. 'But look – fully recovered.' Which was true, barring the momentos of a few lingering aches and pains. 'Now, sit down. And thank you for coming. I know you are a busy man. A pastis?'

Lucchi's gold-capped teeth twinkled as he accepted the drink. As Marcus had expected, he was full of questions, wanting to know every detail of the attack. Had there be no warning or threats prior to it? Who did Marcus believe was its instigator? Had the police made any progress in their investigations? Marcus looked him in the eye and said that neither he nor the police had the slightest idea who was behind the outrage.

'Still you must fear that your enemy will persist in his efforts,' said Lucchi cunningly. 'You're like a politician or film-star with your guards around you.'

'Just a precaution,' Marcus parried. 'I hope it won't be necessary for long.'

'I hope so too. Let me wish you a happy and a prosperous New Year.' He raised his glass. 'May the change of year mark a change in your fortunes.' A sentiment which Marcus was happy to endorse.

He had thought long and hard about who he might approach for help in dealing with Jarman, and how he might best do it without compromising himself. In the end he had selected Lucchi, partly because of his remarkable range of contacts amid the international fraternity of mercenaries, gun-runners and war-lords and partly because he could be bought.

He wasn't the ideal co-conspirator. He was too given to gossip and boastfulness to be that. Though perhaps even this could be seen as a saving grace. Those who knew him were accustomed to taking his stories with a pinch of salt and so were likely to do the same if he were ever to betray Marcus over one too many Pastis.

Besides, there was no easy way of having a man killed. Dealing with Lucchi was a small risk compared to what would follow.

As Marcus ran the arguments in his head – the pros and cons of killing Jarman that had obsessed him since his arrival home from hospital – Lucchi launched into a rambling account of what he referred to as 'the merchandise of Vietnamese origin'. Which Marcus interpreted as the fabled American arsenal Lucchi had all but promised to deliver to him when they had met in Paris, the day before he was gunned down.

Apparently there were problems. (Hardly a surprise, but Marcus kept a straight face and listened patiently.) The supplier was proving elusive and unreliable, on top of which there might be political difficulties: rumoured changes of heart in Hanoi among those who had seemed on the verge of authorizing the release of the munitions onto the international market. Lucchi stressed how he was continuing his best efforts to circumvent these problems.

The whole thing, with lots of talk and no action, was typical of the Algerian. Endearingly so under other circumstances; now it made Marcus wonder if he had, indeed, chosen the right accomplice. (Then reminded himself that there was probably no such person as the *right accomplice*; only some who were less dangerous than others.)

Deciding it was now or never, Marcus said, 'Actually there was one other matter I wanted to consult you about.'

'Yes?'

Marcus spoke carefully and gravely, wanting to impress the other man. Even frighten him if possible. 'It is a very delicate matter. I am relying throughout on your total discretion.'

Lucchi responded instantly, assuming an expression of fierce solemnity. 'I flatter myself that it is what I am best known for.'

'I am acting on behalf of a friend of mine. Someone to whom I owe a debt of honour. Forgive me if I don't tell you his name.'

'I understand.'

'He needs someone to carry out a job for him and is willing to pay a large amount of money to the right man.'

'And what sort of job would this be?'

'An execution.'

Lucchi's mouth fell open in surprise.

'I wonder if you might know of such a man,' Marcus continued. 'A professional. A man who could be trusted.'

119

It mattered little whether Lucchi believed his lie about the friend and the debt of honour. It was a small smoke-screen that would at least leave him guessing. If it ever became necessary, Marcus would simply deny that the conversation had ever taken place. It was one reason he had persuaded Lucchi to come to his home, exaggerating his own immobility following his treatment in hospital. Here, there could be no witnesses or possibility of their conversation being recorded.

Lucchi had regained his composure. Though Marcus detected a new wariness about him, caution replacing surprise. 'There are such men, yes,' he said.

'You could put my friend in touch with one of them?'

'Well, it would not be easy – '

'Something I should have mentioned. I will, of course, be paying you for your services.'

'Ah, no, no – ' Lucchi began to protest.

'I insist,' said Marcus. 'Otherwise we must forget all about this. I am employing you as an agent. I must therefore pay you for your services.'

'Well, if it makes you happier . . . ' said Lucchi, with a gesture of helplessness. It meant he would accept the money.

This was progress, more than he had dared hope for, yet Marcus felt himself sweating. Part of him had not expected Lucchi to take the bait; or perhaps he hadn't truly believed himself capable of offering it. Anyway, extracting the wad of thousand-franc notes from his desk drawer, he had the unnerving feeling that he was about to release forces that might prove impossible to control, forces of evil that were as likely to bring himself down as to bring down his enemy.

Still, there was no going back, not now. He thrust the wad of notes towards Lucchi. 'For you.'

'This is very generous – '

'Not at all. But, Francois, let me make myself absolutely clear. My friend does not want some wild cowboy from the Bekhar Valley. Nor does he want some pot-bellied mercenary. What my friend wants is a professional.' He spoke slowly, his eyes fixed on the Algerian, who was pocketing the notes and looking thoughtful. 'Someone who will complete the job swiftly and leave no complications behind him.'

'I understand,' said Lucchi.

At least Marcus felt he had managed to impress Lucchi with the seriousness of his task. He had to be made to realize that this was one time that his blustering would not suffice.

'Quite honestly, Francois, I would much prefer that you should tell me now if you have any doubts about this.'

Lucchi looked as though he might well be having doubts. But he had already pocketed the notes and made no move to return them.

'I will not fail you,' he said.

'Good. One more thing then. When you find such a man, he must not know who I am. You must simply contact me and tell me where and when my friend can meet him. Then you must please forget all about this. Wipe it from your memory forever.'

Seeing Lucchi to the door and instructing Eduardo to take him to the airport, Marcus was assailed by misgivings and fears. What was he doing but descending to the same level as his enemy? Hiring killers, not even at first hand but through an accomplice, attempting to distance himself from the eventual and brutal outcome. Could he ever hope to free

121

himself in this way? Or would his hands remain forever so stained with blood that he would never escape his own conscience but be re-visited nightly by nightmarish visions of assassins and murder?

Still, the first step had been taken. Whether it would ever lead to a second now rested in Lucchi's tiny hands.

For Lauren the week following Marjorie Daniels' visit and the revelation of James' *fling* was the most awful of their marriage. There were periods when she despised and hated her husband and wanted an end to the whole charade of their continuing together – wanted an end now, and to hell with the adoption. One morning she even got as far as half-packing a suitcase but then couldn't go on and just sat on the bed and wept – shedding endless tears in a way she hadn't done since her girlhood, with loud, gasping sobs and her shoulders heaving – till the door went downstairs, announcing James' return. In a sudden panic, she slid the suitcase under the bed, to be unpacked later, bolted herself in the bathroom and sat on the bidet till she was sufficiently composed to go down and face him.

Then there were other times when, seeing the misery on his face, she was overwhelmed by pity for him and wanted to take him in her arms and comfort him, telling him that none of it mattered and she still loved him. Till she would remind herself what he had done, which made her hold back. They ate in near silence and, although still sleeping together in the same bed, did so without touching, each keeping to their own sides as though their lives depended on it.

James had tried twice to get her to talk about the issue again, tentatively asking how she was feeling, then backing off quickly when she retorted sharply How did he expect? or What did he imagine? Yet she did want to talk about it and knew that they couldn't go on living like this forever, in a state of cold war.

Eventually it occurred to her that perhaps the only way forward, towards a resolution of whatever sort, was to put themselves in the hands of the agency and let them decide whether this marriage was to survive and even be enlarged into a family or whether it was beyond salvation and should be left to wither and die.

It was the tactics of desperation, she knew that, risking everything on one throw of the dice; still she had to do something.

She waited till James had left the house, not trusting herself even to talk to him about it, lest the wrong emotions should surface and she would be shouting at him again. He left early for the Garden Centre, though what he found there to occupy himself at this time of year she couldn't imagine. Perhaps it was merely an excuse to be out of the house and away from her and he spent the day doing nothing but moping forlornly among the seedlings? Anyway, she waited till she heard the Land Rover drive off, then rang Stella at the agency.

'Oh, hi,' said Stella, recognizing her voice. 'Well, and how are things?'

'Oh, could be worse. At least we're still together,' said Lauren, wanting to avoid an outright lie.

'I'm very glad. And so do you want to continue with the adoption application?'

'Yes,' said Lauren. 'Yes, definitely.'

'Well, I'm glad about that too. Because I honestly think you should.'

Lauren was grateful for her approval, though she

knew she was obtaining it under false pretences. Stella didn't know the extent of the rift still there between her and James; she would hardly have sounded so enthusiastic if she had. She explained that not only would she have to call again but that, after all that had happened, Marjorie Daniels would want to see them too. Would that afternoon be convenient or did they want a little more notice to prepare themselves?

They sat in the lounge, Marjorie Daniels smoking, Stella on her chair in the corner, and Lauren and James side-by-side on the sofa. Though they were still not touching, each keeping carefully to their own end of it.

He had been surprised and, she thought, a little alarmed, to receive her call summoning him back to the house. She didn't tell him that it was she who had phoned the agency but let him believe that they had contacted her.

'But don't we need to talk?' he asked, 'the two of us, before they get here?'

'What is there to talk about?' she said, still unable to be anything but off-hand with him. 'We still do want to adopt, don't we?'

'Well . . . yes. Yes, of course but – '

'Then that's what we'll tell them. Everything else is up to them.'

But she knew he was still uneasy, probably fearful she would be unable to contain herself and would have another of her outbursts. Well, she couldn't guarantee that she wouldn't. All she knew was that this was something they had to go through, whatever the outcome.

'I'm sorry we had to spoil your Christmas,' said Marjorie Daniels. 'But I'm sure you can understand that we had no choice in the matter.' They neither of them said anything. She turned to Lauren, 'So, Mrs Eaglesham, can I ask you first. How do you now feel about this relationship your husband had with this Mrs . . . '

'Brandon,' said Stella.

Lauren took a breath, then blurted out, 'I don't think it matters. I honestly don't. I mean it happened quite some time ago and it never threatened our marriage, even then, so I don't see why it should now. James and I . . . well, we've talked about it and . . . well, if nothing else, it shows we can survive something like that, doesn't it. It shows we both value our relationship too much to throw it away lightly.'

She stopped, surprised at herself. Was all this true? Well, yes, perhaps not the whole truth, but true in that they had survived Suzie Brandon's letter and were there together to prove it. (By the skin of their teeth but Marjorie Daniels could work that out for herself.)

'And has knowing what you now know made you feel any differently about James?'

'No, not . . . well, no. I still love him and I know he still loves me.'

There, it had taken an effort, one that had left her heart pounding, but she had said it. Another partial truth presented as absolute. She felt James' hand on hers but she still couldn't bring herself to look at him and so sat staring at Marjorie Daniels, whose expression gave nothing away.

Then, suddenly and without prompting, James began to speak.

He explained, as he had already done to Lauren but now more calmly, how the short-lived affair had come about and how little it had signified. He said

125

he had been devastated to find the whole, unhappy episode, which he had believed dead-and-gone, brought to life in Suzie Brandon's letter. Worst of all, he feared what it might have done to their chances of adopting. For he was as desperate as his wife that they should be successful. He admitted he might not always have shown this. He had perhaps been remiss in leaving it to her to make all the running. Now he wanted to put the record straight and make it clear he was every bit as anxious as she was that they should one day soon welcome a child into their home. He would never forgive himself if his foolishness had sabotaged that prospect.

As he spoke, Lauren felt herself warm towards him. More than that, it was as if she were falling in love with him all over again, re-discovering this honest, decent man who would go to the ends of the earth for her. And, if she had ever had any doubts about his keenness to adopt, well, now they were gone too.

She squeezed his hand, wanting to convey her gratitude and her love. It was the most she dared do with Marjorie Daniels still eyeing them from three feet away.

Still showing not a flicker of emotion, Marjorie Daniels asked: 'Does anyone else know of this relationship you had with Mrs Brandon? Her husband for example?'

Lauren wondered what could be the point of this, but James was already shaking his head. 'No,' he said. 'I'm sure not.'

'Did you ever talk to Mrs Brandon about the possibility of you leaving your wife for her?'

Lauren wanted to protest. Hadn't the woman been listening? Hadn't James explained how it had been no more than a seven-day wonder, certainly not the kind of thing you threw over your marriage for?

'Never,' said James. 'It was something I regretted . . . well, I regretted it almost as soon as it had happened.'

'So why didn't you tell your wife about it?'

'There didn't seem to be any point. Of course, if I'd known this was going to happen, well, I certainly would have told her, yes.'

She's still suspicious of us, thought Lauren. If it were left to her, she'd tell the Panel we can't be trusted with a puppy, never mind a child.

Marjorie Daniels stubbed out her cigarette and said, 'Well, I think we'll leave it at that. Unless, Stella, you have anything you'd like to ask . . . ?'

'Not really,' said Stella. 'It all seems to have been settled as far as I can see.'

Marjorie Daniels gave her a look and said, 'We'd better be going then.' Interpreting the look, Lauren thought – they're going to argue about us. The minute they get in the car, they'll be disagreeing about everything. With Stella on their side and Marjorie Daniels against. And Marjorie Daniels was the principal social worker at the agency, which meant Stella would be out-ranked.

It was all she could do not to grab Marjorie Daniels and shake her and say, look, just what do we have to do to prove that everything's all right? Of course you can trust us with a child. After this you can trust us with anything!

Instead, she grabbed James when he returned from showing the two women to the door. She threw her arms round him and hugged him, saying, 'I'm sorry. I'm so sorry . . . !' And he was telling her no, that it was his fault and that he was sorry too. Till they were close to arguing about who had the most right to be sorry and ended up necking on the sofa and from there went upstairs to bed.

They had made love and were lying together in near darkness, listening to their neighbours on the Avenue returning from work when the phone began to ring.

'It'll be for you,' said Lauren, reluctant to move.

James groaned but swung himself out of bed, pulled on his dressing-gown and hurried downstairs. Lauren was dropping off to sleep when she suddenly realized he had returned and was sitting beside her on the bed.

'What?' she said, blinking up at him.

'It was Stella Priestley.'

Now she was wide-awake. 'Yes?'

'She says there's no need for a final interview. They're going to present their report to the Panel and we should hear within a couple of weeks.'

12

Two weeks came and went and there was no word from the agency. Desperate for something to happen – almost anything would have been better than the waiting – Lauren questioned James: 'When Stella spoke to you on the phone, did she say *two* weeks or *a couple of weeks*?' James considered and said he was fairly sure it had been *a couple* of weeks. 'But that could mean anything!' she exclaimed in dismay.

Otherwise, with Christmas well and truly over, life had resuméd its familiar pattern. James was at the Garden Centre, while she was back selling Toyotas, of which they had just received a new batch so that the garage was chock-a-block. Good to be busy, she told herself, though, in truth, it didn't seem to make much difference. However rushed off her feet she might be, she could not put the Panel and their decision out of her mind.

Suppose the verdict went against them and they were refused? Was her marriage now strong enough to withstand such a blow or would it slowly crumble in the aftermath? She could only try and shut such a nightmare from her mind. Wait, she told herself. Just be patient and wait for the Panel to decide.

Rachel had given birth to her third child, another girl, and there was a small christening party to celebrate. Lauren was given the child to hold but found herself dangerously close to tears and passed her back to her mother. Both her sister-in-laws were keen to know how the adoption was proceeding but she had warned James in advance to say nothing, remembering how her announcement at their last gathering had been so swiftly followed by near-catastrophe. She talked vaguely of 'endless interviews' and 'getting to know sometime soon' till they lost interest.

Each morning she rushed to the post, sifting through it for anything that wasn't a bill and had a local post-mark and so might be from the agency. Then gave a groan of disappointment when there was nothing. It was now close to three weeks since that final visit by Stella and Marjorie Daniels.

James suggested they took the bull by the horns and rang the agency but Lauren was opposed to this. She knew it was pure superstition but felt that such a show of impatience might somehow count against them. 'Anyway, what's the point?' she said, trying to be rational. 'Obviously the Panel haven't met yet. If they had, we'd have been told by now.'

Then, next morning, when there was still no letter, she pursued the postman down the Avenue, insisting he check his bag to make sure there was nothing else for them he might have overlooked.

In fact, the news, when it came that afternoon, caught her completely unawares.

She was preparing a Corolla GT for a test drive. Not one of the batch of glittering, new cars but second-hand, with 28,000 miles on the clock. Similar to the one she drove herself but nippier and bedecked with fog-lamps and spoilers. She let the engine rev and used a rubber scraper to clear the thin film of snow from its bonnet and windscreen. The test drive would be a test more of driver than of car, with icy slush on the roads.

She had a theory that test drives were fairly useless anyway, no more than a bit of ritual to let the customers feel he was getting the full treatment. Most of them were self-conscious about driving an unfamiliar vehicle with her sitting beside them and were happy enough to get back to the garage in one piece.

One day she would write a thesis on the subject.

Greg came from the showroom, hugging himself against the cold. 'Phone for you,' he called.

'Who is it?' she called back, thinking, damn, it would be her customer cancelling his test drive, frightened off by the bad conditions.

'No idea. Woman's voice.'

She stamped her boots clean and went inside, through the showroom with its potted plants and spot-lights and into the office, where it was too warm and made her nose run.

'Hello? Lauren Eaglesham here . . . ?'

'Lauren, it's Stella. Stella Priestley.'

She felt thrown off-balance and put a hand on the desk to steady herself. Oh, no, she wanted to protest. Not now. I'm not ready for it. While another part of her brain was desperately trying to assess the other woman's tone of voice and what kind of news it might herald.

'Oh, hello,' she managed to gasp.

Just tell me, quick.

'I've got some good news for you . . . '

Good news . . . ! That must mean . . . had to mean . . .

'. . . The Panel met last night and they've approved your application.'

131

Lauren gave a cry of joy and relief and saw Greg, sitting at his own desk, look round in surprise. 'Really?' she said, aware that she was grinning broadly.

'Yes. Really,' said Stella. 'I must admit though it was touch-and-go at first. There was a fair amount of discussion but then, the longer it went on, the more they began to swing to your side.'

Letting the voice continue in her ear, Lauren gazed slowly round at the familiar, cluttered office. The clock said three twenty-seven. She wanted to remember this moment and every detail of it for the rest of her life.

'I don't believe it. I really can't believe it,' she heard herself saying. Greg was staring at her and she had to turn away to stop herself laughing aloud at his expression of bewilderment. The relief, after the days and months of waiting, engulfed her like a flood. 'Oh, it's wonderful!'

She heard Stella's pleased laugh at the other end of the line. 'I've put a letter in the post but I thought you'd like to know as soon as – '

'Oh, yes, thanks. And I mean thank you ... thank you for everything. I still can't believe it. This is real, isn't it? I am awake?'

'Wide awake. And, like I say, you'll get the letter tomorrow to prove it.'

They talked further, Stella asking how they were keeping and warning that it still might be some time before a child was found for them, but Lauren was barely conscious of her own replies. All she knew was that they had been accepted. Against all the odds. Well, against the odds that Suzie Brandon had so cruelly stacked against them at the last minute. They had come through all of it, the interviews and her doubts about James and her worrying

132

about what kind of impression they were making . . . they had come through it and been accepted as adoptive parents.

She had to tell James. James whom she loved and would always love. If only Stella would stop talking, then she could ring him. It was all she could do to remain polite as Stella went on about the need for patience in waiting for the right child, until finally she was saying good-by and Lauren was able to put down the phone.

'Sounded like good news,' said Greg wryly.

She looked at him, unable to stop smiling. 'Greg, will you do me a big favour please and go outside for five minutes then I can make a phone-call?'

He gave a groan of mock-protest. 'I promise not to listen.'

'Please,' she urged. 'I'll tell you what it's about later. But there's somebody else I have to tell first.'

He got to his feet, picked his jacket off the back of his chair and moved to the door. 'It's not that husband of yours coming between us again, is it?' But she was already dialling and didn't answer.

James was working outdoors and there was a delay while he was brought to the phone. The moment she heard him begin to speak, she said, 'James, it's me. I've heard from the agency. Stella has just phoned.'

There was a pause. 'And?' he said. But he sounded hopeful. She knew she hadn't been able to keep the excitement out of her voice.

'They've said yes! Can you believe it? Apparently the Panel met last night and – 'She broke off, hearing him laughing with relief, and laughed herself. 'Yes!' she said, feeling triumphant. 'They said yes!'

She heard him muttering, 'Marvellous . . . bloody marvellous.'

133

'We're going to get a letter tomorrow.' And she told him how Stella had hinted that it had been a close-run thing, going against them at first, then swinging in their favour. They agreed it must have been the Suzie Brandon business initially turning the Panel against them and then, presumably, sterling work by Stella to win them round. Thank God for Stella.

She was stopped by Greg making faces through the glass door to tell her her customer had arrived. She told James she loved him, he promised he would try to be home early and she rang off.

Going out, she said to Greg, 'We've been accepted by an adoption society.' Now she wanted everyone to know.

'You're going to be adopted?' he said. But then called after her, 'Hey, no, I'm very pleased. Seriously I am.'

The test drive didn't quite produce the expected sale. Nothing wrong with the car but she suspected the customer was made uneasy by the happiness she couldn't hide. Perhaps he could see that her mind was elsewhere. So what? Who cared anyway?

When she got back to the office, Greg had drawn a makeshift card which said 'Congratulations', above a picture of a stork with a baby in its beak. 'Jumping the gun as usual,' she said. 'We've been accepted, that's all.' But she was pleased, feeling that, yes, they deserved to be congratulated. After all they had gone through, they deserved a telegram from the Queen.

Though, of course, this was only the beginning. Now would come the weeks and perhaps months of waiting till a suitable child was found for them. Then there would be another call and only after

that would she be holding in her arms a child that
this time wouldn't be Rachel's or anybody else's but
that would at last be her own.

13

Marcus stood inside the doorway of the conservatory, sweating under the weight of his overcoat, and peered out across the still, snowy landscape of the Botanical Gardens. Winter was persevering into spring in Geneva. The trees remained bowed under their burdens of frozen snow; the landscape around them was an unbroken, shimmering whiteness.

A door crashed closed at the far end of the conservatory and he swung round, startled, his grip tightening around the pistol he was carrying in the pocket of his overcoat. He peered through the tangle of rubber-plants and giant cacti, then relaxed. It was two women who had entered, stamping the snow from their boots and laughing. He released his grip on the pistol and moved back to where he had been standing. Outside, the silvery parkland remained empty.

The man had said ten o'clock. Marcus looked at his watch and saw it was now ten-past. It surprised him that his contact should be late; their dealings to date had suggested someone who liked things to be precise and who might have been relied on to be punctual.

Besides, he was nervous enough about this encounter and had wanted it over quickly. Suppose he were noticed, loitering there amid the cacti? The two

136

ladies had reached him. He muttered, 'Excuse me,' and moved aside to let them pass.

He had heard nothing from Francois Lucchi for over a month and had begun to think that the diminutive Algerian, not for the first time, had taken the money and scarpered. Then had come a phone-call from Lucchi, saying he had located someone who might be suitable for the work Marcus had in mind. The man's name was Paolo – nothing more, just Paolo – and he could be contacted via a Rome number. Lucchi spoke guardedly, soberly even. He said he believed that this Paolo had the experience and the ability required for the task in hand.

Marcus thanked him, than asked, 'What have you told him of me?'

'Only your first name. So that he might recognize you when you make contact.'

'Can I trust him?'

A pause then, 'Probably.'

It was as much as he might have expected. After all, who could he trust? Jarman had already struck at him twice when he had believed himself safe. Now he believed himself safe nowhere. Even at home, with the guards still deployed in the garden, he had become suspicious of delivery-men or messengers, faces he didn't recognize.

At least with a professional killer the mistrust was an accepted element of the relationship.

It had already occurred to him that his own phone might be bugged. The police, under Inspector Marti, had seemed to lose interest in him; all the same, it would be foolish to take the risk. He waited till that evening when he had, anyway, arranged to call on Ragula Veuillet, then asked her if he might use her phone, though, of course, without telling her why.

137

Her willingness to pursue their budding relationship had been a pleasant surprise. After all, both their lunch together and then the promised dinner at her flat had ended in violence. It would have been understandable had she decided that enough was enough and given him a wide berth. Yet she had phoned him when he was out of hospital and accepted his invitation to her to visit him. They had become lovers later, in the small bedroom of her flat, and now their affair had reached that comfortable, undemanding stage where each had discovered the limits of the other. Though passionate between the sheets, she had a hard-nosed selfishness about her: he knew she would never allow their relationship to carry her further than she wished to go. Well, fine, he told himself. Had he really any right to expect more? Their meetings – no more than one or two a week – had become part of his convalescence.

He wondered whether perhaps he had at last met his true soul-mate. Someone destined to remain slightly detached, never giving more than a measured part of herself and so not asking too much in return.

He had told her nothing about Jarman and she had ceased to question him about the attacks, as though accepting that it was his business and so his right to tell her as little as he chose. Certainly she showed no inquisitiveness about his request to use the phone and directed him downstairs to the gallery, where he would be alone.

After all his precautions, it was something of an anti-climax to ring the Rome number Lucchi had given him and find it to be an accommodation address that did no more than take messages. He rang off, to give himself time to think, then dialled the number again and said, 'This is Marcus. I can be contacted on Zurich 70–35–82.' It was a transportation firm with whom he did business and who, he knew, wouldn't mind operating as a halfway house for any messages.

In fact, it was three days before he heard from them – with a message that simply asked him to ring a further number, this time in Naples. He did so and found himself speaking to another answering-machine. He gave his Zurich number and, three days later, received a message saying Paolo would be in touch.

Had Lucchi conned him into this elaborate charade or had Lucchi himself been conned? Or was the whole roundabout way of making contact no more than an excess of caution, which Marcus should have been welcoming? He had demanded that Lucchi found him a professional, not some gun-toting maniac. Perhaps this elaborate routine was a sign of such professionalism and should be welcomed?

Then, without warning or further preliminaries, Paolo had made direct and unexpected contact. Marcus was eating breakfast and glancing over the pages of 'Zurcherzeitung' and 'Barslerzeitung', the two newspapers he took regularly, when the phone rang. He answered it and heard a voice say, 'I am Paolo.'

It took him a moment to realize the significance of that simple announcement and to collect his wits before he could answer, 'And I am Marcus.'

'If you still wish to do business,' said Paolo, 'then be in the main conservatory of the Botanical Gardens in one hour's time. That is, at ten o'clock.' He had rather a hoarse voice, speaking French with a heavy Italian accent.

This was a further surprise. Where was he ringing from? Could he really be so close?

'The Botanical Gardens ... what, here in Geneva?'

'Yes. Do you know it?'

'Well, yes, I certainly do but – '

'One hour's time if you still wish to do business.' And there was a click as the phone at the other end was replaced.

Marcus felt outmanoeuvred, even slightly panicked, by the sudden arrival of this man practically on his own doorstep. No doubt it was a deliberate ploy to gain the initiative, aimed at making Marcus feel at Paolo's beck-and-call, instead of the other way round.

Again, it could be seen as a point in Paolo's favour. He was a man who planned ahead and did so effectively.

Strange, then, that with his watch now showing ten-twenty Marcus was still alone amid the tropical plants of the Grande Conservatoire. The two women had completed their tour and departed. Even though still edgy about the meeting, he was becoming impatient, tired of pacing up and down the crazed pathway, his eyes aching from scanning the luminous landscape beyond the glass.

Ten-thirty.

Suddenly, materializing as if from nowhere, a man in a blue coat was approaching at a hurried pace, his head down as he trudged through the snow. Paolo. It had to be. Marcus had just time to realize that he must have emerged from one of the gazebos close to the conservatory. He must have been there all along, watching and waiting, even before Marcus had arrived.

Was he making sure that Marcus was alone? So

140

was he also fearful of some kind of trap, trusting nobody?

But now he was at the door and pushing it open. Marcus stepped back, his hand tightening around the pistol in his overcoat pocket.

The other man was about Marcus' own height, with thin features and large, brown eyes. Hungry-looking. When he unwrapped his scarf, Marcus saw that his jutting jaw was softened by a neatly-trimmed, dark beard.

And he was young. No more than twenty-five or six. Yet, Marcus wrily reflected, he was probably several years the senior to the two youths who had ambushed him in the Rue de l'Athénée.

'You are Marcus?' he said, his voice low as it had been on the phone.

'Yes.'

'I am Paolo.' Marcus nodded and they shook hands. 'And you wish to place a contract on someone's life?'

'I do, yes,' said Marcus, finding the American slang unexpected but encouraged by the brisk, direct approach. This was hardly the kind of business that would benefit from small talk or a shared lunch.

'For what reason?'

'Self-protection. He is out to kill me.'

Paolo considered that, then shrugged as though to say, well, it was as good a reason as any. He reached into his pocket, a gesture that made Marcus flinch, then pulled out a cigarette-lighter and a packet of Marlborough. 'Tell me about the target,' he said, shaking out a cigarette from the packet.

Marcus hesitated, fearing that to do so would reveal too much of himself. Still, it had to be done. He could hardly hire the assassin without giving

141

him the information he needed to find his target. He began to talk about Noel Jarman, telling everything he knew save for the details of his own past association with him. Paolo pulled a small face at the mention of South Africa but didn't interrupt. They were both distracted by the sound of the doors opening and the rush of cold air. A young woman with two small children in bright galoshes entered. Marcus fell silent and both men stepped back from the pathway to let them pass.

'I must be honest,' said Marcus, when the woman was out of earshot, 'this is a dangerous and resourceful man I am talking about. He will not be easy to find, much less to . . . ' – he shied away from the crude truth and took refuge in the euphemism – '. . . to eliminate.'

'Which is why my fees will be high,' said Paolo.

Marcus gave a grunt of assent. He could hardly contest that after the warning he had just issued. Nevertheless, he would not have had it retracted; it was both right and expedient that this young man should know the odds against him.

'Anything else?' asked Paolo.

'How old are you?' asked Marcus on a sudden whim.

Paolo stiffened. 'Is that important?'

'No. I just wondered.'

A moment then: 'I'm twenty-four.' And, with a touch of sarcasm: 'Do you still wish to proceed?'

'Yes.'

After all, wasn't it always the young men who were sent to do the murderous bidding of the old? And often with less reason than this, knowing less of the cause but going anyway.

'OK,' said Paolo briskly. 'Now let me tell you how I work. Firstly, if you wish to proceed, you must pay me ten thousand Swiss francs. This is to cover my expenses. Then I will go away from here and do a little research into this man you have told me about. If, after that, I decide that I will make the hit,' – the American slang again – 'I will contact you and at that point you must telex one hundred thousand Swiss francs into an account, the number of which I will give you. Then, when I have made the hit, you will pay another hundred thousand francs into the same account.'

It was much as Marcus had expected. Of course he had to trust that Paolo wouldn't simply take the first hundred thousand and disappear but such a gamble had been inevitable from the outset. Certainly he had kept his promise that his fees would be high – two hundred thousand and ten thousand in all – but this was hardly the kind of job for which there could be a going rate. The money could be found. How much was it costing him now to protect himself against further attack? Besides, he sensed that there would be no point in haggling. Paolo's quiet statement of his terms suggested that Marcus could take them or leave them.

Well, he had come this far and so would take them. He gave a small nod of assent.

'Very good,' said Paolo. He dropped his half-smoked cigarette and ground it out. 'Do you have the money for me, the ten thousand?'

Marcus had come prepared, taking money from his safe before leaving the house. He took the wad of notes from his pocket and counted out ten thousand francs.

'Thank you,' said Paolo. 'Well, then I think that concludes our business.'

But Marcus was curious. 'How will you find your . . . ' – searching for the right word – 'your target?'

143

'From the information you have given me.'

'You will remember it?' Impossible surely. Marcus' account had included names and addresses which Paolo had never asked to be repeated.

Paolo gave a quick smile, his first. 'Not necessary. This will remember it for me.' He took a small device from his pocket. It was some kind of recorder, no bigger than his packet of cigarettes. Marcus glimpsed the tape still running. 'But don't worry,' Paolo said, before he could express his doubts. 'The tape will be destroyed. Afterwards, when the job is done, everything that could connect me to it, or me to you, will also be destroyed.'

Marcus nodded. It wasn't just a matter of trusting the man but recognizing that these precautions were in both their interests. Besides, he was impressed by Paolo's calm and organized approach, the absence of swagger or boastfulness.

They shook hands again and Paolo left first, holding open the door for the woman and her two children who were leaving at the same time. Marcus gave him a few minutes' start, then set out across the snow.

It would not be the first time in his life he had been an accomplice to murder. When he was only fifteen, already wise to life in the tenement blocks of Marseilles, he and his brother, Hervé, had become distressed by the violence inflicted on their mother by her latest boy-friend, a boorish street-trader in African knick-knacks. He was a man who seemed unable to take more than a single shot of absinthe without having to lash out at someone. They had, more than once, found their mother nursing a bruised and bleeding face. Hervé, two years his senior, had become enraged and talked of killing the man. Accustomed to such wild talk and not

144

believing it would come to that – not to *killing* – Marcus had gone along with his brother's plan to waylay the street-trader that night as he staggered home from a local bar. They had waited in the shadows till late into the night. Marcus was beginning to fall asleep, his head lolling, when Hervé muttered excitedly, 'He's here, he's here . . . !' Everything else had happened within seconds. Marcus heard the sound of uncertain footsteps and saw Hervé pulling something from his pocket. It was a knife. Two knives. One of them was for him. Then Hervé was shouting, 'Now!' and they charged from their hiding-place, striking out together at the reeling figure. He had tottered and fallen with barely a sound and they had left him there on the pavement, throwing the knifes into the harbour before running home.

Nothing had come of it. No investigation, no police, nothing.

When next Marcus had ventured down the street where it had happened, there was only the slightest stain on the pavement to suggest that it had not been some terrible nightmare. His mother never mentioned the man again, finding others to take his place. Marcus had wondered about it and had even tried confessing it to his parish priest but the priest had refused to believe his halting account and had chased him from the confessional, threatening God's wrath on those who abused his Holy Sacraments. Shortly afterwards Hervé left home to begin his service nationale and the matter had never again been raised between them.

Was he now hoping that Jarman's death might be achieved with so little consequence? That the police would show no interest and that even God – through his representative on earth – would seem to dismiss the whole thing?

That had been thirty and more years ago. He had

been a boy, ignorant and careless. Now he was older, with more to lose, and so more easily terrified. His days of waiting in the shadows, knife in hand, were over. He would remain in Geneva, pursuing the life of the blameless citizen, and would pay this Paolo – little more than a boy, with a boy's wildness about him – to wield the knife on his behalf.

A week after their meeting in the conservatory, he received a message from Paolo. 'Yes,' it said, 'I will accept the commission according to the terms agreed. Awaiting your first payment.' And it gave the name of the bank – conveniently, a Swiss one – and the number of the account into which Marcus was to transfer the money.

The positive response did not surprise him. Young as he may have been, Paolo had struck him as serious and workmanlike. Oddly, after their single meeting, he found he had confidence in him. Perhaps, after all his agonizing and then the tortuous negotiations, it might be simple after all and he would now need to do no more than make the payment and wait patiently for news of Jarman's death. He had the vivid memory of his burning car and the puckered wounds in his own flesh to help banish any remaining qualms of conscience. He rang his bank, arranged for the money to be made available in his current account, then gave instructions for its transfer to Paolo's nominated account.

It was done. He had made the decision and signed the warrant for Jarman's death. Now Paolo was beyond his reach so that he had no way of granting a stay of execution, even should he wish to. Well, so be it. Jarman had brought it on himself. If only for the murder of the innocent waiter, he deserved what was coming to him.

Yet it was a terrible thing to order the death of another human being. Marcus spent the remainder of the day distracted and uneasy, trying to absorb himself in business – contracts, shipping-orders, end-users' certificates – without being able to shake off the awareness of what he had done.

At five o'clock, he had an appointment to see Doctor Gerrone at the hospital. (Another Italian. What was it about them that they seemed, in their different ways, so at home with the business of life and death?) It was a routine check-up following his release. Eduardo drove him to the hospital. As he breathed in the atmosphere of antiseptic and quiet urgency, he felt to be back on familiar, comfortable ground. At least here they had asked nothing more of him than that he stayed alive and did as he was told.

'Good . . . good,' muttered Doctor Gerrone as he prodded and poked. 'You are a very fortunate man. Very fortunate indeed.'

Marcus smiled but made no reply.

'All right, thank you. You may put your clothes back on. And I don't think there will be any need for you to come and see me again. Unless, of course, you particularly wish to.'

'Thank you, Doctor,' said Marcus, not surprised at the diagnosis. His strength had returned and the niggling aches and pains now almost vanished.

But Doctor Gerrone had more to say. 'You are not married?'

'No,' said Marcus, finding the question a curious one.

'And you have no children?'

'No.'

'Hmm.' He said nothing for a moment or two, then began to pace about the room, as though

147

preferring to lecture Marcus rather than converse with him. 'One thing I have not mentioned to you before. Because there was no point, not until now when you are well again.' Marcus waited, unable to guess where this might be leading. 'The bullet which entered your abdomen took a downward trajectory and inflicted damage and trauma to the base of the bladder and surrounding area. It also damaged the prostate gland. My main concern, in operating, was to maintain the normal urinary functions. Are you following me?'

Well, yes, he was. But still without being able to see the direction in which they were heading.

'In doing so it was necessary to reduce the dimensions of the channels that carry the sperm from the testicles to the urethra. But everything is healed, everything is fine. You have nothing to worry about.'

But the reassurance was too late. Marcus' mind was racing, trying to anticipate the blow that was about to fall. 'So why are you telling me – '

'Because there is one possible side-effect. It may well be that you will be unable to father children.'

Marcus' first reaction was one of surprise but hardly of shock, not yet anyway.

'I see.'

'But I only say may be unable. No-one can be certain. It is a matter, if you like, of probability.'

'Yes.'

Had it ever been probable anyway? He had never planned to have children. He had never seen himself as a married man with a family. But nor had he ever taken the decision *not* to marry, *not* to have children. He was a bachelor by omission rather than design.

Perhaps all this talk of probability was Doctor Gerrone's way of trying to break the news gently.

Perhaps what he was saying was that he had, in fact, been sterilized. Either way – whether it was a matter of mere probability or of cast-iron certainty – Marcus remained unsure of his own reactions and so sat without speaking, nodding to show that he had heard.

'You understand?' asked Doctor Gerrone, sounding puzzled that his patient had taken the news so passively.

'I think I do, yes.'

'And one thing I must stress. In case you are concerned. This will not in any way affect your sexual ability. Not in the slightest.'

Marcus gave him a smile of thanks, though actually that had not been one of his worries. Thanks to Ragula, he already had had sufficient confirmation on that score.

'So, anyway, there it is,' said Doctor Gerrone. 'Perhaps some day you will come to see me with your large family and tell me I am wrong. In which case, I will be delighted. But for the moment I would be failing in my duty if I did not tell you that your chances of having children are less now than they were before the operation.'

At least the news that he had received a gratuitous vasectomy (assuming that was what it really amounted to) had distracted him from thoughts of Paolo and the murderous contract between them. He related his conversation with Doctor Gerrone to Ragula as they sat over dinner. She was about to leave for America on a trip that was part-business, part-pleasure and would mean an absence of some weeks.

'And so how do you feel?' she asked cautiously.

He smiled. 'Well, that's the point. I don't really

149

know. I don't suppose it's ever likely to matter anyway.'

'But you're still young.'

'Forty-six.'

'My own father was in his sixties when I was born.'

Well, yes, that had occurred to him: that, God willing, he still had enough of his life left for new and unguessed-at relationships. Though, if his track record were anything to go by, they would remain transient and stop well short of marriage and children.

'You don't feel it makes you any the less of a man?' she asked. She was still, he thought, trying to assess his real response. Well, and so was he.

'No,' he said. 'Nothing like that.'

'Well, then,' she said. 'Look on it as a bonus. Many men would envy you.'

He laughed, saying that he would recommend they had their vasectomies by more conventional means than resorting to wayward machine-gun bullets. And they talked about her holiday, where she was to visit and the acquisitions for her gallery she was hoping to make.

Afterwards, when he had left her, with both of them promising to write, he wondered how honest he had been, passing the matter off so lightly. It wasn't that he felt the affront to his manhood that she had asked about. He had been honest enough with her there. But, since his visit to Doctor Ger-rone, he had been haunted by a feeling of regret and even of disappointment. It was a feeling he could neither account for nor manage to shake off.

After all, he had never planned on marrying; never planned on having children. The nearest he had come to it, and only then in a romantic, gloriously impractical way, was when he was nineteen and head-over-heels in love with the beautiful daughter of a bicycle manufacturer from Provence. Nicole she had been called, with raven hair and hazel eyes that had driven him wild with desire. Till her father, disapproving of this penniless nobody, had spirited her away to Paris. Marcus had spent a week getting drunk, then a year laying every woman he could find. And the rest of his life getting rich, if only to demonstrate to the bastard of a bicycle manufacturer how wrong he had been.

Since when he had seen himself as a bachelor and growing old as one. His will stipulated that his estate should go to his brother and, through him, to his brother's children. Why then should Doctor Gerrone's words matter one jot?

The parcel was about the size of a hat-box but square. It appeared to be of thick cardboard, with reinforcings on the edges and double reinforcings on the corners. It was addressed to 'Marcus Revachier' at his home address and had been delivered by private courier. The word 'PERSONAL' was stencilled boldly across it and a torn Swiss customs clearance certificate was attached to one side.

It was Térence who had carried it up from the gate. Térence, an ex-Legionnaire, had become one of the regular members of Marcus' contingent of guards. He had taken to wearing a pump-action shotgun across one shoulder and a belt of red cartridges across the other so that, with his cigar clamped between his teeth, he had the appearance of a Mexican bandit. He arrived with the parcel in the open doorway of Marcus' study.

'This has just been delivered, Monsieur. Do you wish me to leave it here or – ?'

Marcus glanced at it. 'What is it?'

'I don't know. It says Personal. I've run the metal detector over it. Not a peep.'

'All right. Leave it.'

'Certainly, Monsieur.' He came into the room and placed it on a chair. 'OK, Monsieur. It's all yours.'

When he had gone, Marcus continued working for a while but then, wanting a break and, anyway, curious about the parcel, he got up from his desk and crossed to where it rested on the chair. He picked it up, finding it lighter than its size might have suggested, and gave it a tentative shake. Whatever was inside moved slightly. He placed it on his desk, took his paper-knife and began his attempt to cut his way into it.

The plastic-coated cardboard proved difficult to puncture. He had to hack away at one spot before the protective skin finally gave way and he was able to slide the knife through and begin sawing his way along. It was still hard going, so much so that he thought of abandoning the attempt and summoning Térence to take over. Still, it was marked 'PERSONAL', odd on an item of this size, and so he persevered.

Reaching the end of one side, he forced the knife through a ninety-degree turn and continued the slow progress along a second side. Then stopped as his nose caught an unpleasant, sweetish aroma seeping up from inside the box. He raised the flap of cardboard but could see nothing through the limited opening. The smell was now almost overpowering, making him step back. Whatever was inside must be rotting or decaying. Surely nothing could be intended to smell like that?

He should take the parcel into the garden before

it stank out his study. But first he wanted to know what it contained. He sawed away at the top till he reached another edge and so could now fold back a flap of cardboard and get a better look at whatever was inside.

He saw something dark and matted and put in his fingers to touch it. It felt like hair or some kind of fine grass, with long, matted strands. Tilting the box, he was able to make the object move so that he could see . . .

He let it fall and stepped back. What he had seen was a head, a human head. With dark, matted hair on top and the white features just distinguishable below.

He tried to tell himself he was mistaken. Perhaps it was a facsimile of a human head, in plastic or plaster . . . ? But no, the smell – the smell was what convinced him it was no facsimile but the real thing.

He felt himself gagging and moved to the door. He took big mouthfuls of air, as much to try and stop himself shaking as to drive out the smell. Then he heard footsteps along the corridor and withdrew into the room, closing the door and locking it. Though his revulsion for the obscene object on his desk kept him standing there, unable to bring himself to approach it again.

Yet he had to know more. If it were a head, then whose head? And why had it been sent to him in this ghoulish fashion? He forced himself to step up to the desk again and take up his paper-knife. Averting his eyes from the shape within, he began to cut across a third side, sawing recklessly till he had reached the edge again. Now the whole of the top could be pulled back.

He put down the knife, took hold of the cardboard and prised it open. The smell arose and surrounded him till he was again forced to step away.

But this time he had seen enough. The large, brown eyes and the sharp features ... the dark growth of beard. It was Paolo. Paolo's severed head.

He gave a cry of despair and fury, filled with anger at this new barbarism, one that this time he was partly responsible for. He had sent the assassin, he had paid for this, and now Jarman had returned his assassin to him.

He forced himself to look again inside the box, in search of some message or of anything that might explain the abomination, but there was nothing, just a caked mass of blood on which the head rested. And why should there be? Jarman must have known that the brutal contents would need no further explanation.

Marcus sank onto the sofa, feeling helpless and defeated. His plotting now seemed puny, against the might of an enemy whose viciousness knew no bounds.

What had happened he could only guess. Perhaps Paolo had made an attempt on Jarman's life and been killed himself in the process. Or, worse, had been captured and then executed in this brutal fashion. He might even have attempted to double-cross Marcus and do a deal with Jarman. What did it matter? One way or another he had come to this terrible end.

It was some minutes before Marcus could bring himself to act. His brain told him that he must dispose of the parcel and its contents, and do so quickly before it might implicate him in some way, but his body refused to move. What was the point? His adversary was stronger and more resourceful. Hardly a man at all but the devil himself.

It was the telephone ringing that roused him from his stupor. The call was from his warehouse manager, routine and unimportant; it was the act of taking it while the parcel, its top gaping open, was there on the desk beside him that pushed him into action.

He wedged the top back into place, hiding the grisly contents. Then opened the windows of the study. A plan had come to him, one that was simple and straightforward and which he hoped he was capable of carrying out.

Tucking the box under his arm, he made his way out of the house, meeting no-one. He had his own set of keys for the car and so need not trouble Eduardo. He wedged the box in the back of the car, then drove out through the front gates. He saw Térence and the other guard watching him curiously.

He drove into Geneva, praying that there would be no hold-up or accident, and then to the lakeside where there was a stretch of marina, the power-boats and yachts in regimented lines. Among them was his own boat, the Aurora, a 25-foot cabin cruiser with outboard motor, which he had bought on a whim three years ago and used only occasionally since. He parked the car as close to it as possible, then spent frustrating minutes removing the tarpaulin which had been lashed tight over the boat's superstructure.

In front of him the harbour fountain was still climbing skyward. Some of the tourists who were photographing it turned their attention to him as, with the tarpaulin now removed, he fought to pull-start the motor that was reluctant to come to life. Mercifully the petrol-gauge showed half-full. As his arm was beginning to tire, the exhaust kicked out a thick cloud of black smoke and the motor fired. Marcus muttered a prayer of thanks as the tourists lost interest and moved away. He eased the motor down to a steady tick-over, then hurried back to the car and, with a quick glance round to check that no-one was paying particular attention, he opened the back door and lifted out the parcel. He carried it to the boat, placed it carefully on the deck, then cast off and headed out towards the centre of the lake.

All he wanted was a stretch of open water with no other boats in close attendance. Finally, when he judged himself a sufficient distance out from shore, he pulled back on the throttle and allowed the Aurora to settle.

There was a set of tools on the boat, stowed under a bench. He dragged them out and selected the heaviest – a monkey-wrench and some spanners – which he then proceeded to place inside the parcel. His actions were clumsy and forced, trying to avoid touching the head itself yet wanting to fill the space around it. He was haunted by a vision of what would happen should he fail: the obscene head rising from the lake floor and bobbing shoreward on the waves.

In the end the box was weighted to a point he could scarcely lift it. He staggered to the side and heaved it over. There was a small splash, then a gurgling sound as though the head were breathing its last. For a few seconds it was visible, descending through the clear water with a stream of bubbles behind it, then it was gone.

He thought of the lines from the funeral service: 'Out of the depths have I cried to Thee, Oh Lord. Lord, hear my voice.'

Already he was assailed by doubts. Would the

parcel stay there? After all, it was basically no more than cardboard. Would it not rot and release its dreadful contents? Too late for such considerations. At least now he was rid of it, a consolation that outweighed everything else.

He rode back slowly. He wasn't dressed for sailing at this time of the year and felt the bitterness of the cold air. He was exhausted by his efforts, and disheartened and sickened by Jarman's brutal victory. Paolo might have been a professional killer and so hardly deserved a prolonged period of mourning; nevertheless, returning home past the puzzled gaze of his guards, Marcus felt himself soiled with his blood.

He had been relying on Paolo to free him from the threat to his own life. Well, Paolo had failed and had paid a terrible price. The whole bungled operation had achieved nothing but to give Jarman even more cause for his obsessive vendetta. If Marcus had imagined that his enemy might eventually tire and let the matter rest, he now knew better. This would remain a fight to the finish, one in which he had lost the initiative and could now only wait for his enemy's retaliation.

14

The mild winter had given way to a bright though windy spring. The blossom was snatched from the trees almost as soon as it appeared; the coloured flags on the garage forecourt fluttered like so many tormented doves.

There had been nothing more from the agency since the letter confirming that their application had been accepted, not even a phone-call just to say hello, how are you. Or a letter to say Don't worry, you haven't been forgotten. Lauren told herself that this was only to be expected: there was always going to be a hiatus while the agency searched for a suitable child. (*Suitable* child . . . ? Wasn't it *any* child that she had gone seeking? Now here she was slipping into social worker jargon.) Even so, after the triumph of their acceptance, it was a slow torture to have the days and weeks pass and hear nothing.

Following the family tradition, they went to Rachel's for Easter Sunday. It was Rachel's husband, Russell, who was James' partner in the garden centre. Their house was a converted barn, on the moors outside Preston, roomy and substantial with exposed stonework and an old cider-press in the garden. It was another house of children, with small wellingtons lined up inside the back porch and crayoned drawings pinned along the kitchen walls.

This year the new-born baby was the centre of attention. Taking her turn to bill and coo over her, Lauren wondered whether she would ever take to motherhood in that natural, unselfconscious way that her sisters-in-law seemed to manage. As though they had been born to it. Of course, they had heard how she and James had been accepted by the adoption agency, though Lauren had made it all sound very straightforward, anxious that they should never know how close a call it had been. They were full of promises of help for when the time came, baby-clothes and sterilizing-units to be passed on, baby-buggies and play-pens that were stored away in lofts, waiting.

After lunch, the two older children, plus Sarah's four, went out into the garden on an Easter egg hunt. Lauren stood in the big lounge window, watching them. She would have all this to learn for when her child got older.

Five weeks later, a morning in early May, she was lying in bed still half-asleep, when she heard the telephone ringing in the hallway below. At first she didn't move, knowing James was already up and would answer it. Then wondered – who could be ringing so early? She tried to push the thought of the agency from her mind; after all, it could be anybody, anybody ringing. She held her breath and listened intently.

The ringing stopped and she heard James recite their number. Then he said, 'Oh, hello,' as though surprised. Or was she imagining the surprise? Unable to resist any longer, she slipped out of bed and padded to the top of the stairs, from where she could see his head through the bannisters. All she wanted was confirmation that it was just an ordinary, run-of-the-mill call, then she would go back to bed again.

159

But he looked up, catching her there. And his expression told her that no, this wasn't an ordinary, run-of-the-mill call. Her heart leapt and she put her hand to her mouth to stop herself crying out.

'Lauren's here,' said James into the receiver. 'I think you'd better tell her yourself.'

'What? What?' she said, now running down the stairs.

'Stella Priestley,' he said quietly, handing over the phone.

And she knew then that this was it, the moment she had been anticipating ever since the agency had accepted them, the moment she had been fearing would never arrive. She marvelled that she could even hold the phone. James had put his hands on her shoulders.

'Stella, hello,' she said.

'I was just telling James we have some good news. There's a baby about to become available for adoption and we think it would be right for you.'

Lauren said nothing. There was nothing she could say, so stunned was she that the moment she had imagined so often had at last arrived. Yet it had. There they were, standing in the hallway, with the morning's newspaper partly unfolded on the mat and the directories stacked where they always were beside the phone, numbers scribbled on their covers. It was real, and it was happening now.

'Yes?' she gasped. 'You're sure?'

A stupid thing to say, of course. She heard Stella laughing. 'Yes, I'm sure. I've even seen him'

Him. It was a boy. Up to that moment she had thought – when she had dared to think about it, to risk admitting to a preference – that she might have opted for a girl. Now, faced with the fact of a boy, she knew immediately it was a boy she had wanted all along.

'A boy,' she said to James.

He nodded and smiled. Unable to think of what to say to him either, she grabbed him and kissed him. Till she heard the small voice from the phone and had to jam it back to her ear to catch the end of what Stella was saying. ' ... Whether you could come to the hospital later this morning?'

'This morning? Yes. What, you mean we can see him this morning?'

Could things really be going at such a helter-skelter pace after all the days and weeks of waiting? She looked down at her nightdress. She would have to change. And then how long would it take to drive to the hospital?

But Stella was sounding a note of warning. 'You can see him, yes. But remember that this is only a first visit. It's just so that you can have a look at the child. You won't be able to take him away with you.'

No, of course not. 'So when ... when will we be able to take him?'

'Well, I think it's best if we talk about that at the hospital. Could you both be there for, say, eleven o'clock?'

Lauren said yes and they arranged to meet in the main entrance. Then she wondered why eleven. Why not ten, or even nine? But it was too late. Stella was saying goodbye and ringing off.

Lauren put down the phone and stared at James. 'You heard her?' she said.

'Yes, I heard her.'

'So it's true . . . ?'

He gave a shout of laughter and grabbed her round her waist so that she was lifted from the floor. We did it, she thought, clinging to him, the hallway spinning about her. We've had a child. Even when he put her down, she stayed in his arms, holding him tightly, not wanting him to see the tears that were rolling down her cheeks.

'You go and get ready,' he said gently. 'I'll make us some breakfast.'

She kissed him again, then ran back upstairs and shut herself in the bathroom. Along with the elation, she felt suddenly nervous and unprepared, though knowing, as Stella had reminded her, that they wouldn't be able to bring the child home with them and so there would be time enough for assembling everything that would be needed.

(*Him.* It was a boy. The more she dwelt on this, the more it felt like some great, unlooked-for bonus. Their son.)

She threw on some clothes and tried to do her make-up but found her hands were trembling. Slow down, she told herself. Plenty of time. They don't want us there until eleven o'clock. But she still went on hurrying, brushing her hair back and then, using one hand to steady the other, managing to apply enough lipstick and eye-shadow to get by.

Below her, she heard James ringing the garden centre to explain why he wouldn't be in. She heard the pride in his voice as he said, 'They've found a baby for us . . . a boy.' She raced downstairs to join him for breakfast.

'Did Stella say anything else about him?' he asked as they ate.

'No.' She wasn't sure what he meant. 'Anything else . . . ?'

'Well, anything about his parents or the sort of background . . . ?'

'No. Nothing.' What did it matter? Did she even

162

want to know about his parents? They were going to be his parents.

They arrived early at the hospital and so had to hang around, killing time. The hospital had been established in the nineteen-twenties as a charity institution and constructed in red brick; since when glass and concrete extensions had sprouted in all directions. The main entrance was part of the original building and still displayed in letters of faded gold the names of those benefactors who had subscribed to it. Lauren read and re-read the list – 'Mr W. Bancroft, Doctor J. Crabtree, Mr N.D. Storey . . . ' She was grateful to them all, grateful to anyone who had contributed however distantly and slightly to the hospital in which her child had been born.

'We're like two expectant fathers,' James joked, referring to the way they were both pacing up and down.

Lauren kept returning to the door, looking out onto the car-park for signs of Stella arriving.

'I suppose it's our turn now to make the decisions,' said James, joining her.

'What decisions?'

'Well . . . whether this is the child we want.'

She looked at him, suspecting a joke, but no, he was serious. 'Why shouldn't we?' she said.

He took her hands as if to reassure her. 'No, I'm just saying – they are offering us the child. We can still say no if we want to.'

'Well, I know we can,' she muttered, not wanting to consider that. So, all right, he was simply reminding her of the formalities, as they had long ago been outlined for both of them by Stella. But she didn't want to be reminded, not now.

And then suddenly Stella Priestly was there, coming through the doors, a big smile on her face.

Lauren went forward to embrace her, then got a small shock, seeing Marjorie Daniels following. She still saw Marjorie as their prosecutor before the Panel, and Stella as their heroic defender. Though even Marjorie was smiling today so that Lauren brought herself to shake her hand and say hello.

Marjorie ushered them towards a row of stacking-chairs. 'Let's just sit down a minute, shall we,' she said.

Stella said to Lauren, ' He's beautiful. I nearly took him home myself.'

'He is?' said Lauren, her heart beating.

Stella nodded. 'Beautiful.'

'And what about the mother?' said James.

Lauren glanced at him, wondering why he should ask. But Stella seemed to find it a sensible question and, after a look at Marjorie for her cue, she explained that 'Baby Smith', the alias given to the child by the nurses on the ward, had been born four days ago to a woman who had decided in advance that she wanted her baby to be adopted. She was unmarried, had no permanent relationship and claimed that the father had no idea of the pregnancy. (Good, thought Lauren.) The baby had been removed from her at birth and then, when interviewed later, she had remained adamant that she wished the child adopted. (Even better.)

Now it was Marjorie's turn. 'So the first question we have to ask you – do you still want to go ahead with the adoption? It doesn't have to be this child. You can tell us that after you've seen him. But do you still want to adopt?'

It seemed so unnecessary a question that Lauren found herself hesitating. James said, 'Yes, I'm sure that we – ' and then she found her voice and said, 'Yes, of course.'

Marjorie smiled. 'Well, I thought so, but we still have to ask.' Can we go now, pleaded Lauren silently. Can we go and see him? But Marjorie had more to say: 'Stella has told you about the mother's attitude. Obviously we can't give you her name but we can tell you that she's English and she's white. Thirty . . . '

'Thirty-four,' prompted Stella.

'Thirty-four years old and in good health. Doesn't have any history of infirmity that we know of. And the child is in good health. And, of course, we can't tell you anything about the father, because she won't tell us anything about him.'

'And is that liable to be a problem?' asked James. 'I mean when it comes to the legal aspects – '

'No,' said Marjorie. 'None. Don't worry about that. I only mention it because it means we can't give you as full a medical and social background to the child as we'd like to.'

It's all right, thought Lauren. In fact, all the better. He would have no 'social and medical background' but for the one they would give him.

'And will we have to meet this mother?' asked James.

Lauren waited for the answer. She hadn't thought of this and couldn't decide immediately whether it was something she wanted to do or not. Probably not.

But Marjorie was already shaking her head. 'She's made it clear that she doesn't want to meet you. Of course, she's been told a certain amount about you, the kind of people you are. But not who you are.'

'So we don't meet her?' said Lauren, wanting it clear.

'No.'

Good, she decided suddenly. It would help them

see the baby as theirs, given them by the hospital. And, anyway, what kind of unnatural woman must this mother be that she was willing to give away her new-born son to a pair of strangers she didn't even want to meet? Lauren knew she would never understand, not in a million years; still, she should be glad at the woman's decision, however perverse. And now could they go and see the child please? Hurry things along before the mother could change her mind?

But Marjorie had more to say. 'Now, as I think Stella's already told you, you're here just to see the child. Not to take him home.' Lauren gave a reluctant nod. 'If you want to go ahead after seeing him, then it'll be another couple of days before you can come back and collect him. For one thing, we like the mother to have been discharged from the hospital first.'

Why? thought Lauren. Why all this consideration being given to a woman who didn't even want her own baby while she and James, who wanted only to love and care for it, were being kept waiting in the wings?

But now Marjorie was at last pulling herself to her feet and they were all four of them moving off down the corridor. Lauren caught up with James and took his hand. They passed beneath signs that spoke of decay and disease and mortality, with the one exception, the one they were following, which pointed towards the maternity ward. They came to its doors and Marjorie said, 'Wait here a minute,' before disappearing inside. Beside them was a long window through which Lauren could see rows of babies in cots, some awake and crying, others asleep. Some were strong-looking, beefy even, while others were tiny, so tiny they appeared miniaturized.

166

Which one was theirs, she wondered.

Marjorie popped out from the ward and said, 'You can come in now.' Lauren stumbled forward and felt James' steadying hand on her elbow. They followed Marjorie, not onto the ward itself, but into a smaller room, the walls of which were covered with cartoon characters and a rainbow which snaked from one corner, across the ceiling and down again. A nurse had followed them in. With a thrill of excitement, Lauren saw that she was carrying a small, white bundle.

'Here we are then,' said Marjorie, and gestured to Lauren to take the bundle. Hardly able to move, Lauren held out her arms and the nurse placed the bundle across them. Lauren saw a tiny head of dark hair and then staring, blue eyes.

'Hello, Baby Smith,' she said.

She felt overwhelmed, numb even, to be holding the flesh-and-blood reality of what for so long had been a dream. She saw that his hair was fine and he had long eyelashes. His features seemed less chubby than those of most babies. 'Oh, he's beautiful,' she breathed.

'We'll give you five minutes alone with him,' said Marjorie, and she and Stella left the room.

Lauren turned to James. 'Look,' she said. 'Oh, look.' And now, with the two social workers gone, she felt free enough to raise him to her face and place her cheek against his.

James cleared his throat. 'Can I hold him?'

'Of course you can,' she said, handing him over, then hovering at James' elbow, immediately wanting him back. 'We are going to have him, aren't we?'

'Yes,' said James, sounding bemused. She saw her own feelings reflected in his face: that he, too, couldn't believe that here at last was *their* child, to be held and cuddled like any other. (Only more beautiful than any other, she told herself.)

She took him back from James, knowing she was being unfair but unable any longer to deny herself the pleasure of holding him. 'You're going to be ours, Baby Smith,' she said. She saw his tiny, pale red lips move and cried, 'Oh, look, he's smiling!' Of course, Sarah and Rachel – the experts – would have claimed it was no more than wind making him grimace, but she knew he was smiling at her to tell her he was as keen on the adoption as she was.

There was an apologetic knock on the door as Marjorie and Stella let themselves back in. Lauren tightened her grip around the bundle, fearing the moment when she would have to let go. 'You like him then?' said Stella, smiling broadly. Lauren realized it must be a big day for her too, in her role as midwife to the whole process.

'Like him? Oh, he's beautiful, absolutely beautiful!'

Stella laughed and came to stand beside Lauren so that she could get another look at him. 'I take it then I don't need to ask whether you still want to go ahead?' said Marjorie drily.

'Try and stop me,' said Lauren, even warming to Marjorie now. Warming to everybody.

'Can't we take him home now?' said James.

Lauren saw he was joking but still waited anxiously for the other two to react. Had they given the slightest sign of this being possible, she would have implored them, beseeched them, to make it so. But they only smiled. Marjorie said, 'Sorry. No can do.'

The nurse had reappeared. Lauren steeled herself to hand back the bundle that contained her son, first planting a kiss on his forehead to claim him for her own. Then, placing her faith in the procedures that, after all, had carried her this far, she allowed the nurse to lift him from her arms.

'Oh, yes, we want him,' she said to Marjorie. 'Please.'

Marjorie smiled and gave her hand a squeeze. 'I don't think there are going to be any problems,' she said. 'Just have to be patient for a little longer, that's all.'

They retraced their path through the maze of corridors and came out into the sunshine. The two social workers went off, calling their goodbyes. Lauren gave a long sigh of pure joy, then stood on her tiptoes, held her arms out and slowly pirouetted till she had come full circle.

'I know you won't believe this,' she said, 'but I'm missing him already.'

James took her in his arms. She was aware of other people in the car-park staring at them as they passed but she didn't care. 'Only two more days,' he said. 'Three at the most.'

'I know,' she said. 'But I want him now. I want to take him home now.'

As they drove homewards in the Land Rover, she wondered again about the mother. This woman they would never meet yet who was presenting her child to them. The child she had carried for nine months, then laboured to deliver.

And what had Stella said? That she had already decided to have the child adopted even before giving birth to it, before she had seen it. Well, all right. No doubt she had her own reasons. But could she stick to such a resolution, once she was feeling stronger and about to leave hospital? Could she – could anybody in their right mind – leave such a child behind them?

These new fears gripped her, stifling the elation. Almost choking her.

'Suppose she changes her mind?'

James glanced at her. 'Who?'

'The mother.'

'But she won't. You heard what they said – '

'But she can! And, if she does, well, then she can take him back, can't she.'

He drove in silence for a little way before replying. 'Yes, she can,' he said quietly. 'And, if that happens, then there's nothing we can do to stop her.'

Lauren felt a sudden wash of despair. 'I wish we hadn't even seen him!' she cried.

She knew it was absurd to react like this, now of all times, when she could still feel his tiny weight in her arms. But they had come so far and were now so close that even the slightest risk of failure was unbearable.

James pulled the Land Rover over to the side of the road and stopped. He turned to face her. 'Look, you're upsetting yourself about nothing – '

'No, I'm not. You just said yourself – she can take him back and there's nothing we can do to stop her!'

'In theory she can take him back – '

'Yes!'

'But in practice she won't. Marjorie and Stella wouldn't have put us through that if they thought there was one chance in a million that she'd change her mind. You know that.' When she said nothing, he repeated, 'You know that, yes?'

'I . . . I suppose so,' she said, wanting oh so much to be able to agree with him.

She felt better, regaining some of her confidence, once they were home. Anyway, there was too much to do to indulge her fears. She couldn't risk bringing

170

the child home to a house that wasn't ready for him. For the next two days she threw herself into the plans which she had carried for so long in her head, beginning with calls on Sarah and Rachel to collect the baby paraphernalia they had promised her. Of course, neither of them would let her get away till they had heard every last detail of the visit to see Baby Smith. Their delight in what she had to tell them, as well as the act of re-telling it, buoyed her up and she left them elated, her spirits restored. She re-arranged one of the bedrooms, turning it into a nursery, then embarked on a shopping binge and to hell with the expense.

With, all the time, the hours passing, cutting down on the opportunities for disaster.

She called in at the garage and explained to them what had happened and why she couldn't come in anymore. She felt a touch guilty, throwing in the job without giving proper notice, but felt a pride too when she told them her reason. Greg said, 'You know you're breaking my heart. Why can't you adopt me as well?' She gave him a kiss and promised to keep in touch.

Stella Priestley phoned next day. Recognizing her voice, Lauren was re-visited by her terrors – did this mean the mother had changed her mind after all? But no, Stella only wanted to arrange a time for them to meet again at the hospital. When this was done – three o'clock, same place as before – the conversation got round to why the Eagleshams had emerged as front-runners for Baby Smith when, as Stella admitted, there had been three suitable adoptive couples all together, two others beside themselves, on the agency's books. In the end it had been the mother's choice. She had been given details of the three couples and asked which she preferred.

171

'And do you know what it was that made her choose you?' said Stella.

'Go on.'

'We'd mentioned that you'd once been a dancer and had wanted to take it up professionally. And that seemed to strike a chord. I honestly don't know why but, once she'd hear that, she wasn't interested in the other two.'

Her dancing . . . ? It had all been down to that? Lauren caught her breath, horrified by the thought of how much had turned on such a random detail of her early life, something so far behind her that she might even not have bothered to mention it in their application.

'But why – ?'

'I don't know. It just seemed something she was able to relate to.'

Well, thank God for that. But there was something more that Lauren had to ask. 'Is the mother still there, in the hospital?'

'I think so, yes. I think she's leaving tomorrow morning.'

So she still had time to change her mind. How could she be in a bed in the same hospital as her child and not creep along the corridors to view it? And, having viewed it, how could she not fall in love with it?

Lauren sat up late, drinking sherry and waiting for the phone to ring with the bad news. James, bless him, tried to make conversation, but conversation was the last thing she wanted and she insisted he go to bed and leave her. When the clock showed midnight and the phone still hadn't rung, she went to bed herself, though sure that she would never sleep. Then she lost consciousness immediately and dreamt of babies, rows and rows of them, all with the same dark hair and bright blue eyes.

The following day was sunny and warm, the best yet. James went into work after breakfast, leaving Lauren to potter about the house and watch the clock. She remembered Stella saying that the mother was leaving the hospital 'in the morning' and so wasn't able to relax until midday had come and gone. Only then did she feel that the mother must have stuck to her resolution and they were home-and-dry.

She felt relaxed and happy as James drove her to the hospital. They went in, hand-in-hand, to find Stella, alone this time, waiting to greet them. 'Well,' she said, 'and so you've come to collect your son?'

Lauren's heart soared.

Hand-in-hand with James, she followed Stella along the corridors to the maternity unit. Once again they were admitted to the room with the cartoon characters and the rainbow climbing across the ceiling. It was a different nurse that appeared but she was carrying what seemed to be the same white bundle. This time Lauren went forward confi-dently and took it from her.

And there he was, staring up from among the folds of the cotton blanket – her son. She held him as tightly as she dared, saying nothing. Even forget-ting to thank the nurse, who had left the room. James and Stella were talking, then James was sign-ing something.

'OK,' said Stella. 'That's it.'

She couldn't believe it.

'What, you mean . . . ?'

'He's yours. We can go.'

She gave a little cry of surprise and delight – at the suddenness of it, how easy it was. And James laughed too.

They walked back along the corridors, though

173

now Lauren was barely aware of where they were, concentrating on the bundle in her arms. James gripped her elbow, guiding her. Then they were outside again and Stella was wishing them luck and moving away to her own car.

'Oh, but thank you,' called Lauren. 'Thank you for everything.'

But Stella only laughed and said that they might not feel like thanking her once the broken nights started.

James held open the back door of the Land Rover and she climbed in awkwardly, still holding the baby. He had offered to take him from her but no, she wasn't having that. Nobody was ever going to take him from her.

She gazed down at him as they drove homewards. Her child. It didn't seem possible. He wore a plastic hospital bracelet round one wrist. She twisted her head to read it: 'Baby Smith.'

'We can't keep on calling him Baby Smith,' she said.

'Pardon?' said James, up front and driving.

'What're we going to call him?' she said, raising her voice above the engine.

This had been a taboo subject, to be avoided lest they might seem to be taking too much for granted and be punished for their presumption.

'I don't know,' called back James. 'What d'you think?'

'Adam,' she said, on an impulse. It wasn't something she had thought about or, come to that, a name used before in either of their families. Yet it seemed right. 'Adam,' she said again, trying it out the sound of it.

'Yes, all right,' said James. 'Sounds OK to me.'

'Adam,' she said to the child. 'Do you think you can remember that? Adam Eaglesham.'

15

Vernon Angelis was a tall man with a pointed ginger beard. Rather like an elongated pixie thought Lauren, seeing him on the doorstep.

He presented his card and introduced himself in grave, almost self-mocking tones, as 'the Reporting Officer sent by the court to oversee the final phrase of the adoption process'. Then looked heavenwards as though to say – can you believe such a thing! Lauren laughed, feeling herself immediately at ease with him.

'Come in,' she said, stepping back. 'Though everything's in a mess. You'll have to promise not to look.'

Vernon nodded solemnly and tiptoed after her through to the lounge, where Adam was lying in the middle of being changed, the soiled nappy beside him and, beside that, a mound of dirty clothes that were waiting their turn to go into the washing-machine that was churning away in the kitchen, as it seemed to have been churning away night and day since the minute they had brought Adam through the door.

'Cup of tea?' said Lauren, surveying the wreckage of what had once been her neat and tidy home.

'Oh, well, only if – ' said the pixie, who had perched on the edge of the sofa. Lauren noticed he was wearing open-toed sandals and had a folded, spotted handkerchief protruding from his jacket pocket.

'Yes, I'm having one,' she said firmly. She went to the kitchen to put the kettle on and, while she was there, re-set the tumble-drier, filled the steriliusing-unit and lined up the next bottle of milk. The breakfast things still hadn't been washed and upstairs was . . . well, upstairs was a *disaster*.

It was the chaos she had long dreamt of and longed for and she was proud of it.

She was especially proud of it when visitors came. Even as she said, 'Oh, ignore the mess,' she didn't really want them to ignore it but wanted them to notice it, to nudge one another, bringing everyone's attention to it, so that they would know she was a real, fully-fledged mother at last and that this adoption wasn't some sort of second-class, easy-payment way of doing things. And visitors there had been aplenty. As well as Vernon, who was still waiting for his tea, there had been Mrs Revell, their Health Visitor, Lauren's sisters-in-law (almost tieing in their race to be the first) and the rest of their families and then a whole parade of neighbours and friends wanting to see Adam, all agreeing, even without her prompting, that he was gorgeous. Greg came from the garage with a model of a Toyota Supra, which was sweet of him, even though the gift would have to be hidden away for a couple of years yet.

Going back into the lounge, she found Vernon Angelis making clucking noises at Adam while he stared up, wide-eyed and unblinking.

'Oh, thank you,' said Vernon, taking the tea. 'And so how's motherhood?'

'Wonderful.' Saying it because she meant it, not caring anymore what kind of impression she made.

'Hmm, yes. Well, it will be with a little chap like this.'

She got on with the task of nappy-changing. Whatever this nice man from the court had come to say, she could hear him just as well on her knees as sitting on a chair. (*This nice man from the court . . . ?* The baby-talk that they used to Adam was already beginning to infect her brain. She had heard her sisters-in-law talking to one another as though they were three-year-olds and wondered at it; now she understood.)

'As you know,' said Vernon, 'the court still has to make the adoption legal and binding. And it's my job to advise on this. Which is why I'm here today and which is why I'll probably have to visit you again.'

'Any time you like,' said Lauren, fearing nothing. Anyway, with so many visitors pouring through the door, what was one extra?

'Well, thank you. The other thing I have to do, of course, is to go and talk to the natural mother. Just to make sure that she hasn't been under any kind of undue pressure to give up the child.'

Lauren glanced at Adam to see whether he was listening but, if he was, he showed no signs of being perturbed by this reference to his previous life. 'But even if she wants him back – ' she said, trying to remember what she had been told by Stella.

'Oh, well, no. There's nothing automatic,' said Vernon, eager to reassure. 'Not any more. Even if she were to want him back – which I'm sure won't be the case, by the way – that happens so very, very seldom – but, even if she were to do so, the court might well decide it was in the child's best interests that he should stay with you.'

Lauren nodded and then added, 'In case she should change her mind again.'

'Well, yes. Or she might just be judged not to be a suitable parent. Now that she's relinquished the child, she can't just turn round and ask for it back.'

'Well, she can ask – ' said Lauren, wanting things clear.

'Oh, she can ask – '

'But it would be up to the court.'

'Absolutely.'

Strange how she could now talk about these things without any qualms or fears. Oh, she would be glad when the adoption was confirmed; of course, she would. Then Adam would be theirs as surely as if she had given birth to him herself. But in the meantime, having him there in the house, she felt a new, delightful confidence about everything. They had come through the emotional whirlwind of the last year and were now into calm waters. She had found her son, and he had found her, and if there were still t's to be crossed and i's to be dotted, well, she wasn't going to let that worry her.

She hadn't time to let that worry her.

'Of course she still hasn't told us who the father is,' said Vernon.

Lauren looked again at Adam. Close your ears, son, she thought. I'll explain all this to you when you're older.

'Now I daresay you probably don't care who he is,' said Vernon. 'But the court has a duty to try and find out, and so that's another reason why I have to go and see her.'

'But suppose she still won't tell you?' asked Lauren.

'Oh, well, then we'll just have to give up and leave it at that. But she might. I've found before that, once they're out of the hospital and the whole business is behind them, then these mothers are sometimes more willing to talk.'

178

Well, yes, she could understand that. And perhaps it might be better if this natural mother did tell all. (It was an unwieldy title – 'natural mother' – but Lauren was sticking to it; she had already claimed the simpler title of 'mother' for herself.) After all, it could hardly affect them. And perhaps one day Adam would be curious about his origins and it would be a shame if they had to admit they could tell him nothing.

Vernon drank his tea and departed, promising to keep in touch, shaking Adam's hand as well as her own. 'He's a fine, little fellow,' he told her. 'A fast bowler surely, look at those hands. Or a spinner.'

At the weekend, they held a small christening party. Russell came up trumps with some bottles of champagne and they drank a toast to Adam. The other children gathered round him curiously, wanting to touch and being warned by their mothers to be careful. Lauren was happy to see him being passed around, wanting him to grow up with cousins and aunts and uncles, like any other child.

Though the best time was when they had gone and she and James had him to themselves. His cot was still in their room and sometimes at night she would awake for no reason and gaze across at him, watching for the rise and fall of his breathing. His presence with them still struck her as a miracle, something fabulous that had touched her life and transformed it.

Among the usual trawl of the morning's mail Marcus caught sight of an embossed coat-of-arms and the heading below it: 'Palais de Justice. Place de la Blourg-de-Four'. Intrigued to know what he had done to attract the attention of such an august department, he slid a thumb beneath the flap of the envelope and pulled out the single-sheet letter.

179

'Dear Mr Revachier,' he read, 'We are instructed to inform you that you have been named as the natural father of a child recently born to one Claire Jane Tempest in Preston, county of Lancashire, England. The child is at present the subject of a court hearing regarding its adoption. You are being informed of this so that, should you wish, you may exercise your right to make representation on this matter. However, our understanding is that there is no obligation on you to do so.'

He gasped with astonishment. Then re-read it, thinking he must have misunderstood. But no, it stated quite clearly that Claire had had his child . . .! Claire with whom he had had no contact since, well, yes, it must have been a good nine months ago. Even so, he could scarcely believe . . . It wasn't that he wished to deny any responsibilities. The letter hardly seemed to be accusing him or making demands. It was the way it had come out of a clear blue sky that left him stunned and still slightly incredulous.

He read it for a third time, telling himself it was certainly not a joke and was hardly likely to be a mistake. The staff of the Palais de Justice were noted for neither. He must take it then at its face-value and accept the truth of it. After all, it was simple enough. Claire had been pregnant, though she probably didn't know it, when she left him and now she had given birth to their child. He was being informed only because the child was being adopted. So did that mean that she didn't want it? Or that she wasn't in a position to support it? Or perhaps it simply meant that Claire, with her beguiling honesty, had looked in the mirror and realized she wasn't the mothering sort and never would be.

He found himself smiling as he thought of her.

She belonged to a more innocent part of his life, before the deadly games with Jarman had so reduced and demeaned it. Though, of course, she had been with him when the car had exploded. It was that that had sent her fleeing back to England.

The letter, this amazing letter, said that he was not obliged to do anything. Indeed, to read as though that was the last thing its author expected or possibly even wanted. The Palais de Justice were doing no more than passing on a message; its clear suggestion was that things in England would take their course without his ever needing to become involved. He rose from his desk and paced about the room, then came back to the letter.

Looking at it again, another thought struck him. Clearly Claire had not particularly wished to involve him. She may even have wished him never to know. After all, she could have contacted him anytime but had chosen not to do so. Well, it was her decision of course. Her decision, too, if she wished to have the child adopted.

Though he couldn't help but see it as an grotesque trick of Fate, to reveal him as the unsuspecting father so soon after Doctor Gerrone had warned him of his probable impotence. If there were a joke to be found anywhere in this, then perhaps that was it. And perhaps that was how he should regard the letter – as one of nature's little jokes, which he would do best to ignore.

What else could he do?

He put the letter determinedly aside and turned to the remainder of his mail, which was mercifully free from such surprises.

However, the thoughts that the letter had provoked were less easy to shift and remained to nag at him. The idea that there was a child, a baby, living in Preston, the county of Lancashire, England and that he was the father of that child . . . it was a notion that, try as he may, he could not ignore but that disturbed and excited him. He felt an urge to act, to respond in some positive way. After all, he had just been told that he was a father.

Unthinkable, yet it was true. Here was the evidence, on the stiff notepaper of the Palais de Justice. He could hardly toss it into the waste-paper basket without a second thought.

The signature to the letter was indecipherable but beneath it was typed the name, 'Philippe Lommer.' Marcus reached for the phone, though as yet with no clear idea of what he wished to achieve. Simply that he couldn't take the implied advice of the letter and leave well alone. He dialled the number on the letter-heading and was put through to Philippe Lommer.

'My name is Marcus Revachier,' he said, 'and I've just received a letter from you.' He saw that there was a reference number in the top corner and recited it.

There was a pause, then Philippe Lommer said, 'Ah, yes. How . . . how can I help?' It was the voice of a young man, sounding defensive, as though he feared being dragged into some scandal.

'I assumed you received this information from England?'

'We did, yes. From the court in Preston, which is dealing with the adoption.'

'And did they tell you anything else about it?' He knew it was a vague question but couldn't be specific since he didn't yet know what he wanted out of this conversation, save that he was trying to explore his own feelings and see where they would take him.

He heard a rustling of papers, then Philippe

182

Lommer said, 'Well, not much. Apparently the child was born some three or four weeks ago . . . oh, and it's a boy. I didn't put that in the letter. But it's a boy.'

'A boy.'

'Yes.'

He felt that he had taken a step closer. 'And this adoption – I can object to it if I wish?'

'Well, I'm no expert in English law – '

'But this is why the court has made contact?'

'Oh, yes. Indeed. And I'm sure they would take note of your wishes. What I can't say is how much weight those wishes would carry.'

'And when is this adoption to be completed?'

'The fifth of next month.'

Which gave him, what, no more than two weeks. But two weeks in which to do what? 'Yes, well, thank you,' he said, now wanting to be alone with his thoughts. 'And so I can contact you if I wish to proceed on this?'

'We can make your intentions known to the English court, yes,' said Philippe Lommer cautiously.

Marcus thanked him again and put down the phone. So what was he doing? Why had he even made the call? Was he considering – seriously considering – contacting the English authorities and contesting the adoption?

No, he told himself firmly. Such a notion would be an absurd fantasy, a dangerous delusion.

Here he was, a bachelor living alone and liable to remain that way, surrounded by armed guards because of the attacks that had already been made on his life. Did he really, even in his wildest dreams, believe that he might bring a child, a baby, to share such an unenviable life with him?

No doubt the child would be well cared for by its

new parents. The court would make sure of that. No doubt everything was being done for the best. The greatest contribution he could make to the child's future happiness would be to throw away the letter and forget that he had ever received it.

Forget that he even had a son.

An hour later, he was still sitting there, still telling himself that he was prey to a fit of crazy sentimentality, one that he must resist. What would he, Marcus Revachier, of all people, do with a baby on his hands? Wasn't it just romanticised nonsense to picture himself watching over and providing for a growing child when the reality was that he was approaching middle-age and living alone in an austere, over-large house that any child would find little better than a prison? The arguments against him doing anything were overwhelming.

And yet.

In all likelihood this was his one-and-only chance ever to have a child of his own, an heir to everything he had worked for and achieved. Perhaps his only chance to give his life the direction that it had lost.

Besides, this was his son. *His son.* Of that there seemed to be no doubt, otherwise why would the English court have gone to such trouble to locate him? No, this was his son, whom he had a right to know and to care for, even a duty to do these things. Claire, seemingly, had abandoned him. Well, he had no wish to judge her, but didn't that only increase the burden on him, the father, to take up not only his own responsibilities but hers as well?

Stupid, sentimental fantasies.

They should never have written to him. What kind of madmen were they, this English court, that they first took upon themselves the task of disposing

184

of his son and then, instead of doing it quietly and without fuss, insisted on parading the fact before him, tormenting him with it? Well, on their head be it. They had told him he had a son and now nothing he told himself could take that knowledge away.

He had never known his own father. How could he now allow his son to grow up and be able to say the same?

He slowly pulled the phone towards him, delayed to read the letter one more time, and then pressed the coded button that put him through to the office of Jacques Martin-Achard.

16

Lauren had bathed Adam and put him down to sleep in his cot. She was coming downstairs again when the door-bell went. 'I'll get it,' she sang out, knowing James was in the lounge, clearing up the debris of the day.

It was Vernon Angelis. 'Oh, hello,' she said, smiling though she was surprised to see him: he had already made the two visits which were all he had said would be necessary. The adoption ceremony was only two days away. No doubt there was something he had forgotten. 'Well, come in. We've just put him down, so you've caught us free for once.'

He was wearing a red bow-tie clipped onto a green corduroy shirt but had kept faith with the sandals, even though it was a wet evening. She saw James' smile, knowing he thought him something of a weirdo.

Vernon said, 'I'm afraid I've got some rather unexpected news.' Then he slumped down onto the sofa so that it seemed for a moment he wouldn't have the strength to deliver it.

Lauren exchanged a glance with James, who was now frowning. 'About the adoption?' she prompted.

'Yes.' He roused himself and spoke quickly, without looking directly at either of them. 'I'm afraid the child's father – the natural father – has now decided to contest it.' He made a gesture of helplessness. 'So.'

Lauren's heart sank. So what did this mean? And where had he sprung from, this natural father, whom she thought everyone had dismissed as having no part to play in all this?

'I'm sorry,' said Vernon. 'Of course, it means postponing the adoption hearing. It must be terribly frustrating for you.'

James groaned and said, 'Damn.' She knew he was looking at her, waiting for her reaction.

'But is it just . . . just a postponement?' she said. 'I mean there's no chance that he'll be awarded custody?'

Such a terrible question that it took an effort to ask. But Vernon was shaking his head with what seemed to be total confidence. 'Oh, no. No, I can't see there being any chance of that. I really can't.'

His words came as a massive relief, particularly since they reinforced what both he and Stella had been telling her all along – that Adam was as good as theirs already. Still, she wanted him to say more, to offer some kind of guarantee. 'You're sure?'

'Well, I'm as sure as I ever can be, yes. I think I told you before the man is unmarried, so he can't be offering much of a home. And till a few days ago he didn't even know the child existed!'

She believed him and was encouraged. Though it was still disappointing to think that they were going to be robbed of their day of celebration by someone who, upto now, had scarcely seemed to exist. Her dismay hardened into annoyance. What right had he to interfere anyway? 'I thought the mother had refused to identify him?' she protested.

Vernon nodded. 'Well, yes. But I think I mentioned to you that I was going to go and see her again – '

'And she decided to tell you,' said James bluntly.

'I'm afraid she did.'

So it's your fault, Lauren wanted to say. But Vernon looked so apologetic, so distressed already at his own role in this, that she remained silent. James took her hand and give it a reassuring squeeze.

'I didn't pressure her,' said Vernon, apologetic. 'In fact, I'd much rather she hadn't said anything. But I did have to ask and . . . well, she just came out with it. His name and address, as simple as that. And then, of course, we had no choice but to let him know what was happening. Even then, I was surprised. I didn't expect that he'd be very interested.'

'But he is,' said James.

'I'm afraid so.'

'Well, it's not your fault,' said Lauren, sorry for him. 'I suppose he has every right.'

She saw James' look of surprise. Well, yes, she was surprised, too, that she seemed able to take this in her stride. It was having Adam there in the house, upstairs in his cot, that allowed her to be strong. He was already hers and could never be taken away. The court, she knew, would see that. The court must see that.

And, anyway, poor Vernon looked so much like a crest-fallen pixie that she hadn't the heart to let him see her disappointment.

'So,' she asked,' what will happen now?'

'Well, we'll still want you to attend court on the fifth. But, instead of the simple ceremony that it was going to be, the judge will now be hearing your counter claims for custody of little Adam.'

There was a moment's silence, then James said, 'Would anyone like a drink?'

Vernon agreed to a beer and Lauren said that yes, she would have one too. As James popped open the cans and provided glasses, Vernon explained again what they already knew but which Lauren was more than willing to hear again: how English law no longer recognized any kind of automatic right on the part of either natural parent. All right, they could contest the adoption – in theory, anybody could contest the adoption, anybody who thought they might make a better shot at bringing up the child – but the judge had every right to reject their claims and award the child to the adoptive parents.

As he will do in this case, Lauren told herself. It was a set-back but they would overcome it, as they had overcome previous ones.

And Vernon clearly agreed. He even seemed to cheer himself up, stressing how high the cards were already stacked in the Eagleshams' favour. They had undergone the rigorous scrutiny of the adoption agency; they had taken Adam into their home and showed themselves more than capable of caring for him. 'To tell you the truth,' he said, 'I wish the mother had kept her mouth well and truly shut. It's almost certainly not going to make a ha'p'orth of difference and would have saved a lot of trouble all round.'

'And what will we have to do?' said Lauren, trying to think practically. 'Will we need a solicitor or –'

'Well, not you personally, no. See, as far as the law is concerned, the child is still under the care of the adoption agency. So it's the agency that will be represented.'

Her pulse began to race at this talk of the legal battle to come. 'Does this mean that we'll meet him – Adam's father?'

189

'No. Oh, no,' said Vernon, adamant.

She was surprised. 'Not even in court?'

'No. For one thing, the hearing won't be in court, not open court. The judge will see both parties in his chambers. And it will all be arranged so that you and Adam's natural father never meet, you needn't worry about that.'

She wasn't sure that she would have been worried about it. It might even have helped to have confronted a flesh-and-blood enemy rather than have him remain a shadowy and mysterious figure, always slightly out of picture. She couldn't help but be curious.

'And what sort of man is he, do you know?'

Vernon shook his head. 'I know very little about him. The natural mother gave me his name and the address where he lives in Switzerland. After that, she wouldn't say a thing.'

Lauren saw her own surprise mirrored in James' change of expression. 'Switzerland . . . ?' they exclaimed almost simultaneously.

'Oh, yes,' said Vernon. 'Sorry, did I not mention that?'

'So what nationality – ' began Lauren.

'He's Swiss. At least I assume he is. Lives in Geneva.'

Did that make things better or worse, she wondered. It probably didn't do them any harm, having a foreigner oppose them. Let's just hope they got a zenophobic judge. Though it was certainly a surprise to realize that Adam had such distant blood in his veins. Under other circumstances, she might have found it intriguing, welcome even, making him even more special than he was already.

When Vernon had gone, she and James sat together in the lounge, saying little.

'Two steps forward, one step back,' muttered James, disconsolate.

'Don't worry,' she said, patting his hand. 'We're going to win.' She meant it too. She still felt that the court would be on their side – well, Vernon was definitely on their side and it was his report that would go to the judge. They also had the adoption agency on their side. Together, they would send this Swiss upstart back to his mountains and his cuckoo-clocks.

Beside, the alternative was so dreadful she could not – would not – even consider it. That way madness lay.

There came a jarring cry from above, which meant that Adam was awake and demanding supper. They went together to see to him and even managed to be quite jolly about it, as if determined to make sure that the bright-eyed six-week-old should catch no hint of the legal storm-clouds looming over him.

Lauren's assertion that they would win became a kind of mantra that she repeated over and over to herself, keeping despair at bay. After which she would remind herself that the agency was now on their side, that Vernon Angelis was on their side and that everyone she spoke to – Sarah, Rachel, Mrs Revell the health visitor, Jane from next-door, even the man who ran the small sub-post-office on the corner – reassured her that this intervention by the Swiss father was too little and too late and would be thrown out by the court.

Stella Priestley arrived to add her voice. 'He hasn't a leg to stand on,' she insisted, holding Adam while Lauren made coffee. 'I mean think about it. Up to a week ago, he didn't even know the child existed, for God's sake.'

'But the court obviously thinks he has a case, otherwise – '

'They've no choice. If he wants to object, well, then they have to listen. But that's as far as it will go.'

Lauren nodded, wanting to believe her. And there was one more thing she had to know. 'Can I ask you something?'

'What?'

'Will the court have to be told about James' affair with Suzie Brandon?' It was an unsettling notion that had come to her in the early hours, when she had been lying awake, watching Adam asleep in his cot.

Stella smiled. 'Hey, listen. Forget Perry Mason. Forget your big courtroom dramas. This is all going to be in the judge's chambers. Very low-key – '

'But even so – '

'And we certainly won't be mentioning it. All we'll be doing is explaining why we thought it right to place baby Adam with you and why we think it right that you should keep him.'

Lauren nodded, feeling that a small ghost had been laid to rest. Perhaps it had been an absurd question, looming large in the early hours but easily disposed of in the light of day.

'Don't worry,' urged Stella. 'If the judge asks you anything at all, it'll be something simple and straight-forward about how you're getting on with the baby. He already knows everything he needs to know to confirm the adoption. It's the gentleman from Switzerland who's going to have his work cut out.'

They went through into the lounge, where the sunlight was flooding through the windows, a promise of the summer to come but also highlighting the room's neglect, catching the circles of dried milk on the mantelpiece and the dust mites in the air. After the court hearing, when it was all over, she would give it a good cleaning, get her life organized again.

Another thought occurred to her, though she hesitated before asking: 'What about the mother?' Then held her breath, frightened that there might be something here they were keeping from her.

Yet Stella seemed unperturbed. 'I shouldn't think she'll have anything at all to do with it. Though I think Vernon is going to have another word with her. Just as a formality.'

'Does she know about the father's application?'

'Not yet.'

Which triggered off a new wave of doubts and fears. Suppose she were to weigh in on the side of the father? Suppose the two of them were to decide to get together again, for the sake of the child?

Don't think about it. 'We're going to win,' Lauren silently recited. 'We're going to win.'

And certainly Stella seemed confident enough. (It couldn't be all an act surely? She was a social worker; it would have taken a RADA-trained actress to have carried off the visit with such an air of calm and certainty if she had any real misgivings. Wouldn't it?) 'And it won't last long. Half an hour at the most,' she said before she left. 'Don't expect a great, drawn-out affair.'

Giving Adam his bath, Lauren rehearsed him in what he must and mustn't say. 'If the nice man asks you whether you like living here, then you must nod and smile. And if you hear the word Switzerland – got that, Switzerland – then start yelling your head off.'

She believed she was doing well, managing to keep the horrors at arm's length. It helped, of course, that she had so many visitors; and James

193

had been so kind, staying at home for as long as he could, making sure he was away at the garden centre for no more than a couple of hours at a time, and even then ringing her on some pretext or other which she knew was really to check that she was bearing up.

Only once, the afternoon before the hearing, did her spirits fail her. She had taken Adam out for a stroll and he had fallen asleep by the time she returned to the empty house. There were no visitors and the phone was silent. She left him in the pram in the hallway and, unable to settle, had wandered through the kitchen and out into the garden, which was looking unkempt. Coming back and into the hallway, she was suddenly choked with tears and trembling. 'No, you can't,' she cried aloud. 'You're my son. They can't take you!' She wouldn't let them. She would run with him from the court, barricade herself in the house, do anything to keep him. Wild fantasies. 'We're going to win,' she recited desperately. 'We're going to win.'

By the time James returned, she had regained her composure. Besides, there was a meal to be cooked and Adam was awake, wanting feeding and changing. The hearing was the following morning, at ten-thirty. At least the waiting was almost over. For how many years to come would they look back on this and laugh at the way she had reacted so jumpily to every obstacle, real or imagined?

God, let it turn out so that they might be able to look back and laugh.

Stella rang that evening, sounding breathless. Hearing her voice, Lauren experienced a renewed frisson of apprehension.

'I've just heard from Vernon Angelis,' said Stella.

194

'You know I told you he was going to see the mother again – '

'Yes?' Holding her breath, fearing the worst, yet unable to guess at what it might be.

'Well, apparently she doesn't want to appear in person at the hearing tomorrow, but she has drawn up an affidavit – '

'A what?'

'Sorry. A sort of signed statement, made before a solicitor.'

'Right.' Though still not understanding. A signed statement about what . . . ?

'The point is that it can be submitted to the court as evidence. Which is what we're going to do. Because she's agreed to support your case against the natural father.'

It took a moment to sink in. 'Against him . . . ?'

'Yes. Isn't that marvellous?'

Oh, yes. Now, understanding, she could see that it was indeed marvellous. 'Wonderful,' she breathed.

'So have a good night's sleep. See you in court tomorrow.'

Marcus flew into Manchester airport, accompanied by Jacques Martin-Achard. It was a relief to be in action at last, doing something. The flight from Geneva had brought him closer to his goal; now it was a short journey to Preston, where they were to meet an English solicitor and barrister to go over the case they would present in court next morning.

It was a case he had already gone through in his head a hundred times, each time becoming more convinced of its transparent validity. He had come to claim his son as his own. Could there be any more basic right? Could there be a court in the world that would deny him?

Of course Jacques' reaction had been all he might have expected – astonished disbelief which rapidly matured into total opposition. He had expected it because it had been his own reaction when he had sat staring at Phillipe Lommer's letter and felt the first stirrings within him, knowing he could not let this alone but must pursue it.

'You must be crazy.'

'This is my child, my son – '

'Biologically, maybe. But in every other sense it's just a child, any child. You don't know anything about it. You only knew the mother for a short time – '

'I know, I know – ' Though he also knew that Jacques would not rest till he had challenged every step of his thinking and so told himself he must remain patient. No doubt it was a good dress-rehearsal for any cross-examination he might face in court.

'And what kind of life could you offer a child anyway? You're virtually a prisoner yourself. You would bring a child to live here, surrounded by high walls and armed guards?'

'I know that this is not ideal – '

'Not ideal? Not ideal . . . ! It would be monstrous to bring a child here!'

'This is not just something – '

But Jacques was into his stride and would not be stopped. 'I don't know where you have got this romantic idea from. Or even why they bothered to tell you of the child's existence – '

'Apparently they had to.'

'But for the sake of our friendship I have to speak the truth. You may not like it, but I have to.'

'And for the sake of our friendship I will listen,' said Marcus patiently.

'You are a businessman and a . . . well, what we used to call a playboy. You're not a family man and you never will be. Besides, you're not married. The child would not have a mother. And, as if all that weren't enough, your life is in constant danger. If you bring a child here, then his life is going to be in constant danger also.'

'I know. You think I haven't considered these things?'

'No, I don't. Anyway, not sufficiently. Otherwise how in your wildest dreams could you have ever thought it possible?'

It was no more than Marcus had already told himself time and again. That he must do nothing and let the adoption process go ahead. Yet he couldn't. It was as simple as that. He needed and wanted this child as he had never needed or wanted anything in his life before, and all these arguments, these powerful and undeniable arguments, were beside the point. Not because they were false but because they were founded on mere reason and could do nothing to quell the emotions that had been growing within him since the moment he had opened the letter.

'Will you listen to me now?' he said, when Jacques seemed to have run out of steam.

'I'm listening.'

'Say what you will, this isn't just any child. This is my child that we're talking about.'

'Biologically yes, but – '

'Biologically is all that any father has to start with.'

'Usually there's a wife around as well.'

Marcus ignored that and ploughed on. 'Also, what you don't know is that this is probably the only chance I will ever have to father a child.' And he told Jacques of Doctor Gerrone's diagnosis.

Jacques stared in undisguised surprise. 'But I did not know,' he stammered. 'Why didn't you – '

'I would have told you but it didn't seem to matter. I never saw myself as a father either. But now . . . now I feel as though I have been offered a reprieve, a chance to have a son as other men have sons.'

Jacques shook his head slowly. 'Even so . . . ' he muttered.

Marcus pressed home his advantage. 'I accept that you've never seen me as ideal material for fatherhood. I've never seen myself that way either. But which of us is until we actually find ourselves with a child to care for?'

'Oh, admitted – '

'Did you ever see yourself as having a child until that moment when you knew Chloe had been born?' Chloe was the elder of Jacques' two daughter, both now grown-up and starting families of their own.

'That may be true,' said Jacques in uncharacteristic retreat. 'And perhaps I shouldn't have phrased things as I did. I just meant . . . well, have you really thought it through? The responsibility you would be taking on, not just for a year or two but forever?'

'Yes,' said Marcus simply. Indeed, he had thought of little else since receiving the letter. 'Yes, I have. Which already puts me ahead of most fathers in history. I don't have to accept this child. I can do nothing and know that I'll never hear another word about it. But I am choosing to accept it. With my eyes open and knowing the consequences.'

Jacques nodded, then said quietly, 'And what about Jarman?'

Here Marcus knew he was on shakier ground. The danger that Jarman posed was a consideration which had already almost persuaded him to forget the child. How could he deliberately involve an innocent third-party in their bloody vendetta?

Yet, in a curious way, it was Jarman's attacks upon him that had forced him to reassess his life, leaving him vulnerable to this Heaven-sent gift. His close shaves with death, the long stay in hospital and now this circumscribed, confined sort of a life had bred in him a discontent for what he had so far achieved and an awareness of his own isolation.

'I know, I know,' he said. 'But the child will be safe. I swear to you the child will be safe.'

'Marcus, I have to remind you why Jarman has mounted these attempts on your life – '

'I know.' Because of the death of his own son.

'It's because he believes that you were responsible for the death – '

'I know.'

'Then think what a danger your own son would be in – '

'Jarman won't even know he exists.' Then, feeling the weakness of that, he added, 'Besides, if I allow him to stop me recognizing my own son, then he might as well have killed me at the first attempt.'

'With respect, that doesn't answer the question – '

'There'll be no danger to the boy,' said Marcus doggedly. 'I'll make sure there's no danger.'

'How?'

'He'll live in this house. He won't go outside this house – '

'A wonderful childhood.'

'He'll live here for the time being. Until the situation is resolved. And, if I didn't think he was safe here, then I would take him elsewhere. Anywhere on this earth.'

He knew it was hardly a detailed plan of campaign. But there would be time for that. The time that was lacking and was already ebbing away was that available for them to approach the English court and state their case before he risked losing the child by default. And for that he needed Jacques' help.

They had talked further, on into the night. Marcus told of his childhood and of the envy he felt towards his brother, Hervé, who had his restaurant in Paris and his family around him. Jacques spoke of his own family and of that time, precious in his memory, when the children had been young and before his wife was killed. It was the first time Marcus had heard him speak in this way or seen him reveal the emotions which were normally so carefully controlled.

'So,' he said finally, 'will you help me in this?'

Jacques hesitated, then nodded. 'Of course.'

Marcus gripped his hand. 'I'll always be grateful. Always.'

'We may not be successful.'

And Marcus had laughed, recognizing the voice of the lawyer returning, the voice of caution. It did nothing to dent his feeling of elation, his new-found confidence in their eventual victory.

Wasn't their case undeniable? He was the child's father: the English court had already admitted as much in going to such lengths to contact him. They were asking only one question: did he wish to assume responsibility for this child?

Well, now he was ready to give them his answer.

Their English legal team were waiting in the Preston hotel and introduced themselves even as Marcus and Jacques were signing in at the desk. There were two of them, one a solicitor, the other a barrister. Though Marcus wasn't clear on the distinction, he had been assured by Jacques that it would be advisable to have one of each. The more the merrier.

The solicitor, a man called Snelgrove, was a beaming heavyweight in some kind of sporting club blazer. He took it upon himself to make a short speech of welcome, while the barrister, who was called Meacham, stood by in silence. He was younger but more austere, in a dark suit.

They went together to Marcus' suite, ordered sandwiches from room service and got down to business. Jacques had already given them the facts of the case and something about Marcus' own past and present circumstances (though omitting all mention of Jarman). It was now a matter, as Snelgrove explained, of familiarizing themselves with their client. After all, it was his character, his suitability to act as father to his own child, that was the issue.

'So what do you want to know?' asked Marcus patiently.

It was Snelgrove who took it upon himself to answer. 'Well, what the court will want to know is why do you want to take on the responsibility of bringing up the child yourself?'

'Because it's my child.'

'But you still don't have to. They have gone to some pains to find a couple who they believe would make good parents for it.'

Marcus felt a faint irritation: he hadn't expected his own motives to be challenged so bluntly by people he was employing, paying good money, to present his case, not question it. 'It's still my child. I have a right to bring up my own child.'

'And you think you can do that better than this other couple? Even thought you're not married? Forgive me, but this is bound to be asked.'

201

'I have the financial resources to provide everything the child could want,' said Marcus evenly.

'Well, yes, but – '

'What about the mother?' said Meacham.

Marcus turned to him, sensing from Snelgrove's deferential giving-way that this younger man was the senior of the pair. 'She was a lady I met some time ago, and who came over last summer to stay with me in Geneva.'

'Well, yes, we have that information. I was wondering why she had chosen to present the child for adoption.'

Marcus shrugged. He had also wondered why Claire should have done such a thing, without contacting him, without even giving him the chance to offer his support. 'You'd better ask her.'

'Well, unfortunately, we're not allowed to do that,' said Snelgrove.

'She won't be in court?' asked Marcus, surprised.

'No. I gather she's keeping well away.'

He turned to Jacques, who gave a gesture of helplessness.

'That might not be a bad thing,' said Meacham. 'After all, she did opt for adoption. That is already her declared preference. It would hardly help our case to have the court reminded of it.'

Snelgrove beamed and nodded, as if applauding his colleague's sagacity. Looking round at Marcus and Jacques, inviting them to do the same. In truth, Marcus was less than impressed with the pair of them, sensing a certain detachment. They weren't quite the bullish, high-powered team that he had pictured. Was it just that they were English or was their commitment less than total?

'Anyway, never mind about me,' he said, trying to inject some pep into the proceedings. 'What about the couple who want to adopt my child? What do we know about them?'

It was Snelgrove who answered. 'Well, they're what we might call a lower-middle class couple. She used to be a teacher and then worked in a garage, selling cars, before giving that up to look after the child. And he's part owner of a garden centre.'

'OK. And so what line are you going to take on them?'

'What line . . . ?'

'What kind of questions are you going to ask? We want to undermine them, don't we. Show that, whatever they can offer the child, I can offer more.'

God, did he have to teach them their job? Spell it out for them? He saw them exchange a glance and then Meacham spoke.

'You must understand the situation we face, Monsieur Revachier. We will not be in open court. There won't be an opportunity for cross-examination. We will present your case as strongly as possible, but that's all we can do.'

Marcus was dismayed. Perhaps he had misunderstood. 'You mean there'll be no chance to question these people?'

'Not directly, no.'

'So what will we be able to do?'

'We'll be able to present your case to the judge.'

'And then they'll present their case?'

'Yes, but privately. They won't hear your case and you won't hear theirs.'

'We're not even in the same room?'

'You won't even see one another.'

He could hardly believe it. He had been prepared for a contest, one to which he had been expressly invited, yet now was being told that his opponents could neither be seen nor questioned. They would be tilting at windmills. 'Will you excuse us a moment?' he said. The two Englishmen murmured their assent. He gestured to Jacques and they went out together into the space between the sitting-room and bedroom doors, where the drinks cabinet stood, its refrigeration unit ticking.

'Just what the hell is going on here?'

'Marcus I tried to explain – '

'We can't even question this couple, whoever they are? We won't even be in the same room . . . ?'

'English law tries to ensure that the adoptive parents never met the natural parents.'

It seemed preposterous. 'Then how can anything be resolved?'

'The judge has to decide. He meets both. He talks to both. And then he has to decide.'

'Jesus Christ,' said Marcus. He felt himself undermined, out-manoeuvred before battle had even begun. 'What can we do?' he asked Jacques in desperation.

'No more than we're doing already.'

'I don't believe this. I don't believe that this is happening!' He slammed the drinks cabinet with his hand. There was a tinkle of bottles; the refrigeration unit hiccuped, then continued its ticking. 'Listen, are these two any good?' Indicating the other room, where the two Englishmen were chewing on the sandwiches.

'I am assured they are very good, yes. But they can only operate within the system. These things are not of their devising.'

'Shit,' said Marcus, feeling that things were beginning to slip away.

'It's no better for the other side. They are just as limited as we are.'

Well, yes, he could see that. In theory, it was all

204

there, still to be played for, beginning at ten-thirty tomorrow morning. So why was it then that, in the short time since they had entered the hotel, he felt the odds lengthening against him?

He saw the distress on Jacques' face and knew that he must not take out his frustration on his friend who had come so far to help and support him. 'I'm sorry,' he said. 'I'm just . . . I don't know, perhaps I'm tired.'

They went back into the sitting-room and to another half-hour of questions and answers, though Marcus now felt himself detached from the whole process. It was as though the case had already been lost before they had even set foot in court. As though it had been lost there, in that hotel suite. He felt, with a dreadful foreboding, that the court had already made its decision. It had probably made it weeks ago.. He had been contacted and his attitude sought only as a legal politeness, with no-one imagining he would take it seriously and rush over like this.

Sitting up late after the lawyers had gone and Jacques retired to his room, he even wondered whether it was worthwhile going ahead with the charade. His child was going to be taken from him by a couple he would never meet and whose suitability could not be challenged in open court. He helped himself to a whisky from the humming drinks cabinet and paced about his bedroom.

He had expected everything to be settled in an English court, by means that would be robust but fair. In which arena he had been confident of success.

Now, it seemed, that was not going to happen. It would all be done in private, secretly, discreetly, with no means of challenging the outcome. An

English judge deciding between an English couple and a foreigner.

His decision, before finishing his drink and climbing into bed, was two-fold. Firstly, that he would attend the court. After all, it would be ludicrous not to, having come this far. Secondly, should his worst fears be realized and it should bestow his son upon these strangers . . . then he would feel himself free to use whatever means possible to retrieve him from their grasp.

17

There was quite a posse of supporters waiting for them in the foyer of the courthouse. Lauren first caught sight of Vernon Angelis, a head taller than those around him, then she saw that Stella and Marjorie were beside him; with them was a young man in a grey suit and paisley tie who was introduced as James Burrows, the agency's solicitor.

How can they all be so relaxed, thought Lauren as they greeted her. She felt herself to be one tight knot of nerves.

Around them were groups of people in huddled consultation, policemen and the occasional wig-and-gown; while at the same time, on the benches around the walls, slumped a line of dispirited-looking men and women – men mostly – waiting in silence. 'I've never been here before,' she said, then wished she hadn't since it seemed an inane, pointless comment.

'Me neither,' agreed James. 'Half of this lot look as though they're here every week.'

Suddenly they were on the move, Vernon leading them. Lauren allowed herself to be swept along, through what seemed a maze of corridors and stairways till they came to a stop before a door marked only with a number – '26'. So what are we doing here Lauren thought, looking at the others but not wanting to ask. Adam lay silently in her arms, staring around him with wide eyes and seeming oblivious to the way each of the adults would, almost in turn, chuck him under the chin or touch his cheek, as though wanting to keep in contact with their lucky talisman.

We're going to win, recited Lauren. She believed it too, especially after Stella had told her about the affidavit that Adam's natural mother had signed. Though she couldn't relax and knew that she must take nothing for granted. Half-an-hour at the most, Stella had told her. Half-an-hour, then it would all be over.

The door opened, catching her by surprise so that she almost cried out. The man standing there said hello to Vernon and smiled round at the rest of them. Was this the judge? Though he was wearing an ordinary suit, Lauren didn't want to take any chances and so gave a small bow of the head, just in case. But then he was inviting them to follow him into the room, which opened out into a commodious chamber with portraits around the walls and she saw another man sitting at a round table. He was wearing a red gown and, although without his wig, was clearly the genuine article. He was perhaps in his early sixties, grandfatherly, with red cheeks and sparse, white hair.

He wished them good morning as they formed a semi-circle before him. Lauren bobbed her head again. James Burrows, their solicitor, addressed him as Your Honour and explained who everyone was. The judge rose and chucked Adam under the chin as everyone else had done.

'My, what a beautiful child,' he said.

Lauren's heart swelled. 'Thank you,' she said, then added, 'Your Honour.'

The judge sat down again, rearranging his robe about his knees. He said that he had read the agency's report and also the report produced by the court's own appointed officer – which meant Vernon Angelis – and was well satisfied with both. His only question was why the natural father hadn't been consulted at an earlier stage. Vernon explained that this had not been possible because of the mother's initial refusal to identify him. Lauren saw his annoyance at the question. *He has told the judge this before*, she interpreted, *and resents being asked again now.* And interpreted further: did it mean that the judge had no real questions to ask at all, that he was perfectly satisfied with everything, and had had to manufacture this one just to show that he was on the ball?

She told herself to calm down and stop trying to find significance in everything. Let things happen in their own good time.

Now the judge was speaking to her and James, asking how they were finding life with a baby and whether he had begun to sleep through at nights. Small talk. Stella had been right: this was no court-room drama, merely a rather stilted conversation between people trying to put one another at their ease and not quite succeeding. Then – really the only formal bit – their solicitor asked His Honour's permission to offer an affidavit from the child's natural mother for His Honour's consideration. The judge nodded, slipped on a pair of dark-framed glasses and read through the sheet of paper which the solicitor placed before him.

Then he took off the glasses and smiled at Lauren. 'That seems to be all in order,' he said. She wondered how she should respond and managed a smile back. The judge went on: 'Now, of course, I have to see the other party in this case, so I must ask you to wait for a little while. Then I shall send for you and will give you my decision.'

The man who had admitted them and who had been standing at the back of the room during this now swung into action. 'If you would care to follow me,' he said and headed for the door. He put Lauren in mind of a theatrical dresser. No doubt he helped the judge on with his robes and generally saw that everything ran sweetly for him.

Now he lead their little team – for this was how she thought of them, the agency team, the good guys, the home side, the ones everyone was rooting for – along further corridors and into a small room that was furnished only by a line of plastic stacking chairs. They filed in and then the judge's dresser said, 'I must ask that none of you leaves here until I return.' With a meaningful look at Vernon as though to say – and you make sure they don't. They muttered their assent and he disappeared, closing the door behind him.

This is so that we shouldn't accidentally bump into the other side, the bad guys, the away team, thought Lauren. She wondered how the judge would receive them, whether he would remain benign and chatty or become stern and give them a hard time. Perhaps he would even put his wig on.

Where they surely had the advantage was that they had got in there and stood before the judge with Adam. Surely it had to colour the judge's view of the rival candidates seeing one of them actually holding the baby and the other one with nothing at all.

Didn't it?

Please.

'I thought that went all right,' said James, giving her hand a squeeze.

'I think so,' she agreed. 'He was nice, wasn't he?' Then turned to Stella and Marjorie. 'What do you think?' For they had presumably been through all this before and so were better placed to read the vibes.

They reassured her that they, too, had thought the judge sympathetic. Extremely sympathetic. Marjorie said she had never known him ask so few questions and, like Lauren, took this as a sign that his mind was already made up, or as good as. She was chain-smoking and James opened a window. Stella offered to hold Adam for a while but Lauren said no thanks, she would prefer to keep hold of him herself.

A quarter of an hour passed. They ran out of conversation and sat around, looking at their watches. We're going to win, Lauren reminded herself. So why was it taking so long?

But for the presence of the others, she would have been tempted to slip out into the corridor, risking the wrath of the judge's dresser. She imagined herself creeping along, peering round corners, and finally catching sight of the away team emerging from the judge's chambers. Looking downcast, she hoped.

In the centre would be Adam's father. For some reason, she saw him as burly and dark-haired.

Then the judge's dresser had returned and was inviting them to follow him. Lauren felt dry-mouthed and tense and had to be careful not to grip Adam too tightly. They none of them spoke as they retraced their route along the corridors. She wondered what she might do if the verdict went against them. Run from the building with Adam in her arms, ushers and policemen calling her to stop and passers-by turning to stare at the commotion?

But the judge was smiling and she knew everything was all right.

211

He was still wigless but now had a cup of tea in a saucer. They stood as before, forming a semi-circle before his table. He looked up at them and said, 'I won't keep you in suspense any longer. I have no hesitation in rejecting the claims of the other party and so am happy that the adoption should go ahead as planned.'

For a moment no-one spoke, then the solicitor said, 'Thank you, Your Honour.' The others murmured in agreement. Lauren could only smile; she thought she was going to cry but managed to hold back the tears. Through blurred eyes she saw James beaming at her.

'Well then,' said the judge, turning to Vernon, 'it's a pity we can't complete everything now, but I gather that the papers – '

'Not quite ready,' said Vernon apologetically. 'Since, of course, we didn't know for sure – '

'Of course,' said the judge. 'But I think now as soon as possible. Don't you?'

Lauren saw that he was addressing her, and managed to gasp, 'Oh, yes. Please.'

He felt cheated and deceived. He had come to England expecting justice and fair play and found himself a bit-player in a high-speed farce, which had ended in a off-hand rejection of his claim. This had been no proper hearing where both sides of the case could be publicly aired and challenged but a private get-together where, so far as he could see, the outcome was a foregone conclusion.

It was a fix. His invitation to participate had been a cruel hoax.

Oh, his counsel had done their best, but they had never stood a chance either. Even the most silver-tongued of lawyers would have been defeated by

212

such a process. Meacham had spoken persuasively of Marcus' upright character and his standing as a man of business. He had stressed the blood-tie between Marcus and the child, seeking to make it the main component in the case.

Yet the judge had rejected it out-of-hand!

He had been courteous enough, thanking them for their attendance but clearly regarded the fact that Marcus was the child's father – a fact which no-one contested – to be incidental and irrelevant. As though the child might have been anybody's, with this couple, picked almost at random, having as much right to it as its own father.

More right to it. Since it was to them that the child had been given.

Emerging from the courthouse, Marcus felt a deep anger and, with it, a resolve that this must not be allowed to rest. When the appalling verdict had been given, he had said nothing but had turned and walked from the room. Now he had left Jacques to deal with Messrs Snelgrove and Meacham and come to stand by himself in the fresh air. Though the earlier rain had petered out, the sky was still grey. It was a miserable, joyless sort of place, this northern English town to which his son had been so casually condemned. Nearby, a Land Rover was pulling away from the car-park next to the courthouse. His attention was drawn to it by two women alongside who were waving and calling as it departed.

Then, as it left the car-park and passed in front of him, he caught a glimpse of the man driving and, behind him, a woman holding what was surely a child on her lap. 'All Seasons Garden Centre' said the lettering on the door of the Land Rover.

With a stab of despair, he realized that this was his own child he had glimpsed, being carried off by the lower-middle-class English couple on whom the English judge had looked with such approval. He had to fight an instinct to pursue the vehicle and wrench open the door.

Jacques came to join him, gazing at him anxiously. 'I'm sorry,' he said.

Marcus shook his head, meaning that it was not Jacques' fault, nor even that of their English lawyers. 'They had it sewn up,' he said.

'There is no appeal,' said Jacques quietly.

Marcus nodded. He knew that; he had been warned of it in advance. Now he simply wanted to get away from this place. They took a taxi back to the hotel and Marcus went to his room while Jacques enquired about flight times.

There was a sense in which the injustice had been so blatant and undisguised that he now felt free to reverse it by whatever means were necessary. He had played by the rules and been treated with contempt; ergo, he need play by the rules no longer.

Suppose there were a way in which he could take this child – a child that was already his own by every natural law in the universe – and spirit it back to Geneva in defiance of this English kangaroo court and its mockery of a system?

It wasn't a prospect to be relished but one to which the morning's shabby pantomime had driven him. Kidnapping was the ugly word for it.

Nor would it be easy. There would be risks, big risks, for himself and anyone else involved in it. Jacques, for one, must have no part of it, or even knowledge of it. He was a man of principle, and lawyer to boot, and would never countenance anything so undeniably illegal.

Yet he would need help from somewhere. He could hardly do it alone.

There was a knock on the door. He opened it to find Jacques there with news of an available flight that afternoon. Marcus listened, then said, 'Good. Then you must get yourself on that. But I won't be coming with you. I've some business to conduct, which I might as well do while I'm here. Then at least the trip won't have been a total waste.'

He saw that Jacques wasn't totally convinced. 'Well, I don't mind staying with you –' he began to protest.

But Marcus over-rode the objections, explaining that he wasn't in the mood for company and would prefer to be left alone. Jacques still looked as though he had misgivings but finally gave way: he would go and make his reservation for the afternoon flight.

The moment he was gone, Marcus moved to the telephone. There was a card beside it showing international dialling codes. France was 01033. Sitting on the bed, a plan already forming in his mind, he called the restaurant on the Rue Poissonniere and asked to speak to his brother, Hervé.

18

Lauren's afternoon was spent answering the phone as family and friends rang, wanting to know how the case had turned out. And how she loved telling them! Not minding having to deliver the same account time and time again; in fact relishing it, adding to it each time of telling as more details occurred to her.

Then, once news got round, there were cards popped through the letterbox by neighbours, and a bunch of flowers – blue irises and yellow tulips in a cloud of gypsophila ('baby's breath') – from Jane next-door. Even the weather responded by clearing up and turning sunny so that Lauren was able to put Adam out in the garden for his afternoon nap.

It was something she was still a touch nervous about, putting him outdoors like this. She covered his pram with a cat-net, checking that it was securely fastened at each corner and placed the pram in the middle of the back lawn so that it was no more than twenty yards from the kitchen window.

The phone rang yet again. It was Sarah, James' sister, ringing with her congratulations. She had already heard the good news from James, though that didn't stop her wanting a full account of everything that had happened from Lauren so that she was kept talking for another ten minutes. Then, before she could ring off, Sarah announced that she would be round tonight to babysit for them. It would be a chance for them to get out somewhere on their own and celebrate properly. Lauren said, 'Well, thanks but I'm not sure – ', nervous about the idea of leaving Adam in anyone else's care. But Sarah would have none of it, cheerfully insisting she would be round at seven-thirty, so that Lauren had to agree.

She went back to the kitchen window, checking that there was no sign of movement from within the pram and that the cat-net was still in place.

James, arriving home and being brought up-to-date on developments, was all in favour of the idea of their having a night out together. He laughed at her qualms as Sarah had done. 'Well, all right,' conceded Lauren, 'but we're not going to be late back.' Then, when Sarah arrived, she insisted on giving her a guided tour of the nappies and the talc and the changing-mat, and the bottle already made-up for when Adam should awake.

'I have done this before, you know,' protested Sarah, amused.

Almost too late, Lauren saw herself in the mirror and realized she was still in the stained t-shirt and jeans that she'd slipped into on their return from the courthouse. 'Just give me ten minutes,' she cried and did a frantic quick-change act, throwing off the t-shirt and jeans and getting into the orange dress that she'd worn for that first visit they had made together to the agency.

That must have been almost a year ago. It felt longer, endless months of waiting, dogged by hopes that had had to be restrained and fears that couldn't be restrained.

Till now it was over.

217

She suddenly felt excited about going out. It was right that she should give some of her time to James. She mustn't allow herself to become monopolised by Adam and forget that she had a husband too. She fixed her make-up, some mascara and blusher, and dragged a brush through her hair.

'You look lovely,' said James, as he ushered her out through the front door. She called to Sarah that they wouldn't be late and Sarah called back, insisting they could be as late as they liked.

I didn't go in to see Adam, she realized, as they drove away. I meant to go back upstairs to kiss his little head and say good-night but there wasn't time, with James looking at his watch and going on about how the table was booked for eight.

I'll ring from the restaurant. Get Sarah to kiss him for me.

The moment they had been shown to their table, she was on her feet, telling James she just had to make this one, quick phone-call. He gave a groan of mock-despair, then had to delve into his pocket to provide her with the necessary change.

Sarah burst into laughter, hearing her voice. 'I knew you'd be ringing,' she said, 'but not this quickly!'

'I forget to say good night to him,' said Lauren, not caring if she sounded foolish. 'So I wondered if you'd mind – '

'I'll go up now.'

'Oh, would you really? I'll wait.'

She heard Sarah's footsteps going away up the stairs. From the phone in the restaurant foyer she could see their table where James was sitting alone, staring at the menu. I'm neglecting him already, she thought, with a pang of dismay. Then Sarah was back on the line. 'He was awake, so I've brought him down to say good night to you himself.' James was forgotten as she glued her ear to the receiver. She could hear a faint gurgling and said, 'Oh, hello, darling. This is mummy. We're out at a restaurant.' More gurgling, and then Sarah was laughing: 'He looks a bit puzzled. I don't think he can quite work it all out.'

'No, well . . . ' She saw James looking impatiently in her direction. 'Give him a kiss from me, won't you.'

'I will. Now you go and enjoy yourself.'

Still, she was glad she had made the call and went back to James feeling happier. Content to know that Adam was awake and so Sarah *had* to be tending to him; not just sitting downstairs watching television while he might have been upstairs crying and unheard.

James had already decided on a lasagne and she chose a pizza with extra chillies. And a bottle of the house red. At last she began to relax, feeling the tension go from her neck and shoulders, tension she hadn't been aware of.

Around them most of the tables were filled; someone in the corner was having a birthday. The waiters came trooping noisily through with a cake, then there was lots of cheering and laughter.

Sipping at her wine, she thought – now I have everything. And she smiled at James, loving him for the support he had given her and because she knew that he, in his own way, was as devoted to their son as she was herself.

'What're you thinking?' he asked.

'Oh . . . ' She was going to tell him how happy she was, something like that, but then, as it came into her mind, she said, 'D'you know who I feel sorry for?'

'Who?'

'Adam's father. Natural father.'

He stared. 'The Swiss – '

'Yes. Well, not sorry exactly. But just a tiny bit . . . ' – then, because she couldn't think of another word – 'well, yes, *sorry*.' Why not? She was allowed to say it; she was entitled to be generous in her victory. 'When you think about it, he did make a tremendous effort, coming all that way. I suppose he must have genuinely felt that Adam was his.'

'Then he was wrong,' said James firmly.

'Oh, yes, I know he was wrong. I know he was wrong. All the same . . . ' She thought of him going back on the plane – alone? – condemned never to seeing his son. She felt they owed him a moment of sympathy. 'Well, I just hope he gets over it,' she said.

'He'll have to.'

She saw that James wasn't going to give an inch and so left it at that. He wasn't vindictive by nature and so she could only suppose he felt he was protecting her. Protecting her from her own feelings. He was a lovely man, this husband of hers, and would protect her even from herself. She found she was smiling at him again.

'What?' he asked, startled.

And this time she kept it simple and said, 'I'm just so happy. I can't believe . . . I can't believe I've got everything I want.'

Their main course arrived and they began to eat. Beside the birthday celebrations going on in the corner, there was another party, some kind of anniversary gathering, to the side of them. Champagne corks were being popped and one of the men at the table was attempting to make a speech, shouting against the noise around him. When he had finished, there was applause. Lauren joined in, even though she hadn't understood a word. The other people turned towards her and raised their glasses. Both she and James began to laugh, raising their glasses in reply. It was as if all this was for them, even if they were the only ones who knew it.

She had a *strega* with her coffee, and then another one, now talking about holidays they would have and how soon Adam would be old enough for them to take him camping. Not this year, no, but there was no reason why next year . . .

Then she saw the time. Unbelievably, it was past eleven. Past eleven and here they were, still sitting in the restaurant – after all she had promised Sarah about getting home early!

Trying to calm her, James called for the bill, but she was already on her feet, making for the door. She felt panicky, and furious with herself that on this, their first night out, she should have been so careless as to lose track of the time.

Perhaps she should ring, reassure Sarah that they were returning. But that would only delay things further. And now here was James hurrying to join her, stuffing his wallet back into his pocket.

Ten minutes later they were home. She was first into the house, calling out, 'I'm sorry, we forgot the time . . . !' and seeing Sarah getting to her feet in the lounge, looking blank-faced as though she had been asleep.

'It's all right,' she said. 'He's been as good as gold – '

But Lauren was already on her way up the stairs, leaving James, who was coming in through the front door behind her, to talk to his sister. She reached the top, crossed the landing and pushed open the door to their bedroom.

There he was, her son, in his cot, breathing steadily. He was lying on his left side, with his right arm stretched out, his hand gripping the blanket. She bent low over him so that she might catch that smell that was already distinctly his own. He whimpered softly in his sleep. 'It's all right,' she said, and touched his forehead with the tips of her fingers.

He opened his eyes – just for a second, opened them quite wide – then closed them again and continued sleeping.

19

The weather seemed to have taken a permanent
turn for the better. The following day presented
blue skies and enough sun for Lauren again to risk
putting Adam outside for his afternoon nap. Though
he was unusually unsettled, whingeing when she tried
to leave him. She stood by the pram, rocking it
gently.

Looking around, she observed the neglected
garden: the grass needed cutting and weeds were
beginning to flourish. Well, perhaps she might get
out later and do something about it, but only perhaps. Priorities had changed. She understood now
how her sisters-in-law had remained indifferent to
the clutter around them and their bedraggled gardens.

She heard the phone ringing inside the house.
Adam had quietened, though he was still awake.
She took a couple of tentative steps away from the
pram, prepared to return if he should start yelling.
When he didn't, she hurried across the garden and
managed to grab the phone before its ringing
stopped.

'It's Vernon, Vernon Angelis,' said the voice at
the other end.

'Oh, hello.' She picked up the base of the phone
with her free hand and carried it as far into the

223

kitchen as its cable allowed. At least from there, with the kitchen door still open, she would hear Adam if he started to wail.

'I just wanted to congratulate you on your famous victory.'

'Thank you. and I mean thank you as well for all the help.' Vernon demurred but she insisted. 'I'm sure it impressed the judge enormously, having that statement from Adam's mother supporting us.'

'Yes, that was something of a bonus.'

'I was wondering actually. What made her decide to do it?'

It was only since the court hearing that she had allowed herself to think of Adam's natural parents and their feelings. Even to admit that they might have had feelings.

'Oh, well, she's a sensible lady,' said Vernon. 'And I don't think she was ever that closely involved with the father. So she just took the view that all she wanted was whatever was best for Adam.'

'Good for her.' She even wondered if she might thank her in some way but then dismissed the thought: no doubt it would be frowned upon, breaking the rules that said there must be no contact between them.

'I agree,' said Vernon. 'But listen. The real reason I'm ringing – '

'Yes?'

'They've set a date for the adoption hearing. It's a bit short notice but what would you say to tomorrow morning?'

Lauren didn't hesitate. 'I'd say yes please. What time do you want us there?'

'Ten-thirty. Same time as before.' Though he explained that it would be quite unlike yesterday's drama. Now that the natural father's objection had been dealt with and put behind them, this would be a straightforward, even perfunctory matter, taking no more than a few minutes. The judge would sign a paper and Adam would be theirs for life.

'Wonderful,' said Lauren. 'I can hardly believe it.'

'You will,' said Vernon, and promised to be there in the foyer, as before, to meet them and take them to the judge.

She wondered whether to ring James immediately with the good news, but first replaced the phone and went back outside to see whether Adam had settled. Certainly he had quietened and the pram was still. She approached cautiously, unable to see through the gauze cat-net until she was standing by the pram.

He was asleep. Flat out, with his blankets in a muddle around him where he had wrestled them. She gave a little laugh, seeing him like that, then skipped back into the house for the camera and, standing on tip-toes to get the angle right, took a picture of him.

The Day Before Adoption, she would entitle it.

Then she covered him up, replaced the cat-net and left him to his slumbers.

James expressed himself delighted with the imminent adoption hearing. 'Then it'll really all be over,' he mused. 'Can you believe that?'

'No. I told Vernon I couldn't.'

'I mean except for having to look after him for the next God-knows-how-many years . . . !'

When they had laughed about this – the notion that anything was over when there they were with an eight-week-old baby on their hands – and James had confirmed that of course he could take tomorrow morning off, Lauren decided to give Jane a ring to let her know the good news. After all, she had been one of the referees; she now taken to referring to herself as 'Aunty Jane' in honour of the fact. Now, rather than talk on the phone, she came hurrying round and they sat in the lounge. Lauren brought her up-to-date on Adam's sleeping and feeding habits and Jane reminisced about when her own sons had been that age.

It was the kind of conversation Lauren had once warned herself against, the kind she had endured for years in the company of James' sisters, who totalled seven pregnancies between them. Mustn't become a baby-bore, she had resolved when they had first brought Adam home.

Now she only thought – what the hell. Since he was the most important thing in her life, what was more natural than that she should talk about him?

'I've got to be going,' said Jane finally. 'Is he really still asleep out there?'

Lauren laughed. 'He likes his naps.'

'You want to thank your lucky stars. I used to have to dose my two upto the eyeballs to get a wink.'

Lauren glanced at her watch as she went through to the garden. Perhaps he had been asleep for longer than usual. She couldn't remember just what time it had been when she had put him down. Her step quickened.

Then she gave a gasp of horror as, even from the doorway, she could see that the cat-net had been pulled back from across the pram.

'Adam,' she cried, and ran across the grass, willing him to be there, knowing he must still be there and that she would be holding him in her arms and laughing with relief in a moment.

And knowing also that he wouldn't be there at all but had gone.

The pram was empty. She felt as though her life-blood had drained from her; she had turned to stone. She couldn't move, could do nothing but stare down at where he had been. But where had he gone . . . ? How . . . ? She forced herself to turn her head and look around her.

'No, no, no . . . ' she murmured, refusing to believe. Wasn't this just a nightmare? Wasn't there some way of wakening up from it?

She ran her hand around the inside of the pram, in the absurd hope that he might yet be hidden beneath the blankets. Pulled them from the pram and threw them onto the grass.

But this was no nightmare and there would be no awakening. He had gone. He had been taken. She had left him out here, neglected him, failed to watch over him and now he had gone! She was to blame and would never forgive herself.

She ran back towards the house, calling, 'Jane, Jane . . . !', then stopped, not know what she was doing – only that she must do *something* – turned and began running towards the bottom of the garden, where a wooden gate let out onto a narrow lane. She wrenched the gate open and began to run up the lane. But she could see nothing. There was no-one there. She turned and ran the same distance in the opposite direction, then stopped again, beside herself with despair, and came back into the garden.

On a forlorn hope, she went back to the pram. Perhaps she had been deceived? But no, it was still empty, the blankets still strewn on the grass around it.

'What is it? What's the matter?'

Jane was standing in her own garden, peering over the dividing hedge.

'He's gone,' moaned Lauren. 'Adam's gone.'

Hoping that Jane might tell her no, he's in the house. Don't you remember taking him inside? But she only said, 'I'm coming,' and then ducked out-of-sight. Confirming, if further confirmation were needed, that this wasn't a nightmare but was real.

Lauren ran to the gate, to meet Jane entering the garden. 'I just came out and he'd gone!' she wailed, grabbing her hands.

'Oh, my God,' said Jane, glancing at the empty pram. 'We must . . . we must ring the police.'

The police? Well, yes. And James. No, not James. How could she ever tell James?

But now Jane had pulled herself from her grasp and was hurrying away, towards the house. 'I'll ring them,' she called. 'You keep looking.'

Keep looking, yes. She must do that. Though she didn't know where to start and found herself going round and round the garden, looking beneath bushes and shrubs, even ones that were too small to hide anything, never mind a baby. Knowing all the time that Adam could not have climbed unaided from his pram. Someone must have lifted him out. Having done that, they would have taken him away, not hidden him somewhere.

Could it have been children? Perhaps with the best of intentions, hearing him crying and believing the house deserted? Intending only to take him back to their own homes, to their own mothers?

It was a desperate hope but it was all she had. It sent her running back out into the lane that ran between the backs of the houses. This time, ignoring the brambles that tore at her and stumbling on the uneven ground, she followed it till it came out into Highgate Avenue, which was a busy thoroughfare, with shops and passing traffic. She looked wildly about her but could see nothing of any children, who anyway, she realized with a fresh lurch of despair, would still be in school.

'Have you seen a child?' she demanded of a man who was passing. 'A little – ?'

'Sorry, no,' he said, barely breaking his step, and then glancing back curiously at her.

Of course this was futile. She couldn't question all these people. She should be at the house; she should never have left there. And so ran back along the lane and into her garden, where Jane was emerging from the back door.

'I've rung the police,' she said, putting an arm round her. 'They're on their way.'

'Someone must have taken him,' moaned Lauren.

This was more than she could stand. She wanted only oblivion and escape, yet knew also that she would never rest, would never again close her eyes in sleep till he was found.

She thought of crazed women and child-murderers. The kind of thing she had seen on television: parents making their helpless appeals and then the announcement that a body had been found . . .

She might even have blacked out for a moment, she didn't know. Jane was escorting her towards the house, saying, 'James is at work, is he? You tell me the number and I'll ring him.' Then they were standing in the hallway. It wasn't James who answered the phone – she was glad of that, welcoming even the tiniest of respites – but someone else to whom Jane spoke briskly, asking that a message be given to Mr Eaglesham telling him to return home immediately. Then, even as Jane was still speaking, there was a knock at the front door and it was pushed open. 'Hello? Police,' called a male voice.

Lauren felt an unexpected surge of hope at the sight of the uniforms. 'It's my child,' she said. 'He's been taken.' Pointing towards the garden. And waiting desperately for them to say he had been found, or anyway to promise that he would be found.

But they did neither, these two policemen. Instead, the older one, who had a pudgy face and heavy eyebrows, insisted she sat down in the lounge and told him just what had happened. His partner, who was younger and taller, was taken out into the garden by Jane to look at the empty pram.

'He was out there sleeping, and then, when I went to check on him, he'd gone . . . just gone!' Why did it seem so difficult for him to understand? Now the police were here, she wanted them out of the house and organizing searches, not painstakingly noting down names and times in a notebook.

'And the baby's how old?'

'Eight . . . just over eight weeks.' She felt herself to be gabbling and was surprised he could even understand her.

'And his name . . . ?'

'Adam. Adam Eaglesham. He's adopted.'

'Adopted . . . ? Is he now.'

Why had he said it like that – 'Adopted . . . ?' – and given her a look of, well, of suspicion almost, before bending to write in his notebook? Did he think that it made Adam any the less hers? Or was it something else that he had in his policeman's mind, something that now began intruding itself into her own consciousness. A possibility that brought with it huge implications, the limits of which she couldn't yet make out.

The limits of which she didn't dare to make out.

But now, suddenly, James had arrived, white-faced, still wearing his gardening overalls. 'Darling . . . ' he said, putting his arms out to her.

'It's Adam . . . ' she began, but he stopped her.

230

'I know. I know.'

She wanted to say more – that it was her fault, that she would never forgive herself – but she couldn't and so clung to him, sobbing. As he, cradling her, turned to the policeman and shouted with a sudden vehemence that made her gasp, 'It's the father! Well, it's obvious, isn't it? It's the bloody father that's got him!'

Time had passed, must have done, though she wasn't aware of it, only of movement, people coming and going. Everything else had stopped, been frozen, at the moment when she had looked into the empty pram and realized he had gone.

There were more police uniforms among the crowd in the lounge. A policewoman, with green eyes and her hair tied back in a pony-tail, was sitting beside her, holding her hand. James was explaining to someone about the contest there had been over the adoption. Stella Priestley had arrived and now she was sitting beside her in place of the policewoman.

But how long all this took Lauren had no idea. She felt numbed and increasingly remote from the bedlam around her. All she knew was her grief which gripped like a dull ache.

So it was the father, was it? The father from Switzerland who had stolen Adam from them. That at least seemed to be the general opinion. Was that preferable to some maniac, snatching Adam for no understandable reason? She supposed it meant that he would be cared for and would come to no harm; though it also suggested that this was a planned and calculated act, unlikely to be resolved within a few hours.

Unlikely ever to be resolved . . . ?

James was leaning over her, explaining that they were mounting a house-to-house search. She nodded. He told her they were also pursuing Adam's father, alerting airports and ports to be on the watch for him. She nodded again.

People offered her tea and asked her if she would like some food but she shook her head. Even so, she found herself with a cup in her hand. Then someone else was bending over her, speaking to her. 'Now then, Mrs Eaglesham, I'm just going to give you something to help you relax.' It was their doctor, a youngish man she had last seen – the bitter irony struck her even through her numbed, helpless condition – when she had consulted him on her inability to conceive.

She watched him take a hypodermic from his case and inject a purplish liquid into her left forearm. 'Thank you, Doctor,' she said.

There were now fewer people coming and going, a lessening of activity which only increased her fears. The abduction had become a fact; Adam had gone. James was constantly on the phone, returning to give her bulletins which she found increasingly difficult to follow.

Now there were people – Stella, James, the policewoman – trying to persuade her to go to bed, but she refused. Adamantly refused. She would stay where she was till there was news of Adam.

Then, even as she was still protesting, she found there were sheets covering her and realized she was in bed anyway. Across from her, the light from the landing edged around the door and outlined the empty cot. She put out a hand towards it, then lost consciousness.

She awoke and remembered everything. The empty

pram, Adam gone. There was no period of half-awake realisation, no gradual awakening. She opened her eyes and knew immediately. She gave a groan of dismay at having come back to consciousness and having to face the horror of it again.

She could see it was daylight, bright behind the curtains, but her eyes wouldn't focus to read the face of the alarm-clock. She peered hard and decided it was ten or eleven o'clock, something of that order. So how long had she slept? As she struggled from the bed, she saw that James' side was still turned down. Had he been up all night? What had happened?

She found herself staggering, still half-drugged, as she crossed to the bedroom door. She was wearing her nightdress, though who had put it on her she had no idea. She felt a faint, fluttering hope that something might have happened during her long sleep.

The cot was still empty. And the house silent.

She went out onto the landing, trying to call out, but her mouth was parched and she could manage no more than a croak. Putting her hand against the wall to steady herself, she went into the bathroom. She sat on the side of the bath and managed to reach a glass on the shelf above the wash-basin. She filled it from the tap and took great gulps until she had emptied it.

She heard James calling softly – 'Lauren?' She struggled back to her feet and went out onto the landing in time to meet him as he came up the stairs. His face was puffy and red as though he hadn't slept. He took hold of her, saying, 'Careful. The doctor said you hadn't to –'

But she pulled herself away, shaking her head.

233

She didn't want to hear what the doctor had said. 'Any news?' she said hoarsely. 'Have you heard – ?'

'We've heard something, yes.'

She stared, waiting. Then found herself swaying. He gripped her elbow, steadying her.

'They've found him?' she said. Meaning – is he alive?

'They know where he is. And he's all right.'

For which she thanked God. Though knowing at the same time that it meant, wherever Adam was, he wasn't here. They hadn't managed to get him back.

'So where – '

'Look, come and sit down – '

'Where is he?' she cried.

James sighed and said, 'It's like we thought. The natural father, he's the one who took him. The police got a call late last night. He admitted he'd taken him and said that we were not to worry, he'd take good care of him.'

So it wasn't a maniac. Would she have preferred a maniac? She didn't know.

'Did you speak to him?'

'No. The police – '

'They spoke to him?'

'I don't know who they spoke to. But this was the message.'

'That he's the one – '

'He's the one who took Adam. And he's going to look after him.'

She could only nod. Knowing she should welcome the good news that Adam wasn't in any danger but knowing also that this wasn't good news. There was a sense in which it was the worst possible. It meant they were up against a resourceful and ruthless enemy. Even though James had to help her downstairs, she could think clearly enough to see the implications.

If this man had rung the police, he had done so knowing they were helpless to restore Adam to them. In effect he was taunting them, saying – yes, he's here with me. Out of your reach.

Passing the hall table, she saw that the phone was off the hook. 'Why ... ?' she said, indicating it, since it struck her as an ominous portent that needed explaining.

'Oh, the press have been on. In the end that seemed the only solution.'

She let that go and allowed James to lead her into the lounge, which smelt stale. Windows needed opening. She moved towards them, then fell back onto the sofa. What did it matter anyway? What did anything matter anymore, other than what this man had said.

'When he rang them – '

'The father?'

'Yes. When he rang ... where was he ringing from?'

James, who looked deadly tired, his hands trembling as he gestured helplessly, said, 'They seemed to think he was ringing from Switzerland. I don't know how they knew that but – '

'Switzerland.'

'Yes.'

'And will they be able to get Adam back?'

He looked at her, seeming surprised. 'It's kidnapping,' he said.

'Well, yes, but – '

'Kidnapping. It's a crime.'

'So will they – the police I mean – can they just go out there and bring him back?'

She wanted to be told yes, that that was what

235

they were already doing. But she saw James hesitate. 'No . . . ?' she prompted. Wanting the truth. Even if she were half-drugged and he looked as though he needed to be, she wanted the truth, not some palliative, to be rescinded later, when she was stronger, able to bear it.

'It might take a little time,' he said.

'How long?'

'I don't know. I don't think anybody does yet. But the main thing is – no harm's come to him.'

She nodded and managed a smile, seeing that he only wanted to offer her some consolation, something positive. And that he was at the end of his tether. For his sake, if for no other reason, she needed to clutch the straws of comfort he was offering her.

'Yes,' she said, 'Of course it is.'

He seemed relieved to hear her say it. 'How're you feeling?' he asked.

'Still pretty groggy. What did they give me?'

'I don't know. Can I get you something? A cup of tea?'

She nodded. Though again it was for his sake. She saw that he needed to be doing something. 'And a couple of paracetamols,' she called, as he went out to the kitchen.

She stood up and went to the window. Outside, the grass looked trampled. The pram had been removed. She took some deep breaths, trying to clear her head.

She must be strong, she told herself. For Adam's sake. And for James'. She could not, must not, remain the helpless, near-hysterical female of yesterday. She must face this new world in which she found herself and do whatever was necessary to regain her son.

20

It had been a dreadful business, taking the sleeping child. He knew it would be seen as kidnapping, the ugliest and most cowardly of crimes. Of course he believed himself justified, believed himself compelled to such desperate measures by the travesty of justice he had suffered at the hands of the English court.

All the same, there was a moment, as he leaned over the pram and took the baby into his arms, when it had felt like kidnapping, an act of desecration.

It was the sighting of the Land Rover outside the courthouse, with the tell-tale name on its side, which had given him the lead he needed. He had rung the 'All Seasons Garden Centre' and discovered that the proprietors' name was Eaglesham. The phonebook had supplied their home address. A short drive to the outskirts of town and he had found himself looking at a semi-detached house halfway down a suburban avenue. There was a pram standing on the back lawn with some kind of netting over it.

So this was the place. This was where they lived, these people on whom the court had looked with such disproportionate favour.

At the bottom of the garden was a narrow pathway, snaking between other gardens and allowing

237

him to approach the house unseen. He could have taken the child there and then, had he been so minded.

But that would have been futile, a crazy gesture, doomed to failure. He must first plan his escape, the route by which he might spirit both of them out of this god-forsaken country and back to Switzerland. He would hire a plane: that was his first thought. His second was that he would avoid the major, international airport at Manchester, through which he had arrived and where security was water-tight, and would instead try Blackpool, which was smaller and probably more easy-going. And about the same distance away. He drove there next and, by paying what struck him as well over the odds, managed to charter a six-seater jet, to be standing by ready for take-off from noon onwards the following day. The hire-car he was using could be simply dumped at the airport.

He knew, of course, how easily this route of his would later be traced, each transaction a gigantic, unmistakable footprint, but what did it matter? He was relying on outstripping his pursuers, not baffling them.

Indeed, he wanted them to know that it was he who had taken the child. He had come to England not as a criminal, under cover, but openly, happy to comply with all the formalities. It was they who had forced him to resort to abduction and subterfuge. Once he was out of their grasp, he wanted them to realize this.

His only qualms, which grew till they almost caused him to cancel everything, were over Hervé, his brother. In response to Marcus' call, he arrived from Paris the morning after the court hearing and placed himself at Marcus' service.

238

He was bigger than Marcus, two inches taller and more heavily built. Though their lives had taken different paths, crossing only infrequently, there had remained a deep sympathy between them, an acceptance that each would always be there for the other. If Marcus had ever been tempted to think himself the smarter, the one who moved in a wider world, he had always recognized qualities in Hervé – a dependability, a solid, no-nonsense straightforwardness – that he might envy. As he might also envy his brother's wisdom in knowing when to settle for the restaurant and the wife and family and being able to find his happiness in those things.

All of which he was now asking him to risk on a wild and highly illegal enterprise that could land him in an English jail, separated from that family for years to come.

He had phoned him on impulse, before such considerations had had time to surface. Now he agonized over the enormity of what he was asking. Telling Hervé in the same breath what it was all about and then urging him to return to Paris, saying he had been wrong ever to ask for his help in such a venture.

But Hervé simply ignored such exhortations, wanting to know only about the practicalities of the plan. Could they view the house without being seen themselves? How long would it take them to get to the airport?

'But what if it goes wrong?' Marcus urged. 'No, I must do it myself. It was wrong of me ever to think of involving you.'

Hervé smiled. 'So speaks the bachelor. Have you ever tried driving a car and looking after a baby at the same time?'

'That's beside the point – '

239

'You won't think so when you try it. And, anyway, I'm here. I'm coming with you whether you like it or not.'

'And what if things go wrong?'

'They are already wrong,' said Hervé. 'It is our task to put them right.'

And so, that same afternoon, Marcus checked out of his hotel and drove with his brother to the house where his son – 'And my nephew,' as Hervé kept reminding him – was being held. They parked at the end of the pathway that passed by the back garden. Hervé waited in the car while Marcus went to look into the garden and check what was going on. Part of him felt it would be a relief if the pram had disappeared. At least then he could tell Hervé that the whole thing was off and pack him off home, back to the safety of his family.

But, no, the pram was there. With the netting again stretched over it, presumably covering the sleeping child. Marcus felt a sickening mixture of excitement and fear, knowing he must act now or resign himself to losing his son forever.

His heart racing, he looked around. There was no-one to be seen in any of the adjoining gardens. The mother would surely be inside the house. She might even be watching at that moment – he had no way of knowing or of finding out. It was a chance he had to take. He unlatched the gate, knowing that that act alone compromised him, and stepped inside the garden.

It was four strides to reach the pram, a moment when he fumbled to release the netting stretched across it and then he was reaching in for the child.

He barely looked at him, save to register that he was asleep. His own ears were training to hear the cry of alarm and challenge that must surely come from the house. The gate had flapped closed again, so that he had to shuffle the child into the crook of one arm before he could pull it open and pass through.

And still there was no warning shout. All he could hear was his own laboured breathing and the tearing of brambles on his coat as he broke into a stumbling sort of run, back along the pathway.

Hervé, who had been leaning idly against the side of the car, threw down his cigarette and wrenched open the back door so that Marcus was able virtually to dive straight into it. Then had come the desperate drive to the airport and the tantalizingly slow formalities of take-off. Until at last, unbelievably, they were leaving the ground, shaking off whatever hue-and-cry might be developing behind them.

Only then did they have time for the child, to look at him properly and exclaim over his beauty. He was awake now but silent, staring up at them with large eyes.

'Is he all right?' shouted Marcus over the noise of the engines. 'Shouldn't we give him something?'

'He's fine, he's fine. Look at him,' said Hervé, laughing. 'He's enjoying this.'

Still high on adrenalin, Marcus reacted with delight to the child's every movement, watching him greedily. Now that the deed was done, he felt the need to explain himself yet again and to have Hervé tell him over and over that yes, of course he had done the right thing. He was a father refusing to let the whim of a court separate him from his son. That was the simple truth of it, however anyone else might choose to see it.

And what a son, thought Marcus, his heart swelling. A sturdy, bright-looking infant, as fine a son as any man could wish for.

It was only when they were back in the house at Geneva that he felt truly safe and able to rejoice. With Hervé still accompanying him, he carried the child upstairs to one of the bedrooms, then sent out the startled housekeeper to buy a cot and whatever else might be necessary. He and Hervé, exhausted and exhilarated, tended him between them, washing and feeding him in what was no doubt a haphazard fashion but one which seemed to suffice. At least the child didn't complain, beyond a short spell of whimpering which Hervé confidently put down to tiredness and which, true enough, stopped once they had been able to offer him a bottle, which he took like a champion, draining it without seeming to draw breath.

A similar process of trial and error got them through the first night. It was fun even, a blessed release, to have the whole of life's problems and uncertainties reduced to the single task of keeping this tiny, helpless infant fed and watered.

Still, it couldn't go on. Marcus was no wet-nurse and Hervé had his restaurant to run, his own family to get back to. When next morning finally came, Marcus contacted a local nursing agency and arranged for them to provide round-the-clock cover. Starting immediately. It was important that the child received every attention, not simply for his own welfare but also for the sake of those in authority who, sooner or later, would want to know about such things.

He had already, late the previous night, phoned the English police in Preston and left a short statement to the effect that it was he who had taken the child and that they could be sure it would be well cared-for. It seemed a small, safe gesture for him to make but one which he hoped might help to put minds at rest.

Hervé left for Paris and his own life. Marcus thanked him for all he had done, for the risks he had taken, but his brother seemed embarrassed and shook his head. 'At least now I'm an uncle,' he joked. 'Just wait till his cousins hear about this. And Marie! She's going to drive me mad with her questions until she can see him for herself.'

Marcus smiled. It pleased him to think of his son taking his rightful place in the world, with cousins to grow up alongside. Later they would get to know one another, perhaps sharing holidays and Christmases. He might even consider buying a villa by the sea for the use of the whole family.

He answered the door to Jacques Martin-Achard, shook his hand and led him immediately up the stairs. This was going to be tricky. It might, if he got it wrong, sever their friendship forever.

He had already decided on a direct approach, one that he hoped would demonstrate his own belief in what he had done.

'Something I want to show you,' he said. 'A little gift I brought back for myself.'

And he took him to the improvised nursery where the nurse, who was called Anna, had the child on her knee and was feeding him.

Jacques stared, open-mouthed with astonishment. 'But what . . . I mean who . . . ?'

'Jacques, I want you to meet my son,' said Marcus. 'Here. Hold him. You're always telling me what a capable father you were. Let's see you in action.'

He took both child and feeding-bottle from the nurse and thrust them upon Jacques, who struggled for a moment to manage them.

'Now, have you ever seen a more beautiful baby?'

243

'No, but – '

'This is my son. And I want you to be his god-father.'

'Your son? The child that – '

'Yes,' said Marcus quickly, not wanting him to say too much in front of the nurse. 'And I'm told you have to tilt the bottle, otherwise he swallows air and that's bad for him.' Showing off his small and recently-gained knowledge. The nurse smiled and nodded her approval.

'Marcus, how on earth does this child come to be – '

'Wait,' said Marcus, stopping him again. 'Before we talk about anything else, I want to know – will you be my son's godfather?'

'I really have to ask – '

'Will you?'

Jacques sighed, then said stiffly, 'I would regard it as a great honour. Now can we please – '

'One moment.' Marcus lifted the child from him, knowing he could stall things no longer. 'Let's leave Anna to see to this young man and go to my study, shall we.'

Jacques said nothing as they returned down the stairs. His face was full of misgivings as he sat in his usual chair and waited.

Avoiding his eye, Marcus plunged in and gave a brief summary of how he and Hervé had spirited the child away from its adoptive parents and back to Switzerland. Even to his own ears it was a fairly damning account and Jacques' outrage was inevitable.

'But this is . . . this is monstrous! It's . . . well, it's kidnapping! You understand that? What you have just described to me is kidnapping pure and simple!'

'Possibly.'

244

'For God's sake, Marcus, what were you thinking?'

'I was thinking of my son. My son that the English court was kidnapping from me!'

Jacques sighed. 'You may not have agreed with the court's decision – '

'And neither did you.'

'No, but they had every right to do what they did. Whereas you – '

'I had every right to do what I did.'

'No – '

'Ask anybody. Ask any other normal human being what they would have done in my situation.'

Jacques sighed again and put his head in his hands, as if despairing forever of his recalcitrant client and friend. Yet he hadn't walked out. And he hadn't demanded that Marcus surrender the child to the authorities. Perhaps beneath the lawyer's outrage, there lurked a sneaking sympathy for what Marcus had done. Not that Jacques would admit it, of course; not until he had first thrown the book at him.

Jacques lowered his hands and addressed him again. 'And so what do you think will happen now? Do you really think for one minute that the English court are going to say OK, fine, and let you keep him?'

'No.'

'No,' echoed Jacques grimly.

'So what will they do?' asked Marcus. It was a question he needed answering.

'What will they do? What can they do! They'll demand that you return him.'

'Well, OK, but what does that mean? In legal terms what will happen?'

Jacques hesitated. 'Well, I'm no expert on English

245

legal procedures. But whoever has legal custody of the child – and that would depend on whether the adoption was ever officially completed – whoever has legal custody will apply to the court for his return.'

'And then?'

'Well, and then that application will be forwarded to the courts here with a request for enforcement.'

'Will it be granted?'

This time Jacques paused for some seconds, tugging at his ear and frowning. It gave Marcus encouragement to which he clung gratefully: it wasn't all so clear cut then.

'I don't know,' he said finally.

Marcus seized on the admission, wanting to know more. 'You mean the Swiss courts might decide in my favour?'

'Well, it's complicated. Like I say, looked at from one point-of-view, this is straightforward kidnapping.'

'Which I don't accept.'

'You may not, but the court may disagree with you. And, if they do, then it's not just them returning the child that you'll have to worry about. They'll also be issuing a warrant for your arrest.'

'I shan't worry about it. If I lose the child, the rest is incidental.' It came out sounding like trite heroics but he felt himself to be speaking no more than the truth. His life, once diffused and unfocused, was now centred around the child he had first held only two days ago.

'As your lawyer, it might not be incidental to me,' said Jacques drily.

'I know, I know,' said Marcus, apologetic. He hadn't been intending to score points or to deflect Jacques from telling him the worst. Now he tried to

246

move them back onto the important point, the one that preoccupied him. 'But there's a chance that the Swiss court won't go along with this request for enforcement . . . ?'

'The nationality of a child is usually decided by the nationality of its parents. Now in this case . . . father Swiss, mother British . . . on top of which we have the question of whether the adoption was ever completed . . . As I say, it's complicated.'

Good, thought Marcus. Wonderful. The more complicated, the better. If the case were straightforward, it would be straightforwardly against him, he recognized that. What he wanted was to hear of legal entanglements, delays, appeals, the case foundering under its own weight in the murky waters of international law.

As much as anything, he was counting on the traditional and deep-rooted Swiss mistrust of foreign intervention, their wish to insulate themselves from the doings of other nations, their resentment of interference.

'I know it's complicated,' he said. 'Which is why I need your help.'

Jacques looked at him but said nothing. No doubt he knew the game Marcus was playing and knew that he did indeed need his help, now more than ever.

Marcus persevered. 'Can you tell me this? Are the courts likely to make any sudden move? Is there any chance they'll turn up one morning with a piece of paper and tell me they're going to take the child away?'

Jacques considered. 'You're not intending to deny you have the child here?'

'No.'

'Well, I suppose no-one could claim he's in any danger or not being well cared-for so – '

247

'They'll leave him with me.'

'I would think they'll be content to leave him here until all due processes have been exhausted.'

It was all he had been hoping to hear. In truth, Jacques' censuring of his actions had been less severe than he might have expected. Perhaps his ploy of letting him see the child and hold him had worked. Perhaps for once his lawyer's heart had been softened.

And, if the worst ever did come to the worst, well, then he would take both himself and the child away to some country where neither Swiss nor British laws could reach him. It wasn't an enticing prospect: he had no particular wish to leave Geneva and begin a new life in Turkey or Peru. Though he would do if forced. The option was there as a fallback position, a last resort if the Swiss authorities ever did the unexpected and agreed to toe the British line.

In the meantime there were other formalities to be observed as well as the merely legal. He must arrange to have the child baptised.

His invitation to Jacques to be godfather had been sincere as well as a device to enlist his support. Marcus regarded himself as a Catholic, even though he wasn't a regular attender at mass and paid more attention to some commandments than to others. He knew his duty where the child was concerned. Having provided for its physical well-being, he must now see to its immortal soul.

'I'm going to name him Max Philippe,' he told Jacques.

'But surely he already has a name . . . ?'

Marcus made a dismissive gesture with his hand. He didn't even want to consider such a possibility: it would have been an admission of the rights of others over him. 'This is my son and I shall name him.'

He would contact the Monseigneur at the Church of Notre Dame the following day. Suddenly it seemed important, a matter of urgency, that the new name should be bestowed as soon as possible and the child's new identity – his real identity – thus confirmed.

Besides, it would do no harm to be able to present him to a Swiss court, should it come to it, complete with a good Swiss name and to be able to tell the court of the baptism that had marked the child for eternity in a way that no adoption ceremony ever could.

Most amazing was how the house itself was transformed by the arrival of baby Max.

Where once Marcus had paced through uninhabited rooms and immaculate gardens, sometimes without seeing a single soul, these same rooms and gardens now seemed to have spawned a bizarre family to fill them, to a point where he even found himself retreating to his study in search of seclusion. Of course some of this 'family' had been there in the house all along – his housekeeper and gardener and Eduardo, his chauffeur – but he knew they had always been wary of him, keeping their distance until summoned. Then, of course, had come the guards. But they, too, had kept to their own private world, deferential but distant.

Max had changed all that, bringing the house to life, giving all of them a shared concern. How was he? How had he slept? How was he feeding? They were all in this together, and were joined by the rota of nurses, who all seemed to be called Anna or Cecile or Ruth and who wore the agency's blue-

and-red uniform with a white frilly cap, which they each of them professed to hate and removed immediately they were inside the house.

He had brought home a son and, to his surprise, found himself head of a huge family. Even more surprising, he found himself delighting in it.

A date for the child's baptism was set. A week, two weeks passed, and still nothing was heard from the courts. Though he remained on his guard, Marcus was beginning to feel increasingly confident. He had feared a pre-emptive strike by the courts and social services, men arriving in the night to take the child from him. Now he felt that to be less and less likely with every day that passed.

In the longer term, if the courts did nothing, locked in conflict or simply ineffectual, then time itself would resolve the issue in his favour. There must come a point, with Max growing under his roof and growing also to know him as his father, when it would become plain ridiculous for any court to insist he be taken away and transported to a foreign land where he would be faced by an English couple who would be strangers to him.

21

The bottom, right-hand drawer of his father's desk was crammed with photographs, mostly black-and-white and of people he didn't recognize. He lifted them out and spread them on the desk-top. As he did so, he uncovered beneath them a number of folders, their covers yellowed with age. They had his own name on the cover: 'WILLIAM ARNOLD SANGSTER'. It took him a moment to recognize them as his school reports.

He opened the topmost one and found it was a report on his fourth year in what had been a boys-only grammar school. Strange how he had forgotten even what the reports had looked like. Or was it strange? Since he could remember so little of anything else. His seven years there had fused into a blurred impression of sports-days, on which he had thrown the javelin, prayers recited in crowded assemblies, and exam rooms where they were allowed to take off their blazers and place them over the backs of their chairs. But these were dim recollections; he could recall nothing of what it had felt like. Only the report, a single page, on which his achievements and deficiencies were recorded in various hands, connected him to the boy he had once been.

'ENGLISH: Relies too much on natural ability and not enough on application and hard work.

SCIENCE: A better term, though still too easily distracted.

MATHEMATICS: Good. Should consider doing this subject at A-level.'

Reading it now did nothing to bring the past back into focus. The news that he had ever been good at maths came as a surprise. Overall, he had come seventh out of a class of thirty-two. His form-teacher (and who could that have been?) had written by way of summary: 'A lively and popular member of the form. Needs to settle down to some hard work to fulfil his potential.'

Well, he'd never quite managed the hard work. Or the settling down for that matter. And whether his form-teacher would regard a career as a freelance foreign correspondent as fulfilling his potential he found hard to say.

How much of all this flotsam should he save?

The photographs, yes. They would be interesting to keep. The older ones in particular appealed to him, with their formal and unsmiling family groups arranged before the photographer's studio back-drop. Then there were the snapshots, taken on sea-side holidays. In some of them he could recognize himself, in short trousers and Fair Isle jumper. (But only because he had been *told* that this was him.) His mother appeared in a variety of broad-brimmed hats and floral dresses, more attractive than he had remembered her. Whereas his father . . . his father alone was instantly recognizable, stern and straight-backed even when young, and always in a heavy worsted suit, the direct descendants of which were still hanging in the wardrobe upstairs.

So he would keep the photographs, but the other stuff would have to go. The wads of correspondence and bills, the boxful of cloth samples from the mill where his father had been works manager – all would swamp his tiny London flat.

The furniture was to be carted off and sold as a job-lot. The house was in the hands of an estate-agent. All that remained to be dealt with were these accumulated bits-and-pieces. His father had been a brisk and unsentimental man, insisting that he be cremated. 'It will save all those journeys to the cemetery with flowers that only get blown away.' No doubt he would cast an approving eye if Bill disposed of what was left in much the same way. He would have a bonfire, here and now, before he left. Grabbing an armful of cloth samples, he made his way out into the garden.

Where, to his surprise, two men were busy with crowbars, attempting to remove the ornamental stone fountain that had stood in the centre of the lawn, and as dry as a board, for as long as he could remember.

'Hey,' he said. 'What the hell do you think you're doing?'

They appeared just as startled to see him as he was to see them and said nothing, remaining as they were, caught in the act of prising the fluted basin from its supporting plinth. They were both tall and lean, with unkempt, dark hair, gypsies at a guess. There was a battered Transit van backed up on the drive beside them.

'I said what the hell do you think you're doing?' repeated Bill, feeling a rush of anger. The fountain had been part of his childhood; it grieved him to see it being vandalised like this.

'And what business might it be of yours?' retorted the older of the two men, straightening up.

Bill eyed the crowbars, sensing the makings of a confrontation. One in which he was clearly out-num-bered.

'This is my house,' he said, opening his arms and letting the cloth samples fall to the ground.

The older one spoke again. 'Man whose house it is has died.'

'My father, yes,' said Bill. 'Which makes it mine. And I still want to know what you think you're doing.'

'We bought this off him a week or two ago.' Knocking his crowbar against the fountain. 'Now we've come to collect.'

The young man with him nodded eagerly and said, 'That's right.'

It was his eagerness that gave them away. He wasn't so much agreeing, Bill realized, as applauding his partner's inventiveness. They've seen father's death recorded in the local paper and have come to see what pickings there might be.

'I don't believe a word of it,' he said. 'Now will you please get off my property.' And he took a step forward.

The younger man looked to his partner, who, Bill saw with a sinking feeling, was setting himself defiantly, the crowbar held in both hands before him. 'We've paid good money for this,' he said. 'And we're not going without it.'

'Fucking right we're not,' leered the younger one, taking his cue.

Bill thought of the police. The phone in the house was still connected. But how long would it be before they arrived? And what damage might be done in the meantime?

'We'll see about that,' he muttered, turned and walked back into the house.

Behind him, one of the men guffawed and there was the clang of a crowbar striking stone.

He had been gripped by an idea, a notion of how

254

he might drive them off. It was crazy, he knew that, but he was in the mood for it, provoked by the effrontery of these grave-robbers. He raced to the dining-room, where the old shotgun was still mounted in its place of honour above the sideboard. Like the fountain in the garden, it had been there as long as he could remember and had been something of a family joke.

'If it ever worked, it would take your hand off,' his father had said more than once. 'But not to worry, because it won't. When I'm gone, you can give it to some museum.'

Still, the intruders in his garden weren't to know that. Standing on a chair, Bill lifted the gun from its mountings. It surprised him with its heaviness so that he had to step down quickly.

I must still be drunk to be doing this, he thought. He had got involved in the boozy session that had followed yesterday's funeral, swapping stories with cousins he had last seen when they had been young men together, before leaving school and going their separate ways.

He held the gun in as convincing a fashion as he could manage and strolled back outside. He allowed the door to close noisily behind him and the two men looked up.

'Fucking hell,' said the younger one.

'Right,' said Bill, as they gaped. 'I'm going to count to six and then, if you're still here, I'm going to blow your balls off.'

He saw them exchange a look. Please, he silently urged them. Just go.

'One,' he said. There was a pause as nothing happened. 'Two.'

'You're not going to blow anything off with that old thing,' said the older one.

255

'Three.'

Why had he said six? Why not ten or, better still, twenty?

'Four.'

He raised the gun so that it was now pointing directly at them. He saw them exchange a glance and wondered if they might be going to rush him. And wondered what on earth he might do if they did.

But they didn't move. The silence lengthened.

'Five,' he said, with no alternative.

'Fuck it,' said the older one and spat onto the ground. 'Come on.'

And, to Bill's immense relief, he walked quickly to the van and climbed in. The younger one scuttled after him, shouting, 'Mad bastard,' over his shoulder towards Bill. The van coughed into life as he pulled himself in.

'Six,' said Bill, light-headed with the realisation that he had got away with it. As a joke, now that they were on their way, he pulled the trigger.

The gun exploded in his hands, its butt recoiling into his side. There was another, almost simultaneous whumph as the back doors of the van took the force of the shot and crumpled inwards. The van screeched into the road and accelerated away.

'Christ,' said Bill, and let the gun fall to the ground. 'Oh, Christ.'

He was so shaken he could do nothing for a moment, then he began to laugh. Then he gave a 'Ooh' of pain and put a hand to his side, which hurt where the gun had whacked him. Still, it couldn't prevent him laughing, wondering who he had scared the most – himself or the gypsies in the Transit with their back doors being blown in behind them.

So the old relic of a shotgun had been primed and

loaded all along. Suspended there over their heads while they had eaten their Sunday dinners and none of them knowing. Or perhaps his father had known and had stressed its derelict condition for his mother's peace of mind?

It was nice to think he would have enjoyed seeing it brought into action after all those years.

Bill picked up the gun gingerly. It was the first shot he had fired in anything like anger and it had left him exhilarated. And not a little proud of himself for the way he had seen off the intruders, returning home after so long away to defend the family honour.

The phone began to ring just as he was gathering his things together, preparing to leave the house and go in search of lunch.

The ageing files and papers and cloth samples had made a small bonfire, which had now reduced itself to a few embers and could be safely left. Only the photographs would be going back to London with him. The gun he had returned to its pride of place on the wall.

He picked up the phone and said, 'Hello?' Expecting it to be one of those cousins he had met yesterday or perhaps some old crony of his father who hadn't yet heard the news.

'Found you. Wonderful,' said a voice that it took him a second to place.

'Jason . . . ?'

'Yes. How are you?'

'Oh, not too bad.'

Jason Smith. They had worked together in Blackburn as fledgling local journalists; Jason now worked as a news editor on the 'Guardian'. Their long, infrequently renewed acquaintance might just explain the call; on the other hand ... Bill felt himself grow wary, wondering what was coming.

'I gather you've been attending your father's funeral. I was sorry to hear – '

'Well, he had a good run. Eighty-seven.'

'We should be so lucky.'

'Exactly.'

'Listen, I'll come clean. Can you cover a story for us?'

Bill groaned aloud. It was what he had been fearing, not wanting to have to say no.

'Does that mean yes?' said Jason wrily.

'No. It means that, just as soon as I've cleared up here, I'm going to have the holiday I've been promising myself for God knows how long.'

'Only promising yourself?' said Jason, quick to interpret. 'So you haven't actually booked it? It could wait for a day or two?'

Bill considered lying, insisting he was at that moment on his way to the airport, but knew he wouldn't be believed. 'It means I'm not available. Out of commission,' he said. It had seemed proper that his father's death, which had brought him back to his native town after so long, should be followed by a spell well away from other people's wars and disasters.

'I need a favour,' said Jason wheedling. 'Just a one-off, couple of hundred words. You could do it in an hour.'

'Even so – '

'Look, you're in Preston, right?'

No point in denying what he already knew. 'Yes.'

'Well, then it's there, on your doorstep. You won't even need a passport.'

That surprised him but it also made it easier for him to object. 'So why me? There must be a dozen other people you could use – '

258

'No. I swear there's nobody. Our usual local freelance is down with chicken-pox and the other man we sometimes use is already doing a piece for us and has his work cut out. If you could see me, you'd see I'm on my knees here.'

Bill groaned again.

'You're wonderful,' said Jason. 'I owe you one.'

'I haven't said I'll do it,' protested Bill. Though, even as he did so, he felt his resolve eroding. He had never been good at saying no, a weakness that in the past had seen him posted where other, wiser hacks might have feared to tread.

'Usual fees, plus we'll say you're working out of London,' urged Jason.

'What sort of story is it?' Which was as good as saying yes, he would do it. But then a holiday. Then definitely a holiday.

'It's a child that's been snatched. He was on the point of being adopted when his natural father turned up and grabbed him and flew him back to Switzerland or somewhere. You've heard about it?'

'No.'

Jason sounded surprised. 'Everybody's carried it.'

'Sorry. Doesn't mean a thing.'

'Well, never mind. Means you'll have a fresh mind.'

'Is there really nobody else who – '

'Nobody. Look, all we want is an up-date. Just talk to the couple who were supposed to be adopting and find out what's happening. And, Bill, I'm grateful. Really I am.'

Bill fumbled in his pockets, coming up with an old credit card receipt and a felt-tipped pen. He took the top off the pen with his teeth and turned over the credit card receipt so that he could write on the back.

'OK,' he said wearily. 'So what's the address?'

22

'Mrs Eaglesham?'

'Yes.'

'I'm sorry to trouble you. I just wonder if I could have a word . . . ?'

She knew immediately that he was another journalist. Perhaps it was the way he led with the apology for disturbing her or the tone of voice, which promised fairness and sympathy. But certainly he was another of the scribbling rat-pack sent by some newspaper or radio station to discover what she was feeling – which was the one thing she could never properly explain to anyone.

Still, she said that no, she didn't mind talking to him and invited him to step into the house. For one thing, it was a policy they had decided upon – herself and James and Stella and Marjorie and the solicitor – that publicity could only help and so they should accommodate the press in every way possible. For another, it helped fill her time, of which she had altogether too much for comfort. Going back to work at the garage was out of the question, even if they would have her. It would have been an admission of defeat on her part, a sign she no longer really expected Adam to be returned. She now spent her days roaming the house, waiting for the phone to ring, even though it constantly betrayed her, bringing only sympathetic enquiries or the kind of encouragement that was supposed to help her keep her chin up, when what she wanted was news of action, of something being done.

She led the reporter into the lounge and invited him to sit down, realizing that she hadn't taken in his name or, indeed, anything else he had told her on the doorstep. She glanced at the card he had handed her and read: 'Bill Sangster. Foreign Correspondent,' and then an address in Maida Vale.

It struck her as odd that a foreign correspondent should be sent from Maida Vale to Preston. Never mind. She placed the card on the mantelpiece, along with the others which had accumulated over the past two weeks. Two weeks and one day if you counted the actual day it had happened.

She realized that he was asking her a question.

'I'm sorry . . . ?'

'I said how long have you lived round here?'

'Oh . . . nine years, just about.'

'Amazing how it's changed.' Then he added by way of explanation: 'I was born and bred here. Till this job took me away. When I was a boy, this was all fields.'

She nodded and smiled and set herself to think of fields – ploughed fields, meadowlands of grasses and wild flowers, poppy fields – but she could picture none of them without seeing, somewhere in the middle distance, a child running towards her. It was Adam, of course, grown older and sturdier, as she might never see him.

'I'm sorry,' she said. 'Can I offer you a cup of coffee?'

'Well, only if you're –'

'Yes, I was just going to have one. Shan't be a minute.'

And she went quickly into the kitchen, needing the time alone to compose herself, knowing that if she didn't get it, and if the images kept returning, she would end up in tears. Normally they rang, these reporters, to make an appointment, which gave her the time she needed to prepare herself, to do the crying before they got there. This one had taken her by surprise, turning up on her doorstep. So she needed these few moments, bustling about the kitchen, taking deep breaths, to calm herself, in the hope she might get through the interview without bursting into tears.

She took in the coffee. She saw now that he was fair-haired, about her own age and probably tall when he stood up. Casually dressed in denim shirt and cotton trousers. She noticed his hands as he took the cup from her, slender but marked by small, brown freckles. They somehow seemed in keeping with the relaxed, almost sleepy air he had about him.

He gave a yawn, which he quickly tried to smother, bringing up a hand to his face.

'Oh, I'm sorry,' he said quickly. 'Sorry. I – '

'That's all right.'

'Had a rather late night.'

'You're here for some sort of celebration?' she hazarded, recalling his earlier comment about having moved out of the area.

'Well, not exactly. I've been burying my father.'

'Oh, I'm sorry – '

'No, no,' he waved his hand. Then said, choosing his words, 'I suppose you could call it a celebration of a sort. He'd had a long life so . . . ' And a smile.

She tried to think of something to say but now he was asking her another question, changing gear. 'Can you tell me what's happened since your son was taken?'

'Well – '

But he was already adding: 'That's if you don't mind me referring to him as your son?'

'No. That's what he is.'

He was avoiding her eye. 'Of course, yes. Well, since he was taken . . . have there been any developments?'

She sat at right angles to him, so that she could gaze out of the window, and said steadily, 'Not a lot. I'm told that he's been made a Ward of Court and that there's been an application made for his return.'

'And have you been given any indication of how the Swiss authorities might respond? It is Switzerland he's been taken to, isn't it?'

'Yes. And no, we haven't really been given any indication, not yet.'

'But surely it's a fairly straightforward case? I mean I don't know too much about the legal side of all this but – '

'The problem is that the adoption was never completed,' said Lauren, who now did know quite a lot about the legal side. Too much for her own good: she could no longer take the optimistic up-dates she received from Stella or the solicitor at face-value but had begun to suspect they were all lying to her, trying to hide the real difficulties of the situation.

'That makes a difference, does it?'

'All the difference in the world. It means . . . ' Well, wasn't it obvious? Did she really have to spell it out? She forced herself to continue. 'It means that Adam was never legally adopted and so the man who took him, the natural father, he still has the right to apply for custody.'

'And has he done this?'

'Yes.'

'So the Swiss court has to weigh your application for the return of Adam against his application to keep him . . . ?'

'That's basically it.'

'And when do you expect them to decide?'

'I've no idea. Nobody seems to have any idea. Or, if they have, they're not telling me.'

She felt her voice waver and cleared her throat. If she felt the tears coming on, she would run from the room rather than remain there, weeping before this stranger.

'So you think this might go on for some time?'

'I . . . they've warned me that it might, yes.'

'Months or years?'

She took a deep breath before answering, fighting for control. 'Months or years, yes.'

'And how do you . . . No, I was going to ask you how you feel but I suppose I don't need to, do I. You must be devastated.'

She turned towards him and managed a small smile, grateful that he was telling her how she felt and not asking her to describe it, analyse it, put it into words. It was the words that brought the tears she was trying so hard to avoid.

She had had to instruct James to stop asking her how she was feeling since her attempts to answer only rendered her helpless. They now talked about the case only if there had been some new development, some legal step forward, something factual which she could report to him or he to her. Her doctor had prescribed valium, which she took only in extremis, on those days when she felt so overwhelmed by it all that she was unable to do the simplest things, brush her teeth or comb her hair.

'And how do you regard the father? The man who took the child?'

The unexpected question startled her. Most of her interviewers had wanted little more than the basic facts and a picture of her standing by the empty cot. (Which she wouldn't give them. No pictures – she had drawn the line at that.) She found herself searching for the honest answer; at least the question was a distraction and moved them for a moment away from the danger area of her own feelings.

'It varies,' she said. 'Sometimes I hate him. Well, I suppose there's part of me always hates him, but then sometimes I can see that he might have had reasons of his own. I don't know.'

'But you believe you have the stronger claim to the child?'

'Oh, yes.'

'Why?'

He spoke gently, not as a challenge. And, because this, too, dealt with matters in the public arena, she felt able to answer.

'This man didn't even know of Adam's existence until he was, what, four or five weeks old. And, even then, it was just the *idea* of a son that attracted him. It had to be since he hadn't even seen Adam.'

She saw that the reporter was writing in a small notebook that was resting on his knee. Perhaps he had been writing all along and she hadn't even noticed. Beyond the window, she saw two of her neighbours, an elderly couple who lived along the avenue, pause and glance towards the house as they passed. No doubt they were wondering how she was managing to survive; how normal life could be possible after what she had experienced. She could have told them that it wasn't possible and that she felt as thought it would never be again.

'And do you plan to try anything else to get the child back, on top of what's being done already?'

265

'Not really.' Having been told again and again that there was nothing else to be done.

'You're just waiting.'

'Yes,' she said.

And, suddenly, even as she thought how well she was doing, to have got to what seemed to be the end of the interview, the tears started to flow. She could do nothing about them but sniff and gesture hopelessly.

'Oh, I'm sorry – ' he said, looking alarmed and starting to his feet.

She shook her head and managed to say, 'No, no, it's not – ', wanting to absolve him from blame. She had to be alone and be able to give way to her sorrow. She stumbled from the room, not caring what he might think, ran up the stairs and flung herself on the bed. Burying her face in the pillow, she could think only of Adam and of her own desolation.

Stick to what you're good at, Bill told himself, hurrying from the house. Which in his case was war and rumours of war. Not interviewing highly emotional women who've recently had their babies abducted.

He had called up the stairs, asking if she was all right, advancing upwards a couple of steps each time he got no answer. Then he heard a muffled sobbing coming from the bedroom and, calling again, had finally received a faint 'Yes' in reply. He had taken this as his cue to leave and let himself out of the house.

Oh, not that he didn't have sympathy. She had been an intelligent woman – good-looking too, though that was hardly relevant – who was clearly on an emotional tight-rope from which it would

266

take only the slightest tremor to dislodge her. He hadn't realized till towards the end, when it was too late, just how fragile was that rather bright and willing-to-talk exterior or what awful desperation lay behind it.

Still, he assumed there were people around to help. And he had been witness to worse disasters and then to the human resilience that had kept the survivors going, burying their loved-ones before resuming whatever scrap of a life was left to them.

As this woman would no doubt resume hers.

He reached the hire-car that he had rented for the trip to Preston. When he had called at the solicitor's, he had been informed that the completion of the house-sale could not take place until the following morning, which was a disappointment and would keep him hanging around for another twenty-four hours. Well, he could use some of that to write up his interview with poor Mrs Lauren Eaglesham, then he would be high-tailing it for London and from there off on the holiday he had been promising himself.

The Church of Notre Dame, the main Catholic church of Geneva, boasted high, Gothic stonework and stained glass that shredded the sunlight into its primary colours. The main altar was dominated by the huge blue-and-white statue of the Blessed Virgin suspended above it. Smaller altars, dedicated to other saints, nestled in alcoves down each side of the church, between the wooden confessional boxes and the stone-carved stations of the cross.

It was a cool and airy building, even on a warm afternoon in early summer.

Standing with his small party, Marcus felt both pleasure and pride in the ceremony going on before him. Though not a regular attender, he regarded this as his church. It was here that he came to receive Confession and Communion on the Feast Days, as well as contributing to its building fund. How fitting and proper it was then that he should be standing here now, watching his son being baptised into the Holy Faith.

The baptismal font stood in one of the side altars, beneath a painting of Our Lady of the Ascension, depicted being borne aloft by cherubim and seraphim. The font itself was carved from oak and topped by the figures of Christ and St John the Baptist. Now, of course, it had been removed so that the child's head could be held by the priest above the basin of holy water.

'I baptise thee in the name of the Father and of the Son and of the Holy Ghost . . . ' intoned the priest. His voice carried across the near-deserted pews and came back in a distant echo. As he spoke he allowed the holy water to trickle from his cupped hand onto the infant's forehead. Max Philippe didn't flinch but gazed up in silence.

The priest now turned to address Marcus and Jacques Martin-Achard, who was standing beside him in his capacity of godfather. 'Understand that by this baptism Our Lord claims this child for his own. It means he is now a member of the Roman Catholic Church on this earth and can look forward to life ever-lasting with Our Lord in Heaven.' The priest gave a small smile at this as though, thought Marcus, he were aware of how weighty were the sentiments and how small the child. 'Let us pray that God may grant him the grace to resist the devil and all his pomps.'

Now he gave a larger smile, indicating that the solemnities were over. He stepped towards Marcus and returned the child into his arms. 'Congratulations,' he said.

Marcus nodded his thanks. It surprised him to find how deeply moved the bestowing of the sacrament had left him. He had never doubted that the child must be baptised. It was the final step of the birth process, freeing the soul as the body had already been freed. What he had not expected was to feel the bond between himself and the child confirmed.

Now Jacques was adding his congratulations, and others too, the friends who had accompanied them. Marcus stood at the centre, proud to be holding his son while they milled around him, each wanting to bestow their blessing and all marvelling at how quiet he had been, not alarmed by the water or the strangeness of it all.

They left him in the arms of one of the nurses while Marcus and Jacques followed the priest into the sacristy and signed the baptismal certificate. Coming out, back into the body of the church, Marcus caught sight of the two guards he had assigned to accompany them, standing at a discreet distance and in suits for the occasion.

He took Max back into his arms. They would now go back to the house and celebrate. He carried him carefully down the main aisle and out through the door, into the bright sunshine and the din of the passing traffic.

23

Lauren went to the window, peering cautiously round the side of the bay so that she might see who it was who had rung the door-bell before deciding whether or not to answer.

She couldn't face any more reporters, not today. Come to that, she couldn't face anyone, certainly not anyone who might want to talk to her about the case and ask her how she was feeling. The session she had had with the newspaper reporter this morning had been enough. It had taken her over an hour and two valiums before she had been able to stop herself sniffing and sobbing and been able to embark on even the most trivial of household tasks.

This time it was a woman, a stranger. Another reporter? Though this woman looked altogether too stylish for that: her blonde hair was sleekly coiffured and she was wearing a crimson suit and high heels. She had the kind of pert, chiselled features that sold magazines.

No, Lauren didn't want to speak to her. She didn't want to speak to anybody who had so little to do with her life that she should think dressing-up so important.

Still clinging to the edge of the window, she caught sight of herself in the oval mirror opposite: hair dishevelled, grim-faced, wearing an old t-shirt

270

and out-at-knee jeans. Such a grotesque contrast to the woman on the door-step that it almost made her smile.

The door-bell rang again.

Lauren moved away from the window. She wasn't going to answer the door: of that she was certain. Though now it began to worry her that this woman's chic appearance made her so impossible to place. She looked so unlike any of the reporters who had called, yet Lauren was sure she hadn't met her before. She hesitated in an agony of indecision. After all, she had promised Stella and Marjorie she would do anything that had the remotest chance of helping their cause. And here she was, unable to bring herself to answer the door to a total stranger.

If she were a reporter, then she needn't let her in, just put her onto Stella or somebody else. And never mind the state of her own hair: she was well beyond worrying about that.

She rushed to the door and opened it as the young woman was already walking away down the path.

'Hello?' called Lauren.

The young woman turned and stared. 'Oh, hello,' she said. 'I thought there mustn't be anybody – '

'I know. I was . . . I was upstairs.'

She came click-clacking back up the path towards Lauren, then stopped.

'You're Mrs Eaglesham?'

'Yes. But if you're a reporter, then I'm afraid – '

'No. No,' she said, 'I'm not.' There was a pause. She gave a quick, nervous smile, then said, 'My name's Claire Tempest. I'm the mother of the baby you wanted to adopt.'

Adam's mother. Never in a million years had Lauren dreamt she might set eyes on her. Or wished to, for that matter. Leading her into the house, her mind whirled, trying to guess what her arrival like this, out of the blue, might signify.

'I hope you don't mind me calling like this – ' Claire was saying.

'No – '

'I know that normally we're not supposed to meet but, well, after what's happened – '

'Yes. I mean . . . I'm very glad to see you.'

She remembered the affidavit presented to the judge: this woman had been on their side all along. Now she had come seeking her out when she could have remained well out of everything. She deserved a warmer welcome. Lauren tried to gather her wits.

'Can I get you a cup of tea or something?'

'Oh, no, really.'

'Well, sit down.'

'Thank you.'

'It really is good of you to call. I'm sorry if I seemed surprised. I just didn't expect – '

'No, well, I didn't know whether . . . I mean I read about it in the newspapers. What he's done. That's how I found out who you were. And I just wanted to call and say I think it's terrible, and if there's anything I can do – '

'Yes, of course,' said Lauren, wanting to convey that she understood and that there was no need of further explanation.

Claire gave her another quick smile, then bit her lip. Lauren realized that, beneath the artfully-applied make-up, she was probably scared to death about being there. Knowing she was breaking the agency's code anyway and probably frightened of how Lauren would react, what her state of mind might be. Simply coming to the house must have required a deal of courage.

272

'Have you had to travel far?' she said, trying to put the woman at her ease while her own mind was still going round in circles. What was it she should be asking her? There must be something to be gleaned here, information she could get from no-one else.

She felt as unprepared as she had been for the reporter earlier. Though this time she must retain control. No more break-downs.

'Well, I've come from Birmingham. And I'm on my way to Newcastle, so –'

'I see.'

'It wasn't too difficult to stop off.'

'No.'

'Do you have any more news about the baby?' said Claire, who didn't seem any more up to small talk than Lauren was.

'No, nothing. Apparently it's all in the hands of the lawyers and all we can do is wait.'

'It must be terrible for you.'

'Yes, it is,' said Lauren simply. No point in deny-ing that. And then said, realizing, 'I suppose you must have found it upsetting too.'

It struck her that here was a genuine ally, a fellow-victim. It had been her baby too that had been snatched. What was more – obvious, but this was what really excited her – *here was someone who actually knew the father*. Someone who had known him to the point of sleeping with him and bearing his child. This woman was unique in actually know-ing the man they were dealing with. If nothing else, she might serve as a guide as to how he might retaliate to any moves made by their side.

'It was a shock to hear about it,' said Claire. 'I just hope the baby's all right.'

'I think he is,' said Lauren, and then blurted out,

'Tell me about him. I mean his father, the man who took him? Who is he? What . . . what sort of man is he?'

Claire stared. 'You don't know?'

'Not much. I mean I'm not supposed to, am I. Just as I'm not supposed to know much about you.'

She seemed to understand that, and to be willing to talk. 'Oh, right, yes. Well, he's called Marcus Revachier. And he's about forty-three, forty-four years old. And he's – '

'Do you mind if I write some of this down?' said Lauren, interrupting.

'Oh, no,' said Claire. 'Please do.'

She took a notepad and biro from the bureau. It wasn't that she had any specific intention or could as yet foresee how she might use the information. But, with this being probably her only chance to obtain it, she couldn't afford to let it go to waste.

Settling herself again, she got Claire to repeat his name. Marcus Revachier. Even writing it down seemed a step forward, though in which direction she didn't yet know.

'And he's Swiss,' said Claire, who seemed to be relaxing at last. 'Though he was born in France. Oh, but he speaks English. I mean almost perfect English, though with an accent.'

'Do you have his address?'

'Yes.' And she recited this slowly, so that Lauren could write it down, beneath his name. 'It's a big house. A mansion I suppose you might call it. But he's not married. Never has been so far as I know.'

'How does he make his money?'

'Through guns.'

'Guns . . . ?' Thinking she must have misheard.

'He deals in them. Armaments. He has this enormous warehouse in France which is just full of them.'

274

'I see,' said Lauren, her image of the man doing an abrupt somersault. The info they had received from the agency had simply described him as a 'professional man', which had given her a picture of a businessman in a suit, operating from an office, perhaps in insurance or finance. To learn that he dealt in guns threw a new, shadier light on everything. Perhaps then his abduction of Adam was more in character than she had been able to imagine.

'Someone tried to blow him up while I was there,' said Claire.

'Really?'

She nodded earnestly. 'Some rival I think it was. That's why I left. I couldn't stand it.'

This was even more disturbing. Now all her preconceptions were going out of the window. She had at least been able to console herself – to attempt to console herself – with the thought that Adam was safe and being well cared-for. Now here she was hearing of guns and bombs.

'So it's a pretty risky business he's in?'

Claire nodded. 'Uh-uh. There's a creepy side to a lot of what he does.'

'Illegal you mean?'

'I don't know. All I know is, like I say, there was somebody trying to kill him.'

It was frightening – terrifying – to learn that Adam might have been taken to a place not of safety but of mortal danger. Now she had to get him back, and not only for her own sake. Of course she had to get him back so that they might be a family again but, on top of that, it was his own small life that was at risk here. Or so it seemed if Claire's account was one to be believed. (Which it surely was. Why else would she have sought her out and come to the house but to tell her the truth? Doing so because she, the natural mother, also feared for her child.)

It was also oddly liberating. The 'professional man', doing battle through the courts, had now been transformed in Lauren's mind into a modern-day pirate, a mafioso, who didn't give a damn for legality save when it suited him. It freed her to reply in kind, to fight dirty if necessary. Though how to translate this feeling into practice she had no idea. She needed to know more, and wanted to hear everything that Claire could tell her.

'Suppose the courts ordered him to return Adam? What do you think he would do then?'

'Adam . . . ? Oh, is that what you've called him?'

'Yes.'

'It's a nice name.'

'Thanks,' said Lauren, smiling but feeling also the threat of tears returning from far-away. 'So what would he do if the courts decided against him?' she said, wanting to hurry things along.

'I don't know.' And she fell silent so that Lauren started on another question – 'Well, would he – ' – before she began to speak again, looking Lauren in the face: 'I don't think he'd accept it.'

'He wouldn't . . . ?'

'No. In fact, I'm sure he wouldn't. I'm sure he'd do . . . well, he'd do anything rather than obey them.'

'He might send Adam away to another country?'

Claire nodded. 'Anything. He's very determined. I thought I was in love with him for a while. You know how you do?'

Well, no, Lauren wasn't sure that she did, but she nodded anyway.

'Because he always seemed to know what he wanted and wouldn't let anybody stop him.'

276

'Ruthless,' said Lauren softly.

'Yes. I suppose you could say that. But he can be very kind as well. He was very kind to me anyway.'

In a way it was the worst news possible. Her son had been taken by a ruthless gangster who would do everything within his considerable power to keep him.

Still, she felt it was a step forward to know even that. As though by knowing it she could move nearer to him and could size him up. She wouldn't be shadow-boxing any longer.

'What do you think I should do, Claire?'

The question seemed to startle her. 'Well, I don't know . . . '

Lauren persisted. 'What would you do if you were in my shoes?'

But Claire was not to be drawn and shook her head. Lauren sensed she was still intimidated by this man, even at this distance and after this time. Or perhaps it was that, having once loved him, she felt still honour-bound to display some loyalty towards him.

Lauren persevered. 'Well, would you go to Switzerland and talk to him? I mean, if you were me, would you go over there and talk to him? Try and persuade him that what he's done is wrong and not in the child's best interests?'

Claire considered, then said, 'I don't think it would do much good. I don't think he'd listen.'

No, thought Lauren, neither do I. Not hearing what she had just heard. The idea of going over there to confront Adam's kidnapper had been a wild idea that she had secretly entertained as a last resort, not even speaking to James about it. Now it seemed almost laughable.

'I suppose you must think . . . ' began Claire, then stopped. She was looking away.

'What?' asked Lauren, mystified.

'Well, giving away my baby like that. I suppose you must think I'm a pretty awful sort of person.'

'No,' urged Lauren, seeing the desperate look in the other woman's face and realizing that she was looking to her for reassurance. For a kind of absolution even. It was a shock to realize this – after all the sympathy and reassurance that she had received herself from so many people and yet had rejected, allowing her own sense of loss to all but overwhelm her. 'No,' she said, reaching across and taking her hand.

Claire said, 'See, I know me. And I know I wouldn't have been much of a mother. I'm in show business. I'm a singer. So I travel a lot and . . . well, it just wouldn't have worked. I know it wouldn't.'

Lauren embraced her, feeling her trembling and knowing now, at last, what a gigantic effort it must have cost her to come to the house and face her, the woman to whom she had given up her child. She felt an overwhelming gratitude, not just that she had done this or for the information that she had given, but for the fact that she had turned to Lauren in this way, seeing her not as a bundle of inflammable emotions, to be circled around and approached with caution, but as someone stronger than she was, someone who had taken on a responsibility she could not accept.

It made Lauren feel suddenly strong, releasing her from the burden of self-pity and self-absorption that had threatened to dominate her and swallow her up. She insisted they had a drink – never mind that it was the middle of the afternoon – and showed Claire the photographs of Adam that James had taken. They were photographs she had put aside, feeling she would never be capable of looking at

278

them again. Now it was as though the jinx had been removed and she was, if not her old self, then something near to it.

Most of all, she felt Claire's faith in her. It rekindled her own faith in herself and her determination to fight for Adam with all the resources and cunning at her command.

'Bill. Many thanks. We're going to use every word.'

Jason, of course. 'Hi,' he said into the phone, and took a sip of his whisky. 'Just don't tell me it was so good you want me to do another one.'

'I won't. Actually I didn't know whether I'd find you there. I thought you might have been off on this holiday you were talking about.'

'I should be. There was a delay at the solicitor's. I have to call in there tomorrow morning. After that, you won't see me for dust.'

Nor here again, he thought, gazing round at the room, now stripped of all that had made it familiar and homely. He had lingered here long enough, paying due homage to his father (and driving off marauding gypsies) but also discovering in the process how far he had grown away from this town of his childhood. He would probably, he reflected, never set foot here again.

'So the woman was happy enough to talk, was she?'

'Who?'

'This Mrs . . . Mrs Eagelsham.'

'Oh, yes.' Or rather no, he thought, not happy. Not by any stretch of journalistic vocabulary could she have been called happy.

'That's good. Only we're thinking of doing a follow-up.'

'No,' he said. 'No, no, no.'

He almost put the phone down there and then. A favour had been asked and a favour had been delivered. He had repaid any dues owing from their friendship and would do no more.

Besides, he would not relish having to return to torment Mrs Eaglesham any further. She had been too vulnerable, too devoid of any protective self-interest for him to take it in his stride. He still felt a pang of guilt, wondering what he must have put her through and whether she was still prostrate up there on her bed, sobbing her heart out.

'Look, I told you – '

'I know you did,' said Jason quickly. 'And I'm not asking you to do it. I'm really not.'

'You're not?'

So what did he want then?

He heard Jason chuckle. 'No. It's not even my baby anymore. Sorry, no pun intended. It's Features. They want to do a follow-up for the Woman's Page. Tell her story and link it with other, similar stories, that sort of thing.'

'Best of luck to them.'

'Well, yes. Only what they're asking. And they've asked me to pass this onto you – '

'What?'

'Is whether you'll just have a word with her and let her know what we have in mind. I mean since you're the contact. You're the one she knows.'

'No,' said Bill, determined to be stubborn.

'Well, I've asked you. I said I'd ask you, but I'm not going to try and persuade you.'

There was a silence between them. A persuasive silence.

The thought insinuated itself into his mind that, if he went back there, he could at least satisfy himself that the woman was still alive and kicking and being cared for. If necessary, he could try and speak to someone else – her husband? – and make them aware of the looming despair he had detected in her.

Strange, he now realized, that she hadn't mentioned her husband. In the whole of the interview, so far as he could remember, there had been no direct reference to him. As though it were *her* tragedy, a situation she had to face on her own.

'But you don't want me to write it?' he said into the phone, wanting to be sure.

'No. No, just to let her know that there's going to be somebody else – '

'OK,' he said, cutting him short. 'I'll do it.'

'You will?' He sounded surprised.

'Why not,' said Bill.

Jason began to thank him, but he didn't want that either. He had his own, private motives for going back there and didn't want them dressed up as altruism. He told Jason that he would go and see Mrs Eaglesham the following morning and inform her of the newspaper's intentions. After that, in Jason's immortal words, it would be somebody else's baby.

Their conversation left him thinking about the woman he had interviewed. He had felt sorry for her certainly; and been less than proud of his own hasty departure from the house. For the first time for a long time, it had left him wondering how the story would end.

Would she ever see her child again? And, if not, how would she survive?

He had believed himself immune to such involvements, made insensitive by exposure to death and destruction on a major scale. Yet this had been something different. Someone whose life he had

281

touched – when perhaps, let it be admitted, he was in a somewhat vulnerable condition himself – and which it had troubled him to walk away from.

Lauren, she was called, Lauren Eaglesham. Perhaps Jason had told him or he had picked it up at the house. Anyway, that was her name.

Was he drunk, he wondered, that he should be so unable to shake off the memory of this woman whom he had met only at the insistence of Jason Smith and who had struck him as emotionally disturbed, bursting into tears in front of him and rushing from the room?

Or was he just not drunk enough? Caught in that maudlin and sentimental state where every chance encounter seemed charged with significance?

He poured himself another whisky. 'To hell with it,' he said aloud. He had promised to re-visit her and he would do that. After which, he would take himself off to somewhere where there were no wars, no child abductions and, most importantly, no news editors on the other end of telephones.

She lay awake long after James had fallen asleep beside her, listening to the rhythm of his breathing. She had told him nothing of Claire's visit or of what she had learnt. The piece of paper on which she had made her notes she had hidden in a dressing-table drawer.

She saw now how close she had been to giving up. And close to what else besides she could only guess. Total break-down? Suicide? Or a long, slow decline under the insupportable burden of her depression? She realized, too – or was she imagining this? – how those around her had been attempting to prepare her for the worst. Never openly admitting that the legal struggle to regain Adam might be a vain one but stressing its protracted nature . . . the non-cooperation of the Swiss . . . the legal quagmire resulting from the fact that the adoption had never been completed. Softening her up for the inevitable. The reassuring phone-calls from Stella and the rest had become a way of marking time, with nothing new to report.

Even James, who had been a tower of strength throughout – let that be admitted – supporting her and patiently talking her through the blackest periods of her depression, had somewhere along the way slipped into the habit of saying 'If we get Adam back . . . ' in place of 'When . . . '

It was time itself that was the greatest enemy. She remembered how quickly Adam had become hers. Within days, hours even, of their bringing him home from the hospital, he had become her child as surely as if she had borne him herself. Now she was losing him with each day that the stalemate continued. He was growing and becoming someone else, while being tended by different hands. Soon the time that he had spent with her would be all but obliterated.

On top of which there had been the warning from Claire that this Marcus Revachier was unlikely to abide by any court decision that went against him. By the sound of it, he had the means and the wilfulness to spirit Adam away to . . . well, she didn't know where but to somewhere that would place him forever beyond their reach.

She would wait no longer.

James shifted in his sleep, muttered unintelligibly, then resuméd his regular breathing. She gently pulled up the duvet to cover his exposed shoulder.

He would know nothing of her plans. Oh, she loved him and longed to take him into her confidence, but she knew that she must not if she were to remain free to act. It was in his nature to be cautious, to foresee the pitfalls. Besides, he would be concerned for her, worrying about her safety and perhaps even about her mental state that she could even consider such a notion. He would do everything to oppose her, putting obstacles in her way, pointing out the problems, ridiculing the very idea that she might succeed where the resources of the court could not.

She would go tomorrow. That way there would be no time for him to detect what she was up to. Or for her own resolve to falter. For she knew that, buoyed up as she was now by Claire's visit, the depression that had so immobilised her had not gone so far away. It could still return, with its squalls of tears and crushing hopelessness, to lay her low.

Tomorrow then. She would do it while James was away at the garden centre. She would take her car and go to that foreign land where Adam was prisoner and she would rescue him. Exactly how she had no idea. But, as he had been taken from her by a combination of stealth and brute force, so she would feel at liberty to use whatever tricks and deceptions might be needed to bring him home.

24

It was hard to contain her excitement. She knew that James was watching her, as he did every morning before leaving for work. He was concerned for her, still reluctant to leave her alone. She must do nothing on this particular morning to alert him to the change she felt within herself and so settled for saying little and seeming abstracted as she went about making breakfast.

Even so, he commented, 'You're looking well this morning.'

She gave a quick smile. 'Yes, I feel . . . more rested.'

'Still taking the tablets?'

'Yes.' Which was a lie.

'I'm sure you should. There'll be plenty of time to wean yourself off them later.'

'I might try and get out today,' she said. 'I think I'm spending too much time in this house.'

She said it so that he shouldn't worry if he later rang the house and got no reply. (Was it a symptom of her recovery that she could be cunning and deceitful like this?)

'Good,' he said. 'Yes, I think you should. Look, do you want me to take the day off and come with you?'

'No. No, don't do that,' she said, trying not to

sound too insistent. 'I was just thinking of wandering around the shops. That sort of thing.'

To her relief, he backed off immediately, not making an issue of it. 'Oh, right, fine. You do that.'

'It's just I think it might do me good to –'

'Of course, yes.'

And nothing more was said.

They had been this way with each other since Adam's abduction, prickly and self-conscious, each trying to assess the other's mood and then over-reacting to it. Treading on egg-shells. Love-making had been avoided altogether, each careful to keep to their own side of the bed. It reminded her of why she had first loved him: he was always considerate, never demanding.

Which she, of course, was now exploiting. Showing by the speedy way she cleared the breakfast table almost before he had finished eating that she wanted him gone from the house.

He kissed her on the cheek and said, 'I'll be back about six. But don't forget you can ring me anytime.'

And was finally gone.

She looked at her watch. It was eight-forty-five, which meant she had nine and a quarter hours before his return. Would that be enough to get her across the Channel and into France? If she could do that, she would feel to be beyond his reach. Oh, he might pursue her and catch her even then. In France, though, she knew she would be able to resist him; whereas, if he were to catch up with her here, in England, she doubted that her resolve would be strong enough. And, anyway, here he could enlist the support of the adoption agency or of her doctor or even of the court in an attempt to stop her.

She still didn't care to think too far beyond

France. What she would do once she got to Geneva was a blank. She had never been there before and knew little about it save that it was just over the border from France and on the shores of a lake. (Lake Geneva? It would be logical.) That morning she had had a waking dream of herself stalking a nurse-maid who was pushing a pram through a public park. She had got nearer and nearer, close enough to see into the pram ... before she had woken up.

Well, it might come to that. She felt herself capable of anything. She could only hope and pray that Adam hadn't already been taken from Geneva to somewhere else. What she would do then she couldn't even begin to consider.

It would be a test not only of her courage but also of her command of French. At school she had studied it to A-level and put it to modest use since on the camping holidays which she and James had taken over there. But that had been simple stuff, exchanges with waiters and shopkeepers. How effectively it would carry her through this desperate business was another question altogether.

She threw an assortment of clothes into a bag, not caring much what they were but only making sure that she should have plenty. She took her passport from the bureau drawer where it lay beside James' and checked to see it was still valid. On the page across from her photograph was a blank section headed 'CHILDREN'. She hesitated, then took a pen and wrote in Adam's name and date-of-birth. It was a sign to herself of her own confidence: she would need it for the return journey when he would be with her.

Maps.

She grabbed the handful that they had accumulated over the years and stuffed them into the side pocket of the bag. No point in wasting time studying them now. That would be something for the boat. Then she ran back upstairs and took from her dressing-table the piece of paper on which she had written Marcus Revachier's address, folded it and placed it in the side-pocket along with the maps.

Money.

It was now nine-fifteen. The banks wouldn't open until ten. Still, she would need time to drive into town and park.

The nearer she got to leaving, the more she was gripped by a sense of panic that James might for some reason return and catch her in the act. Should she leave a note for him, explaining what she was doing? Or should she leave nothing and ring him the minute she landed in France? She hesitated over this, taking out the notepad and starting to write, then tearing out the paper and throwing it away. What if he should return home prematurely and find it? Then her eight hours' start would be in jeopardy. But then what if she reached the south coast in the nick of time for an evening crossing and then was unable to ring him from the boat? No, she couldn't do that to him. She couldn't put him through the torment of wondering what had happened to her lest he assumed the worst. Assumed . . . well, anyway, she couldn't. A note then, with a phone-call to follow whenever she got the chance.

'Darling,' she wrote, 'I have gone to Geneva to see what I can do there about getting Adam back. Will ring soon. Don't worry. I am well and feel better doing this than sitting at home doing nothing. Love, Lauren.'

It would alarm him anyway, but there was no avoiding that. At least she wasn't leaving him completely in the dark. She placed the note on the kitchen table, using a cup as a paper-weight.

Twenty-to-ten. She felt as though the count-down had now started, triggered off by her writing of the note. It was now a little over eight hours before James' return. She would need at least five, probably six, of those hours to get to Dover. She had no idea of times of sailings and couldn't delay herself by enquiring or attempting to make a reservation. She would turn up and take pot-luck.

She came out of the house, feeling furtive. Not that it mattered who witnessed her departure. Still, she was relieved there was no-one around. She threw her bag into the boot of her car, checked that she had locked the front door and drove out of the drive and along the avenue.

She felt calmer now, having made her escape from the house, trying to shut out of her mind the haunting vision of James returning and reading the note. He'll forgive me when I return with Adam, she thought. Won't he?

There was still the town centre to be negotiated. She had to drive twice around the one-way system before she could find a parking-space, cursing the delay.

Ten past ten. At least now the banks would be open.

She forced herself to walk the short distance from the car to the bank, not wanting to attract attention. Then, even as she came to the very door of the bank, she caught sight of Jane, her neighbour. She hurried forward, not wanting to be seen, but Jane was already calling: 'Lauren . . . ! Hello. How are you?'

So that she had to stop and smile. Another few minutes wasted. 'Oh, fine,' she said. 'Just in a bit of a hurry, that's all.'

'There's no news?' said Jane, putting on a grave face.

'Nothing new, no.'

'But they did say it would take some time – '

'Oh, yes.' She had to force herself to remain on the same spot, chatting like this.

'Well, any time you want to talk, just come round and – '

'Oh, I know. Thanks.'

Finally Jane was saying goodbye and Lauren was able to enter the bank. She was struck by an awful thought: was this one of the days on which James brought in the money from the garden centre? She waited in the queue, watching the door, until at last it was her turn. She wrote a cheque for one thousand pounds, noticing how her hand was shaking. It seemed a large sum but she had no idea how long she would be away, days or weeks, or what expenses she might have. If she spent up, she would have her credit card to fall back on.

She hurried back to the car, stalled it in her anxiety to be away and then, at last, was leaving the town. It was ten-thirty. Seven-and-a-half hours before he would return and find the note.

It was only when she was on the motorway and heading south that she was able to breathe easily. She even felt a spurt of excitement at the thought that she was on her way at last, every mile taking her closer to Adam. It was a warm day and, as the clouds cleared, a sunny one. She pushed open the small sun-roof and switched on the radio. Behind her, the travel-cot they had bought was still strapped in position across the rear seats, empty but for a blanket and a couple of plastic rattles.

He rang the bell again, hearing its distant chimes

inside the house and realized that no-one was going to answer. The house *sounded* deserted. He realized, too, that the car which had been standing in the driveway when he had made his previous visit was now absent.

Well, he had done his best. He couldn't be expected to hang around here forever. Yet he felt a twinge of disappointment that he wouldn't be seeing her again. He would have welcomed the chance to apologize for the way he had upset her. And to reassure himself that his visit hadn't done worse damage.

Then, even as he swivelled on his heels away from the door, he was confronted by a Land Rover turning in at the gate and pulling up beside him.

He waited as a man climbed out, a tall, thin-faced man wearing jeans and a denim shirt.

'Hello?' the man said. 'Can I help?'

Must be the husband, thought Bill. The one she had barely mentioned in her account of her sufferings.

'I'm Bill Sangster,' he announced himself. 'Newspaper reporter. I called yesterday – '

'Oh, yes. You talked to my wife.' He thrust out a hand, which Bill took. 'James Eaglesham.'

'Pleased to meet you.'

It was a relief that this husband showed no hostility. The wife must have survived her outbreak of weeping then. Perhaps she hadn't even mentioned it to husband James, who was now unlocking the front door. For some reason, which he couldn't really have explained, Bill had a strong suspicion that there might be many things she didn't mention to him. James Eaglesham threw a casual 'Come in' over his shoulder, and Bill followed him into the hallway.

291

'I was doing a piece for the Guardian – '

'Yes, Lauren said. Sorry. Be with you in a one minute.' And he went away into the lounge, leaving Bill hesitating in the hallway. He had the impression of a brisk, rather single-minded man, for whom dealing with people was a chore. One to which he would apply himself but only in due course, keeping them waiting until he was ready. Not like his wife at all. With her Bill had felt an immediate contact, uncomfortably so since she had been so desperate and vulnerable.

The husband came back from the lounge, raising his empty hands in dismay or failure. 'Left some paperwork here. Something I should have taken in with me this morning but – '

'Right,' said Bill.

'Must be here somewhere.'

And now he had disappeared again, this time into the kitchen. Bill waited, not minding the other man's indifference towards him. Perhaps it was his way of coping with the disaster that had befallen. Sticking to his daily routine, concentrating on the minutiae of life.

Then, when the other man didn't reappear, Bill took a step towards the kitchen door. Through it, he saw James Eaglesham standing by the table, staring at a piece of paper he was holding.

Bill began to speak, if only to alert James Eaglesham to his presence. 'I've only called because they want to do a follow-up article . . . '

Then he saw James Eaglesham's expression – of shock? disbelief? – and stopped. He was intruding on something here. James Eaglesham gave a groan of dismay. 'She's gone,' he said. 'Just set off.' And he held out the paper. Bill took it and read: 'Darling. I have gone to Geneva to see what I can do about

292

getting Adam back. Will ring soon. Don't worry. I am well, and feel better doing this than sitting at home doing nothing. Love. Lauren.'

It astonished him and yet he felt he understood. He had seen her despair; he had almost felt it as a palpable thing that she carried with her, and had feared that she might collapse beneath it. Instead, if the letter was any guide, it had driven her to stake everything on this wild throw. Exhilarated, he wanted to exclaim Wonderful and Good for her but checked himself, aware that the husband's eyes were on him.

'And you had no idea?' he asked, already knowing the answer.

James Eaglesham shook his head. 'None.'

He was clearly stunned by it. He shook his head again, then said, 'I mean what can she . . . ', before falling silent, leaving the question incomplete.

Observing him, Bill was gripped again by the strange notion that, after only one brief meeting – which had ended in tears – there was a sense in which he knew this woman better than her own husband did. He was surprised at what she had done, yes. But not totally confounded, as this James Eaglesham seemed to be. He could see that she was the sort of woman who might do this. He saw also, with a feeling of soaring excitement, that, having once embarked on her desperate quest, there would be no limits to how far she would go.

The other thing he realized was that he wished to protect her. Help her even. Which he could only do by stalling this husband of hers, who, once his wits returned, would be out to stop her and bring her home.

Never minding what that would do to her. To what further suffering it would condemn her.

'You didn't know anything about this?' Bill asked again.

'Nothing.'

'And you saw her this morning?'

'Yes.'

James Eaglesham looked at his watch. Bill sensed he was coming back to life. In a minute, unless he could think of some way to deflect him, he would be ringing the police and moving heaven and earth to have his wife dragged back here. If he were to stop that, then he needed to know more, and know it quickly.

'What time did you leave her this morning?'

'Well . . . some time around eight-thirty, nine.'

And it was now eleven-thirty. She had a slender lead, even assuming she had fled the house within minutes of her husband leaving.

'I've got to stop her,' said James Eaglesham. 'If you knew the state she's in – '

'Does she know where your son is being held?' asked Bill, wanting to delay him, to keep him from rushing into action. 'I mean the actual house?'

'No. Well, unless she's somehow found out. I don't know.'

'And what do you think she has in mind? To talk to this man? Try and make him see sense?'

'God knows. You've seen what she's written.'

He had seen it, yes. And, so far as he could see, it could mean anything. It could even mean that she wasn't out to talk at all but to try and snatch the child back, repaying the abductor in his own terms.

He wondered if James Eaglesham had realized this. It was to be hoped that he hadn't, though, with his defensive, guarded manner, it was difficult to tell.

'I mean what's this going to do to our chances of

getting him back legally?' said James Eaglesham, talking to himself as much as anything. 'It's only going to turn everybody against us!'

'Let's assume that she's not flying to Geneva,' said Bill, trying to put himself in Lauren Eaglesham's shoes. If she were hoping to return with the child, then she would be more likely to be making the whole journey by car. 'Where will she be making for?'

James Eaglesham hesitated, then said, 'Might be . . . Dover.'

'Yes?'

'That's where we've always crossed before when we've been to France on holiday.'

'Listen, I'm going to suggest something. I'm heading south myself. Now, if you'd let me ring the paper, with their help I might be able to find her.'

James Eaglesham stared, as if this was all beyond him. Or perhaps he was trying to work out Bill's motives, which would be difficult since Bill himself would have found it near impossible to explain why he was plunging in like this, involving himself in this desperate woman's escapade.

Except that suddenly, more than anything else, he wanted to see her get away with it. Or, anyway, be given the chance to. With the odds already piled against her, didn't she deserve to have somebody, *anybody*, in her corner?

'How?' asked James Eaglesham.

But he didn't want to answer that, not yet. Not till he had worked out himself just what it was he had in mind. 'Look, forgive me but we're wasting time. Could I just use your phone?' Trying to hustle him into agreeing.

'Well, yes but – '

'Thanks. By the way, I hope you don't think I'm rude, but I couldn't half use a coffee.'

'Oh . . . well, yes, I'll, er – '

But Bill was already back in the hallway, where the phone stood on a small table, directories beside it. He rang the London office of the Guardian and stood waiting impatiently for his call to be answered. Behind him in the kitchen he could hear a kettle being filled.

So, all right, there was a story in this and one that he couldn't ignore. But also, hand on heart, he believed that Lauren Eaglesham should be given her chance. That was his main motive. Even if she were to fail, that would surely be better than being hauled back here by her husband.

It was arrogant of him, he wouldn't deny it, to believe he knew what was best for these near-strangers. But other people's conflicts had been his speciality for long enough; this one was simply more localised than most.

'Can I speak to Jason Smith,' he said, when he was finally connected. Then waited anxiously. He didn't know how long James Eaglesham would remain docile, allowing him to run the show; he needed to keep things moving.

Mercifully, Jason was available. 'Listen,' said Bill, cutting through his greetings. 'I'm at the house of that Eaglesham woman you persuaded me to do the piece on.'

'Yes?'

He lowered his voice, conscious of James in the kitchen. 'She's taken off in her car, heading for Geneva. I think she's going to try and grab the baby back again.'

Jason gave a 'Ha' of surprise.

'So I'm going to go after her. See if I can tag along. Now the odds are she's sailing from Dover. What I need is to know which ferry she's on.'

'How the hell am I supposed to – '

'Come on, Jason. I'm doing you a favour here. Do you want this story or you want me to take it to somebody else?'

'We might. We might. Just give me time – '

'I haven't got time.' He raised her voice to the kitchen. 'What's your wife's car, Mr Eaglesham?'

James Eaglesham appeared in the doorway. 'A Toyota Corolla.'

'And the number?'

'F 124 NEC.'

'Thank you.'

James Eaglesham hovered for a moment, looking uncertain, then disappeared again. Bill relayed the information. 'Send somebody down there. I'll ring you when I arrive and you can tell me which boat she's on.'

'Look, I'll do what I can but I'm not promising – '

'I'll call when I get to Dover,' said Bill, and put down the receiver.

He returned to the kitchen. Two cups of coffee were standing on the table, the note lying beside them. James Eaglesham was frowning. 'Now look –' he began, in a voice heavy with reservations.

'They're going to try and track her down,' said Bill. 'Watching the ports and all that.' Making it sound like a large-scale dragnet operation rather than the hit-or-miss ringing around that was the most Jason might achieve. 'And I'll let you know as soon as there's any news.'

'Can I just say,' said James Eaglesham, frowning.

'Yes?'

'This is my wife we're talking about.'

'Of course.'

'I'm the one who has to find her. I'm the one who has to talk to her – '

'Oh, and you will, yes. I wouldn't try and do anything other than simply put you in touch with her.'

But the husband still looked suspicious. He began to shake his head.

'Look at it this way,' said Bill, inspired. 'Suppose we're wrong? Suppose she's not going to Dover but is going by another route altogether? She might even be flying.'

'Well, yes, I know – '

'The note says . . . ' He turned it on the table top so that it was facing him. 'Yes, look, it says – Will ring soon. Which means here. She's going to ring here.'

He paused, letting James Eaglesham see the inference for himself: how his place was in this house, by the phone; he had to let Bill go alone. He nodded slowly, though still looking unhappy.

Bill took a swig of the hot coffee, then set the cup down again, by the note. 'Mr Eaglesham, I'll do everything I can to find your wife. And, when I do, I'll get her to contact you, OK?'

'I'd be very grateful,' said James Eaglesham. Though the words sounded as though they were being dragged out of him.

'Only the sooner I go, the better chance I have. So excuse me if I don't stand on ceremony.'

He was already backing out into the hall, and then leaving the house almost at a run. James Eaglesham was shouting something about medical help but Bill didn't stay to argue that, calling goodbye as he hurried to his car which was parked on the road outside.

He was doing this because . . . well, because he felt a strong sympathy for the woman Lauren Eaglesham.

And because there might be a story in it too good to ignore. And because he had nothing else to do anyway but drive south and head for the sun, which would have taken him in the same direction anyway.

Even put together, they didn't add up to the strongest of reasons or succeed in quelling the small voice inside his skull which nattered away at him, asking what the hell he thought he was playing at, pursuing emotionally disturbed women across Europe and involving himself in the serious issue of kidnapping. In truth, he was involving himself because . . . well, it was the boldness of it, the sheer, crazy courage of this woman that attracted him. The way she had pulled herself back from the despair in which he had left her and set out on this death-or-glory mission.

It was that that he found irresistible.

Perhaps when he caught up with her – if he caught up with her – then he might discover that her husband was right and she was, after all, in need of medical treatment.

Or perhaps he would find her sitting on the quayside at Dover having second thoughts.

Or perhaps he would never find her at all.

Whatever happened, he still nursed the absurd and arrogant belief that it would be better he should find her than that her husband should. Somewhere amid the jumble in the boot or on the back seat of his hired Sierra was his trusty travel-bag, containing toothbrush and passport. She could be no more than an hour-and-a-half, two hours at the most, ahead of him. Settling on the motorway, he pushed his speed up to eighty and headed south.

25

Lauren stood in the stern of the car-ferry, watching the cars filing into its belly beneath her. They seemed to move at a snail's pace; it was already ten minutes after the time given for sailing. She willed them to be quicker, desperate that the boat should be away before James might appear on the quayside, scanning the decks and calling out her name.

She couldn't bring herself to move from the rail but remained there, gripping it, till at last the procession of vehicles tailed off and the giant doors rumbled closed. A young man with a cigarette in his mouth ambled along the side of the ship lifting the thick mooring-ropes from around the metal bollards. He looked up towards her and waved. Before she realized it, she had waved back.

Feeling the deck move beneath her, she was visited by an immense relief. Now at last she could let go of the rail and step back from it, looking around her. It was mid-evening but still light and warm and the deck was well-populated by her fellow-passengers, who were mostly holiday-makers in anoraks and sweaters. Many of them had children and were standing in family groups, pointing things out to one another.

She felt herself to be a spy among them, embarking on a life-or-death mission, of which they, with their simple, holiday concerns, could know nothing. Despite the long drive, she felt wide awake, elated even. As much as anything, it was the feeling of having escaped from all those who had encouraged her to remain calm and patient and accept that she could do nothing. They had been well-meaning, of course; yet they had come close to suffocating her. She tasted the sea air and knew she was now beyond their reach and free to act as she might choose.

They cleared the harbour, passing a horde of small boats bobbing at anchor. The sight of the white cliffs receding put her in mind of past holidays with James when they had stood together, arms around one another, reluctant to leave the deck till the cliffs had shrunk to a thin strip. It had become a superstition with them, a way of guaranteeing that the holiday would be a success. And so she remained there now, keeping the cliffs in view until they had merged with the horizon.

She was hungry, hungry and thirsty after the long drive. She had stopped only twice and then only to purchase a bar of chocolate and a carton of orange-juice, not wanting to lose time standing in queues. Her fear had been that she would miss the evening crossing and so be stranded in Dover till the following morning; in fact, she had arrived with ample time to spare and had had no difficulty in purchasing a ticket.

She went below decks, following signs that said 'Self-Service Restaurant' and came to a cafeteria that, mercifully, wasn't too crowded. Presumably most people had eaten before boarding. Especially those with children, whose meal-times would be earlier. (Seeing these things, as she did, through the eyes of a mother.) She picked up a tray and loaded it with a chicken salad and some bread and, by way of celebration, a half-bottle of white wine, paid for it in English money (reminding herself that she must change some of her thousand pounds into French francs before disembarking), and found an unoccupied table. She opened out the maps she had brought from the car and spread them around her, hoping to deter anyone else from joining her. Conversation of the and-where-are-you-going and have-you-been-before variety was the last thing she wanted.

Besides, she need to plan her route for tomorrow. It would be foolish to attempt more driving tonight. A small yawn escaped her: perhaps she was just a little tired. And sticky and dirty too, in need of a good bath. She would find somewhere – anywhere, it didn't matter – in Calais to doss down and then be underway first thing, aiming to reach Geneva without another overnight stop. It was what? She did a rough measurement using her thumb. Four hundred and fifty miles? Perhaps five hundred, depending on the route she selected.

And she must ring James. She winced at the thought that, even if he had worked a full day at the garden centre, he must by now have been home for some time and so would have read her note and be panicking. Well, she was sorry about that and would ring immediately she was off the boat.

She pushed aside the remains of her chicken salad, wiped her fingers on a paper napkin and poured the rest of her wine into her paper cup. Now she could turn her full attention to the maps. She wanted the fastest route. Never mind the scenery, cathedrals, chateaux and everything else *la belle France* had to offer. She was interested only in getting from Calais to Geneva in the shortest time possible. She bent over the map, tracing her route with a blue felt-tipped pen. She would take the A26, heading south-east towards Paris. Then she had a choice. Lifting the pen and considering the alternatives. Either she could take the A1, which was the more direct route but which took her via Paris itself and so brought with it the risk of being swallowed up in that city's notorious ring-roads, or she could take the A2, which then became the A15 and took her to Liege, quite a detour east but one which would leave her with a more-or-less straight line south to the Swiss border.

'Anyone sitting here?'

There was a man standing over her, holding a cup of coffee. Not wanting to encourage him, she kept her eyes on the map and muttered, 'No. Nobody.'

He sat down across from her. She pulled the maps fractionally towards her, not wanting to be overtly rude but all the same irritated that he couldn't have chosen an empty table, of which there were several around.

The scale of the map was twenty-five miles to the inch. Using her thumb again, she began to measure the first route, the one that took in Paris, so that she might compare it with the alternative and decide whether it was worth sacrificing distance for time.

The man spoke. 'You look like you're planning quite a trip.'

'Yes, I am,' she said shortly.

Go away, why don't you? She resolved that, if necessary, she would collect her things and move herself to another table.

'To Geneva?'

She was going to say yes, resolving it would be the end of their exchange, then wondered how he could have guessed that. Now, for the first time, she looked at him, and was shocked to see a face that she knew.

'You're . . . '

He smiled. 'Bill Sangster. Nice to see you again.'

Was it? Was this just a chance meeting then? She felt herself flushing and made a half-hearted attempt to fold up the maps, hiding them from him. How was she to explain her solitary trip? Especially when he already knew so much about Adam, all that she had told him herself, and seemed already to have guessed her destination.

'I'm sorry if I seemed to be ignoring you. It's just that – '

'No, that's OK.'

She managed a little laugh. Why should she even feel the need to explain? It was nothing to do with him; let him assume what he liked. 'I didn't mean to be rude,' she said.

'Well, you might be in a minute. When I tell you why I'm here.'

She stared again. Now alarm-bells were beginning to ring. So this wasn't coincidence at all. Was that what he meant?

'What do you mean?' she asked, fearful.

'I might as well be honest. I've been . . . well, I've been following you.'

'Following – ?'

'Been driving like a maniac trying to catch up with you. See, I called at your house this morning. And your husband . . . well, he'd got there about the same time I did. And he found the note you'd left him.'

Her heart sank and she gazed round wildly, looking for James. She could almost hear his voice, wanting to know what the hell she was doing.

All her feelings of escape had been an illusion. They had waited till she was on the boat with nowhere to run to and were now closing in.

Even when he said, 'Your husband's not here. There's just me,' she couldn't believe it, still seeing herself as caught in a trap.

'And so what're you supposed to do?' she said, struggling to fold the maps, preparing for flight.

'To do . . . ?' He shook his head as though not understanding.

'You're supposed to take me back. Is that the idea?'

'No.'

Still she wasn't persuaded. She looked around again but could see no-one else she knew – not James anyway – at the tables around them. She felt the urge to get to her feet and run but of course it was absurd. Where was she run to? She was on a not very large ferry in the middle of the English Channel.

She told herself to be calm and face this man. If he really were alone – though she didn't believe that yet, not fully – then who was he anyway but some reporter, with no authority over her nor any right to be following her like this.

'And so would you mind telling me just what this is all in aid of?' she said, striving to keep her voice firm and stop the shrillness from creeping in.

'Well – '

'I mean I assume you don't just make a habit of following people?'

'Not a habit, no.'

'So then – '

'Look, I haven't come from your husband, don't think that. I mean he hasn't sent me to bring you back or anything.'

'No?'

Now she was completely lost. All right, things might not be as she had initially feared: it was not a

305

trap; James was not going to materialize behind her. But that only made the newspaper reporter's sudden appearance all the more baffling.

'So what – '

'I was there at your house because the newspaper wanted to do a follow-up story.' She stared at him, not knowing what to say. 'It's true,' he urged. 'I mean why else – '

'And that's why you've followed me?'

'Well, when I found out what it is you're trying to do . . . I just couldn't resist it.' And he gave another of his smiles.

Lauren set herself not to smile back. She wasn't going to be won over by this display of boyish charm. The self-effacing shrugs, the toothy grin, it was all too transparent a tactic, asking let's be friends and telling her I'm on your side.

Though now she was beginning to breathe freely again. If he really were alone, as he was claiming and as she was now inclined to believe, then what did she have to fear? It meant he was no more than a nuisance, to be brushed off. He might have cornered her on this boat but he would hardly be able to keep track of her once they were landed and in France. Besides, she wasn't going to permit it. She wasn't going to allow herself to be pestered like this.

'Well, I'm sorry but you've been wasting your time,' she said.

'Oh, I don't think – '

'I'm certainly not going to give you an interview, or whatever it is you want. And I've got to ask you not to follow me any further.'

He appeared to think about that, then switched on another smile. This time she even allowed herself a small, tight smile of her own in response, feeling she now had the measure of him.

'There was another reason as well,' he said.

She waited.

'I think you're doing the right thing. Trying to get your baby back like this. And, well, I just thought you might be able to use some help.'

'No, thank you,' she said abruptly, and began gathering her maps together.

'Well, you don't know. I mean once you get over there – '

'I don't want any help. Not from anybody. And I certainly don't want to be followed anymore. Now, excuse me.'

She stood up and walked out of the restaurant, not hurrying or looking back but walking briskly, as though she knew where she was going, wanting him to see that he didn't worry her anymore. The encounter had been a surprise – she was still trembling as she came up the steps and back onto the deck – but now she felt sure that it was not the trap that she had at first feared. This newspaper reporter was on her trail in search of a story and for no other reason. Well, he was wasting his time because she would give him nothing, except for some sharp words if he should try it on again.

She stood on the deck by one of the lifeboats, watching the choppy, blue-grey seas. Ahead, she could make out the coast of France as an uneven line. They would be there within the hour.

With time to recollect and, as always, to regret that she hadn't handled things differently – handled things better – she wished now that she had found out a little more from the reporter before marching off like that. After all, he claimed to have witnessed the moment when James had read the letter. How had he reacted to it? For that matter, why hadn't he

307

come after her himself? Or had he been unaware of the reporter's intentions?

She glanced along the deck and saw him ambling towards her. Perhaps he would carry on straight past; anyway, she wasn't going to run away or hide. No doubt that was the kind of challenge his sort thrived on. No, she would remain where she was, letting him see she was no longer concerned whether he saw her or not.

She was aware of him stopping beside her. He was leaning on the rail so that they were shoulder-to-shoulder. She didn't turn her head but remained looking out to sea. She was determined she wouldn't be the first to speak, then was surprised to hear him laughing.

'Bit of a silly situation, isn't it,' he said.

Now she did turn to look at him. 'I don't find anything amusing about it.'

'No, I'm sure you don't.' There was a silence that extended itself till she almost forgot he was there. The sun was setting, dropping in a spread of orange behind the French coast. 'Look,' he said finally, 'I'm not here to try and persuade you to change your mind. Why should I? What's it got to do with me?'

'Nothing.'

'Exactly.' He sounded encouraged by that, though she couldn't think way. 'Except that I'm a reporter. And OK, maybe I'd like to write up the story one day. But only with your permission and when you feel you want it doing.'

'Which will be never.'

'Well, then I'll be the loser. But in the meantime, like I say, I might be able to help.'

'Why should you if it's nothing to do with you?' she countered.

'Because I happen to think you're right in what you're doing.'

She realized she didn't know what to say to that, not wanting to agree but unable to disagree. 'I don't want any help,' was the best she could manage.

'You have a plan?'

She didn't answer. Her plan was to get Adam back, the simplest plan in the world.

He tried again: 'So what happens when we get off the boat? Are you going to stay over in Calais?'

She hesitated. 'I haven't decided.'

'Only I know a place I can recommend – '

'No, thank you.'

Another boat, similar to their own, was passing them, heading back to England. It looked festive, bedecked with lights. And unreal, in its smooth, silent progress across the darkening waters. Lauren wondered how long it would be before she would be making that return journey, pray God with Adam in her arms.

Now that the reporter – what was his name? Bill? – seemed to have abandoned his attempts to attach himself to her, she felt confident enough to satisfy her curiosity about James.

'You say you were there when my husband found the letter?'

'Yes. I'd just arrived.'

'And how did he . . . I mean what did he say?'

'Oh, he seemed pretty staggered. Tell you the truth, I don't think he knew what to say. Then we talked about where you would be most likely to cross and, since I was going to be travelling south anyway – '

'I suppose he thinks it's a crazy thing to do.'

Bill hesitated, then admitted, 'Well, yes.'

'I'll ring him when we get on shore.'

'I did say that, if I came across you, I'd ask you to do that.'

'Well, now I've saved you the trouble.'

'Do you know Geneva?'

'Not . . . I've never been there, no.'

'It's not the most exciting place in the world.'

By which I'm supposed to understand that he does know it and is available as guide, should I want one, thought Lauren. Well, thanks, but no.

'And this man who's got your child, do you know where he lives?'

She hesitated, but there seemed no reason to lie. Indeed, it would be nice to let him know that she wasn't so totally unprepared as he might suppose. 'Yes, I do as a matter-of-fact.'

'Really? Only, when I interviewed you the other day, I thought you said – '

'Whatever I said, I know his name and I know where he lives.' She was pleased to have surprised him on this at least. 'So, you see, perhaps I don't need as much help as you think.'

Now the coast of France was looming larger, showing clusters of lights. They passed a beacon flashing red and a small fishing-boat with its own light shining onto the water.

'So, all right,' he said, 'you think you can rescue your son from this man – '

'Yes.'

'But then how're you going to get him back, all the way across France, with the police alerted and looking for you?'

'I'll find a way.'

'You might do better with two cars.'

Ah! So this was what he had been leading up to. Still not giving up, still determined on tagging along. Did he think she was so simple-minded, so weak-willed that if he pestered her for long enough she would cave in and say yes, all right? Or that she was at heart the helpless woman, secretly yearning for a man who would take over the whole enterprise?

'No, thank you.'

'OK, suit yourself. Only I thought the only thing that mattered was getting your son back.'

He spoke roughly, aggressively, so that she was taken aback for a moment and stared at him.

'It is,' she said.

'Then why don't you stop being so damned obstinate and accept that you might not be able to do everything on your own? You don't know what's going to happen over there. I might just be the difference between getting him out and not getting him out.'

Still she wanted to tell him to go away and leave her alone. It wasn't that she any longer felt threatened by him or saw him as an emissary from James; it was just ... well, even *talking* about rescuing Adam seemed to risk diluting her will to do it.

'You'd rather lose him than accept my help,' he persevered.

Well, of course she wouldn't, no. She didn't know how to explain it anymore, not to him nor to herself, and so she said nothing.

The lights of Calais were spreading themselves ahead of them. There was a tannoy announcement, first in French, then English, asking passengers to return to their cars.

'At least let me show you this hotel I know in Calais,' Bill urged her. 'You are going to stay in Calais ... ?'

Was she? Yes, she supposed that she was and nodded.

'So at least let me show you this hotel. It's cheap

311

and, anyway, all the tourist ones are going to be crowded. And I'd say you need a night's sleep if you're going to get to Geneva tomorrow.'

Why was she fighting this? She needed a hotel, yes. She was weary and in no state for driving further. What did it matter if she allowed him to lead her to his blessed hotel?

'All right,' she said, raising her hands as if to fend him off. 'Yes.'

He smiled and said, 'Great.'

Seeing his smile, she thought: he thinks he's got me. He believes that he's broken down the defences and insinuated himself. But I'm more cunning and stronger than he thinks. As there will be time and space enough in France for him to discover.

They had agreed that whoever was first off the ferry should pull up immediately after clearing customs and wait for the other. Lauren did this and sat, now feeling quite calm, watching the other cars pass her, their back windows and often their roof-racks as well piled high with camping equipment or suitcases. She saw one of them, a Ford Sierra, flashing its lights, then recognized Bill Sangster waving through the windscreen. She waved back and then pulled out to follow him.

Let him take her to his hotel. Tomorrow she would rise with the lark and disappear into the vastness of France before he had so much as opened those china-blue eyes of his.

Sticking to his tail through a confusion of streets, and once nearly losing him around a busy square, she found herself pulling up beside him in the car park of what looked like a medium-sized and rather scruffy hotel. 'La Bonne Auberge,' read the neon-lit sign.

'Well done,' he said. 'I'll book us in and you can go and ring your husband.'

'I'll book myself in, thank you.'

She carried her own bag too, going with him to the desk. Behind it a plump young woman with her hair tied back looked faintly disbelieving at Bill's request for two single rooms. It irked Lauren to hear him speaking French that was considerably better than anything she might have managed. Never mind. She was weary and had more important things to concern herself with. They were asked to sign a card and hand over their passports. The young woman handed them each a key, which had a large, pink plastic disc attached to it.

'Would you like something to drink? Something to eat?' Bill said, indicating a noisy bar off the foyer to their left.

She shook her head. 'I'm going to ring James and then get to bed.'

'And what time do you want to get off in the morning?'

She had to stop herself smiling at the thought of her deception. 'About nine?' she suggested.

He nodded. 'OK. See you then.'

'Good night,' she said, and headed for the small lift, not waiting to see whether he was going to follow her, assuming he would be making for the bar.

Her room was small but clean and adequate, with a shower off. She dropped her bag to the floor and tried the window, which at first resisted her attempts to open it, then gave way suddenly, admitting a draught of cool air and the traffic noises of the town. She wanted nothing more than to collapse onto the made-up bed but first she must ring James. There was no phone in the room, so she had to return to the lift and descend to the foyer. At least Bill Sangster had disappeared, which was a relief. There was a phone, in its acoustic hood, by the reception desk. She would need change, though she didn't know how much, and had to ask the plump young woman for help. It was the first test of her French, which, miraculously, carried her through. Supplied at last with change and the international code, she dialled her own familiar number.

James answered on the second ring. She had an image of him standing in the hallway, looking drawn and pale and running his free hand through his hair.

'It's me,' she said.

There was a moment's silence, then he said, 'Where are you?'

'I'm in France. Calais.'

She heard him sigh. 'Lauren, I want you to come back.'

At least he sounded less agitated than she had feared but then, of course, he had had all day to get used to the idea.

'And I will come back,' she said, trying to keep her own voice steady. 'Of course I will. Only first I have to go to Geneva and . . . and see what I can do there.'

'Meaning what? See what you can do. What does that mean?'

'Well . . . I don't know till I arrive but – '

'If you try and take Adam back, then you're playing into his father's hands. You know that, don't you? You'll just be proving that you're no better than he is.'

She said nothing, not wanting to provoke him further. There could be no point in a shouting match that would leave her wretched and destroy the night's sleep she had promised herself.

'I want you to come home now,' James urged. 'Come home and we'll talk about it.'

'No,' she said, steeling herself.

'Why not?'

'I can't. I just . . . just can't.'

'Then tell me where you are and I'll come over.'

'No, please, James, I don't want you to do that.'

'Why not? Just tell me why not.'

This was the most difficult thing. How could she tell him that she didn't trust him to support her but that she knew that he would want only to sabotage her efforts and get her back to England and to the legal stalemate that might go on for months or years while all the time Adam would be growing away from her and, ipso facto, becoming the other man's son?

'Look, I don't want us to argue. For one thing, I'm dead tired. Let me ring you tomorrow and we'll talk then.'

'Lauren – '

'And I'm running out of money. I don't have any more change.' Not true: there was a stack of ten-franc coins before her but she felt it to be a forgivable lie, in both their interests. 'But listen. Can I just ask you one thing. Have you told anybody else about this? The agency or anybody?'

There was a pause, then he said, 'Not yet, no.'

'Oh, good. Because I don't think . . . I mean it might be best if they didn't know, at least not yet.'

She didn't wait for his agreement, now wanting to bring the conversation to an end, and quickly. It was enough that she had done her duty in calling him. 'And don't worry about me,' she said. 'I'm fine, better than I've been for weeks.' And she again used the excuse about running out of coins to force him into a hurried goodbye before she put down the phone with a sigh of relief.

She hadn't mentioned Bill Sangster, she was aware of that, but then what good would it have done when she anyway planned on giving him the slip tomorrow? Besides, James hadn't mentioned him either, not asking whether he had managed to find her. So, if deception had been practised, it had been practised by both in about equal measures.

She thanked the young woman behind the reception desk and asked her, in halting French, if it might be possible to have an alarm-call tomorrow morning.

'Oui, madam. A quelle heure?'

'A six heures, s'il vous plait.'

'Six?' said the young woman in English, as if wanting to be sure that there wasn't some mix-up in translation here.

'Oui. C'est une probleme?'

'Non. Pas de probleme. Six heures.'

'Merci.'

'Merci, madam. Bon soir.'

From where he was sitting in the bar, nursing his glass of red wine, Bill Sangster had seen Lauren use the phone. It struck him as a short conversation and one that didn't seem to have upset her unduly. There she was chatting to the receptionist before disappearing out of his view.

He wondered whether the husband had pleaded with her to return or whether, once he'd got used to the idea, he had given his wife his blessing and told her to get on with it. Deciding that the latter was unlikely. On their admittedly brief acquaintance, James Eaglesham had not struck him as the kind of man to endorse a half-baked kidnapping attempt.

So she'd probably given him short shrift, told him what she was doing and that he could either like it

316

or lump it. He would probably never know; nor did he expect to. If he had learned anything from all the years of being single in a world in which most of his contemporaries had got themselves paired off, it was that other people's marriages were among life's greatest mysteries. Perhaps if you got married yourself it gave you an insight: as a bachelor he couldn't say. All he knew was that couples who were apparently blissfully happy in public often turned out to spend their time in private tearing lumps of flesh out of one another; while other, more overtly brittle partnerships seemed to survive and prosper.

So never take sides. One of the basic commandments of the foreign correspondent – which meant everybody where other people's marriages were concerned – was to observe what was going on and faithfully record each side's version of it, but to award neither the status of absolute truth.

Getting back to Lauren Eaglesham, though, he was struck by how different she seemed from the depressed and unstable individual he had encountered when he had called to interview her. She seemed to have been brought back to life by her mission. He realized, with something like admiration, that she would probably go to any lengths, regardless of the risk.

What he couldn't be sure of, not yet, was how far she had reconciled herself to his accompanying her. She had done her best to shake him off on the boat and he had won a temporary respite only by sheer persistence. Tomorrow might prove a different story.

He considered this – the fact that she might still elude him – then finished his wine and went outside to where their two cars were parked.

26

She saw him come into the dining-room and look around before raising a hand in greeting and heading for her table.

She sat with her fourth cup of black coffee in front her, her arms folded, and allowed him to take the chair across from her before she spoke.

'I suppose you think you've been very clever.'

He stared as though not understanding, though she knew he understood perfectly and that this was merely a pantomime for her benefit. Then there was the boyish smile again and, 'Sorry?'

'I've been here since a quarter-to-seven,' she said, 'thanks to your stupid games.'

He looked at his watch. 'Really? You should have said – '

'Oh, don't try and pretend you don't know what I'm talking about!'

'I don't.'

'Oh, you don't?' she said icily.

'No.' He indicated the remains of the croissant on her plate. 'I'm afraid the breakfasts here aren't up to much – '

But she didn't want to hear about the breakfasts. 'So somebody else moved your car? Somebody else moved it so that I'm blocked in and can't get out?'

More pantomime as bewilderment was overtaken

by a slow realization. 'Well, no, I admit I was the one who moved it but – '

'Exactly.'

'But I wasn't intending to . . . I mean they wanted to move some other car and asked me if I'd move mine. So I thought, since we'd be leaving at the same time, it wouldn't matter if I parked up behind you.'

She could have hit him, except that she couldn't reach and she knew anyway that she would end up apologizing if she did. Besides which the waiter had arrived, asking if monsieur would like coffee. She turned away and gazed out of the window, at the shuttered building opposite with the mangy dog on its front doorstep, a scene she had already had over an hour to commit to memory. She had also had over an hour to consider what she would say to this deceiving, conniving newspaper reporter when he finally appeared.

Now the waiter was asking her if she would like more coffee. 'No,' she said, and he went away.

'Well, I'm sorry about that,' said Bill, taking one of her maps and spreading it before him. 'But I didn't realize – '

'Oh, I'm sure you didn't, no.'

'But it doesn't really matter, does it? You said as long as we were away before nine . . . ?'

He looked up at her, smiling – that boyish smile again – as if to say we both know the game you were playing, why not admit it?

But she wasn't going to admit it. She wasn't going to admit anything, and looked away again, out of the window. If only he had been there an hour ago, when she had discovered his car nudging her back bumper and penning her in, then she would have lambasted him to hell and back and never mind that she wasn't being totally fair since all he had been doing was meeting her trick with a trick of his own, playing her at her own game. Since then she had had a long hour for her anger to evaporate, try as she might to keep it stoked up.

'Did you sleep all right?' he asked.

'Yes, thank you.'

In fact, she had slept deeply and been woken by a tap on her door, feeling refreshed and lighter of spirit than at any time since the day when Adam had been taken. She had taken a shower and even done some exercises, before coming down for breakfast, congratulating herself that she would be away so early and excited by the thought of being in Geneva that evening. Perhaps she might even catch her first sight of Adam . . . ! She had packed her bag and checked out . . . then gone outside and seen the miserable trick he had played on her, making sure she couldn't leave without him.

She had been infuriated and come back into the hotel with the intention of banging on his door and dragging him from his bed. But then he would have been awake too and no doubt – given the persistent, never-take-no-for-an-answer devil that he was – he would have insisted on following her. So she wandered back to the breakfast table where the half-asleep waiter had descended on her with more coffee. There had to be some way she could still outwit him, freeing her car and allowing her to make her getaway without rousing him.

Till, an hour later, she was still no nearer a solution when he had arrived to join her, as cheeky as you like. Her enforced wait at the breakfast table had given her time, too much time, to wonder why she was so eager to ditch him anyway. Would it be such a terrible thing to have him in tow? She recalled

320

what he had said on the boat, about how having two cars might prove invaluable when it came to making her escape. Perhaps he was right. Why was she so determined to go it alone?

Probably because she hadn't wanted James along. Wasn't that the truth? James, who saw everything in terms of potential disaster and who would have wanted to keep her wrapped in cotton-wool. It was James she was fleeing from, not this smart-arsed newspaper man.

'So this is your route, is it?' he said, indicating the blue trail she had drawn across the map.

'It is, yes.'

'Well, it'll certainly get you there. But there is an alternative.' She made no response, forcing him to ask: 'Do you mind if I show you?'

'I don't mind, no.'

He used the handle of his spoon to trace a route that went via Douai and Rheims and Dijon, showing how it would be more direct than the motorway network that she had opted for. It would be a shorter distance and, he argued, a saving on time since the roads were close to motorway standard and the major towns by-passed.

'Of course it's up to you,' he said. 'This is your trip.'

'Yes, it is.'

Though at least she paid him the compliment of glancing at the map. Well, perhaps he was right. He certainly seemed to know his way around, which was more than she did. She had been playing safe by opting for the motorways but the route he had sketched did look appealingly direct, an almost straight line from Calais to Geneva.

She felt trapped by his good advice, unable to reject it yet unable to accept, lest by doing so she might seem to be exonerating him from the trick he had played on her. She looked into the window again and this time caught her own reflection: tight-lipped and frowning, a woman of ill-temper. She felt suddenly exasperated – that her energy should be dissipated on such petty games!

What did it all matter anyway? There was only one thing that mattered, and that was rescuing Adam. Hadn't she told herself that all along? Yet here she was allowing herself to be delayed because she couldn't bring herself to give this Bill Sangster the satisfaction of having her agree with him. Pathetic.

She took a decision, two decisions in fact. One was that she would follow the route he had suggested, and woe betide him if it should prove inferior. The other was that, in the interests of progress, she would stop trying to shake him off and would put up with him, for the time being at least.

Though she would make him pay a price. The waiter had appeared from the kitchens with a tray of coffee and croissants and was threading his way between the tables, coming towards them.

'OK, yes,' she said, standing. 'But we go now.'

'Well, do you think I might just – ' Indicating the waiter.

But on this she was merciless. 'I've wasted enough time already. If you want to come – then we go now.'

He made a gesture of helplessness but was smiling. As well he might, she thought, since he was getting his own way. She headed for the door, leaving him to follow. She heard him apologising to the waiter, saying something about the time and their need to be away.

She already had her bag and had checked out, so

that now she had to wait while he disappeared into the lift. 'Shan't be a minute,' he called. Trying to use the time, she took the map and studied it, attempting to commit the route to memory. Douai – Rheims – Dijon. No doubt they would have to stop but she was determined it would be as infrequently as possible.

He came running from the lift. She re-folded the map as he asked for his bill and proffered a handful of notes.

'Did you managed to ring your husband?' he asked, turning to her.

'Yes.'

'And is he, er . . . well, how is he?'

'All right, thank you.'

She would resist his insidious chumminess, for a while anyway. She was still essentially alone in this and was determined to have him realize that.

At last he had paid and was collecting his bill. 'So let's go,' he said. They walked together out into the car park. There was a haze about which promised a hot day to come.

He stood for a moment, contemplating their two cars, their bumpers almost touching. 'I didn't realize it was as close as that,' he said with a grin.

But she wasn't yet ready to admit that she, too, might be able to see the joke in it.

'Well, now that you do,' she said sharply, 'would you mind backing off a little so that I can open the boot of my car?'

She let him go first, then stuck to the back of him as they traversed the tangled streets of Calais, heading inland, away from the docks. They came to two large roundabouts, each time taking the exit marked 'Arras'. And then, as the town petered out, they

323

came onto dual carriageway. The N43, Lauren noticed.

She could relax now as they settled down to a steady speed. She switched on her radio, which was still tuned to BBC Radio Four. It was people talking about a book but she didn't want to have to concentrate to find out what book it was or what they thought of it, nor to be reminded of life still going on back there on the other side of the English Channel, and so pushed her tape of the Drifters into the cassette-player. It was halfway through Save The Last Dance For Me and she joined in, singing along.

Did he always drive so slowly, this Bill Sangster? She looked at her speedometer and saw it was hovering below the fifty mark. What was the French speed limit on roads such as this? She couldn't remember but it was surely considerably higher than what they were doing now. They were in the inside lane, with a procession of cars passing them on the outside. Perhaps he was driving like this for her sake, believing she wouldn't be able to keep up if he put his foot down. (Didn't he know she had worked in a *garage* . . . !) At this rate they would be lucky to be in Geneva by next week.

She waited for a gap in the traffic to her left, then pulled out and accelerated past the red Sierra, giving him a toot on her horn as she did so. Her speed rose to sixty, then sixty-five. Well, that would do. It was what most other cars seemed to be doing, with the commercial traffic on the inside lane doing five or ten miles less. She glanced in her rear mirror but could see only a blue Peugeot behind her, with something behind that might have been a Citroen but which certainly wasn't a Sierra. Then, as the road went into a slow bend, she looked again and this time caught sight of him, four or five cars back. She might have known that he would be there somewhere. The one thing she had learned about this man was that he was not easy to shake off. Now all she had to remember was Douai-Rheims-Dijon. Douai-Rheims-Dijon.

There was even something comforting – she could admit now, to herself – something comforting about travelling in convoy like this, feeling there was somebody there to talk to if necessary. And she didn't dislike him; it was just that yesterday ... well, yesterday had not been the best time to surprise her on the boat as he had done. Today she felt relaxed, more like her old self. She had successfully made her escape from England and knew she would be in Geneva by night-fall. The thought of it thrilled her.

The Drifters were singing Up On The Roof. She sang along to this too.

The ribbon development of warehouses and factories that had accompanied them from Calais fell away and she saw fields of blood-red Flanders poppies on either side of the road. It reminded her of one of their holidays when she had insisted on visiting the war cemeteries but then had found the sight heart-breaking, the row upon uncountable row of white headstones. She knew she was supposed to admire the neatness and careful tending but she couldn't and had exclaimed against the clinical orderliness of it all.

James, reasonable as ever, had pointed out that she would have been even more distressed had the place been neglected or hidden away. No doubt he was right; still, she had burst into tears two days later at the memory of it, even though they were then two hundred miles away, sunning themselves on the beach in the Vendee.

Wanting to put such things out of her mind, she made herself check the car's dashboard, making sure there were no warning lights or that she wasn't running low on oil or water. The fuel gauge told her she still had three-quarters of a tank. She wondered how the car would stand up to this kind of hammer. Three-fifty miles yesterday and perhaps four-fifty today. When had it last been serviced? She couldn't remember but she did remember, word for word, the spiel she used to give customers about the reliability of Toyotas, never let you down. Well, now she would find out.

The size of France, after crowded, little England where towns jostled for breathing-space and where nowhere was really all that far from anywhere else, was what had always impressed her and now it did so again. The flat fields, now full of corn and maize, stretched away on either side, with few walls or hedges to divide them and mark out territories. So much land they could afford to be careless about it.

She had settled into the driving now and was enjoying it. It gave her time to pay attention to the nagging voices that were there at the back of her brain, and had been there since she set out, asking Are you sure? and Don't you have even the smallest doubt about this?

To which the answers were Yes, I am, and No, I don't.

What, you are right and everybody else is wrong? challenged the voices. When your husband doesn't agree and the adoption agency certainly wouldn't and that nice, old judge who awarded you custody of Adam would have a pink fit? Might they not all think you, well, not to put too fine a point on it, emotionally disturbed? Not exactly certifiable perhaps but –

At which point Lauren decided to stop listening to the voices – who the hell did they think they were anyway? – and put on the other side of the Drifters tape, which had come to an end. It began with The Way You Do The Things You Do, which was one of her favourites.

In truth, the voices didn't disturb her. She knew she wasn't mad; while knowing also that the maddest people believed themselves to be the sanest. And, if James didn't support her, well, it was because he was concerned for the consequences if things should go wrong; while the agency had to speak with its bureaucratic voice; and you could hardly expect a judge to be rooting for you if you were hell-bent on breaking international law.

So there.

All the time driving along, telling herself not to count the kilometres or to convert them into miles, which would only depress her with the thought of the miles remaining to be covered. Just follow the road, the not-so-yellow brick road to where the white wizard is holding your son.

She was aware of a large town over to her left, which the road signs named as Douai, when suddenly there was a car behind her flashing its lights. She looked in the mirror and saw it was the red Sierra, Bill Sangster's car. She had almost forgotten he was following. Now he flashed again. She slowed, not knowing what to make of it, then pulled over into the right-hand lane. Bill passed her, then slotted himself in ahead of her. She looked at her dashboard, fearing something was amiss but could see nothing. Then he was indicating right and braking. She did the same and followed him off the road onto the hard shoulder.

He got out of his car and walked towards her as she wound down her window.

'What?' she said.

He didn't speak for a moment, just stood with his hand on the top of her car, a man exhausted, or feigning to be.

'Are you planning on doing the entire trip without stopping?'

She laughed, then said, 'No, I just . . . ' She looked at her watch and saw it was ten forty-five. So they had been driving for, what, an hour-and-a-half? 'Oh, I'm sorry,' she said, meaning it.

'I'm dying,' he said, miming a man at his last gasp, tongue hanging out.

'I just didn't realize – '

'Only you may remember I didn't get any coffee. Not only did I not get any coffee, I didn't get any breakfast. And why didn't I get any breakfast? Because somebody insisted – '

'I know,' she said, though still laughing. 'And I'm am sorry. We'll stop – '

'Please.'

'At the next . . . well, whatever we come to.'

'I'd like that,' he said. 'And let's hope we come to it soon. Because, if we don't, then I'll be dead.'

And he went back to his own car, leaving her feeling a twinge of real guilt. Even though he had been hamming it up, he must have been finding it genuinely hard going while she had been driving without a care in the world or any notion of what time it had got to.

They edged out, back into the traffic. This time she made no attempt to overtake, letting him stay in front. Then, two minutes later, he was indicating right again and she followed him off onto a small exit road. It took them, avoiding the pot-holes, into a little hamlet of a place: a few houses with flaking, stucco walls, then a dump for old tyres. Did he really have any idea where he was going? Then she saw that they had come to a shabby-looking cafe, a low, white building with a Coca-Cola sign along its roof. Bill drew up beside two heavy-loaders and she drew up to the side of him, wanting to make a neat line of it, even though there was an acre of space round them. Inside the cab of one of the heavy-loaders were a pair of Alsatians that began barking through the half-open window as soon as Lauren and Bill climbed out of their cars.

Actually she was glad to stop, now that she had been forced to. She needed to move her arms and legs, get the circulation going again. And to visit the loo.

'I am sorry,' she said again. 'I really didn't realize how long we'd been going.'

'You should have been a rally-driver, did anybody ever tell you that?'

Inside the cafe, there were pin-ball machines and a glass-fronted bar with a coffee-machine in gleaming chrome. 'I'll get these,' said Lauren, feeling she should make amends for the small ordeal she had put him through. She ordered coffee and pastries, still self-conscious about using her French in front of him. Then they went and sat in a booth, sitting at an angle to avoid their knees touching.

He drank the coffee and bit into one of the pastries, while she sat watching, not really wanting her share. She felt . . . light-hearted. She had always enjoyed travelling – the thrill of being set loose – and the morning's drive had anaesthetised the painful memories that she carried with her. There was something to be relished about simply being here, in the middle of nowhere, with this stranger.

'So tell me about your job,' she said.

'What job?' he said between mouthfuls.

'You're a foreign correspondent. At least your card said that – '

'Oh, yes. Yes. Well, when people have wars, I go and report on them. Are you going to eat your . . .?' Indicating her pastry. She shook her head and pushed her plate across to him. 'Thanks. Only I didn't get much breakfast.'

'I know.' And she wasn't getting much in the way of answers. 'And do you do this because it pays well or . . . or, I don't know, for some other reason?'

He shrugged. 'Pays moderately well, yes. But it wasn't something I always wanted to do, like becoming an engine driver. I started off as a regular news reporter and somehow drifted into it.'

'And don't you get frightened? Sometimes?'

He nodded. 'All the time. In fact, you can get hooked on it, find you can't work without the adrenalin. I sometimes think I write better if I think there might be a shell coming through the window.'

This was better, something like a straight answer which made her feel she wasn't being fobbed off. She asked him which wars he had covered and he mentioned the Falklands, Iraq, Yugoslavia . . . She asked him what they had in common and he said, after thinking about it for a moment, that they were all much messier and more confused than it was ever possible to convey in a report. The minute you tried to describe chaos, you imposed an order on it, making it sound as if events were part of an overall strategy when, more often than not, they were unforeseen and random. He told her of generals who sought out correspondents to try and discover what was happening in their own battles.

It was chaos, he said. Chaos fuelled by fear.

Returning from the counter, where he had gone for another coffee, he added that boredom was the other major factor. Waiting around in various degrees of discomfort, reluctantly tolerated by the combatants who both envied and despised your civilian status. Chaos, fear and boredom then.

Hearing him speak freely like this, with the barriers down at last between them, she saw him as the eternal spectator, the little boy who couldn't take his eyes away. She knew that he had gone easy with her on the actual horrors, skating over the details and making one killing field sound much like another.

At the same time she realized, too, that she probably knew more of life than he did. He had spent too long in his ring-side seat, watching the gladiators hacking away at one another, to have been able to notice much else of what might have been going on. It had the odd effect of making her feel sorry for him.

'You're not married?' she said.

'No.'

'And there's nobody . . . ?' She left the question hanging.

'Nobody waiting at home, no. Oh, there's been the odd one that said she would but . . . well, either I never went back or she got tired of waiting.'

Yes, she could see that – how the chaos, the fear and the boredom might well take you away from normal, everyday life with its patient accumulation of ties and responsibilities. How much you might miss by concentrating only on the events of history, believing that they were what was important.

Now she was back inside her car and following Bill's Sierra along the winding, narrow road that would take them back onto the major one. They had agreed – well, he had made her agree – that they would stop for lunch in two hours, not a minute longer.

331

She settled down for the long haul, wondering how long it had been since she had talked like that to someone else about their problems, their life. Instead of having them talk to her about hers and what she must and musn't think and, most of all, how she was not to worry.

Compared to him, of course, she had done nothing spectacular. Nothing glorious. Setting out to become a dancer then not quite making the grade. Becoming a teacher, then chucking that up too. And settling for the garage job, which she didn't regret, no, but ... well, it was hardly the stuff of headlines.

Looking back, there had been a high point of a sort in her second year at University, when she had found her feet and could coast as far as the work was concerned and had had the heady experience of being sought after and popular. She had gone out a lot, slept around a little, smoked some grass and marched to protest about various things, none of which she could now remember. It had been fun trying out different life-styles, feeling there was an infinite number of possibilities to chose from. Then she had met James and fallen in love.

It might have been coincidence but it seemed to her that it was since then – her marriage and their moving to Preston – that things had, well, slowed down. Come to a dead stop even. The experimenting, the risk-taking ... domesticity had descended like a fire-blanket.

Oh, she could have had affairs, of course. There had been no shortage of offers, one or two of which she had idly considered before firmly rejecting. Not Greg, he was too obvious, too much of a pal. But there had been others – a teaching colleague; an old flame from University who had turned up out

332

of the blue; men at parties made bold by a few drinks – so why had she resisted them? Was it really because of her loyalty to James and her fear of hurting him? Or had it been mere timidity, avoiding the challenge of going to bed with an unfamiliar body?

'Oh, come on, come on,' she said aloud. No need to get defensive, to be apologetic because she hadn't been putting herself about. Perhaps she was born to be monogamous and preferred things that way.

And then, of course, had come the years of wanting a child, a yearning that had come to dominate everything. The monthly cycle of hope followed by disappointment; the fertility tests and the biggest disappointment of all. Then the idea of adoption had appeared as a distant and impossible dream, which she had fought for and finally won.

That was when she had reached the second high point in her life, the highest of all, when the nurse had handed Adam to her – Baby Smith as he was then – and she had walked out of the hospital, hardly able to believe that this was her own son she was cradling in her arms.

That moment and the weeks that followed – they had been glorious.

27

They stopped for lunch fifty kilometres beyond Laon on the road to Rheims. Lauren, anyway, had to re-fill with petrol and, since there was a snack-bar alongside the petrol station selling cold meats and salads, fruit and cheese, they decide to make a picnic of it. They carried their trays away from the cars to a grassy bank which gave them a view of the fields and distant hills.

Lauren felt the sun burning through her blouse. If this had been a holiday, she would have been thinking of sun-creams and tanning. As it was, she could think only of Adam. Even talking to Bill required an effort.

'Do you have a house in England?' she asked, when they had begun on the food.

'A flat,' he said. 'In London. A very small flat. Though I've inherited my father's house in Preston. That'll be going on the market as soon as the will is sorted.'

'You don't want to keep it?'

He shrugged. 'What's the point? I doubt I'll ever set foot in the place again. What made you choose to live there?'

The question threw her for a moment. She wasn't sure that she had ever *chosen* to live there. The move had come as part-and-parcel of her marriage to James. 'Well, my husband's family are in the area,' she said. 'And his brother wanted him to go into the garden centre business with him so . . . '

(She supposed she should ring him again once she got to Switzerland. Would he have alerted Stella Priestley or Vernon Angelis about what she was up to? She couldn't imagine, her whole life there seemed such a distance behind her.)

'You're going to stay there?'

'Pardon?'

'You're going to stay in Preston?'

Why not? Where else was she going to go? 'Oh, I should think so,' she said. 'At least for the foreseeable future.'

Though, of course, it wasn't foreseeable, none of it. With Adam she would be able to return and be happy again. She was confident of that and had even fantasized while driving about the moment when she would return home with Adam in her arms and present him to his father. But should she fail . . . then she wondered whether she would ever be capable of facing James again or of rebuilding their life together.

She saw that Bill was watching her.

'Thinking about your son?' he asked.

She nodded and gave a smile. 'Can we get going?'

'Whatever you like,' he said and clambered to his feet.

She was glad to be back in the car and away from him, not because she any longer felt any antagonism towards him but because, with Adam on her mind again, she found it difficult to maintain small talk and, anyway, was impatient of the time they were wasting.

She drove on into the heat of the afternoon, keeping

335

to a steady seventy or thereabouts, the red Sierra behind her, coming and going in her mirror. Vineyards began to appear on either side of the road, the vines staked into neat lines. Away to the east she glimpsed a range of high, rocky peaks.

The city of Rheims came and went on her left. She saw the tips of the giant cathedral but otherwise took little notice, content to lose herself in the act of driving.

She was tired, made so by the heat and the need to concentrate. She found herself yawning and fought to remain alert. She wound down her window so that the warm air tore in at her and sent her hair streaming behind her, but the distraction and the noise was more than it was worth and she wound it up again. She adjusted the air vents so that the streams of air they admitted were directed onto her body.

And she began to sing, bawling lustily over the noise of the engine: '*Are you going to Scarborough Fair? Parsley, Sage, Rosemary and Thyme. Remember me to one who lives there. For he once was a true love of mine.*' And then a whole stream of pop songs which jumped into her head willy-nilly and of which she knew only parts: '*Only the lonely. Know the way I feel tonight. Only the lonely. Know this feeling ain't right . . . Will you still need me. Will you still feed me. When I'm sixty-four . . . Let it be. Let it be. Let it be. Let it be. say these words of wisdom . . .* '

Then a whole medley of Beach Boy numbers – *Sloop John B, Barbara Ann, Help Me Rhonda, California Girls* . . . The last of which turned into a scream of fear as a white Volvo had materialised in front of her. She stamped on her brake and felt her own car judder in protest and heard the tyres shriek. She braced herself for the thud from behind but none came. She dropped back from the Volvo and glanced in her mirror, seeing some kind of van up close on her boot, the driver's face hidden by the reflection of the sun in his windscreen.

She felt herself trembling and slowed still further, pulling into the inside lane. Had the Volvo been indicating and had she been too inattentive or too weary to notice?

She saw Bill, in his Sierra, pull alongside and glance at her. She gave him a wave to show that she was all right, though she was still shaking. Perhaps she should stop after all. She hadn't come all that way to kill herself in some stupid pile-up. She waited until the next petrol station, driving carefully – no more than fifty-five – then pulled off, stopping away from the pumps. She climbed out of the car. Bill pulled up beside her.

'Did he pull out?' she said. 'Or did I just not see him?'

'Don't worry. The thing is you didn't hit him.'

'Can we get a coffee here?'

There was a vending machine inside the petrol station shop that spewed out a thick, dark liquid into a paper cup. She added sugar – two sachets – and went and stood in the shade of the building to drink it. Bill followed her, opening a can of coke.

'Cheer up,' he said. 'Worst part's over.'

'Will we get there by tonight?'

'Only if you take it easy.'

She put down the cup and did some quick exercises, not caring what he thought of her. She bent and touched her toes, then stretched upwards and outwards with her arms. Then moved her head round in slow circles while easing her shoulders back and forth. Loosening up.

'You don't want to stop for a while?' he said, watching her.

'No.'

She didn't even feel tired anymore. The near-collision had released a spray of adrenalin that had left her edgy. Though she still felt sticky and dirty. She saw that the petrol station had toilets and went inside. Finding herself alone, she took off her blouse and jeans, filled one of the basins with cold water, and then used her cupped hands to throw the water over herself. The shock of it made her gasp but she kept going, even dunking her head in it, till she looked as though she might have been standing under a shower. Then she took a handful of paper towels from the dispenser and wiped herself down. Too late she thought of the clean clothes in the boot of her car; all she could do for now was get back into the sweaty blouse and jeans.

She went back outside, wincing at the sight of the large pool of water she was leaving behind her. Still, she felt better. Damp and uncomfortable but refreshed.

'You look like you've had a wash,' said Bill, observing her.

She nodded and ran a hand through her plastered hair. 'We'd better get going before they discover the mess I've left in there.'

'OK,' he said. 'But listen. We do no more than one hour, then we stop again.'

'Stop again – ' she began to protest.

But he raised a hand. 'You're getting tired. I'm getting tired. And, anyway, we have to decide just what we're going to do once we get there. I mean into Geneva.'

She stared, not understanding. What was there to decide? She knew what she would be doing when she got to Geneva and that was finding her son.

He must have seen her puzzlement, for he added:

338

'I mean where we're going to stay. We're going to have to find a hotel or somewhere, aren't we?'

'Oh, yes. Yes.' Stupid of her. Of course they would have to find somewhere to stay.

'So we stop in an hour.'

'Yes.'

And they were away again. The inside of her car had become stuffy and hot while they had been parked up. She drove with her window down, now welcoming the wind whipping in at her and drying her hair. She drove cautiously, self-consciously even, keeping to a steady sixty.

They skirted Dijon. She settled herself for another long haul. She fiddled with the radio but then switched it off: her mind was too full of images of Adam to concentrate on anything else. She tried to blank out all awareness of time or distance, not wanting to know how far there was still to go.

And so was astonished to see a sign saying 'SUISSE 154 Km'.

Which was how far? Divide by eight and multiply by five ... no more than a hundred miles. She was elated. She had believed herself still ploughing through the vast heartland of France yet here she was no more than a hundred miles from her goal.

She increased her speed and pulled out into the left-hand lane.

Five minutes later another sign said 'SUISSE 145 Km', confirmation that she hadn't mis-read the first one. 'Wow,' she said aloud. A hundred and forty-five, that was ... well, something less than a hundred miles. Even allowing for delays at the border and the fact they would have to negotiate the city of Geneva itself and find a hotel, they would surely be there for the early evening, which would leave them

time to seek out the home of this Monsieur Revachier where Adam was being held.

They might even see him. She might even see her
son today!

Well, probably not, she told herself, reining in her
imagination before it ran completely wild. Unless
the Swiss had some weird ideas on child-care which
included nocturnal walks, there probably wasn't
much of a chance of that. Besides, she must be
careful not to rush in like a bull at a gate and
succeed only in warning Revachier of her intentions.
It would be a catastrophic end to this, the longest
journey of her life, if she were to find herself de-
ported and on her way back to England within
hours of setting foot on Swiss soil.

The latest sign said 'SUISSE 104 Km'. She had
stopped translating into miles; kilometres were more
quickly achieved and gave her the feeling of racing
towards her goal. Another hour perhaps. It couldn't
be much longer.

She saw that the red Sierra was behind her and
flashing its lights, then indicating right. A sign told
her they were approaching a rest area, with toilets, a
snack-bar and a playground for children. So this
was where Bill wanted them to stop. Left to her
own accord she would have sailed straight on; but
she had agreed and so began to indicate herself
before pulling over.

Getting out of the car, she did a little jig to try
and release the tension. The feeling of exhaustion
had gone; now she was excited, wanting to get on
and arrive. This time it was Bill who looked as
though he needed the break. He was yawning and
rubbing his eyes as he came towards her.

'You really would just go on forever, wouldn't
you,' he said.

340

'Well, we're almost there. Less than an hour and we'll be – '

'So there's no need to hurry anymore. I want a drink and I want a wash, so let's just sit down for a while, shall we.'

She let him have his way, seeing that he really did look whacked. She even insisted he went and sat down while she went to the counter and bought two cokes. Her watch showed almost half-past four. She would give him ten minutes, she resolved. If he hadn't recovered by then, she would be on the road without him.

'One thing about Geneva,' said Bill, when she re-joined him. 'It's expensive.'

'How expensive?'

'How much do you want to pay?'

She thought of her thousand pounds, which was now down to little more than eight hundred – if that – after the long drive and meals and the cost of the car-ferry across the Channel. And how much would she need to keep by for the journey back? 'Well, I don't have a fortune. Can't we sleep on the beach or something?'

'There isn't a beach. Look, what I suggest. There's a station, a railway station, that's quite central. I can't remember its name but I think I can get us there. Now, where there's a station, there are cheap hotels. So why don't we head for that, get ourselves parked and see what we can find?'

She didn't even pretend to think about it. It sounded sensible and she wasn't going to waste time in debate. 'Sure, yes.' She waited impatiently till he finished his drink, then they returned to their cars.

'How're you feeling?' he asked. She saw that he was observing her.

'Fine, just fine,' she said abruptly, not wanting to

talk about it because how could she anyway? How could she describe what she was feeling, about to arrive in the city where her son was being held captive?

They were back on the road. Now the signs no longer said 'SUISSE' but 'GENEVE'. 'GENEVE 80 Km' . . . 'GENEVE 60 Km'. A range of mountains, formidable and snow-capped, had risen ahead of her. No doubt they had been visible from miles back but only now did she pay them any attention. The Alps. Of course. She laughed at herself for her slowness and wondered what else she had missed, careering through France like a race-horse in blinkers, seeing only the road ahead and the signs which now promised 'GENEVE 21 Km' . . . 'GENEVE 16 Km' . . .

The Sierra's brake-lights came on. She slowed in her turn and saw a bunching of traffic ahead of them. The border. They had reached the border. She felt a rush of apprehension, suddenly fearful that the authorities might have been alerted to stop her. Ridiculous, she told herself. But the fear grew as she followed Bill's car into a queue and fumbled in her bag for her passport.

They edged forward. She told herself to be calm. She was one of thousands crossing this border daily. They would scarcely give her a second glance. The queue moved forward ahead of her. In her rush to follow, she stalled and had to turn the key several times – the gap widening ahead of her, making her conspicuous – before the engine re-fired and she could move forward.

Now there were no more than two or three cars between her and the border post. A man in shirt sleeves was examining the passports as they were handed to him and looking inside the cars. An armed guard stood idly beside him. Lauren saw that a car in a parallel queue to their right, a black Peugot, had been pulled out of line. The driver was being made to open the boot and bonnet, while one of the armed guards was on his hands and knees, peering underneath.

Why had they picked on him? Or was it merely a routine check, one out of every so many? How long was it since someone had been pulled out of the queue she was in?

Suddenly Bill's car had pulled away and Lauren was level with the shirt-sleeved man. 'Passport,' he muttered, and she handed it over, trying to appear nonchalant, hoping he wouldn't notice that her hand was trembling. Now he was looking past her shoulder, into the back of the car. It must be the empty travel-cot strapped to the rear seats, thought Lauren desperately. He's seen that and is suspicious. Why, oh why, hadn't she hidden it away in the boot? Or done anything with it rather than leave it in full view, where it was as good as an advertisement, proclaiming her intentions aloud?

She saw that he was returning her passport to her and waving her through. 'Thank you,' she said through dry lips, tossed the passport onto the seat beside her, put the car into gear and drove forward into Switzerland.

She concentrated on sticking to Bill's tail as they entered the city and the traffic thickened. Around her were tree-lined avenues of houses and flats, then, as they approached the city centre, a cluster of denser and taller buildings. Beyond them she glimpsed a fountain billowing over the rooftops and the glint of flat water.

She was still gripped by the excitement of simply

being here, even wanting to stop when she saw a woman pushing a pram in case the baby inside should be Adam. No time for that though, as they swept around a flower-filled roundabout and came into the tighter, older streets of the centre. She found herself cut off from the Sierra by a tram then managed to catch up with it again at the next junction, squeezing through the changing traffic-lights. They descended into an underpass and, to her surprise, were entering a car park.

She unloaded her bag as he came to join her, carrying a bag of his own. 'All right?' he asked, smiling.

'Yes.' She gave a little laugh, relieved that at least the driving was over.

'Let's go and see if we can find anywhere to take us in then.'

There was a rumble of trains from overhead. They emerged into a concourse of shops and fast-food parlours that were crowded with people, travellers mostly, with luggage of their own. An escalator carried them up into fresh air. Lauren saw they were beside the railway station. There was a large square, with a church on one side. Among the other buildings a good number seemed to be hotels, with cafes and restaurants out front. The first one they came to was the Montbrillant, which had single rooms with bath at seventy-five Swiss francs a night. (Which was how much? Say roughly two-and-a-half Swiss francs to the pound . . . about thirty pounds.)

She saw that he was waiting for her decision.

'Yes,' she said. 'Seems all right.'

Though how long to take the room for was a more difficult choice. In the end she plumped for three nights, telling herself that she could always leave earlier or extend the booking if circumstances demanded it. She saw that Bill had followed her example and also booked for three nights.

'You want to eat?' he said, as they waited for the lift. 'Because I know I do.'

'Can't we go and find the house first?' she pleaded. Then she saw the look of anguish on his face and relented: 'Oh, OK, let's eat then. But I want to find it tonight.'

'I'll see you downstairs in ten minutes,' he said.

She had a quick shower and pulled on a clean top and a pair of light cotton trousers. Wonderful to be clean again. And, yes, she did feel hungry, ravenous even. Though there was something she must do before eating and that was to ring James. She looked at her watch and saw it had gone six o'clock. He would be home and no doubt waiting to hear from her.

There was no telephone in the room so she had to go down into the lobby. She changed some more of her sterling at the reception desk and rang her home number.

'It's me,' she said when he answered. 'How are you?'

'I'm OK. But what about you? Where are you?'

He sounded anxious. She sighed, not wanting to have to argue with him, not now when she had already achieved so much and was wanting only to put the final touch to the day by finding the house where Adam was being held. Never mind where I am was what she really wanted to say; just leave me alone and I'll be all right.

'In Geneva. In a hotel in Geneva.'

'You've driven all the way – '

Yes, she told him. She had driven all the way and, risking annoying him, she said that she was tired and hungry and was looking forward to an early night.

But he wasn't willing to leave it at that. 'Look,

345

Lauren, I've been thinking about this and I can't see that you can do any good by talking to this man. In fact, the danger is –'

'Don't worry.' she said. 'I'm not going to do anything stupid.'

'The danger is you'll turn the Swiss authorities against us, which is the last thing we want.'

'I said I'm not going to –'

'Will you please, please just find where Adam is if you have to. But then leave it at that and come back home.'

She saw Bill emerge from the lift. Seeing her, he pointed towards the bar, meaning that that was where he was going. She nodded.

'I'll be all right,' she said into the phone. 'You're not to worry about me.'

'You're not listening to what I'm saying.'

'Yes, I am.'

But he said it all again, about how she should do nothing for fear of making things worse. How much worse, she wondered. What could be worse than having their son abducted? But she said nothing, promising only that she would keep in touch and giving him the number of the hotel in case he should need to contact her.

She felt sorry for him and also guilty at what she was putting him through. She had escaped from the house, leaving him alone and so in an even worse plight than when she had been there to share things with him. She felt desperately sorry and would one day make it up to him.

But this was not the day. She had enough on her mind – too much – and could only survive by cutting him out and leaving him to fend for himself. She rang off as soon as she decently could, scooped up the remaining coins and hurried into the bar.

Bill had already seated himself at one of the tables set for dinner and handed her the menu. A waiter approached, fastening up his white jacket. Bill asked for a beer and she said she would have one too.

'How was your husband?' he asked.

'Oh, all right. Still thinks I'm crazy.'

He nodded and left it at that. For which she was grateful. It was enough that she had left James behind and not even told him about how this reporter had invited himself along. She must resist being drawn into a further betrayal, confiding in this other man about James.

Poor James. Still, he would forgive her everything when she returned with Adam in her arms. Then would be the time for her to tell him everything, when all this would be behind them and they would be a family once again.

They had eaten and were back on the road, this time together, in Bill's car. 'It's hired,' he said. 'Doesn't matter if we wreck it.' He was driving while she navigated, following a street map which they had collected at reception and with the piece of paper on which she had scribbled down the address given to her by Claire Tempest.

The traffic was lighter now, as dusk descended. They came onto the Route de Fernay.

'It's on here,' said Lauren, barely able to contain her excitement. 'Third ... no, fourth off on the right.'

He counted aloud, 'One, two three ... four,' slowed and turned off the main road onto a small road which served some five or six houses. Large houses in their own grounds. Lauren had cast the map aside and was gazing ahead.

'Stop . . . stop,' she said. 'There.'

The house itself was almost invisible, only its green slate roof showing above the stone wall that encompassed it like the wall of a prison. The tops of trees also showed from what seemed to be a large garden. Then, as they watched, light came spilling out over the wall and through the wrought-iron gate that was at the front.

'What's that?' said Lauren, startled.

'Some kind of flood-lights.'

'Because of us?'

'I shouldn't think so.'

No, she didn't really think so either. It was the kind of house that might well be flood-lit, the kind of house that might well have every conceivable security device surrounding it. She knew that Bill was looking at her.

'Well,' she said, fighting to control the tremor in her voice, 'there it is.'

He nodded. 'There it is.'

What he didn't say, though she knew he must have been thinking it, was that this was no mere house but a fortress. Unlike its smaller neighbours, whose gardens were open and inviting, this mansion which held her son was forbidding and private. More than private. Impregnable.

So this was what she had come so far to behold. An impregnable fortress, built to withstand a siege.

28

Falling sleep, she hoped and prayed that the house would look smaller and less threatening when viewed in daylight; that the walls would have shrunk and the iron gates ceased to resemble the stout portcullis of a medieval castle.

Faint hopes.

She awoke to the sound of trains outside her window and pushed back the shutters. The side of the hotel was still in shadow but the sun was creeping across the street, presaging another hot day. The traffic was already busy, crowding the street below her.

She did some exercises and showered, buoyed up by the thought that she was, after all, here in Geneva. She hadn't dreamt it. She had come from England, across France and was now camped on the threshold of her enemy. Never mind the ominous aspect which the house had last night presented, she was here and had stood before it. Today she might actually see Adam. In fact, since anything was possible – her being here was testimony to that – might she not actually hold him . . . ?

Hang on, she told herself. One step at a time. Yesterday had been The Journey; then in the evening had come The Arrival. Today was . . . well, today might turn out to be anything but, to begin with, it was a day for watching and weighing the odds.

Bill joined her in the dining-room as she ate her breakfast of rolls and strawberry jam. He looked sleepy and complained about the trains which had kept him awake, but she sensed that he was excited too, and pleased at what they had achieved. She found herself glad of his company: no need now of plans to give him the slip or shake him off. It was good not to feel completely alone but that here was someone she could talk to. Though when he asked her, 'Well, what did you think?', meaning her impressions of the Revachier house, she said only, 'I don't know. Wait till I see it in daylight.' She was still reluctant to confide everything in him and certainly didn't want to confess to the dismay she had felt on seeing it.

Besides, she still clung to her hope that this morning it would be different, bathed in sunshine and looking less of a dungeon.

'And so what's the plan?' he said, yawning.

'Oh, I'm just going to go and sit and watch for a while. Find out . . . well, I don't know. Just sit and watch and see what happens.'

'You want me to join you?'

She had been hoping he wouldn't ask but would have announced plans of his own. Now she could only give him a straight answer. 'No, it's all right, thank you' she said, smiling to show that she was grateful for the offer and that this wasn't a renewal of hostilities.

'Or we could take turns – '

'No,' she said firmly. If she were going to see Adam, then she wanted to be alone.

He shrugged and she was relieved to see he wasn't going to press the point. She was happy to have him for an ally but not on equal terms. This had to remain her own operation. She relented only when he suggested joining her for lunch. At least that meant she would not have to break her vigil. They could picnic in one of the cars and she could keep the house in view.

'Anyway, look, I'm going to go,' she said, seeing it was already nine o'clock and knowing that a house with a child in it – any child – would have already been up and about its business for a full hour at least.

But Bill evidently had something yet to ask. 'You're not going to attempt anything, well, you know – '

'What?'

'Anything dramatic?'

He spoke lightly so that it might have been a joke, yet she sensed a veiled warning. (Well, no, not a warning – a plea, a attempt to restrain her.)

'No,' she said, looking him in the eye. 'I'm just going to watch.'

He nodded, apparently satisfied. 'Be careful.'

She headed for reception where there was a small rack of street maps. The one they had used last night was still in Bill's car. She checked her pockets as she moved: car-keys, money, the paper on which she had written Revachier's address and phone-number.

It was ten-past-nine on Day One.

After she had gone, Bill lingered in the dining-room, taking a third cup of the murky coffee. He felt purposeless, set adrift. He had wanted to accompany Lauren back to the house but she had made it pretty clear that she didn't want him there and he could hardly insist. It still worried him that she might do something reckless if the chance presented itself: seizing the child and making a run for it perhaps. But he couldn't keep dogging her heels every step of the way and so could only trust that she would do nothing until she could be sure of success. Though with that house . . . ! He had almost cried out in despair, coming upon it last night after their never-ending trek across France. What a blow it must have been to her. He had wanted to shield her from the sight, saying No, don't look – you'll only upset yourself.

Though she seemed bright enough this morning. Either the horrendous difficulty of her quest hadn't got through to her yet or she was simply rising above it, clinging to her crazy dream of rescuing her son. A lady of considerable courage, he would grant her that.

He left the breakfast table and wandered out onto the terrace where a waiter was wiping down the tables and opening out the umbrellas above them. Well, here he was then, on a holiday of a sort even if it wasn't quite as he had envisaged. With nothing to do till lunchtime when he had committed himself to providing something for Lauren to eat and drink. (What would she have done if he hadn't suggested it? *Starved* herself to death?) What the hell. He must stop worrying about her; stop feeling responsible for her. (Since he wasn't. Not by any calculation could he be said to be that.) He would take a walk down to the lake-side, stop at a cafe and watch the world go by.

Though first, since in a way he had to admit that he *did* feel responsible, and since it couldn't do any harm and just might turn up something of use, he would ring a friend of his in London, a Ms Julia Beardsley, who lived with three cats and her aged

352

mother in an Earls Court flat. She was a free-lance researcher Bill had worked with in the past, a relentless ferreter after information. If there was anything to be turned up on this Marcus Revachier, then she would be the one to unearth it. Know your enemy wasn't a bad precept and, by the look of his domestic arrangements, this one might prove tougher to get to know than most.

Sadly, the walls had not shrunk. If anything, they seemed higher than they had last night, twelve or fifteen feet high with security cameras peering down inquisitively from each corner. Lauren parked a hundred yards away on the other side of the road, hoping she would be out of their range. She pulled down the sun-visor and put on her light-sensitive glasses which she wore for driving, trying to camouflage herself as best she could yet still feeling conspicuous stuck there on the road-side with hardly another vehicle in sight.

Perhaps, if this business were to continue for some days, it would be wise to take up Bill's offer and use his car as well as her own, alternating them.

She moved her car seat back a few notches so that she could spread her legs and be comfortable. Then she reclined the back of the seat till she was half-sitting, half-lying, with her head just above the sill of the car, giving her what she hoped was a better view of the house than anyone inside it might have of her. And so settled herself for her day of observation, which for a long time (though only forty minutes when she looked at her watch) meant staring at those high, blank walls, trying to guess what might be going on inside them.

When the first signs of life did eventually appear, she started forward eagerly: a van stopped outside the gates and something was delivered; then a car, an ordinary enough Fiat, emerged and came up the road, passing her, with a youngish man inside it, driving while smoking a cigarette. But these were the high-lights, the moments to set the pulse racing. Another hour passed and nothing happened, save that the shadows grew shorter and Lauren began to feel sleepy and disappointed.

Of course she hadn't really expected Adam to be paraded past her in a pram. Though it would have been nice if he had. It would have been nice if something had happened that she could have related to him.

She thought bitterly of the contrast between this house before her, this fortress that was the lair of the gun-merchant who had stolen her son, and her own home, so trustingly undefended.

How laughably simple Revachier must have found it, opening the rickety gate at the bottom of the garden, the one that would never even fasten properly, and simply walking in without a security camera or even a watchful mother in sight. Like taking sweets from a baby. Or, as in this case, taking a baby from those who had believed that a court's decision was all they needed to protect them.

Even with the windows open, it was hot inside the car. Lauren eased her jeans from where they were sticking around the tops of her legs and wished she had put on her shorts. She lifted her hair and found a couple of grips in the glove compartment so that she could tuck it up, off her neck. And finally, growing frustrated, and bolder, she opened the car door and stepped out into the road.

She was running the risk of being seen, of course she was. Though the walls that shielded the house from her would also shield her from the house. It

354

was the cameras she must beware of. She strolled towards the house, though without looking at it, forcing herself to take an interest in its smaller neighbours with their carefully tended gardens. She passed them, walking slowly, and came to the beginning of the wall. She put out a hand and touched it, telling herself not to look up at the cameras, one of which was now directly above her.

She counted her steps – forty-two – till she came to the closed gates. She glanced through them, not daring to stop for a proper look, and saw a driveway curling away between trees, areas of lawns and flowers and then the house itself, square and solid-looking, decorated by a veranda and dark green shutters. Then, with a start, she saw something else: a young man, wearing only a pair of shorts, lolling in a deck-chair just inside the gates. He was less than twenty yards away from her. His eyes flickered open and for a moment they were staring at one another. She walked on, her heart pounding.

Who was he? An employee? Some kind of guard stationed there to deter intruders?

The road came to a dead-end, just the driveway to another house, so that she had to return, this time forcing herself not to glance through the gates lest she should again catch the young man's eye. Just keep walking, she told herself. Slowly, casually.

Till she was back in the car and pulling the door closed. She slid down in the seat and looked again at the house.

To her relief, there was still no movement. No-one had emerged; the gates had remained closed.

She forced herself to relax. Perhaps they were accustomed to passers-by wanting to glimpse whatever was beyond the walls. Perhaps she could have paused for longer.

A new worry began to gnaw at her. Could she be absolutely sure this was the right house? She had the piece of paper with the address that Claire Tempest had dictated to her, but suppose Claire had made a mistake? Perhaps only a small mistake, giving her the wrong number, so that it was the house to either side or the one at the end of the road she should have been watching? Or giving her the correct number but the wrong road?

Once the worry had taken hold, it was impossible to dismiss. She took the crumpled paper from the back pocket of her jeans and studied it, as though it might yield some clue. Beneath it was the phone-number that Claire had also given her. Could she use that to verify the address?

She couldn't continue to sit there with her doubts unresolved and, anyway, the prospect of doing something positive was irresistible after the long, slow drag of the morning. She left the car again, this time walking away from the house. It was a relief to come out of the quiet cul-de-sac, where she felt so exposed, and onto the main highway which was busy with traffic. She moved quickly, not wanting to be away from her post for a moment longer than was necessary. She spied a glass telephone kiosk and hurried to it, then winced at the harsh, accumulated heat that met her as she stepped inside. She wedged the door open with her foot while reading the instructions and searching her pockets for coins.

She rehearsed the questions in her head, hoping her French wouldn't let her down, then dialled the number Claire had given her. The phone at the other end rang four times before it was answered.

What Lauren took to be a woman's voice said, 'Yes?'

'Hello. Is that number five Rue des Monts?'

'It is, yes.' Unmistakably a woman's voice. So at least she wasn't speaking to Revachier himself, which was something of a relief.

'And is Monsieur Revachier at home?'

'Who is speaking please?'

Lauren's mind whirled, then came up with: 'Monsieur Revachier doesn't know me. I wish to speak to him on a business matter.'

There was a pause, then the voice at the other end said, 'I will see if Monsieur Revachier is free. One moment please.'

It was all she needed to know. She gave a silent cheer and replaced the handset. She didn't want to talk to her enemy, not yet anyway, but simply to be sure, as she now was, that she had him in her sights.

Also to have spoken to someone inside the house, that in itself felt like a step forward. As though she had electronically pierced its defences.

Her car had become as hot as the telephone kiosk. She lowered all the windows and searched through the clutter of the glove-compartment, finding a couple of ageing barley-sugars to relieve her dry mouth. Why hadn't she thought to provide herself with something to drink? Or with some fruit, sweets . . . anything?

Not much of a planner, am I, she reflected, sucking on the barley-sugar. Never have been. I don't anticipate enough. There's probably a psychological term for it.

A black Mercedes came nosing its way out of the gates and turned towards her. She slid down in her seat. As it passed, she glimpsed a young man driving – though a different young man from the one in the deck-chair, this one with clothes on and curly hair – but anyone else in the car, if there were anyone, was shielded by its darkened windows.

After which nothing happened at all. The house seemed to have settled down for its midday siesta. Lauren yearned to do the same, fighting a losing battle against the waves of sleepiness which were beginning to roll over her.

There was a flash of red in her driving-mirror and the sound of a car drawing up behind her. Stopping so close that it was almost touching. Her drowsiness was dispersed in an instant. She struggled to sit upright and gave an involuntary yelp of panic. Then, twisting round, she saw that it was Bill's Sierra, with Bill already climbing out of it. She gave another cry, this time of relief.

He had an armful of paper bags and she leaned across to open the passenger door for him.

'How's it going?' he asked.

'Oh . . . not much happening.' She couldn't take her eyes off the cartons of fruit juice he was unpacking, barely able to wait for his invitation to help herself before she was opening one of them and gulping it down.

'Hot day,' he said, amused.

'I know. I should have . . . brought something,' she said between swallows.

'Well, there's plenty here. And some sandwiches. Salami, liver sausage, cottage cheese . . . take your pick.'

Actually she didn't have much of an appetite, but she could hardly tell him that after the trouble he had gone to and so chose the cottage cheese, besides opening another carton of juice.

'So you haven't had any sight of the child?'

'No,' she said, as briskly as she could. 'Haven't had much of a sight of anybody.'

'Well, look on the bright side – at least they don't seem to have noticed you.'

True, she supposed. She saw him put down the sandwich that he had bitten into and take a notebook from his shirt pocket.

'And listen. I've been doing some research. Or rather I rang a friend of mine in London and got her to do it for me.'

'Yes?'

'Well, you told me this Revachier character was an arms-dealer so I thought there might be something about him in the cuttings libraries. And my friend – she does this kind of thing for a living, professional researcher – anyway, she managed to track down what there was. Which probably doesn't get us anywhere but still. Apparently this Revachier is quite big-time. Operates in the Middle East, North Africa, India . . . you name it. Used to have a partner, a South African, but now operates on his own. And, according to one account – this was a human interest sort of write-up – he's something of a lady's man, cultivated, sophisticated . . . well, anyway, he's not one of your absolute barbarians. Though a lot of the people he deals with are.'

She could only nod, faintly depressed by it all, confirming as it did the unequalness of the contest.

'So don't take all this high security stuff personally. It's not just you he's trying to keep out.'

She managed a smile. 'No. And thanks. I mean for ringing your friend and -'

'That's OK. No trouble.'

They sat side-by-side in the car, eating and taking sips of the fruit juice and observing the mansion before them. 'We don't even know whether Adam's still in there,' said Lauren quietly. It was a new fear that had come to her suddenly. She had barely had time to consider it before she heard herself speak. Bill said nothing. She turned towards him and said,

359

'He might have spirited him away to . . . well, to any-where.'

'But why should he? What reason would he have?' said Bill, in a calm, measured tone that she knew was meant to steady her.

'Oh, I don't know. I just . . . well, does it look to you as though there's a child inside there?'

'There could be twenty inside there. We wouldn't be able to tell from here.'

She knew that he was right and wanted to agree but still she felt unable to shake off the sudden pessimism that had descended on her like a fire-blanket. It was the aftermath of the long morning weighing upon her, the hours passing at a snail's pace after yesterday's helter-skelter rush to get here.

'You're tired,' he said. 'Why don't you have a snooze? I'll wake you if anything happens.'

'No, I'm all right,' she protested. She had vowed she would spend the day watching the house and wasn't going to give way to him now.

She stifled a yawn and wondered what she might do to establish whether Adam really was inside those walls. Another phone-call? The one she had made earlier had been successful in establishing that they were watching the right house. Could she try again, this time making some enquiry about Adam? Though she couldn't think what. Or perhaps Bill, with his superior French, might make the call for her.

She had a vision of the garden as she had glimpsed it through the gateway, the lawns stretching out of sight, ample room for Adam to play or to be put out to sleep. She would scale the walls after dark and hide herself somewhere in those grounds, then at least she might see him and know for sure he was there. Then she would seize him and run for the

360

gates, her pursuers behind her calling out and reaching to grab her, a hand gripping her shoulder . . .

It was Bill shaking her. 'Lauren, Lauren . . . ' she heard his voice, first from a distance but then close and urgent, recalling her from the sleep that she had somehow fallen into.

'Oh, sorry – ' she began.

But he wanted her attention. 'Look. There, getting out of the car . . . !'

She blinked to bring her eyes back into focus and followed his pointing finger.

An ageing deux-chevaux Citroen, its soft top rolled down, was depositing someone – a young woman – in front of the gates. She was wearing a red-and-blue dress. Though it wasn't so much a dress, more a uniform . . .

'A nurse . . . !' gasped Lauren.

'Exactly.'

The Citroen did a swaying U-turn and came down the road and past them, with the young woman standing waving outside the gates of the Revachier house. Then she turned and, the gates opening before her, she stepped inside.

'Sorry I had to waken you,' said Bill, sounding jubilant, 'but I wanted you to see – '

'I know.'

'And that has to mean . . . ' He left the rest unsaid, waiting for her to agree.

'Well . . . we can't be sure – ' she said, frightened of false hopes.

'Oh, come on,' he urged. 'Has to be!'

But now Lauren was staring out through the windscreen and waved her hand, motioning him to be silent.

'What?'

'Look.'

361

For there, just emerged from the gates and walking down the road towards them, was another nurse. Older perhaps and taller but a nurse all the same and in identical uniform.

'They must have changed shifts,' said Bill.

Lauren hesitated a moment but she couldn't pass up this chance to have the issue settled once-and-for-all. As the nurse approached, she pushed open the car door and stepped out onto the pavement in front of her.

She heard Bill calling after her but couldn't make out what he was saying and, anyway, her mind was full of what she might say, how she might question this young woman without alarming her.

'Excuse me.'

'Yes?' The nurse stopped. Lauren sensed immediately that she was wary of her and on the defensive. She was in her early twenties with a white, frilly hat perched on her ginger hair and carrying a leather shoulder-bag which she now clutched to her.

'Are you a nurse?'

'I am, yes.'

'A children's nurse?'

'Yes.'

Lauren found herself suddenly inspired: 'It's just that I live nearby and I'm looking for a nurse to care for my own children.'

It seemed to do the trick. The young woman gave a smile and shifted her stance to one that was more relaxed, less poised for flight. 'I see. Well, I work for an agency and they do look after children, yes.'

'You're looking after a child at the moment?'

'I am, yes. In that house there.' And she waved an arm behind her, unmistakeably meaning the Revachier house.

It was all Lauren wanted to know, removing her

doubts in an instant. Though also filling her with an envy which she had to fight to control. Until a few moments ago, this young woman standing before her had been caring for Adam, holding him and being a mother to him.

'What I can do, I can give you a card,' the young woman was saying, plunging a hand into her bag and bringing out a white printed card which she held out.

'Thank you,' said Lauren, taking it from her. 'Thank you, you've been very helpful.'

'If you just ring them, they'll tell you the rates and everything.'

Now they were walking in step, coming back to the car where Bill would be waiting and watching.

There was one thing more Lauren had to ask before she could let her go. 'And this child you're looking after now, is he well-behaved for you?'

How could she not enquire after her own son?

The nurse smiled. 'Most of the time, yes. Anyway, I hope the agency can help you.'

'Thank you,' said Lauren again, stopping by the car as the young woman picked up pace and went away along the road.

Lauren ducked back into the car. Bill stared inquisitively as she placed the agency's card on the dashboard.

'Well?'

'Yes,' she said quietly. 'He's in there. Thank God. It's the right house and he's there inside it.'

That evening they went to a Chinese restaurant down by the lake-side. Lauren had had misgivings when Bill suggested it: 'Let's give ourselves a night off. I'll take you out for dinner somewhere.'

There was something faintly shocking about the

notion that she might take time off from rescuing her son in order to enjoy herself. And so she protested: 'Oh, no. No, I don't think that I really – '

'You can't be planning on sitting in this car all night?'

Well, no, she wasn't intending that but, all the same, his invitation seemed . . . frivolous.

'Can't we just eat in the hotel?' she pleaded.

'Let's put it this way,' he said. 'We've got here and we've discovered where your son's being held. Now I think tonight we should have a serious talk about how we get him out of there.'

Still, she had insisted on staying at her post until the light had begun to go. And Bill had remained beside her, though she had more than once suggested he return to the hotel. Perhaps he didn't believe her but thought that, were he to leave, she would spend the entire night there in solitary vigil.

The afternoon had turned out to be as unremarkable as the morning. Around four o'clock the black Mercedes had returned, sweeping past them, then stopping while the gates were opened to admit it. This time a man dressed in cut-off shorts and a brightly coloured shirt had lingered outside the gates after the car had gone, gazing in their direction.

'Is he looking at us?' Lauren whispered, hardly daring to move.

'Could be.'

She held her breath but then the man had seemed to lose interest, turned and looked in the other direction then wandered back inside the gates, which closed after him.

It proved to be the last of their meagre contacts with life inside the Revachier house. The sun edged down behind the Alpine peaks and suddenly the air was cooler. Lauren had insisted on hanging on for

another half-hour or so, aware of Bill sitting with
infinite patience beside her, till even she had to
accept that the day had well and truly ended. She
leaned forward and switched on the ignition, making
him jump.

'We're off?'

'Might as well.'

She moved her seat back to its driving position
while he scrambled out and went back to his own
car. Then, after both had turned awkwardly in the
narrow road, they came in convoy out of the Rue
des Monts and headed back into the centre towards
the Hotel Montbrillant and the luxury of a shower
and change of clothes.

Despite her earlier misgivings, Lauren felt her spirits
lifted by their small excursion to the restaurant and
the novel feeling of being among people bent on
enjoying themselves. It was almost a surprise to be
reminded that this was part of life too. Neither she
nor Bill had come equipped for such nights on the
town and so it was a joke between them how scruffy
they were in contrast to the well-heeled diners
around them. It made Lauren feel all the more of a
spy in a foreign land, sitting there with her fellow-
conspirator, ordering wan tan, with stir-fry prawns
and snow pickles to follow, and bottles of German
beer to drink.

'To Adam,' said Bill, raising his glass.

'To Adam.'

(She hadn't rung James. Oh, well, too bad. She
hadn't even thought of ringing him till now, when it
was impossible: their food was already being arranged before them by two young girls wearing
cham-songs.)

'Right, so what's the plan? Do we have a plan?'

She shook her head. 'Not yet.'

'OK, so let's think about it. We know that the child – Adam – we know that he's in there. And we know that he's looked after by those nurses, who seem to work some kind of shift system.'

'Yes.'

'So perhaps we could bribe one of them.'

Surprised, she looked to see if he were joking. 'Bribe one . . . ?'

'I'm not saying it's a good idea. Just that it's the only one I have at the moment.'

'And what happens if she screams her head off? Goes running to the police or – '

'I said it wasn't a good idea.'

She shook her head decisively. 'It's lousy.'

'OK, so what do you – '

'We wait. We wait till they bring him out and then . . . well . . . ' But she was already running out of steam, not even convincing herself and knowing what Bill's objection would be even before he spoke since it was something she had had the whole long day to realize for herself.

'They might never bring him out.'

She sighed. 'No.'

'It's a big house. Big garden.'

She wanted to argue the point but couldn't. It was all too dispiritingly true. Adam could grow into boyhood without ever setting foot outside those walls.

They ate in silence for some minutes, then Bill said, 'Suppose . . . ', waited till she raised her eyes from her food and then went on, 'Suppose you went to the authorities. I mean play it all above board. Go to the authorities here in Geneva.'

She was immediately hostile. 'And what good would that do?'

366

'Well, it might force them to get their fingers out and get things moving in the courts. I mean for one thing I could try and get you some news coverage.'

She still didn't like it. 'But it would let him know I was here.'

'Well, yes, but – '

'And that's the only advantage we have – that he doesn't know. We'd just be putting him on his guard.'

'The courts can force him to surrender the child –'

'Oh, no. Oh, no, they can't. The courts ruled against him in England and look what he did then!'

It was because she had lost faith in the courts that she was here. The courts were useless, a sham, a fraud. Worse, they were a shield behind which Revachier could shelter forever.

'A man like that, he doesn't listen to the courts! He'll just have Adam taken away to somewhere they can't reach him. Somewhere like . . . oh, I don't know, the other side of the world. He's got money, he's got . . . well, he's got everything on his side, hasn't he!'

It was a plea for fairness, for some just and benevolent god to intervene and level the odds. But, of course, no such god was likely to and the Swiss authorities had shown not the slightest inclination that they might take on such a role.

'OK,' said Bill, 'forget the courts.'

'Well, I just think – '

'I know.'

She smiled, grateful that he should pretend to agree with her, even if he didn't, deep down. Whereas James would have . . .

No, forget James. This was not a night for comparisons.

Bill talked her into having a sweet and they ordered almond jelly and watermelon pond, with china tea to follow. As they ate, with neither of them having any new ideas, they went over the options again. Option one, they could try and bribe one of the nurses or even try and convince one of the nurses of the rightness of their cause and so win her onto their side. Neither of which Lauren really believed was possible. Or they could go to the authorities. Well, this was possible but it wouldn't get them anywhere. It would be an admission of defeat which would advance things not one jot from where they were already and where they had been three days ago when she had jumped into her car in Preston and headed south. Or they could – the ideas getting wilder – try and scale the walls themselves and free Adam in a death-or-glory mission.

It was a notion that made both of them laugh at its sheer absurdity.

'All we've got going for us,' said Bill, as though drawing up a balance sheet, 'is the element of surprise.'

'Yes.'

'Which we mustn't waste. We've got to wait, be patient, and see what opportunities occur.'

She nodded solemnly, feeling that they had reached some conclusions after all, even if they weren't earth-shaking. They had another cup of china tea, then left the restaurant and went for a stroll along the gaily-lit promenade.

She felt herself in a kind of limbo, squeezed between two opposing truths, unable to see how they might ever be reconciled. Looked at squarely, her chances of extracting Adam from his abductor's fortified lair were about nil. Zero. Hopeless. Yet she knew that she would never cease trying.

And that she would one day succeed.

It was the only secret she still had from this man who had become her ally. She would never give up hope. Whereas he, she suspected, already had grave doubts about the mission. Oh, he was being careful not to show it and she was grateful to him for that. She saw that he would indulge her to the limit, discussing and plotting and sitting beside her during long days of fruitless surveillance in the hope she might get the obsession with reclaiming Adam out of her system and not be too broken-hearted when the truth had finally to be faced.

He was transparent, this foreign correspondent. Transparently loyal and honest but not too clever when it came to understanding women and their children. Not that she thought any the worse of him for that. She was moved by his commitment to her and his wish to save her from further pain.

'Thanks,' she said, taking his hand. On impulse, she reached up and gave him a kiss on the cheek.

'Oh. Well – ' He seemed taken aback, even embarrassed, though it was difficult to tell in the twilight.

'I mean for everything. Helping me,' she said, and left her hand in his.

They stood there for a moment, watching as a yacht, coloured lights strung out between its masts, unloaded a group of revellers onto the quayside. Then, without a word to one another, they strolled through the quiet streets of the city back to the hotel.

Catching sight of their reflection in its glass doors, Lauren saw a couple who might have been lovers. Strange how she was neither shocked nor shamed by this. They collected their separate keys from reception, now letting their hands fall apart, then stepped over to the lift. (And still she hadn't rung

369

James, she registered, going past the telephones.) There was a short wait for the lift to arrive. She knew, surprising herself again, that she wanted Bill to take her in his arms, suddenly needing the comfort and security of being held. For a moment, as the lift rose, she thought she was going to do so but then they had reached their floor and were stepping out. They came to her door first. 'Good night,' said Bill, brushed her cheek with his lips and then was striding off along the corridor.

''Night,' she called after him, wondering what she had done wrong or if she had simply misread things, not knowing. She let herself into her room, relieved and yet disappointed. She slid the bolt on the door then flopped down onto her bed, astonished to discover herself overwhelmed by a mixture of emotions. Above all she felt herself weak and helpless – not knowing why, what had happened to change everything like this – and felt the first touch of that bleak despair that had come so near to conquering her in the weeks after Adam had been taken.

She forced herself to stand and struggled to pull off her clothes, weeping now, letting the clothes and the tears fall around her, till she was naked and could crawl beneath the single sheet where she curled up and let her sobs carry her towards sleep.

29

The feeling of distress and panic was still there in the morning. Weaker and more distant, so that she could almost ignore it altogether while showering and dressing and having a quick tidy around the room, which was threatening to turn into a pig-sty – but there all the same. It suggested that last night's spasm wasn't just a one-off, promoted by the drink and her sudden yearning to be comforted, but was the reappearance of her old depression, threatening to re-establish control.

It was those damned walls, she thought, coming down in the lift. Those damned walls and that monster of a house.

She was going to rescue Adam. She was going to penetrate the fortress and bring him out. Of that she was as determined as ever.

But how?

The mood that had swept her across France, the feeling that nothing was beyond her, had begun to evaporate. Now she felt puny, as though she were beating with her fists against battlements of solid rock.

There was a message at reception to say that her husband had rung and would she contact him as soon as possible. Yes, she said, her heart sinking still further. Thank you.

The request to ring James felt like an accusation. Even worse, one that she deserved. She had been so busy last night enjoying herself in the company of this other man that she had forgotten – or, anyway, had not bothered – to ring her husband.

She went to the telephone, then found she had no change and so had to go into the dining-room where Bill was lounging with a newspaper.

'Ah. Morning,' he said, looking up. There was something questioning about the way he observed her, something slightly too animated about his smile, which made her feel oh no, was I as bad as all that? She had embarrassed him with her show of affection and her all too obvious wish for . . . well, for what? Had she really been wanting to sleep with him? Been trying to lure him into her room?

Yes or no, it was the impression she must have given, frightening him off, making him wonder what kind of a mother-turned-whore he'd got himself involved with here.

Now she, too, was embarrassed. 'Have you any change please?' she said, striving to sound matter of fact. 'I need to ring James.'

'Yes, I think . . .' he said and begun fumbling in his pockets. The newspaper, which he had placed on the table, shed two of its pages which slipped to the floor.

'Oh, I'm sorry – '

'No, no – '

And they bent together to retrieve them so that their faces were suddenly uncomfortably close. She straightened up quickly and let him pick up the pages of newspaper. She felt awkward and clumsy and wanted to run from the room but now had to wait until he had produced a handful of change which he spread on the table-cloth so that she could select the two-franc pieces she needed.

372

She thanked him and promised to repay him and hurried out to the telephone. Even the simplest of transactions were beginning to prove difficult and beyond her. And now what would she say to James? That he had been right and she should never had come?

Well, no, not that. Not yet anyway. It was only Day Two. Surely her resolve could stretch for another few hours?

She dialled her own number, hoping he would have left for work, but no. 'Hello, it's me,' she said, hearing his voice.

'Lauren . . . ! What's happened? I mean how are you? Are you all right?'

His desperation exasperated her. It had been only one day that she hadn't rung him. Twenty-four hours, or anyway not many more than that. Why did he have to react as though his life were threatened unless he were constantly hearing her voice? 'I'm all right, yes. I'm fine,' she said, trying to sound it. He was the one who should have been supporting her, encouraging her; while all he did was make her feel guilty, as though she were doing all this deliberately to hurt him. 'And how're you?'

'I'm all right. Have you been to the house?'

'Where Adam is, yes. But I haven't been in and I haven't spoken to anybody.' She wasn't going to tell him what it was like, the fact that it wasn't a house at all but a fortress. To do so would be to admit that he might have been right and that she was wasting her time, and she wasn't going to do that.

Didn't he understand how his tone of shrill accusation only repelled her further and made it impossible for her to confide in him?

'Have you seen Adam?'

'No. Not yet.'

'So what are you going to do?' Then, thankfully, he saved her having to reply – since she didn't know what she was going to do – by going on: 'Though you know what I think. That you shouldn't do anything at all but should get yourself back here. I had Stella on the phone last night – '

'Stella?'

'Yes.'

'You told her?'

'No. No, she said she was just ringing to find out how we were, and then, when she asked if she could speak to you, I had to tell her that you were out, that you'd gone out to a friend's – '

'Good.' She was grateful for that at least.

'Well, yes, but I can't keep doing that. Can't you see? The longer you stay away, sooner or later somebody's going to realize that there's something wrong. They're going to think that you've . . . well, I don't know, that you've left me or something.'

'I haven't.'

'Well, I know. That's not the point . . . '

She held the receiver away from her ear, letting him go on. Thinking – why does this man make it so hard for me to love him? Does he really believe I can simply give up and return without our son?

What does he imagine such a return would be like?

She spoke into the mouthpiece. 'James, listen. I have to go.'

'What? Why, what – '

'Sorry but I'll ring you tomorrow, I promise.'

'Lauren – '

'Bye.'

And she rang off.

'Oh, shit,' she said aloud. Meaning why did he have to make it so that she didn't want to speak to

374

him? She turned towards the dining-room, then said, 'Shit,' again, thinking of the other man waiting there for her, her embarrassed companion of last night.

She had an impression of the growing complexity of everything. That simple idea with which she had begun – to take Adam back by any means – was fracturing and fragmenting, and with it went the power it had given her.

She parked in the same spot as yesterday. Though at least today she had had the foresight to pick up some fruit and drinks on her way. She wouldn't suffer the same ordeal of slow dehydration. Otherwise, everything suggested it was going to be a repeat performance. The walls showed no signs of crumbling or the house of giving up its secrets. Approaching lunchtime, she had recorded only a couple of vehicles arriving and being admitted, then leaving again. No sign of anyone who might have been Revachier, and certainly no sign of Adam.

The nurses would presumably once again change shift in the early afternoon, though she could hardly risk another conversation. It might even be wise to avoid being seen altogether. If the same nurse were to see her parked there again, she might begin to wonder.

Lauren thought of what Bill had said last night – while she had still been rational and before her emotions had driven her loopy – what he had said about bribing one of the nurses or even attempting to recruit one of them onto their side. Perhaps as a desperate last resort they might try it though it still struck her as unlikely to succeed.

But certainly it was the nurses who looked after Adam and so they who might be the key to all this.

They were responsible for him and must sometimes be left alone with him. Could she turn this to her advantage?

But she couldn't see how, even after considering it for most of the morning, and still felt as though she were beating with tiny fists against defences of oak.

It was nearly mid-day, cooler than yesterday with a mackerel sky. Bill had suggested joining her for lunch again and she had agreed, wanting to put their relationship back on an easier footing than that first awkward encounter in the dining-room. He had been folding up his newspaper and ready to leave when she had gone back in after her telephone conversation with James, so they had said little beyond her agreeing to his joining her later.

She could see all too well that he must have been thrown by her behaviour. First doing everything to shake him off then, on the strength of a Chinese meal and a few bottles of beer, becoming close and affectionate. Probably scaring the poor man to death.

She smiled at the thought, though it had dismayed her, and still did, to discover how vulnerable she was. How much she needed an ally. That was it really, she supposed. Not so much the effect of the drink or that she fancied him but that he was the only one she had to turn to in this crazy undertaking. The tougher it became, the more she needed his shoulder to cry on.

Poor man. Probably regretting his impulse to follow her.

Though there he was now, the red car pulling up behind her. At least he hadn't given up on her and fled. She reached over and pushed open the passenger door for him to climb in.

376

'Pizza,' he said, holding out a flat cardboard box.

'Oh, well done.'

'I didn't know how you liked it, so I got a selection. Just help yourself.'

They wedged the box on the dashboard so that the pizza slices were displayed. The heat from them misted the windscreen. Though what did it matter when there was so little to be seen anyway?

'So how's it going?'

She shook her head, chewing on the wedge she had chosen, the one with chillis. 'Nothing.'

'They're not making it easy, are they.'

It occurred to her that there was something she must say. 'Look, I don't want you to feel, you know, *committed* to all this. I mean you've been great and I'll always be grateful but whenever you want to take off, well ... ' It was easier to say sitting side-by-side, not having to face him. 'I mean I don't want you to feel ... *responsible*.'

That was it, she felt she had got it about right: giving him the chance to make his excuses and leave should he wish to.

'And then who'd bring you lunch?'

'No, but I'm serious – '

'I know but ... ' She turned towards him and saw that he was in earnest, chosing his words, trying to impress on her that he was committed to seeing this through, whatever she might say. 'I'm quite keen on seeing that son of yours myself. So I'll just hang around for a bit longer if you don't mind.'

'Oh, I don't mind – '

'Then it's settled. In fact, I was going to suggest that I should take over there for a while. Just in case they have noticed you or they've noticed your car. Yes?'

She hesitated, not wanting to take advantage but

377

all the same seeing the sense in it and already uneasy about being there when the nurses came and went in case she should be recognized again. 'Well, perhaps just for a couple of hours – '

'Take as long as you like.'

And so it was arranged that she would take her car and go back to the hotel, or simply take herself off for a wander somewhere, while he would remain in his and continue to keep watch. 'And, if I see Adam, I'll give him your love,' he joked, as he closed the door on her and went back to his own car. At least now she felt that the embarrassment that had tinged their dealings that morning had been left well-and-truly behind them.

As she came out of the cul-de-sac, she passed the deux-chevaux Citroen bringing the nurse in her red-and-blue uniform. It had been a close shave then. Another five or ten minutes and her colleague would be leaving.

To help while away the time, Bill had brought with him copies of the Herald Tribune and Time magazine. He made a start on the Herald Tribune, conscientiously lowering it every minute or two to check that nothing new was happening in the vicinity of maison Revachier.

Not that he was expecting much. They might as well have been trying to spring the child from a maximum security prison. His main concern was how Lauren would react as this fact was forced upon her. To what desperate measures might she resort as her frustrations got the better of her? He had already wondered whether, instead of aiding and abetting, he shouldn't be trying to make her face up to reality, abandon the attempt and go home.

Then had decided that there was no point. Firstly, because she wouldn't listen; and, secondly, he would immediately lose the confidence and trust he felt she had placed in him. He would be revealing himself as faint-hearted, a traitor to the cause.

And then last night. Well.

He had longed to hold her, to feel her body against his and had even begun to think that it was what was in her mind too, but then they had arrived back in the hotel and his conscience had begun to nag at him – wouldn't he simply be taking advantage of her vulnerability? After all, she was a married woman seeking her child . . .

The sound of the passenger door opening made him turn in surprise. A young man was bending, looking into the car. 'Excuse me, monsieur – '

Then the other door, at his right elbow, was wrenched open and another, older man was crouched beside him, staring. Bill felt a sudden, sickening rush of fear, knowing he was trapped but not yet by whom.

'We just want to see your hands,' said the older man, speaking in French. 'Just let go of the newspaper and put your hands on the steering-wheel.' One of his own hands was thrusting forward inside the pocket of his leather jacket, suggesting he might have been holding a gun.

'All right,' said Bill, pushing the newspaper aside and letting his hands rest on the steering-wheel. 'Yes, fine.'

'Now get out of the car. But slowly and carefully.'

They were either policemen or Revachier's henchmen. Preferably police though he doubted it. 'Look, what is this . . . ?' he began to protest, but got no reply. He could make a scene and shout for help, but he didn't fancy the consequences if no help came. The younger one had come around the front of the car so that there was one of them on each side of him. He was roughly turned and made to stand with his hands on the car roof while they frisked him.

'OK,' said the older one. 'Now just walk on. Nice and slowly.'

Pushing him towards the house.

30

Going through the gates, Bill thought well, I've got myself inside. Now let's concentrate on getting out again.

Was he in any real danger? Could he be, here in neutral, neutralised, deodorised Switzerland with the United Nations complex no more than a few kilometres away?

It depended on what they knew. Whether they'd simply noticed him on their cameras and decided that this was some bozo loitering with intent who needed to be scared rigid and sent on his way or whether they were smarter than he and Lauren had realized and had somehow picked up on Lauren and her madcap scheme to free her son.

At any rate he no longer held out much hope that these were policemen walking behind him and giving him a prod if he slowed down. Something about their demeanour suggested they were at home here. This was their territory, or anyway territory they were paid to protect.

Seen from the inside, the forbidding walls were largely hidden by trees and greenery so that the place had the air of a country retreat, a gentleman's residence. There was a stable-block away to the left, from where he could hear dogs barking. The two men walked him up the drive, to the front of the house, which was of stone, with a wooden verandah. One of them pushed open the large front door and Bill stumbled forward into a lofty hallway. Details blurred as his eyes sought to adjust after the outside glare but he was aware of a marble floor, on which his trainers gave a slight squeak as he moved, and a curving staircase rising ahead of him.

'Wait,' said the older of the two men, then conferred with his companion in lowered tones. After which, the younger one went off down a corridor. The older one folded his arms and remained where he was, between Bill and the door, chewing slowly.

Bill looked around him. There were modernist pictures on the walls, carefully hung, each with its own light above, and some small pieces of abstract sculpture standing on plinths. It might have been the lobby to an art gallery or a culturally-conscious embassy.

Don't be intimidated by it, he told himself, the big house with its objets d'art and the heavies to guard it. I'm innocent and I've been forced in here against my will. Indignation was called for, a belated attempt to stand his ground.

'Look, what is all this – '

'Quiet,' growled his guard.

'You can't just bring me in here – '

'We already have.' And he pulled a gun from his pocket.

Bill stared open-mouthed and raised his hand in a gesture of surrender. It was also a gesture of surprise, since he hadn't ever been convinced, not really and truly, that the pocket contained an actual gun. But now he had to be since there it was pointing at him, some kind of hand-gun he couldn't identify. He went back to looking at the sculptures, feeling himself to be sweating heavily.

382

The younger of his two escorts returned. 'In there,' he said, nodding towards an open door. Bill held up his hands to show that he was willing to co-operate and, with the two of them on his heels, stepped forward into what seemed to be some sort of library. Three of the four walls were lined with books; in the centre of the room stood a chess board with its figures in place, ornate and medieval. No photographs though – this was something he noticed – no photographs or any other indication that anybody actually lived there. There were arm-chairs and a springy maroon carpet on the floor. His two custodians stood just inside the doorway in attitudes of waiting. As though they weren't commis-sioned to do any more than hold him here and were waiting for further orders or, more likely, for some-one else to arrive. The older one had tucked the gun back into his pocket.

They were, Bill realized, as uneasy about being there, inside the house, as he was. They were no longer smiling, enjoying the game, as they had been when they had lifted him from the car, but were looking sullen and impatient as if eager to get this over with and be outside again.

Bugger this, he thought. Gun or no gun, he had played the compliant victim for long enough. He walked over to one of the armchairs and sat down in it.

He saw his two captors come to life, take a step forward, then stop and exchange a glance. 'Stand up,' said the older one.

'No, I'm all right as I am, thank you,' he said, defiant now that he had sussed out that they didn't really know what they were doing with him.

They looked at one another again but he saw that they weren't going to make an issue of it. He could

383

sit there if he wanted to. He could probably do anything he wanted to, save walk out. There was still some test to be passed, some trial yet to be made of him.

He heard the sudden sound of footsteps in the hallway and another man entered the room. A man who was perhaps in his forties, well-built, wearing tan-coloured slacks, a white shirt, a tie with some sort of insignia on it but no jacket. Bill's two captors straightened slightly and turned so that they were facing him.

Revachier, thought Bill. So this is the man himself, arms-dealer, art-collector and kidnapper.

'Monsieur Revachier . . . ?' he said, leaping from the chair and holding out his hand.

'I am, yes. More to the point, who are you?' Though without taking the proffered hand, clasping his own behind him.

'Sangster. Bill Sangster. I'm a journalist from England.' He would stick to the truth as far as he could and blessed the fact that he had rung Julia and got her to feed him some information on this man, information that might just see him through, help him give some substance to the cover story that was already forming in his head.

'English?'

'Yes.'

'And what were you doing watching my house?'

'Well, no. No, I wasn't watching it – '

'You've been parked out there for the past two hours.'

'As long as that? Well, yes – '

'Why?'

There was something faintly imperious about the man, as though this questioning were distasteful to him, the kind of thing he usually delegated to others. Bill found himself disliking him and was glad of it.

'Why? Oh, well, because, like I say, I'm a journal-ist and what I'm doing, I'm working on a series of articles, one of which I hoped might be about you. The general theme is the pattern of armament sales. Which part of the globe supplies which other part of the globe and something about the major players in the game. Which is why I was out there, just sort of getting my act together, before contacting you in the hope that you might agree to be interviewed. And then, well . . . these gentlemen here have saved me the trouble.' Smiling round at his guards, who stared sullenly back.

'And there was also a woman . . . ?' said Re-vachier, sounding unimpressed by what he had heard so far. He turned to the guards for confirma-tion and they nodded and muttered that yes, there had also been a woman, who had been there before this man had arrived and who had since departed in a car of her own.

'She's my assistant,' said Bill. 'She had some material for me and . . . well, we just arranged to meet up here, that's all.'

It was beginning to sound less plausible, even to himself. He had been hoping that they hadn't seen Lauren. The idea of her as his assistant struck him as weak but it was all he could come up with.

Revachier walked across the room and stared out of the tall windows. As though trying to make up his mind. Bill sensed that things hung in the balance. At least no-one had mentioned the cars being out-side there yesterday as well as today, which gave his story a fighting chance. He tried to remember what else Julia had told him.

'I read the article on you that was in the Sunday Telegraph magazine, some two years ago I think it was – '

'Have you any identification?' said Revachier.

'Yes, I've, er ... ' He produced his battered N.U.J. pass from his wallet and held it out. the younger guard took it from him and gave it to Revachier, who glanced at it then handed it back to the younger guard, who handed it back to Bill. 'Thank you.'

'Have you searched him?' Revachier asked. The guards assured him that they had, and found nothing. Then looked nonplused at his next question: 'And did you search the car?'

'No, I don't think you did, did you?' said Bill helpfully, enjoying their discomfort.

'Go and do it,' said Revachier. 'Both of you.'

They nodded and left the room.

He quickly tried to assess what they might find. Not a lot, just the junk that had accumulated during the trip across France. Nothing that he could imagine might be incriminating unless ... an awful thought struck him. Unless Lauren had returned and was out there waiting. Then they would be sunk and no mistake. She could hardly confirm a story that she hadn't heard. He could only keep his fingers crossed that she wouldn't have returned – please God she wouldn't have returned – and meanwhile keep Revachier guessing by continuing to play the pushy journalist.

'And so would it be possible to interview you, monsieur?'

'I'm afraid not.'

'The article wouldn't be hostile. As I say, it's an attempt to profile some of the leading players in the world's arms – '

'I don't give interviews.'

'Ah. A pity. Only I thought you might have welcomed the chance to give your side of the story.'

Revachier turned away and went back to gazing out of the window.

'You have a lovely house,' said Bill, to fill the silence that had descended. The other man made no reply. Arrogant bastard, thought Bill. 'And a lovely garden.' He looked past him, sharing his view through the tall window.

And saw, out there on the lawn, a pram was standing and beside it, sitting in a wickerwork garden chair, a uniformed nurse was holding a bottle and offering it to the small child that she was cradling.

It was Lauren's child, he realized with a shock; it had to be. And here he was, being given an unimpeded view of it while Lauren had waited and suffered and longed for such a moment but hadn't had even the most distant of sightings. Mind, when he considered how she might have reacted if she had been with him and seen what he was now seeing . . .! Perhaps better it had been him alone.

There were now footsteps hurrying through the hallway, reviving his fears that she might have returned and encountered Revachier's henchmen. He strained to catch whether it was two sets of footsteps or three.

But mercifully it was only the two guards, hurrying in and reporting to Revachier that they had searched the car and found nothing of significance. The documents in the glove-compartment established that it was a hire-car, currently being used by someone called William Sangster.

'Me,' offered Bill, feeling as if the jury had returned and declared in his favour. Relieved to the point where he was now even beginning to enjoy the whole escapade that had given him this privileged access.

387

Revachier nodded to the guards and turned to Bill. 'I am sorry,' he said. 'This seems to have been something of a misunderstanding.'

Though his attitude and his dry tone suggested that he was unlikely to lose any sleep over it: indeed, it seemed to blame Bill for the whole silly waste of time.

'Oh, that's all right – '

'I'm sorry if you have been inconvenienced.'

'Not at all. Though I would still be interested in doing that interview if you – '

But Revachier was already leaving the room, saying something to the guards about seeing the journalist off the premises.

'I assume that means no,' said Bill to nobody in particular.

'Let's go,' said the older of the guards, and they went out through the hallway and down the drive towards the gates, Bill now walking slowly, in no hurry to leave, wondering what else he might spot before he was ejected. The library windows must have been to the side of the house, looking out onto a stretch of the garden now out of his view for he could see nothing further of the child and his nurse.

'I noticed that you have a baby here,' he commented to his escorts, but they wouldn't be drawn, saying only yes, there was a baby there all right, and then staying stubbornly by his side until he was out through the gates and onto the roadway.

Lauren had used her time away from the house – time off duty as she thought of it – to wrestle with the idea that she might somehow use the nurses to gain access to Adam. After all, they were the ones employed to care for him; they presumably often had him to themselves. Yet she still could see no

388

way of turning that to her advantage. Sitting by the lakeside, she directed her increasing frustration at the stream of tourists passing before her, cameras slung like identity badges around their necks. She wanted to shake them out of their contentment and tell them of the injustice she was suffering.

The one thing that did occur to her was that, if the agency were a large one, it was likely that the nurses would not necessarily all know one another. They would operate from a central office and perhaps only meet occasionally, when changing shifts. Which meant . . . well, no, she didn't know what it meant; she couldn't make it mean anything that might offer her an advantage.

She forced herself to remain there for an hour, sitting in the sunshine, then went back to her car and took the now familiar route out of the city and back to the house. Though it was a surprise, pulling into the Rue des Monts, to see Bill, not in his car but walking towards it. He seemed just as surprised to see her and quickened his step so that he was beside her open window as she stopped.

'We can't stay here,' he said urgently. 'I'll see you back at the hotel.'

Now, close-up, she saw that he wasn't so much surprised as alarmed. So had something happened during her absence? 'But why – '

'They're onto us. Tell you later. Only they're probably watching so let's go.'

Now she was alarmed also, not knowing what to make of this. She looked towards the house but could see no-one. Bill had gone to his own car and was getting in. She waited until he pulled away and then, feeling she had little choice and now desperate to hear what he might have to tell her, followed him as he turned and led her out onto the Route de Fernay.

She wanted to know everything. Immediately. What it had been like inside the house, what Revachier had been like and what he had said. Listening to Bill, she had to repress a feeling of envy, that it was he who had been frog-marched inside instead of her. The ridiculous thought even came into her head that he had got rid of her on purpose, knowing what was to happen, but of course that was absurd, he couldn't have. And she could appreciate that it must have been terrifying having the gun flourished in front of him and wondering all the time how much they knew.

They were sitting on the terrace of the hotel, having a coffee, with few other people around but for a rowdy group of youths drinking beer and saying goodbye to their girl-friends. Going back to the army by the look of their haircuts.

She saw that Bill was regarding her strangely, as if he were hiding something or was about to announce something that he knew would surprise her.

'What?' she demanded impatiently. 'What is it?'

'I, er . . . I saw Adam.'

She stared and gave a small gasp.

'He was outside, being fed by one of the nurses. I saw him through a window.'

'Adam . . . ?' she cried. 'You actually . . . ?'

'Not close to. He was, what, about twenty yards away.'

She could only shake her head, overcome by the thought and near to tears. She didn't know whether she was delighted by this first, precious sighting of the son she had come so far to find or whether she was dismayed that it hadn't been she who had seen him. Both. Everything. She didn't know what she was feeling.

'Anyway, he looked at though he was being taken

390

good care of. I didn't really get chance to notice anything else.'

'No,' she said, making an effort to control her emotions. 'But was he . . . ' What did she want to know? What was she asking? 'Was he . . . did he look well?'

'Yes. Fine,' said Bill, and gave an apologetic shrug: sorry, but that was all he could report.

Well, yes. To him Adam must have looked just like any another baby. And of course it was good to know that he was being well cared for; and to have it confirmed beyond all doubt that he was there inside the house and not thousands of miles away. She must count her blessings; try and concentrate not on how much she had missed out on but on how much they had achieved in the short time they had been here.

'And so,' she said, trying to remember where they were in the narrative before Bill had shaken her with his casual, devastating announcement, 'so they believed you were just there as a journalist – '

He nodded. 'Wanting to do a feature on arms sales. Which Revachier didn't want to know about. Which was probably a good thing, since I wouldn't have had a clue if he'd said OK, what d'you want to know.'

'What was he like?' Not that it altered anything, whatever he was like; still, she felt a curiosity about her elusive opponent.

'Revachier? Oh, well . . . a man who takes himself seriously. I mean very much seemed to be master of all he surveys. I didn't like him. But then I wouldn't, would I. I'm on the wrong side.' He gave her a smile to go with this, which she returned. 'No, but I'd say he's intelligent and probably quite hard, quite ruthless. I don't know why I say that – just the way

391

everybody seemed in awe of him. And I should think . . . I should think he's a man who's difficult to get close to.'

She nodded, glad if anything that the verdict was unsympathetic. At least she didn't feel obliged to try and understand him or recognize his point-of-view.

'But I'll tell you this,' said Bill. 'He's on his guard against something. Perhaps he's afraid that somebody might try and take the child off him, I don't know. Perhaps he's just paranoid anyway. But my guess is that we're not going to see little Adam outside of those walls, not if we sit there for a month of Sundays.'

He grimaced slightly, as if it hurt him to deliver such an unfavourable verdict. She nodded, unable to deny the probable truth of it, then looked away, not wanting him to see her distress. The youths were wandering off in the direction of the railway station, rucksacks on their backs and arms around their girl-friends. The terrace felt suddenly silent and empty.

'And another thing,' said Bill, sounding like a man determined to get all the bad news over with at once. 'I don't think it'd be wise for us to go back there. They might have swallowed my story once, but if they spot us out there again . . . no chance. And, anyway, I don't know that there's much purpose to be served. I don't see that we're ever going to learn anything that we don't already know.'

'No.'

He looked at her in surprise, as though he had been expecting her to contradict him. Then he said, 'So what to do now . . . ?' And waited.

She shook her head, meaning that she didn't know either. She felt in a limbo between success and failure. Weightless, floating, not knowing where she would come to earth. They had located Adam and even, via Bill, entered the house and seen him. Progress beyond her wildest dreams. And still Revachier did not know that she was in Geneva, planning on retrieving her child. It was all there to play for, if only she could see a way forward.

What she did know suddenly was that she wanted to be alone with her thoughts, her muddled, unhappy thoughts, and have some space and time to see where they might lead her. She pushed aside her coffee cup. 'I think I might go for a walk.'

'You want me to come with you?'

'No. If you don't mind, I think I'd rather – '

But he was already holding up a hand, accepting that. 'Sure. Whatever.'

'I'll see you later.' Then added, lest that should sound like some kind of brush-off, 'Tonight. I'll see you tonight.'

As she was leaving the table, he said, 'You're not going back to the house?'

And, because she wasn't and hadn't even considered doing so, she was able to look him in the eye and say, 'No. No, I'm just going ... well, I don't know where. Just somewhere to think.'

Watching her go, he wondered whether she would ever be able to come to terms with the hopelessness of her situation. Would she linger on here until a shortage of money or some other crisis forced her to return home or did she have it in her to face up to reality, cut her losses and go of her own accord?

He regretted that he couldn't have given her a more optimistic assessment of their prospects but to have done so would have been fooling her and fooling himself into the bargain. Sooner or later, she would have to return to England and to her husband. He regretted that as well. Face it, he had gone from admiring her to being fond of her, dangerously fond of her.

Time to call it a day for all sorts of reasons.

He decided he might as well enjoy the fag-end of the afternoon, collected the Herald Tribune and the copy of Time magazine from his car and walked to the Parc Mon Repos. Then read neither of them but fell asleep on the grass and awoke to find himself chilled. The sun was beginning to spread itself over the distant mountains. He looked at his watch and saw to his surprise that it was a quarter to six. The strollers were out with their dogs. As he walked back towards the hotel, a group of brightly-dressed youths came swishing past him on their skateboards.

Collecting his keys, he was reminded that tonight was the last night of their original booking. So they had judged it about right then. Three days to give themselves a chance of success or, as it had turned out, to discover that they hadn't one.

To satisfy her conscience, she had rung James but then, within a minute of getting through to him, had wished that she hadn't bothered. He had launched into his familiar, whining attack – what was she doing there? how soon would she be home? – forcing her onto the defensive and making her lie to him. Well, not lie exactly but become evasive when it came to telling him just what it was she had been doing. Nothing much, she said, gritting her teeth, she had just been hanging around, seeing the sights. Which only provoked him into more questions: So what was the point of her being there at all? Didn't she see that she was endangering everything and all for no good reason, as she was as good as admitting herself? On and on. Defending desperately, she said that being here, in Geneva, she at least felt close to Adam. Never mind anything else, it was doing her good just being here.

And she had more or less rung off on that. Aware that once again she hadn't mentioned Bill's presence. And pausing to wonder for a moment just why not. What was it she would have been confessing to?

She went to the bar and ordered herself a white wine. She wasn't going to let James upset her, not tonight, her last night in Geneva.

She saw Bill in the doorway and waved to him. 'Let me get you a drink,' she said as he arrived beside her. 'What would you like?'

'Oh, a beer please,' he said, looking at her in barely concealed surprise.

He must have been expecting to find me depressed, she thought, distraught even. She smiled to herself. She wasn't going to enlighten him, not yet.

'So where did you get to?' he asked.

'Oh, I just followed the shore for, well, I don't know how far. I was walking for a couple of hours. And then, when I thought I was going to have to walk all the way back, I found I was at a landing-stage from where there was a regular boat service. Brought me right back to the quayside and only cost four francs.'

'Been doing some sight-seeing after all then,' he said in a gently teasing tone.

'I suppose I have.'

'Good. And so what's on the menu for tonight? You want to eat here or go out somewhere?'

His look of surprise returned when she opted for going out. Nowhere posh though, she said. Couldn't they just try a few bars and see where they ended up?

Where they ended up first was a bar called La Samba, where a couple of black barmen were supervised by a tiny, white woman balanced on a stool beside the till. There was Latin-American music playing and some stuffed – or plastic? – snakes curling around the pipes overhead. They settled at a table with their drinks and Bill said, 'So have you decided anything?'

'Yes.'

He waited, then said, 'Well? You're going to tell me?'

'I'm not leaving here without Adam,' she said quietly. 'Even if it takes . . . well, forever.'

'Oh.'

He looked disappointed. He had obviously taken her mood to mean that she had shaken off her obsession or at least had abandoned any thoughts of direct action in favour of letting the law take its course. Anyway, he seemed dismayed. She felt sorry for him, knowing how much he was concerned for her, worried about what desperate measures she might be considering.

With good reason, if only he knew.

'And so what, er . . . I mean do you have anything specific in mind?'

She nodded and allowed herself a small smile. 'Huh-huh.'

'You're going to tell me?'

'Later. When we've had something to eat.'

They left La Samba and meandered through the narrow streets of the Old Town, settling eventually in a cafe-cum-bar where they ordered Mexican tortillas and a bottle of Chablis. She found herself doing most of the talking. Well, all of the talking. She talked about her past, the life she had led before all this, with Bill nodding and listening as though fascinated by the merest detail. Could he be or was he just indulging her, happy to keep her away from the one subject that dominated all others? She told him stories about the garage, the intricacies of the second-hand market, the pecking order of the dealer-ships. He said I see and Really? and Wow. She gave him accounts of scams and disasters and then a veritable lecture on the art of selling. Was she really such an expert? She heard her own voice, slightly high and excited-sounding. Perhaps she was drunk or, anyway, on the way to being drunk. She ordered a strega with her coffee to help her along.

They came out of the restaurant into a night that was suddenly bedecked with stars. 'Oh, aren't they lovely!' she cried, opening her arms. Knowing what she was doing, (perhaps she hadn't before but now – oh, yes), in fact being brazen about it and so not surprised in the least when she felt his arms going around her and saw his face approaching.

His kiss was tentative, as though even now he wasn't sure. 'Oh, yes,' she said, 'yes.' Making him kiss her again, knowing that she was wicked and could do with him what she liked.

'Lauren – ' he muttered.

'Come on,' she said and grabbed his hand.

'What?' he said, surprised yet again.

'Well, we're not doing it out here. Not when we've two bedrooms!'

Had she said that? What was happening to her? Whatever it was felt delicious and couldn't be stopped.

They walked quickly through the streets, bodies bumping and touching at every step. She wasn't aware of the route yet there they were suddenly at the hotel, their reflections again appearing in the glass doors. Amazingly, the bored-looking girl behind reception who handed them their keys seemed oblivious to the passion hanging in the air between them.

They moved to the lift but had to wait while it descended. Oh, no, thought Lauren, he'll have qualms and start asking me if I really want to do this, and then what will I answer? But he had said nothing by the time the lift came and then they were inside it. She punched the button and held her breath till the doors were closing and no-one else had appeared and they could begin kissing again.

The lift stopped with a ping and they tumbled out. Her room? His room? But he said, 'Mine,' and led her past her own door and along the corridor.

Good, she thought – since that made it even more wicked. Going to his room made her the seducer.

He opened the door and they were inside. She saw his hand going to the light switch and caught hold of it. The room had a late-evening gloom about it which seemed appropriate for what they were up to. They were kissing again and she thought – we'll have to stop this, for a few minutes at least, or we'll never get anywhere. And so broke away and moved to the bed, still feeling brazen in the darkness.

He followed her and began to fumble with her clothes, the buttons on her shirt. 'Let me,' she said, taking over from his awkward fingers.

He cleared his throat. 'Yes.' And began to undress himself.

But she was the quicker, shedding her clothes onto the floor. She crawled onto the bed and pulled a sheet over her. Then wondered why she had bothered, it seemed such a token gesture towards modesty, and threw it off again. He lowered himself to land beside her, suddenly huge and naked, and, with a few adjustments of arms and legs, they came together at last.

'Lauren – ' he said, his voice throaty, but she put her fingers to his lips, not wanting promises or protestations, just wanting . . . yes, that was it. Wanting that. As his hands ran down her body like two inquisitive creatures following a scent or a stream to its source.

'So now are you going to tell me?' he asked in the darkness.

And she did.

31

She awoke in the early hours, hot and sweaty, with a dull headache and dry mouth from the drinking. Lying beside her and with one hand resting on her shoulder, Bill was sleeping heavily.

She carefully lifted his hand, slid from beneath it and placed it on her pillow. He grunted and turned slightly but remained asleep. She slowly raised herself from the bed and stood for a moment, grateful for the cool air from the window on her naked body. Then, moving with an exaggerated caution, holding her breath even, she felt around on the floor for her clothes and pulled them on. Picking up her shoes, she crossed the room, opened the door onto a lighted corridor, stepped out and eased the door closed behind her, hearing the lock click into place.

Padding along the corridor back to her own room, she thought – I have been unfaithful to James after nine years of marriage. In a cheap hotel with a man I hardly know or, anyway, have known only for a short time.

Yet she didn't feel any real anguish or regret. She had done no more than she had wanted and, in truth, she couldn't convince herself that it affected her relationship with James in the slightest.

She fell, unwashed, into her own bed. Beyond the

window a train was arriving in the station. Tomorrow was nearly upon them, when she would either regain her son or be forced to recognize that she had lost him forever. Whether she could then return to her husband or whether she would want to stay with Bill . . . her thoughts growing wilder and less coherent as she was overtaken by sleep.

She was in the dining-room before him, knowing how much there was much to do before her plan could be put into effect. And it had to be done that morning: they must be in position for early afternoon or the opportunity would be lost, perhaps forever.

She was excited and anxious about what lay ahead and so didn't have the time to go picking over last night to see how much she regretted or was ashamed of or wanted to forget. That was already history and would have to wait till she had time in hand before she might consider it and wonder about her own behaviour. For now she could think only of the future, so preoccupied with re-running the details of her strategy in her own head, searching for the flaw that might prove her undoing, that she didn't see Bill arrive until he was pulling out the chair opposite her.

'Oh,' she said, startled.

He leaned over and kissed her. 'Guess what,' he said. 'I woke up this morning and the lady had gone.'

She smiled, relieved that the episode could be referred to lightly. She didn't want a post mortem. Whatever demon had been driving her last night had been sated and now the morning had come with urgent demands of its own.

'I know,' she said. 'I just . . . just thought it better.'

401

'After all, we were paying for two rooms,' he said wrily. The waiter arrived with a jug of coffee and filled Bill's cup. 'So then, you still want to go ahead with this crazy plan of yours?'

'Yes,' she said, and was visited with a new anxiety: was he having second thoughts, wanting to back out now that they had come to the crunch?

He gave a groan of mock-dismay. 'Then I'd better eat a hearty breakfast.'

She saw that he was only teasing her. So that was all right then: he was still with her, still on her side.

'We've only got, what, four hours, four-and-a-half at the most, before the nurses change shift,' she said, wanting to convey her sense of urgency. The minutes already felt to be seeping away. 'And by then I've got to be there with uniform and everything, otherwise forget it.'

'OK, OK,' he said, tearing into a roll. 'So what's first? I have to get another car . . . ?'

'Yes. Well, don't you think – '

But he was already nodding in agreement. 'I'll do it. Just one cup of coffee and then I'll be onto it.'

They had gone over the entire business in bed last night – lying together, heads close on the pillow – and agreed that it would be best to have a car with local plates; and one that wouldn't be identifiable by Revachier's mafiosa. 'OK, give me five minutes,' said Bill, draining his coffee. Better than his word, he was back in four, telling her that he had reserved a car with Hertz, who had an office at the railway station and so were no more than a few minutes away.

'Oh, great,' she said, surprised by the ease of the transaction. Was it a sign that the gods were on their side, that the whole scam was going to go like clockwork?

402

'So remind me,' said Bill, settling down again at the table. 'I'm supposed to be some sort of rep for a clothing firm . . . ?'

'Yes.'

'So what's the firm called?'

'Oh, anything,' she said, unable to come up with a name.

'Did I tell you that it was my father's line of business, textile manufacturing?'

'Really?'

'Yes.'

She wasn't sure whether this was something that was evoking painful memories or whether he found it an amusing quirk of fate. 'Well, look,' she said to distract him, and also because it was a problem that had just occurred to her, 'we really should get you kitted out in something reppy, I mean a suit or – '

'You're serious?'

'Bill, nobody's going to believe you if you go in looking like that.'

'We'll call the firm Eaglesham Leisurewear and tell them that this is all the latest in men's casuals.'

But she wasn't in the mood for jokes; there wasn't time. She stood up. 'Please. Only if we're going to do this, then we've got to – '

'Yes, OK, OK.' Now he was standing too and following her out of the dining-room. 'Look, don't we have to check out first?'

'When we come back,' she said, without stopping so that he had no option but to follow her through reception and out through the glass doors. They had to hurry. The long hours of the past two days, all that sitting around and killing time, had now been replaced by a countdown she could almost hear, a metronome inside her head.

The air outside was already warm and the sky

above a clear blue. It was going to be blisteringly hot realized Lauren as she strode briskly along the pavement. Was that in their favour?

They came to a gents' outfitters, mercifully empty at that time of day so that within minutes Bill had been provided with a navy-blue blazer, grey slacks, a white shirt and striped tie. They had a small confrontation as to who should pay for everything, both offering their credit cards. The salesman discreetly busied himself elsewhere while they argued, Bill claiming that he could well afford to pay for his own clothes and she telling him that these were clothes he would never wear again – she knew that – and so that it was right she should pay for them. 'Oh, and you need some shoes,' she added. 'You can't go around in trainers with this lot.' It opened the way for a compromise: she would allow him to pay for the shoes if he would let her pay for everything else. And, though he still wasn't happy, she insisted on that, calling the salesman back and giving him her card. The shoes were chosen and Bill disappeared into a changing-room with the whole outfit, emerging like . . . well, at least more like a sales rep than he had looked earlier in his faded jeans and button-up tee-shirt.

'Very nice,' said Lauren, fighting the impulse to grin.

He grimaced, observing himself in a mirror. 'I feel a prat.'

'Never mind how you feel,' she urged. 'What's important is what you look like.'

'A prat.'

'No, you look very . . . very smart.' Then she could contain herself no longer and gave a shout of laughter.

Bill eyed her balefully. 'You want to be careful. I might just change my mind.'

'No, you won't,' she said, giving him a hug.

Oh, why am I so at ease with this man? she thought. Am I in love with him or – the more pertinent question – would I be if it wasn't for Adam? I need him to help rescue my son and so believe I'm in love with him because otherwise what am I doing but using him, letting him sleep with me to make him more pliable?

All too complicated to resolve.

They stuffed his old clothes into a bag and left the shop, heading back to the hotel. Though there was still more shopping to be done on the way. Despite Bill's protests, Lauren bought him a peaked cap, which was probably meant for yachting but would also do to suggest a chauffeur. 'Every little bit helps,' she said, this time determined not to laugh. She also bought him a pair of dark sunglasses.

And, with the time now approaching ten o'clock, they called in at a mother-and-child shop, the kind she had once haunted when their adoption application had been going through, to buy baby food and drinks, nappies and wipes which she hoped and prayed would be needed for the journey home. It was a sobering experience, bringing back into uncomfortable focus what this was all about.

She also bought a baby-harness, the type that held the child against the mother's breast. Trying it on for size, she was suddenly close to tears. 'Yes,' she said, removing it quickly, 'I'll take that as well.'

She knew that these purchases, made in her own name and using her credit card, would later stand as irrefutable evidence against her, proving malice afore thought, but she didn't care. By the time they came to light, she would be in England with Adam. If she wasn't, then what did anything else matter?

405

They carried their booty back to the hotel. She began to feel panicky, seeing it was almost ten-thirty. All they had done so far had been the easy part – booking the car and embarking on a shopping spree. And still there was the mundane business of checking out of the hotel to be attended to. She settled her bill, which left her with only a couple of hundred pounds in cash – would that be enough? – cleared her room of her belongings, her hands trembling now, and went with Bill to where their cars were parked together, throwing everything into the boot.

'So now shall we – '

'The hire car,' she said, anticipating him. 'Yes.'

They found the Hertz office easily enough but then had to wait because there was someone ahead of them who was complaining endlessly about something or other and questioning the rates he was being charged. Then they had to wait some more while Bill filled in a long form and offered them his passport and his driving licence and his credit card.

It jolted her to realize how easily he, too, would be traced in the aftermath of all this. Whatever happened, however things might turn out, he was putting his neck on the line just as much as she was. And for less reason. Adam wasn't his child and would never be. Nor was he doing it because his journalistic instincts told him it might result in a good story, or for some abstract notion of justice – helping return a child to its rightful parent. No, he was doing it for her.

She was glad they had had at least one night of love together.

'Thank you,' she muttered.

'What for?'

'You don't have to do this.' Keeping her voice low so that the girl behind the desk shouldn't hear.

But he only smiled and said, 'I wouldn't miss it for the world.'

She was overcome by gratitude and hugged him, pressing her face into his new clothes. Then stepped back quickly as the girl was handing over the credit card receipt for him to sign. There was no time for hugs and kisses, not anymore.

Bill was given the keys and they were told where to find the car, which was in a corner of the station car-park. 'Come on,' said Lauren and they hurried through the lines of parked vehicles, dodging back and forth till they spotted the two-tone Audi with the number that matched the tag on the key.

It was this year's model, with a fresh, just-out-of-the-showroom look about it. 'Matches your clothes,' said Lauren, which made him smile. He unlocked the door and leaned in to put the key in the ignition.

'Wait, you want this,' she said and, as he turned back to face her, handed him the card she had been given by the agency nurse, the one that had the address on the Rue de Berne.

'Oh, right, yes. So. Wish me luck.'

'Good luck,' she said solemnly, then they were suddenly in one another's arms, hugging and kissing one another. 'Oh, go on!' she cried, breaking away. 'We haven't time!'

'Where will you be?'

'I'll be . . . ' She didn't know and could only think of the hotel. 'I'll be in the hotel, in the bar.'

'See you there,' he said, and ducked back into the car, pausing for a moment to adjust the driver's seat, then pulling the door closed.

She stood watching as he reversed out of the space. Good luck, she silently repeated, good luck. He gave her a final wave before accelerating away towards the car-park exit, going off in search of the Rue de Berne on which he would find the nursing agency which supplied the young ladies who cared for Adam, working eight-hour shifts, coming and going through the closely-guarded gates in their red-and-blue uniforms.

She had promised to be in the bar and so had to remain there, though it was agony sitting with a cup of unwanted coffee and watching the minutes pass. If only she could have gone to the agency herself, then at least she would have been active, taking her fate into her own hands and not relying on someone else. But, having to be hard-headed about things, she had had to recognize that her French wasn't up to it. Whereas Bill, the superior linguist, might just carry it off.

Her part would come later. Even then her command of French might let her down but there was no avoiding that. Once they reached the gates of the villa Revachier – assuming they ever got that far – then she would be on her own.

It was a quarter past eleven. Then half-past. The waiter retrieved her cup and she ordered a soda-water.

Then suddenly there he was, coming in through reception. She stifled a cry and got to her feet to meet him. He looked hot and bothered, his tie loosened and his new jacket collecting creases. 'Well?' she said, scanning his face for clues.

'I need a drink,' he gasped, flopping down in the seat which had been hers.

'You can have that,' she said, pushing her soda-water towards him. 'Just tell me what happened!' He was nodding, even as he drank, and she dared to hope. 'Yes? You did it?'

'I did it,' he said.

She gave a cry of delight, then looked at her watch: twenty to twelve.

'At least I think I did,' he said. 'I didn't see anybody ringing the police.'

'But you've found out where we can get the uniforms?'

'Yes. They're called Dufours – '

'And where are they?' Wanting to know everything at once, hurrying him along.

'It's all right. They're in Geneva – '

'Wonderful!'

'On the Rue Marziano, wherever that is – '

'We'll find it.'

It was the break she had been praying for, that whoever supplied the uniforms would be on their doorstep and not a hundred miles away, on the other side of Switzerland or in France or Germany even, which would have meant postponing the attempt until tomorrow and so risking the agency becoming suspicious and making enquiries.

'And look,' he said, pulling things from his pockets. 'I managed to appropriate these while the lady's back was turned.' She saw some sheets of notepaper headed 'Agencie de Berne' and a dozen or so printed cards similar to the one she had been given by the nurse on the Rue des Monts.

'Oh, marvellous. Oh, wonderful,' she said and kissed him. 'So now write . . . you know, like we said.' Thrusting the pen on him that she had been keeping ready for the last half-hour.

'OK, OK. So I'm saying . . . what? Please supply the bearer of this letter with a uniform . . . No, I think two uniforms. I don't think any self-respecting nurse would be happy with one – '

'Yes, two,' she said, anxious only that he should write.

'And, er . . . what name? We have to call you something. Nurse . . . ?'

Lauren cast around and said, 'Priestley.'

'Priestley.' Now writing.

'It's the name of our social worker from the adoption agency.'

'I'm sure she won't mind.'

Lauren thought of Stella Priestley and Marjorie Daniels and Vernon Angelis. They seemed characters from a former existence, when the world had been sane and ordered and following the rules brought its own reward.

'Right, there you go,' he said, handing her the letter, which she folded carefully and placed in her pocket. 'Now what?'

'Well, now we need to ring them – '

'Ah, right – '

'Let them know we're coming – '

He no longer needed urging but was moving with her even as they spoke, leaving the bar and hurrying to reception. Heads together, they peered over the telephone directory and found Dufours, Rue Marziano, then she recited the number while he dialled it.

She held her breath. Would this Dufours establishment be open? Might they not have closed for their holidays or for whatever reason? And, even if open, might they not anyway refuse to hand over the uniforms?

But now Bill was speaking in rapid French, explaining that he was ringing from the Agencie de Berne (at which Lauren shot a glance at the girl behind the reception desk, but no, she didn't seem to be taking any particular interest) and that they were in urgent need of uniforms for one of their new recruits. No, it had to be immediately. Today, yes. In fact, would it be possible for the uniforms to be provided within the next hour if the girl were to call in person?

Now he was listening and saying no, no, it would be better if the girl were to call. No, it would not be any trouble. Yes, he appreciated that but ... And finally thanking them in a way that told her they must have agreed.

'OK, let's go,' he said, replacing the receiver.

'They said yes?' she said as, hand-in-hand, they ran from the hotel.

'Yes,' he said, raising his voice over the sound of the traffic. 'Though they were trying to persuade me to give them the measurements over the phone, then they would send out the uniforms by taxi.'

'Oh, no – '

'Well, exactly. But don't worry. They've said yes and they're expecting us.'

His car, the hired Audi, was illegally parked half-way onto the kerb close to the hotel. They piled in and Lauren spread the street map over her knees, tearing it in her haste to get it open. 'Rue what?'

'Marziano.'

She ran her finger up down and across, seeing every name but the one she wanted and was about to turn in despair to the index when there it was, leaping out at her. 'Yes! Here, look!'

But he had already started the car and was pulling out into the traffic. 'I can't.'

'Well, go ... go into the centre. Then you have to cross the river. Then it's just two blocks along and we turn right.'

The clock on the dashboard showed ten minutes past twelve, which gave them ... well, hardly more than an hour. It had been early afternoon when she had intercepted the nurse coming from the villa

411

Revachier, not before one o'clock, she was sure of that, but she doubted it had been much later, not as late as two. Perhaps half-past-one if they were lucky. And they still had to get the uniforms, return to her own car and then get themselves out to the villa Revachier. Impossible.

'Next right, next right!' she cried, as they sped across tram tracks and squeezed through lights in what was, mercifully, the quiet time for traffic.

Bill was giving an account of his trip to the Agencie de Berne: ' . . . I said I wanted to see the person in charge of ordering uniforms. And, well, I had to wait around and then finally I got in to see this lady who was the . . . I don't know, the manageress or whatever. Anyway, I told her my firm would like to quote her for supplying all their uniforms and she said don't bother, they were happy with the suppliers they had. And I said, getting into the part, I said I was sure we could undercut whatever they were currently paying – '

'It's on here somewhere. Slow down!'

'But she kept saying no and then finally, just when I thought she was going to show me the door and I'd blown it, she finally said it. Just casually, as she was talking, mentioned the name of their current suppliers. Well, of course, that was all I wanted to know and so – '

'Here, here. Stop!'

It was a large, square building in red brick, more warehouse than offices, with the name 'DUFOURS' blazoned across the front. There was a forecourt for parking and some shrivelled-looking shrubs in pots on either side of the door.

Bill switched off the engine. 'Over to you.'

'I know,' she said, glad that it was and yet terrified.

412

She felt in her pocket for the letter and got out of the car. The sun struck her, making her gasp. Without looking back, she crossed the few yards of cracked concrete and pushed open the door.

Her French almost fell at the first hurdle, leaving her speechless. She came to the open door of an office where a young woman with auburn hair and round, red-rimmed glasses was sitting eating a sandwich. They stared at one another for a moment, then the young woman asked something that Lauren didn't catch. She then spoke again at some length, leaving Lauren mystified and with the impression that she had been mistaken for somebody else.

She advanced a couple of steps into the office, holding out the letter as some sort of talisman or token of good intent. 'I have a letter,' she said carefully.

The young woman put down her sandwich, wiped her fingers on a tissue and took it. 'Ah, yes,' she cried, on reading it. 'Of course. I'm sorry, madame ... ' And then delivered an explanation which Lauren no more understood than she had the original greeting.

And all taking time. Using up precious minutes that might yet be the difference between success and the most dismal of failures.

The young woman spoke into the telephone, then said, 'Come with me please.' She led Lauren into a large space which was hung from floor to ceiling with garments of every description and in all the colours of the rainbow, each encased in its own transparent bag. Lauren supposed they were all uniforms, though she could only guess at what most of them might be: some were military-looking; others suggested catering, hotel staff, waiters; there

413

was a whole block of flashy sportswear, then rails of drab overalls. It was a world of uniforms. With nurses, she hoped, somewhere among them.

Now they were joined by a large and heavily-built man who was perspiring in the heat, wiping himself with a green cloth. He was wearing a uniform of his own, a white coat that strained to meet around his stomach. 'Yes, right, thank you,' he waved the auburn-haired girl away and turned to Lauren. 'Madame is from the Agencie de Berne, yes?'

'Yes.' At least she could understand him, thank God. She held out the letter but he didn't seem interested in it. He had produced a tape-measure from his pocket. 'And does madame know her measurements or . . . ?'

Yes, she did. 'Thirty-four, twenty-three, thirty-five.'

He nodded, but then she thought wait – I might be that now but what will I be this afternoon?

'Ah, no,' she said quickly. 'I mean thirty-six, twenty-six, thirty-eight.'

He looked at her in surprise.

'At least,' she added.

'But madame is so slim,' he said.

'I know,' she said, feeling foolish. Why, oh why hadn't she realized in advance that the uniform would have to be bigger – considerably bigger – than she was? It was stupid to be caught out like this, wasting time and placing everything in jeopardy. 'I just want something, you know . . . ' Lost for words, she gestured as though to suggest that she was expanding, that any minute she would become huge, a fat roly-poly of a woman.

Then realized that she was mimicking the man's own girth and let her arms fall. 'Loose,' she said desperately. 'I want it loose.'

414

He gave a tired smile. 'For the heat?'

'For the heat, yes.'

'One moment, madame.'

He disappeared into the rows of garments, then returned with an armful of polythene bags through which she could see the familiar red-and-blue of the agency uniform. 'Oh, yes, thank you,' she said, wanting to go there and then. But he wouldn't let her, not until he had taken two uniforms from their bags and had her hold them up against herself to check the length.

'If madame would like to try them on . . . ' he said, indicating a door away to the left. But no, madame had delayed for long enough and was becoming frantic to leave. She grabbed the uniforms and made for the exit.

'Madame,' he called after her. 'Madame, wait . . .!'

She would run for it, let them try and stop her if they could. Then she saw that he wasn't trying to stop her at all but was simply wanting to give her more things to take with her – a blue, woollen cape and two frilly, white hats, each in their own small polythene bags. 'Oh, yes, thank you,' she gasped. And now he was holding the door open for her and she was going down the corridor and was outside at last, to where Bill was waiting in the Audi.

'Any problems?' said Bill, once they were back on the road. The clock on the dashboard now showed twelve-forty. Then, even as she stared at it, jumped forward to twelve-forty-one.

'No,' she said, deciding against trying to explain how she had been delayed by her need for a uniform bigger than the ones she was entitled to and that were now piled on her knee. Though she was grateful for the blue cape which the helpful fat man had

415

bestowed on her as she left and which might yet cover a multitude of sins.

'I mean they didn't seem at all suspicious?'

'No.'

'Well, let's just hope they don't decide to ring the agency.'

Well, yes, just hope was all they could do. She knew how vulnerable they were to any such phone call, whether it was Dufours wanting to check that all was well or ringing with some query about the submission of their invoice or ... well, any contact between the Agencie de Berne and Dufours, for any reason, could upset the apple cart. She also knew that they couldn't do a damn thing about it but for what they were doing already, which was to keep moving, hoping to stay one step ahead of disaster.

'Listen,' said Bill, 'I want to see you afterwards.'

It took her a moment to realize what he meant, then she cried, 'No – '

He insisted, 'I can't just dump you outside that house and never know what happens.'

'Well, I know, but I just don't see how – '

'Just two minutes. Just so I know that you've made it.'

'But I won't be able to stop. I mean once I get out of there – '

Surely he understood. Once she had Adam in her arms, she would have no time for leaving-taking or farewells but would be high-tailing it for France and then back across France to the Channel. Of course she would have liked to have seen him again, to have been able to say thank you properly and even to have introduced him to Adam; all the same, it just wasn't possible.

He didn't look at her, concentrating on the driving, but pulled a folded map from beside him and placed it on top of the load of wrapped garments that were lying heavily on her lap. 'Just look at that.'

'Bill, I really won't be able – '

'Just look at it. Please.'

She opened it out and saw it wasn't the street map of Geneva, with which she was familiar, but another, larger-scale map, showing the entire region, up to the border with France and beyond. Presumably it had been among the sheaf of documents that had come with the car.

'Now there's a stopping-place just before the border. I've put a circle round it. You see it?'

'Yes.' A couple of miles before the border, marked with a symbol that meant it was a rest area and petrol station.

'I'll be waiting there.'

She tried again. 'But I won't be able to stop – '

'You're going to have to change out of the nurse's uniform, aren't you?'

'I suppose . . . yes,' she admitted, thinking about it for the first time.

'Then you're going to have to stop. All I'm saying is – if you stop there, that's where I'll be waiting.'

Well, yes, but it might not be that simple; it couldn't be that simple. 'And suppose I get there before you do?'

He gave a resigned smile. 'Then you must go.'

'Well – '

'Oh, sure! You can't sit around, waiting for them to catch up with you. If I'm not there, then you forget about me and go.'

'I won't forget,' she said quietly.

Nevertheless she would go; she would have to.

They were now joining the swirl of traffic that

417

seemed to circle the railway station day and night. Bill edged to the left so that they were in position to take the ramp down to the car park. They came to what Lauren had come to think of as 'their level' and stopped beside the Sierra and Toyota, which were parked side-by-side. She wondered what Bill would do afterwards, with two hire-cars at his disposal but didn't like to ask because of the time the answer might take. It was almost one o'clock and they still weren't ready to go: first she had to get changed.

She rummaged through the boot of her car, taking out the baby harness and dumping the spare nursing uniform and cap. The blue, woollen cape she threw into the car for later. And collected the old cushion from off the back seat while she was about it, the one with tassels around the edges that had matched their first suite and had then been relegated to car duty when the suite had been exchanged.

'Two minutes,' she called to Bill, who was standing waiting, experimenting with the chauffeur's cap and sun-glasses. Clutching her small bundle of clothes and cushion, she ran up the flight of concrete steps that led to the station concourse. The ladies' toilets were straight ahead, she knew that, and so didn't have to pause but just kept running until she was inside. There was a cubicle free. She closed the door, shot the bolt into place, tore off her jeans and top, then took the baby harness and pulled it around her. She struggled to adjust the unfamiliar fastenings, first making it too tight and then too slack so that the cushion simply fell through onto the floor. At last she had it about right, with the cushion held firmly against her stomach. Then she pulled on the uniform, only just managing to do up the buttons over the bulge of the cushion.

She felt awkward and conspicuous, sure that anyone seeing her would wonder what she was doing with a cushion strapped across her stomach but it was too late now for such misgivings. She grabbed her clothes from the floor, opened the door and stepped out of the cubicle.

And saw herself in the long mirror that ran over the wash-basins. A rather dishevelled-looking nurse, in the wrong footwear but distinctly ... pregnant. She stood for a moment, startled and moved by this image of herself.

Then, carrying her pregnancy before her, she hurried out back towards the car park.

32

It was one-fifteen when Lauren arrived, driving her Toyota, outside the Revachier villa. She could hardly believe that things were working out. Or had the nurses switched shifts already and she was too late?

She climbed awkwardly from the car, the cushion hot against her stomach. She had also pulled on the blue cape, which was making her sweat under the blazing sun but which might well be essential later.

She had stopped close to the gates, this time not wanting to hide but to be seen, trusting in the uniform that was to be her passport into the house.

She tried not to think of the myriad ways in which she might still be discovered: if her French should fail her, if the routine of the nurses had been changed, if she should encounter the nurse she had spoken to previously. Only the thought that she was minutes away from holding Adam in her arms allowed her to conquer her fears and begin the walk from the car to the house.

I'm pregnant, she thought, trying to concentrate on her role. I must think pregnant, act pregnant. If only James could see her now. All those desperate months of trying to conceive; now here she was waddling along a Swiss road with a cushion fastened to her abdomen.

420

She came to the closed gates. Through them she saw the young man lolling at his ease in the deck-chair, the same young man she had glimpsed the other day and who might well have seen her too. Now he got to his feet and came forward, to pull open one side of the gate and admit her.

'Good day, madame.'

She was encouraged that he neither seemed to recognize her nor to find her presence there a surprise. But still she had to ask in order to be sure: 'There hasn't been another nurse arrive in the last few minutes?'

He seemed puzzled. 'No. No-one.'

'Well, then I must wait here. I have a message for her.'

He shrugged but didn't seem unduly perturbed, coming to stand beside her, stretching and yawning. Please don't talk to me, Lauren silently pleaded. Her opening lines she had been able to rehearse in her head and so had off pat. Casual conversation would be something else. But he seemed happy to lean against the wall, cat-like, in a patch of sun. She saw his eyes go to her swollen stomach, then look away.

'I am sorry, madame,' he said. 'Would you like to sit down?' Gesturing towards the deck-chair.

'No, thank you,' she said. 'I'm all right.'

Still, it was nice to think that he really did believe her to be pregnant and not some mad woman who went around with a cushion strapped to her. It gave her confidence in her disguise to know it had passed its first test. Perhaps it was a double disguise really. Not only did she have the nurse's uniform to distract from her identity; her apparent pregnancy was another decoy.

There was a car approaching. She stepped back

through the partly-open gate and saw, with a feeling of relief but also apprehension because now things were about to start in earnest, that it was the deux-chevaux Citroen, the one that had delivered the nurse previously. It skidded to a halt just a few yards behind Lauren's Toyota and the nurse got out, leaning over to kiss the driver before slamming the door closed.

Lauren held back, not wanting to be seen too soon. It was vital the Citroen should depart and the young woman be left without transport of her own. That way she would be dependent on Bill, who was parked up in the Audi at the end of the road.

The deux-chevaux did a U-turn, mounting the kerb with one wheel, then was going away, a hand waving through its open roof. The nurse, looking smart and cool with her make-up in place and a half-smoked cigarette between her lips, was almost through the gateway before she saw Lauren and stopped with an 'Oh,' of surprise.

Lauren smiled and delivered another of her prepared lines. 'I was told to wait for you. Apparently there's been some kind of mix-up at the agency.'

The girl removed the cigarette and sighed. 'Oh, not again. It's always mix-ups . . . !'

Lauren felt a further surge of relief and confidence. She had been fearing some kind of challenge, a demand she should identify herself, but no, the sight of the uniform seemed to have done the trick.

'They want me to stay here and you to go somewhere else,' said Lauren, becoming bold.

'Go somewhere else . . . ? And how am I supposed to do that – walk?'

'No, there's a car waiting on the corner. The driver brought me and he has instructions on where to take you.' She pointed to where the Audi was just visible. 'He's there, look.'

But the young woman wasn't looking; she was still exasperated; it struck Lauren that she was also putting on something of a show for the benefit of the young man who was leaning on the gate and gazing appreciatively at her long, slim legs. 'So why couldn't they have just left me here and given you the other job?' she said, exhaling smoke. For an awful moment Lauren thought an answer was expected and struggled to find one. But no, it was just part of the display of exasperation and pouting annoyance at the stupidity of her employers. 'One day it's here, next day it's there . . . I don't believe they have a clue. And there's a car where?'

Lauren once again drew her attention to the distant Audi.

'OK, right. I suppose I'd better go.' She dropped her cigarette and ground it beneath a foot. Then she paused, as though seeing Lauren properly for the first time. 'Are you new?' she asked.

'Yes. Just started,' said Lauren, fearing what questions might follow and wondering how she might get away.

But the nurse's eyes had dropped to Lauren's stomach. 'Pregnant?'

'Yes. Still got to work though.'

'Haven't we all. Ciao.' And she went away along the road towards where Bill was parked.

So this was what it was like being pregnant, thought Lauren. Nobody looked you in the eye; all they saw was the shape. 'Well, then,' she said, turning back to the young man, 'I can go in now.'

He didn't move for a moment, still absorbed in contemplation of the nurse's backside as she swayed gracefully away along the street. Then he roused himself, gave Lauren a smile and stood back to let her pass. 'Certainly, madame.'

She was inside. She had passed through the walls, the impregnable outer defences of this fortress, and was walking up a drive of white gravel towards the house. She was also hot, and sweating heavily with the cushion and the cape. Where was Adam? she thought. How long before I can see him?

She also thought of Revachier, the man who had kidnapped him and whose house she was now approaching. Would she see him too?

Walk slowly, she reminded herself. Remember you're pregnant. As well as being scared to death. Well, perhaps that wasn't so unusual; perhaps the two did often go together. She tried forcing herself to pay attention to the gardens around her, which were lush and extensive beyond anything that might have been guessed from the other side of the surrounding walls. She saw cherry trees and lilacs and rhododendrons with large, fragile flowers of magenta and pink. Till her eyes were drawn back to the house, scanning its windows for signs of life. Was anyone watching her as she approached?

She came to the front door, wondering suddenly if she should be here at all. Might there not be another door through which she was supposed to enter? Still, no-one could expect her to know that. She was new here, a new nurse sent by the agency. She reached up and rang the bell.

She waited and was about to ring again when she heard footsteps approaching. She braced herself, the door swung open and she found herself looking at a middle-aged woman in a dark dress. Rather servere-looking, with her hair tied back. 'Good afternoon, madame – ' she began, but the woman had already responded to the sight of the uniform and was saying something about the garden and gesturing towards the side of the house.

'I see, yes. Thank you, madame,' said Lauren, though not really understanding. Was she supposed to find another door or was she being told that the baby was in the garden? Too late to ask: the front door was already being closed on her. Well, all right then, she would go in the direction in which the woman had gestured. Maybe, once she rounded the corner of the house, things would become self-evident.

All the time feeling the unreality, the impossibility of what she was doing – that she should be inside her enemy's camp like this, wandering around, almost having the run of the place!

She rounded the house and came into a small orchard of apple and pear trees. Suddenly she wasn't alone but was conscious of a figure coming between the trees, a man with two large, black dogs on leads. She drew back, startled, as the dogs pulled towards her but the man, who was swarthy and bullet-headed, wearing only a vest and shorts, reined them in to allow her to pass. 'Good day, madame,' he said, eyeing her swollen belly.

'Good day,' she muttered and edged past the dogs who growled softly.

The encounter had distracted her so that she had to look around to re-establish her bearings. The house to her left, the fruit trees around her and then, beyond them, she saw a huge willow tree, beneath which a nurse was standing beside a pram, idly rocking it with her hand.

Lauren wanted to cry out and rush forward but forced herself to walk slowly, her hands clasped across the cushion. She mustn't spoil it now. Not now. She had come so far – oh, so far – for this moment.

The nurse, a stocky, even chubby young woman, had stopped her rocking of the pram and was staring at Lauren as though puzzled, no doubt surprised not to see her regular replacement. Lauren told herself that she mustn't look into the pram, not yet; first she must speak to this girl. Get rid of her and then she would have all the time in the world to greet her son.

'Hello. My name's Lauren. I've been sent to take over from you.'

'Ah. And you are new?'

'Yes.'

'Well, he's had his feed. Next one's due at seven. I've been trying to get him off to sleep but I don't think he's very keen.'

She had turned away and was searching on the ground for her discarded shoes. Unable to deny herself any longer, Lauren stepped up to the pram and there, lying there with his eyes open and gazing up at her was Adam. Her son. She gave a little moan of joy, then put out her hand and touched his soft lips with her forefinger. As if to tell him that he mustn't cry out either; they must both restrain themselves until this stranger had gone.

The nurse had now put on her shoes. 'So you haven't been here before. You won't know where anything is.'

Lauren caught a note of impatience in her voice. She wanted to be away, not to be delayed showing this rookie around.

'Oh, I'll find things, don't worry.'

'Well, the nursery's through that door over there,' said the nurse, sounding relieved. 'Go up the stairs, then turn left and it's the first room you come to. I'm sure you'll find everything you need.'

'I will. Thank you.'

And now she had noticed Lauren's bulging figure. 'You look like you're having one of your own.'

'I am, yes.'

'Well, you'll be lucky if you have one as well-behaved as little Max here.'

'Max?' She couldn't prevent the question: the unexpected name had caught her almost as a blow.

The nurse stared. 'Yes. Didn't they even tell you his name?'

'Oh, yes, I'd just . . . just forgotten.'

Stupidly, it was something she had never foreseen, that his abductor might want to re-name him. Max. It struck her as strange and ill-fitting but it didn't matter anyway since she would never use it. He had been Adam before and would be Adam again.

'OK, well, I'll be going. Might see you tomorrow.'

'Bye,' said Lauren.

'Oh, and watch out for Gerard . . . ' Then she took another look at Lauren's stomach. 'Well, no, maybe you won't have to.'

'Gerard . . . ?'

'He's one of the guards. Has a thing about nurses. Bye.'

And she was gone at last, moving away through the trees so that Lauren could now turn back to the pram and take a proper look at her son, a long and greedy look at his fine features and the eyes flickering uncertainly between sleep and wake. Then she could restrain herself no longer and had to hold him. She hoisted him from the pram into her arms, surprised to find how heavy he was. And how he had grown! Twice the size that she remembered. She had told herself he would have grown, of course she had, but she hadn't anticipated just how different he would feel. She hugged him clumsily, hampered by the strapped-on cushion.

427

'Adam,' she whispered. 'Adam, it's mummy. It's mummy come to fetch you.'

Yet she knew she must keep control and not be carried away by emotion or by the urge that had suddenly come over her to keep hold of him and make a run for it there-and-then. She must stick to the plan, her own plan that had carried her through the walls and to her son. And she must act quickly, before either of the nurses she had met could speak to the agency about their new colleague and thus cause the alarm to be raised.

She looked around but could see no-one. Nevertheless, she had no way of knowing who might be watching, out here in the open. She must take Adam into the house, to the privacy of the nursery.

Keeping him in her arms, she left the pram where it was and made for the side door that the nurse had indicated, then had to struggle to pull it open. Inside was a small hallway with a green-and-white tiled floor and a narrow staircase ascending. It was cooler here, out of the sun. She listened but could hear nothing.

She started up the staircase, finding climbing difficult with the double burden of the child and the cushion. At the top was a shadowy corridor. Turn left, she remembered. And there, through the first door she came to, was the nursery, with bright, cream walls and a wooden cot in the centre.

So this had been his home – or rather his prison, the room where he had been hidden away. Well, not for much longer. 'Don't worry,' she muttered, 'we're going home. You're going home with mummy.'

She placed him on his back in the cot, then went back to the door and pushed it closed. There was a wash-basin in the corner of the room, and cupboards and drawers on the wall facing the windows. She found a feeding-bottle and a carton of sterilised

428

milk from among a small stock. There was also an electric hot-plate.

Working with feverish haste, she took out the small medicine bottle she had earlier taken from the glove-compartment of her car and stashed in her uniform pocket. The typed label said: 'VALIUM. TO BE TAKEN AS RECOMMENDED.' They had been given to her by her doctor in England to help her through the aftermath of the abduction. Now she shook one of the lemon-coloured tablets out into the palm of her hand and used a spoon to break it in half, then to crush one of the halves and mix it into the inch or so of warm milk she had prepared in the feeding-bottle.

'Now, Adam, she whispered, taking him on her lap and presenting him with the feeding-bottle, 'please, please, drink this.'

His head came up at the sight of the bottle though his lips wouldn't open as she tried to force the teat between them.

'Oh, come on,' she pleaded. 'I know you've had your feed and I know you're tired but please just take this little bit more.'

He allowed the teat to pass into his mouth, then began to suck. 'Oh, good boy. Oh, yes,' whispered Lauren. The level of the liquid in the bottle seemed not to fall at all, then, almost imperceptibly, it began to drop. It was half gone when his sucking movements stopped. She saw that his eyes were closed and felt him begin the heavier, deeper breathing of sleep. 'Oh, no, no, you've got to take the rest!' she urged, giving him a shake. His eyelids fluttered open and he began to suck noisily. Within a few seconds the rest of the milk had gone.

'Oh, marvellous, wonderful,' she breathed. 'Oh, you wonderful boy.'

She eased the teat from his mouth. He gave a small grunt, as though complaining, then his eyes fell shut and he was asleep again.

'Yes, that's it. Now you can sleep all you want,' she said, and placed him back in the cot.

She looked at her watch and saw it was two-fifteen. She thought of Bill, in his dark glasses and chauffeur's cap, driving around Geneva with the nurse – the genuine agency nurse – in the back of the car. How long before she would smell a rat and demand she be allowed to phone the agency? It was already the best part of an hour since Lauren had sent her off up the road.

She looked and saw that Adam was sleeping soundly. No reason for further delay. She began to unfasten the buttons of her uniform, then stopped, hearing footsteps outside the door. They were coming along the corridor, approaching the nursery.

Not daring to guess who it might be or why anyone might be arriving now, at such a moment, she quickly re-fastened the buttons so that the cushion and the harness holding it were hidden. Just in time as the door was pushed open and a man appeared. A tall, blond-haired man, who smiled and gave a small bow of apology for the intrusion.

'Do you mind if I come in and have a look at my son?' he said.

She could only stare, witless and dry-mouthed, as he entered the room and approached the cot.

33

She stood on the opposite side of the cot from him as he looked down at Adam. If he should try to pick him up, then she knew she would be unable to stop herself leaping forward and trying to wrestle the child from him. But he did no such thing. He simply looked down at Adam, then looked at her and gave a smile of collusion – as though they were accomplices rather than mortal enemies.

'He is a strong boy, yes?'

She stared, mesmerized, believing she could never speak again, then heard her own, small voice saying, 'Yes,' and feeling her face stretched into the rictus of a smile.

'He has had his feed?'

'Yes.'

Her enemy wasn't as she had imagined him. Not the dark, saturnine figure of her nightmares but this rather formal and courteous man, a few years older than she was, a few inches taller. He smiled again, showing white, even teeth. Perhaps he sensed her nervousness and wanted to put her at her ease, believing it was only because she saw him as her employer and that a few smiles and pleasantries might do the trick.

He passed a hand lightly over the head of the sleeping child. 'The sleep of the innocent,' he said.

Then, alarmingly, he switched his attention to Lauren herself. 'By the way, I don't think we've met before. I am Max's father.'

Oh, no, you're not, she wanted to say. And he's not Max either.

But what she heard herself saying was: 'Yes, I am new with the agency, thank you.' Her French beginning to fall apart. Any more of this torture and she would be left speechless, her mouth opening and closing like that of a stranded fish.

'You aren't Swiss?' he asked.

'No, no ... ' She hesitated, wondering suddenly whether admitting to being English might not be dangerous, offering him a clue to her true identity. But she could think of nothing else to say and, anyway, she no doubt sounded English. English and half-witted. And so she confessed: 'Not Swiss, no. No, I'm English.'

It at least brought her some relief, as he switched into an English that was almost accentless. 'I see. And have you been in Switzerland for long?'

She felt her scattered wits to be returning and improvised quickly: 'Only two months. Just over. My husband was transferred here. He works for . . .' – her eye caught the range of baby lotions – '. . . works for a pharmaceutical firm. Roche.'

'Oh, yes, I have heard of them. And you were a nurse in England?'

'Yes. I trained in London, at Guy's hospital, and then I worked there till we left.'

It was the only London hospital she could think of. Why was she offering these unasked-for details anyway? She must fight this urge to babble on, which only took up time and risked complicating her alibi.

But this Revachier, this kidnapper of her son, he

seemed in a mood for talking. Or perhaps he still felt himself under an obligation to put her at her ease. 'I have heard that English nurse training is the best in the world. Isn't that so?'

'I, er . . . I don't know.'

'I think it is, and so I'm happy that you are caring for my son. If there is anything you need, please inform the house-keeper.'

'I will. Thank you.'

Would he go now? Please God he would go. Every minute that passed made discovery more certain. Bill surely couldn't divert the other nurse forever; sooner-or-later she would contact the agency, who would ring the house . . . leaving Lauren trapped along with her son, not rescuing him but joining him in his captivity.

But no. He wasn't going, not yet. Like all of them he had noticed her bulging uniform. 'And you are expecting a child of your own?'

'Yes,' she said.

He smiled. 'And what do you want, boy or girl?'

'A boy,' she said, risking the bold reply.

'That I can understand.' He trailed a finger over the baby's cheek. 'I worship my own son.' He moved away from the cot, but not towards the door. With a stab of despair, Lauren saw him cross to the chaise longue which was beneath the window and sit on it, leaning forward, hands clasped and resting on his knees. 'I am not disturbing you, am I?'

'No. Of course not.'

She was beginning to feel physically sick. The cushion strapped to her stomach seemed to be burning its way into her. She was hot and frightened, near to giving up.

And was suddenly gripped by the awful conviction that this was all a charade: he knew who she was

433

and had known all along. He was simply tormenting her; he had no intention of ever letting her leave but would keep her there forever.

'I like to be in this room,' he said. He leaned against the back-rest of the chaise, making himself comfortable. 'I like to be with Max, even when he is asleep.'

Bill had watched anxiously as Lauren talked to the nurse outside the gates of the villa Revachier, then had given a silent cheer when she disappeared inside and the nurse had begun to walk up the road towards him. So she had pulled it off then. They were in with a chance after all.

He put on his dark glasses and pulled down the peak of his cap, still regretting that it was Lauren who had had to go alone into the lion's den and that he could do no more than play second fiddle.

Still, he would play it as well as he could. He looked at his watch and saw it was one-thirty. His job now was to do whatever was necessary to keep this nurse from reporting back to the agency and so alerting them as to what was going on.

She was leggy, like a young foal, but made-up to look older than her, what, nineteen or twenty years at the most. Bill got out of the car as she approached and opened the rear door for her.

'Bonjour, mademoiselle.'

'Bonjour.'

She spread herself along the back seat with a sigh of boredom. She's fed up with being messed about, thought Bill. Well, too bad. She's got a hell of a lot more of it to come.

'I have to phone the agency for instructions,' he said, getting into the car himself.

'What, you don't know where we're going?' His mirror showed her exasperated expression.

'No, but they'll tell me. You just sit back and enjoy the ride.'

'Always the same,' she grumbled. 'First here, then there.'

He made sympathetic noises, while slowly turning the car around. Driving with exaggerated caution, he took them out of the cul de sac and back into the traffic, heading toward the centre of the city. But making sure that they didn't come too close to the Rue de Berne where his passenger might take it into her head that she wanted to call at the agency office.

He saw her light a cigarette, judged that she was comfortably ensconced in the back of the car, then pulled up beside a telephone kiosk on the Rue de Saint-Jean. 'One moment, mademoiselle,' he said and leaped out before she could suggest that she might come with him or even that she might make the call herself.

He shut himself in the kiosk, keeping one eye on the car, and went through the motions of feeding money into the slot and dialling. His watch said one forty-five, which meant that Lauren had had fifteen minutes. He must give her an hour at least, more if at all possible. So that he might appear to be speaking, he recited the Lord's Prayer into the mouthpiece, surprised at how well he remembered it. In front of him, above the telephone and its paybox was a map of the area. His eyes wandered over the names, none of which meant anything to him, till he settled at random on 'Russin', which was in the top right-hand corner of the map and seemed to be some sort of village. From where he was, he needed to head out towards the United Nations buildings, then right and more-or-less straight on for another fifteen or twenty kilometres. 'OK, Russin it is,' he

435

said. 'Been nice talking to you.' And put down the receiver.

The nurse was still where he had left her on the back seat. 'Well?' she said, as though expecting the worst.

He didn't answer until he had started the car and pulled out into traffic, lest she should decide to get out herself and give the agency a piece of her mind. 'We have to go to Russin,' he said.

'Russin! But why?'

'Apparently that's where the job is.'

'Russin!' she repeated, as though it were the end of the world. 'But how am I supposed to get back?'

'They promised they would send someone to fetch you.'

'Christ,' she said, and lit another cigarette. She then treated him to a long tirade on the deficiencies and stupidities of the nursing agency. Apparently nurses were swapped around all the time, never knowing where their next patient would be. 'And you want to know why?'

'Why?' asked Bill, who was driving as slowly as he could without actually becoming a hazard to traffic.

'Because they're frightened we'll start making our own deals. You know? That we'll get to know the clients and they'll get to know us and then we'll agree to work for them privately instead of through the agency. Not that it's going to worry me for much longer.'

'No?'

'No, because I'm going to be leaving.'

'Really?'

And she told him of her plans to quit nursing altogether and join her boy-friend in his doughnut-making business, which was better pay and where she would be her own boss.

'Good for you,' said Bill. A sign warned him that Russin was only six kilometres away. With the lighter traffic, away from the city, he would be there within minutes. He looked at his watch and saw it was now almost ten past two. How long could he stall her once they got to Russin? Then he saw a petrol station and stopped at the pumps. Even though his tank was already three-quarters full, he made as lengthy a job as he could of topping it up and paying, using his credit card because it would take a few seconds longer than cash.

A quarter-past-two, and they were back on the road with Russin approaching fast.

It turned out to be a tiny hamlet of a place, picturesque but impossible to get lost in. Bill drove slowly around the main square, which had a post office, a church and a cafe.

'What are we looking for?' asked his passenger from the back. He had been hoping that she would have fallen asleep, but no.

'It's called the Villa des Arcacias,' said Bill, keeping his fingers crossed that there would be nowhere with such a name.

They had gone three times around the square and he decided to stop before the cafe, which was showing the only signs of life in the place. 'Wait here,' he said, confident by now that she had little inclination to do anything else, and went inside. The proprietor, who was an unshaven, taciturn man, confirmed that he knew nothing of any Villa des Arcacias – which was a relief. There was a pay-phone on the bar, which Bill went through the motions of using, conducting another one-sided conversation which took up more precious minutes. The nurse had wound down her window and was looking out at him as he emerged. 'Well?'

437

He made a gesture of despair. 'Another cock-up by the sound of it.'

She rolled her eyes. 'Shit.'

'I know.'

'Still, so long as they're paying me, what should I care.'

'True. Anyway, nobody here knows this Villa des Arcacias. So I rang the agency. They've said that they'll make enquiries and will ring us back here.' It was an idea that had come to him even as he spoke but it seemed a good one, offering an alternative to more aimless driving. 'So we might as well have a cup of coffee while we wait, eh?'

And he opened the back door of the car, giving her no option but to get out. She did so, shaking herself and stretching, and clattered after him across the pavement to one of the tables that stood outside the cafe.

He ordered two coffees and encouraged her to a slice of chocolate gateau, which she wolfed down greedily. Then she lit a cigarette and sat back, hitching up the skirt of her uniform to let the sun get to her legs.

Bill glanced at his watch and saw it was now over an hour and a quarter since Lauren had disappeared into the enemy's lair. Well, he had done her proud then, going already well beyond the hour to which he had pledged himself.

'And they said they would ring here?' the nurse said.

'Who?' he said, caught off-guard.

'The agency.'

'The agency. Oh, definitely, yes. I gave them the number here and they said stay there and we'll ring you.'

She glanced towards the door. 'Even so, I wonder if we should call them.'

He sensed her growing unease. Perhaps he had taken this game to its limits and should get out while he was ahead. 'I'll tell you what,' he said. 'I've got a little bit of business of my own to complete while we're here. Just give me ten minutes, then I'll be back and we'll give them a ring then, OK?'

He half-expected a challenge, that she would demand to know what this 'little bit of business' might be, but she seemed unperturbed and only nodded, settling back and raising her head towards the sun. He wondered if she had any money with her. Possibly not, in which case she was heading for a nasty wrangle with the cafe-owner that would further delay her telephoning for help and so give Lauren a few more precious minutes.

'Shan't be long,' he said and, leaving her where she was, walked to the car and drove away.

She wanted to scream but didn't. Or to run from the room, anything to be out of his sight, but she didn't do that either.

Instead, she moved about the nursery, trying to occupy herself, tidying and cleaning, shifting around the stocks of bottles and jars, all the time with him watching from the chaise longue, the imperious dictator who ruled her life through his grip on her son. She felt herself to be awkward and unconvincing, the stage nurse with no real understanding of her role and so busking it, and wondered how much longer she could sustain the pretence. For that matter, how much longer would she be allowed to, before events outside the house would catch up with her and her cover would be blown?

Then she heard him speaking: 'Well, I have things to get on with and I'm sure you do too.'

She saw that he had stood up and was moving

across the room, pausing to glance into the cot and then making for the door.

'Thank you, monsieur,' said Lauren.

'I hope we'll see you here again,' he said, and then was gone.

She stood without moving until she could no longer hear his receding footsteps. Did she still have time or was this reprieve no more than a cruel illusion?

Still, if there was a chance, half a chance, she must take it and take it now. She frantically unbuttoned her uniform, pulled out the sweaty cushion and hurled it away. The harness hung loosely about her, though she now wondered whether it would accommodate Adam, he had grown so big. She heaved him up, out of the cot, and, holding him against her with one arm, tried to manoeuvre the straps around him with the other. It was no good, they were too tight and would not go around him!

She put him down again into the cot, then tugged at the straps till she had extended them to their limits. This time yes – only just, but yes – she could fit them around him so that he was held tightly to her, his head lolling sleepily between her breasts and his legs dangling around her hips.

Now she had to pull the uniform closed but it wouldn't fasten. The material strained but there was a gap between buttons and buttonholes that could never be crossed.

Well, all right, then leave it. At least she had the cape to cover her. She placed it over her shoulders and pulled it closed before her, enveloping Adam. I'm sorry, my love, she told him. I know it must be a squash and awful but it won't be for long. She could feel him breathing against her. Be still, she prayed, be still for just a few minutes more.

Going out of the door, she caught sight of herself in the mirror above the wash-basin. She looked like a comedy pregnancy or a shop-lifter who hadn't known when to stop. But perhaps no-one would notice, already believing her to be pregnant and so not inclined to look too closely. She left the nursery, went down the stairs and out into the garden.

There was no-one there. Please God that Revachier wouldn't suddenly appear. Or that the dogs wouldn't come sniffing round her. All she wanted now was a clear run through the trees and to the gate.

Though it wasn't a run at all but a steady trudge, with the weight of Adam pulling her earthwards. She felt him move against her, twisting in protest against this new imprisonment. Be good, she urged, be good for just a little longer.

She came out of the trees and saw that there were now two men beside the gate, resting together on the grass: the young man who had admitted her and the older, more sinister-looking one who had been patrolling with the dogs. They both turned at her approach and got to their feet.

'I have to go out for a little while,' she said, a line she had rehearsed.

They looked at one another, neither moving towards the gate.

'Please,' she said. 'I'll be back in a few minutes.'

Had they had instructions not to let her out? Adam wriggled again and she pulled the cloak tightly about her. If he should cry out now . . . ! She was beginning to panic and wondered what they would do if she were to try and open the gate herself, then realized they were asking her whether someone could not be sent in her place; it was, after all, a hot day and madame in her condition . . .

They were not suspicious at all but concerned for her.

'You're very kind,' she said firmly, 'but I have to go myself.' And she stepped forward, right up to the gates, so that there was no alternative but for one of them, the young one, to hurry past her and open them for her.

'Thank you,' she said, and was outside, walking to her car, telling herself she mustn't run. Her sense of desperation grew rather than lessened. She was so nearly there. Adam gave a whine of complaint. Shush, quiet, she told him. Unlocking her car, she glanced back and saw the young man disappearing back inside the citadel.

Now, quickly, regardless of everything, she pushed herself into the narrow back seat of the car. Inside was bakingly hot but it could hardly be worse for Adam than being swaddled up against her. She threw off her cape and hoisted him clear of the harness. Though still asleep, he gave a yelp of dismay as the straps scraped his arms and legs. Sorry, oh, sorry, she told him as she lowered him into the travel-cot. Her uniform was still unfastened but there was no time to worry about that. She thrust her legs between the two front seats, then scrambled through till she was in the driving seat, though with her skirt ruckled up beneath her.

She pushed the key into the ignition with trembling fingers and at last was away. She had done it! She began to laugh, a rather wild, hysterical laugh. It was the tension she had been under, the awful, unendurable strain, finally releasing itself.

But no, she mustn't. She mustn't let herself go like this. She had achieved nothing yet. This was only the beginning and there were still so many miles to go.

Miraculously, she found the road out of the city which took her westwards, towards the border. She managed to fasten up her uniform while driving, though she knew, of course, that she must change out of it at the first opportunity. She would keep her promise to Bill and stop at the rest area, which had already been signposted, a thousand meters ahead.

Though she wouldn't wait for him. On that she was adamant. It had been part of their agreement and, anyway, she couldn't risk everything on some sentimental farewell. Bill had been an angel sent from heaven and she would be forever in his debt; all the same, she would not wait.

She came to the exit, braked and pulled off the road, finding it to be an area of scattered trees and picnic-tables. There were other cars, with their occupants sitting at the tables or standing, stretching their legs. But she could see no sign of the Audi.

She stopped in as remote a spot as she could find, away from the other cars. Adam was still asleep in the back, snoring lightly. Bless you, she thought, bless you for being so good and so quiet. She took the rolled-up jeans and cotton top she had thrown into the car, stripped off the uniform and pulled them on, not caring if anyone was watching. She wasn't going to risk leaving Adam for a moment, never again. There was a waste-bin some twenty yards away. She ran to it and dropped in the nurse's uniform.

She was running back, telling herself that she couldn't wait for Bill – almost relieved that she wouldn't be delayed – when she saw the Audi arriving behind her own car, its lights flashing in greeting.

So he had caught up with her after all. She

wondered suddenly whether she would have preferred it otherwise, whether it might have been better if she could have avoided this.

Bill jumped out, pulling off his cap and dark glasses. She allowed him to take her in his arms and hug her.

'You did it, yes?'

'Look,' she said, and showed him where Adam was lying asleep.

'Marvellous,' he said. 'Bloody marvellous.'

He embraced her again. But now, grateful to him as she was, loving him as she did, she was impatient to be gone, bitterly regretting every second wasted.

'Bill, I've got to go. I've got to.'

'I know. I left the girl out in some village somewhere, but the penny must have dropped by now – '

'I'll never forget you. Thank you.'

But he was holding her hand and wouldn't let her go. 'Let me come with you.'

She winced, feeling betrayed by this breach of their agreement, which after all had been his suggestion. He had promised that he would not delay her and she had believed him.

'No,' she said. 'Please, I've got to go.'

'Just to see you across France,' he urged. 'I might be able to help – '

'No,' she said, now almost hating him, despising him for this weakness. Surely he knew that she must now go back to James and do so alone, returning his son to him?

She suddenly saw that she was harder than he was. Tougher, with choices to make that he would never understand. He would cling on, believing that she would never be able to turn her back on him.

Not seeing that, with the adoption not yet completed, he was no longer an ally but a threat.

'I'm going,' she said. 'Don't spoil it.'

'Lauren, please – '

'No!'

She stared at him until he let go of her hand, then she turned and walked quickly to her own car, knowing that his eyes were still on her and were imploring her not to abandon him like this.

But abandon him she would. She had already.

'I could follow you,' he called, as she got into her car.

She stopped, knowing that she had to end this now. She could not run the risk of having him trail after her back across France. 'No, you mustn't,' she said. 'Please, Bill. Promise me!'

He looked puzzled, like a small boy who was being punished and didn't understand why. Then he shrugged, accepting it. 'It's your life.'

'Thank you.' And now at last she could get into the car, knowing that he wouldn't follow.

She heard him call, 'Good luck,' as she pulled away but she didn't look back. She knew she had been cruel but knew also that, for Adam's sake, she could not have decided otherwise. With more time she might have been kinder; but the result would have been the same.

Within what seemed like seconds she was at the border post, taking her place in the queue of cars waiting to cross. (If she had not been delayed by Bill, she might have been, what five, ten cars ahead in the queue, but she tried not to think about that.) She waited helplessly, edging forward, counting and re-counting the cars ahead of her. Trying to assess how long each one was taking to cross and so how much longer she would have to wait.

She knew, of course, what would happen and was

resigned to it. She had seen enough films and read enough books to know that the fugitive was always allowed to reach the brink of freedom before having it denied at the last possible second.

Behind each official and his accompanying policeman was an office. And in that office, Lauren could see through the open door, was a telephone. It was that telephone that would ring with the instructions to detain her.

Just one car in front of her now. She watched the telephone, willing it to ring. After all, it was going to. Better that the whole thing were over and done with.

The car in front pulled away, the barrier dropped behind it and she edged forward, knowing the barrier would stay down, keeping her there forever.

'Passport please.'

She handed over her passport, the one in which she had written Adam's name. The official looked past her, into the back of the car.

'He's a good traveller.'

'Pardon?' Her attention had been on the phone. 'Oh, yes. Yes, he is.'

'All right.' He was handing her back the passport. 'Have a good trip.'

'Thank you,' said Lauren.

The phone, missing its cue, had remained silent, the barrier went up and now she was in France and heading westwards like a bat out of hell.

She had done the unthinkable, going to the heart of her enemy's fortress – past his guns and his guards and his dogs – and had brought out her son. Now there lay only the bulk of France and the thin ribbon of the English Channel between them and home.

34

'No . . . !'

He wouldn't believe it, couldn't believe that such a thing had happened. And yet the look on Gerda's face, her usually stern features distressed and fearful, told him that it had.

'Max has gone . . . ?'

'It was the nurse, monsieur, the new nurse. The agency rang and so I went to check – '

But she had told him this already, bursting into his study and telling him that Max had gone, Max had been taken by the nurse who was an impostor. Impatiently he pushed past her and ran along the passageway and into the hall. Térence and Beat were standing there, stepping back as they saw him, as though they, too, were afraid of what his reaction might be.

'The nurse,' said Térence, making a gesture of helplessness. 'She must have smuggled him – '

But Marcus didn't stay to listen, taking the stairs two at a time, then racing along the landing to the nursery. It was how he had left it not more than an hour ago but now the cot was empty, with just a faint whiff of talc and milk hanging in the air above it, a tantalizing after-image of his son.

He gripped the sides of the cot and gave a groan of despair. That this should happen after he had

447

surely done as much as mortal man could to ensure the safety of the child ... ! He wanted to blame someone – anyone – to strike out at those who had let this happen. He turned as Gerda and the two guards appeared in the doorway.

'How?' he shouted. 'How could you allow this?'

'Monsieur, we are desperately sorry,' said Térence. 'It was the nurse, the one who – '

'You should have searched her!'

Only his house-keeper of the three of them had advanced towards him; only she had the courage to do so; the two men remained outside the door, as if poised for flight.

'She fooled all of us, monsieur,' she said. 'All of us. And now we must inform the police.'

'Yes,' he said, though still without moving. He thought of Jarman, his enemy, who had come after him with bomb and bullet and who now had without a doubt inflicted this mortal blow. How he would revel in his triumph, having captured not Marcus's body but his heart and soul.

The rail of the cot snapped beneath his grip. 'Oh, God!' he cried. 'Oh, God!'

Gerda was at his elbow. 'Please, monsieur,' she urged, 'it is best that you ring the police. And quickly.'

'Yes,' he said, and allowed her to lead him back towards the door. Ring the police. And quickly, yes, while there might still be a chance of detaining the impostor and her charge. For Max's sake, he must not allow himself to be petrified by shock or distracted by his anger at those he believed negligent.

Besides, she had fooled him too, the nurse. Hadn't he spoken to her, lingered in the nursery while she fussed around, all the time waiting only for him to leave so that she might make off with the boy? It was a bitter thing to have to admit, that she had fooled him too. He could hardly blame these dolts who had stood while she had carried Max out past them when he himself had spent so much time with her and noticed nothing, even chatting about her own supposed pregnancy, going out of his way to put her at her ease, supposing her nervous on her first day.

(Remembering her answer when he had asked her whether she wanted a boy or a girl. A boy, she had said.)

Perhaps such a complacent fool as he had been deserved to be surrounded by the purblind and the half-witted.

Back in his study, he rang the police and told them what had happened. He heard himself becoming insistent, frantic even. They must catch this woman. They must do whatever was necessary to apprehend her. She couldn't be more than . . . well, he didn't know, but not far away. They must catch her and return his son.

'And could you describe the woman, monsieur?' asked the policeman.

For a moment his mind was blank. 'Shut up!' he yelled at Gerda and the two guards who were conversing in low tones outside the open door. They fell silent and he turned his back to them. He must concentrate, try and remember the nurse as he had seen her with Max in her arms or leaning over the cot.

'Mid-thirties,' he said. 'Slim and quite tall. Fair hair, fair skin and I think blue eyes.' What else? 'Oh, and English. Did I say that? Definitely English. And wearing a nurse's uniform, a red-and-blue nurse's uniform.'

'And how old is the child?'

449

'Oh, just . . . just a few weeks.'

'A boy?'

'Yes.'

'And this is your own child, monsieur?'

'Yes. My son.'

It hurt him to admit these things, to confess his failure that he had not managed to protect his own son.

'And was he taken away in a car?'

'Yes.'

'What kind?'

Marcus turned to the cowed-looking trio at the door. 'Her car?' he snapped. 'What was it?'

They exchanged looks till it was Beat who said, 'I think a Toyota. Or anyway Japanese. A sort of silver colour.'

Marcus relayed this down the phone. The policeman promised that they would put out an immediate alert for the woman. And that somone would be calling round to see him.

'Thank you,' said Marcus and put down the phone.

What else? What more could he do? He would ring Jacques – not only because he might have need of his wise counsel but because, as Max's godfather, he must be told personally of the tragedy. Other than that . . .

He could not suppress the memory of how he and Hervé had spirited Max out of the garden in Preston and onto the plane that had freed him from the jurisdiction of the English court. What kind of dreadful nemesis was this that he should now lose him in similar fashion to his arch-enemy?

That is . . . if it were, indeed, Jarman behind the kidnapping.

The thought of Preston and all that had gone on

450

there now gave him the faintest flicker of hope. Oh, no more than that, for it still meant that Max had been taken and was no nearer being returned. But the thought of the Eagleshams, the couple he had never met but had only glimpsed in their Land Rover as they had driven away from the court, had made him dare to wonder whether, after all, this might be their doing and not Jarman's.

Suppose they had mounted some kind of crude counter-attack, attempting to drag Max back to England by force? The woman had been English, no doubt about that, and had perhaps been the right age. It was still only a forlorn hope, preferable because it would mean that they would care for Max and because ... well, because they were amateurs compared to Jarman. They would have neither his resources nor his ruthlessness and so might be more easily stopped, even now.

He left his study and went to find Térence and Beat, who were sitting in the garden. They got to their feet, looking nervous at his approach.

He lifted his hands in a gesture of conciliation. 'This woman who has taken Max,' he said, 'it's possible she is going to try and drive across France with him, heading for England. Can you go after her? I know it's a long shot but – '

Yes, yes, they were assuring him. They would depart immediately. Clearly anxious to be seen to be doing as much as possible, however slim the chances of success.

'And any of your colleagues. If they can also – '

Yes, yes, they would contact them and no doubt they, too, would be on the road immediately.

'If you can bring him back then you will find me very grateful,' said Marcus. 'Very grateful indeed.'

They hurried away, calling back more promises

451

that they would do all they could and were sure
their colleagues would do likewise.

Marcus stood for a moment, then turned and
began to walk back across the lawn, still cursing
himself, cursing all of them, that they had been
fooled so easily. The saw that he was approaching
the willow tree and that Max's pram was still standing beneath it, with toys and a woven rug scattered
on the grass.

He wheeled away, unable to face such things, and
headed for the front door of the house.

It was Inspector Marti who arrived, the same Inspector Marti, thin-faced and in a grey suit, who had
questioned him after the bomb had exploded beneath
his car behind the Grappe d'Or restaurant and then
questioned him again in the hospital after he had been
gunned down on the Rue de l'Athénée. My guardian
angel, thought Marcus bitterly, though one who
clearly resented the assignment. Even today, with the
life of a child at stake, the Inspector's expressions of
concern seemed formal and the minimum necessary.
Was it a personal antagonism, wondered Marcus, or
a matter of the Inspector's practised eye telling him
that here was a man who used the police when it
suited and shut them out when it didn't?

No matter. So long as none of this interfered with
the pursuit of Max's kidnapper.

They sat in Marcus' study. Inspector Marti took
out a pair of steel-rimmed glasses and stared through
them at a piece of paper he had taken from his pocket.

'We do have some news,' he said.

Marcus held his breath.

'A woman matching your description crossed the
border into France . . .'

Marcus gave a groan of dismay: so she had

slipped through that particular net; they had not moved quickly enough to stop her. Still – small consolation – it was evidence that Max might have been taken not by Jarman, his mortal enemy, but by the Eagleshams, whom he had cause enough to hate but not to fear. The woman had held onto the child rather than delivering him to someone else, and she was heading westwards, in the direction of England.

'. . . The border guard confirms that there was a child in the car but, alas, the alert had not at that time been issued.'

'You have informed the French police?'

'Certainly.'

So he was now in their hands, those forces of law that he had for so long mistrusted and kept at arm's length. Unless, of course, Térence and Beat and whoever of their colleagues they had managed to muster might actually . . . Was it possible they might catch up with the woman in the whole of that vast country?

He saw that Inspector Marti was watching him. 'You have had an unfortunate year,' he said.

Marcus shrugged, resenting that this policeman should think of questioning him now, when he could think only of his son. And yet he needed his cooperation and so finally grunted, 'Unfortunate, yes.'

'Can we take it that whoever was behind the attempts to kill you is now behind this abduction of your son?'

'I have no idea.'

Inspector Marti sighed. 'First we have the car-bombing, then the shooting, and now – '

'I don't know who is behind this,' said Marcus, too engrossed with his own bitter feelings to relish a sparring session. 'I only wish I did. Now please, Inspector, all I want is that you find my son.'

'And you can tell me nothing that might help . . .?'

'No.'

Could he?

Suppose it were the Eaglesham woman, well, then he could talk about the court case in England and the woeful miscarriage of justice that had given his son into the care of strangers but he couldn't see how that would help. Indeed, he felt that would blur the issue and might even cause the police to pause in their efforts. Better they should regard this as a straightforward kidnapping where the sole prioritiy was the safe release of the victim.

'No,' he said again.

'Has there been any kind of demand made?'

'Demand . . . ?' Not clear for a moment what this might refer to.

'For money. A ransom.'

'Oh . . . no. No demand.'

Strange how this was the one option he hadn't considered: that Max might have been taken, not by Jarman or even by the Eagleshams, but by someone else altogether with the intention of demanding money for his safe return. (But would a woman be involved in such an enterprise? It felt unlikely.)

'No. There has been nothing,' he repeated.

'Well, it's early days as yet. But you will tell us if there is? If there is any kind of communication from these people, then you will tell us immediately?'

'Of course.'

Knowing that he would do no such thing but would enter eagerly into any financial transaction that might return Max to him. If only things could turn out to be that simple. No matter what the amount demanded, he would raise it and pay it without hesitation.

454

As so often before, it was only to Jacques Martin-Achard, his long-standing friend and counsellor, that he could open his heart and speak freely. Jacques arrived as Inspector Marti was leaving and embraced Marcus with tears in his eyes.

'To take a child, an innocent child . . . the man is a monster!'

So he, too, had made the same assumption – that it could only be Jarman who was responsible. It made Marcus uneasy: was he deluding himself in thinking of the Eagleshams, desperate that it should be them since they were, by any calculation, the lesser of two evils?

'You think it must be Jarman?' he said, pouring himself a drink.

'Of course. Who else? And this time you must surely tell the police. You must tell them everything you can – '

'It was a woman,' said Marcus.

'Well, yes. But there can be no doubt who is behind – '

'And she was English.'

Jacques frowned, failing to see the significance.

'And there was a man watching the house. He was also English.'

Now Jacques gave a start of surprise. 'What, you think it might be . . . ' he said, and stopped as though struck by sudden doubt.

Marcus waited, wanting him to spell it out, needing the reassurance that others beside himself might see an English connection to all this.

Jacques began again. 'You think it might be . . . ' – and this time completed – 'those people who were wanting to adopt . . . ?'

'I want you to tell me,' said Marcus eagerly. 'Am I being foolish or – '

'No, I suppose . . . of course it's possible – '

'What do you think?' insisted Marcus.

Jacques hesitated. As if his opinion might later be tested in court and so must be weighed carefully; or perhaps he was only afraid of raising hopes that might later be dashed.

'But would they be capable of something like this?'

'I was,' said Marcus simply. Becoming certain, even as he spoke, that it was the Eagleshams – not Jarman but the Eagleshams – who had taken Max.

'And you would rather it were them?' said Jacques.

'Well, at least they'll care for the child. So in that respect . . . I suppose yes, I would,'

Though, even as he spoke, he was overwhelmed by the futility of all this speculation. Even were the Eagleshams to ring and confirm that they had Max, how would that help him get him back, which was all that mattered? So what if it were the Eagleshams or Jarman or somebody else altogether? What mattered was that Max should be returned to him, otherwise his life would be a mere remnant, a mechanical charade to be pursued without purpose.

Jacques had come to stand beside him and placed a hand on his shoulder. 'Whoever the woman is,' he said. 'She can't possibly get the child back to England. Someone will see her.'

'You think so?' said Marcus, wondering why he suddenly felt such despair. Such hopelessness.

He had wanted Jacques to agree with him – that the Eagleshams were, indeed, the most likely kidnappers – and Jacques had as good as done so. So why had this depressed him where only a short time before it had seemed a life-line, something to cling to?

456

Was it because he now knew, for the first time, how Lauren Eaglesham must have felt in those days after he had taken Max from her? Odd how he now felt close to her, suddenly knowing her and what she had felt. Knowing how she must have despaired of a life without the child she had come to regard as her son and so had risked everything to reclaim him.

He now saw how his blindness to her feelings had been his downfall. He had always regarded Jarman as the danger, the threat to be feared; not realizing till now when it was too late how much more dangerous and cunning an enemy he had made in this woman.

Better if it had been Jarman. He would have wanted the child only for the hold it gave him over the father. He might have been willing to trade, to state a price for Max's return.

Whereas the Eaglesham woman . . . with her there would be no trading and no price. If she did indeed have Max, then the one certain thing was that she would sacrifice everything and go to any lengths in order that she might keep him.

By midnight Lauren was on the N44, approaching Chalon-Sur-Mere. The signs told her that; otherwise she had little idea where she was, save she was in her car, somewhere in the middle of France and heading north-west. Or, anyway, had been heading north-west the last time she had been able to read her map which was lying on the seat beside her. Her eyes were swimming with exhaustion so that she could barely see the road. Just lights. Red lights to be followed; yellow lights that passed her on her left. She was frightened she would fall asleep yet, more frightened of stopping, had continued on and

457

on into the darkness. She also also hungry and
thirsty and stiff from being so long at the wheel.

She told herself that she must stop, that she
would stop at the next service-station or cafe. It was
madness to continue like this, risking both their
lives. Then, when the next cafe came along, the
signs urging her to pull off, she refused to look at
them but fixed her eyes on the red lights of the car
ahead and went on, promising herself that she would
stop at the next one, which would put her just a few
more kilometers ahead of any pursuers.

Or perhaps the one after that.

She seemed to have been driving for as long as
she could remember.

She had stopped only once. That was when, believing Adam still asleep, she had risked a glance over
her shoulder at him and been startled to see him
wide-eyed and looking back at her. So she had
pulled up in a lay-by, amid a clutter of lorries which
shielded her from the road, and climbed into the
back seat where she fed and changed him, using
what she had bought in Geneva on her shopping-
expedition with Bill. She had two cartons of evaporated milk, a packet of rusks and some baby rice.
Iron rations that should have been enough to see
Adam comfortably through twenty-four hours.
What she hadn't thought of was herself. She had
already eaten two of the rusks and searched the
glove-compartment in the hope of finding forgotten
chocolates or sweets but had found nothing.

It had been her failure throughout, this lack of
forward planning. Well, now she would just have to
suffer for it.

Adam had still been dopey from the valium, those
bright eyes ever so slightly out-of-focus and the eyelids dropping. When they had got back onto the

road, he had lay silently, staring at the car roof or dozing fitfully.

But that feed had been what, three or four hours ago, and now he was wide-awake again and demanding attention. So now she would have to stop. No more excuses. The sound of his whingeing couldn't be shut out and was making her edgy. And, anyway, she couldn't continue like this, not without risking killing both of them.

The signs promised her a service area in two kilometers. She would stop at that. There would be no more postponements. This time she would stop, even if the place had a dozen police-cars lining its approach road. At the one kilometer sign she began to slow.

Adam started to wail in earnest. 'Just hang on,' she shouted back. 'I know how you feel but yelling about it isn't going to help.'

Now the service area, its lights showing, was coming up on her right. The reducing bands on the road side showed her where to turn and, steadfastly resisting a last-second impulse to ignore them and try for just a few more kilometres after all, she slowed right down and steered the car onto a vast and near-deserted parking area.

She shut off the engine.

Silence.

Even Adam had stopped his racket, perhaps shocked that the engine noise which had been with them for so long did not have to go on forever.

Lauren gave a great sigh of relief and slumped down in her seat, but then Adam started to gripe again. 'Yes,' she said, 'yes, OK, I'm coming.' She struggled to open the front door and climb out of the car into the night air, wincing at the pain as she forced her body into movement.

There were arc-lights set on tall concrete columns that cast a cold and feeble light over the expanse of tarmac; then, on the far side, a group of low buildings with bright, neon lights and a few caravans and trailers parked around them.

She gave an enormous yawn and then tried stretching this way and that to rid herself of some of the stiffness. She was dirty and sweaty but, most of all, just plain exhausted.

Though she wasn't too tired to be aware of the dangers. No doubt the police had been notified, here as well as in Switzerland. Perhaps they would remember her crossing the border. For her to be seen by anyone was a risk, particularly for her to be seen with Adam, a mother and baby together.

Yet she needed water – water for her to drink and water to dilute the evaporated milk. She dithered for a moment – wasting more time – then said, 'Oh, sorry, love, but I've got to do this,' and locked the doors of the car, trying to ignore Adam's muffled cries from inside.

I'm a terrible mother, she told herself, jogging across the tarmac. Don't ever let the adoption agency find out about this.

The inside of the cafeteria had an eerie, middle-of-the-night feel to it, a few diners crouched over their food, a girl sitting behind the till gazing up at a television set that was suspended from the ceiling showing a pop video but without sound.

Suppose I die here, thought Lauren. No-one would ever know about Adam locked inside the car. It made her positively sprint to the counter and grab two plastic bottles of mineral water, plus a bar of chocolate . . . no, two bars of chocolate . . . and then she was pushing money at the girl and waiting impatiently for her change.

460

So far as she could tell, no-one had paid her any attention. A couple of bikers were coming in through the door as she hurried out past them. Then she was running back across the tarmac, slowing down only as she came near enough to the car to see that Adam was still there inside it, safe and sound, though yelling his head off by what she could hear.

'No, it's all right, love. It's all right. Mummy's here,' she said, wedging herself in beside the cot. Close to, his cries were piercing, making her head ring. Feeling herself clumsy and awkward after the long drive, she managed to mix the mineral water with the evaporated milk, heaved him out of the cot and into her arms and offered him the bottle, which he took eagerly.

Another silence.

It also gave her a respite during which, using her free hand, she gobbled up one of the bars of chocolate and drank the other bottle of mineral water, all the time reminding herself to keep looking out of the windows, on watch for anyone approaching the car.

She then had to wait for Adam to finish his own bottle. 'Come on,' she urged. 'Nearly finished.' She felt her eyes closing and had to keep talking to stay awake. 'Soon be home, won't we. Yes, we will. We'll soon be home and then won't daddy be surprised.'

And now his eyes were closing; the sucking became intermittent and then stopped altogether. She went to take the bottle from him but he resisted, his eyes flashing open. 'Well, make up your mind?' she said. 'Do you want it or not?' His eyes had closed again and this time she was able to ease the bottle from his lips till it came away with a wet plop.

461

It must be the valium still working. Well, good. Let's hope it would go on doing so at least until they reached the Channel.

She lowered him into his cot and pulled the blanket over him, then climbed backwards out of the car. She gave another yawn. She looked at the road beyond the barrier of trees, the headlights of passing cars coming and going between them.

Oh, no, she thought. No, I can't.

She had intended to drive on, stopping only when it was essential to tend to Adam, but otherwise to drive on through the night and into the following day until she arrived at Calais. Now she knew it was beyond her.

I can't drive anymore, she thought. I just can't.

She felt the tears fill her eyes – at her frustration with her own weakness, her failure – but shook her head, refusing to cry, telling herself no, no, she would not give way like this. All she needed was a few minutes' sleep, a cat-nap, then she would feel refreshed and able to continue.

She adjusted the driver's seat so that she was lying back, with room to stretch her legs and her head close to Adam in his cot. She looked at her watch and saw it was a quarter-to-one in the morning. She would allow herself a ten-minute snooze, fifteen minutes at the most. She lifted a weary hand to check the doors were locked, said, 'Good night, Adam,' and fell asleep.

She was home, in her own bed. It was early morning but not time to get up, not yet: she could allow herself another few minutes before Adam would have to be fed and James got off to work. Another day to be faced. Later on, she would set about cleaning the house, which had become unaccountably dusty and smelling of stale milk.

Except that she wasn't at home, was she. The discomforting realisation gnawed at her and brought her out of her sleep. She wasn't at home at all but was in the car, hunched up in the driver's seat, with Adam sleeping behind her, giving the odd shrill, little snore, and the sky outside lightening with the promise of morning.

She gave a cry of alarm and pushed herself upright. It was a moment before her eyes would focus to read the clock on the dashboard.

It was ten minutes to four.

'Oh, no,' she said. 'No.' But her wrist-watch told her the same. She had been asleep not for the ten minutes she had promised herself but for three hours.

She looked around frantically, half expecting to see a posse of police-cars but no, everything seemed much as it had been when she had first stopped there, the car-park all but deserted and the lights still burning in the distant buildings. Well, that much was a relief, but to have lost so much time . . . ! She cursed herself as she struggled to bring the seat back to upright.

Still, she had to admit she felt better. No longer bone-weary but capable of driving again. First, though, she must find a loo. She couldn't put that off until Calais. And perhaps she might grab something to eat and drink while Adam was still sleeping.

Perhaps this unplanned stop would turn out to be for the best, allowing her to complete the rest of the journey in one long haul.

There was a welcoming chill to the air as she stepped out of the car. She shook herself, as a dog might have, feeling grimy and unwashed, but there was no time to worry about that. A quick sprint

463

over to the cafe buildings, a glance back to see the car was undisturbed, then she was inside, first finding the loo and then into the cafe. She grabbed a polythene-wrapped roll from the counter and was sorely tempted by the smell of percolating coffee but no, there wasn't time for that and so she took a carton of orange-juice instead. It was a different girl behind the till, one who who looked at her brightly and wished her good morning. Lauren mumbled something, collected her change and purchases and hurried back outside through the swing doors.

It was then that she saw that another car, an ordinary-looking green saloon, had stopped close to her own. She gave a gasp of fear and began to run.

And instantly considered every possibility: that it was the police who had caught up with her; or, more hopefully, someone who had noticed Adam left on his own and who had become concerned; or nothing more remarkable than someone else choosing a quiet spot for a sleep.

Oh, God, let it be the last, she prayed.

But then saw the car doors opening and the two men stepping out and knew that it was worse than any of these. They were the two guards – she recognized them immediately – who had been at the Revachier villa when she had taken Adam: the young one who had opened the gate for her as she left and the older one who had been leading the dogs across the grass.

'No! Oh, no ... !' she cried, pleading that this might not be so. Her run came to a jarring halt and she stood looking at them. She saw that the older one was smiling. She thought of turning and running in the other direction but, of course, she couldn't do that, not without Adam, who was there inside her car, already in their power.

So she had to walk towards them, panting and desperate. If only I had gone on, she thought. If only I hadn't been so feeble as to fall asleep!

She saw that they were also dishevelled and weary-looking. Though their manner was now bold, swaggering even, as they waited for her to approach.

'What do you want?' she said, trying to match their bravado but her voice came out plaintive and weak.

'Good morning, madame,' said the older one, the one she for some reason thought of as Mexican. 'You've caused quite a lot of trouble, did you know that?' And he chuckled.

'He's my child,' she said. 'Oh, please. Please, you've got to believe me. He's my child.' She directed her appeal to the younger man, remembering his solicitous manner when he had believed her pregnant. 'He was my child before the man you work for came and took him away from me!'

The younger man gave a small shrug, which might have been of apology or just shamefacedness at what he was about to do.

'You can't take him away!' Lauren beseeched, latching on to this smallest hint of possible sympathy. 'Not again!'

But he had turned away, refusing her appeal, and it was the Mexican who answered. 'We don't know about these things. We're only doing our job.'

'Oh, no, you can't. You can't, not again . . . ' she heard herself pleading, while part of her was also calculating: she still had the car-keys in her hand so if she could only get past them and into the car . . . or perhaps she should leave Adam locked inside where he was and run back towards the buildings in the hope that . . .

But, even as she hesitated, the Mexican stepped forward and tugged the keys from her grasp.

'Thank you, madame.'

'No! Give me those . . . '

She grabbed at his arm, digging her fingers into the rough weave of his shirt, but he shook her off, then she felt her own arms being held by the young man who had moved behind her.

'Let me go! Let me – '

Then she was being pushed into the back seat of her own car, beside the cot. Too late she realized what was happening and began to hit out and shout till she was pitched forward onto the floor of the car and the door slammed shut behind her.

Sobbing, she turned and strove to push the door open, but the younger man was standing against it, preventing her from moving it. And now Adam was awake, whimpering. She tried to control her sobs, not wanting to alarm him. 'It's all right. Mummy's here,' she said. 'Don't cry.'

Whatever happened, she wouldn't allow these two brigands to drive away with her son and return him to his prison. She would shout and scream. She would make it impossible for them to leave. What did it matter who heard her now? The more, the better. Even the police who might – just might – be persuaded to recognize that this was no simple kidnapping but an attempt to put right a grievous wrong.

She held Adam to her and looked out through the car windows. The younger man was still positioned by the back door while the Mexican had gone to their own car. So far as she could see, he was speaking into a car-phone, no doubt seeking instructions from his master.

She wound down the window, seizing the chance to speak to the younger man while he was alone.

'This is my child,' she said. 'If you take him from me, then you'll be kidnapping him. Do you understand that? You'll be the real kidnappers, not me.'

Her French had become miraculously fluent, but the young man only shook his head, meaning he wouldn't listen, it was none of his business.

'Don't you have any children of your own?' she persisted. 'Or brothers or sisters? Don't you understand what I'm trying to tell you?'

'Please, madame . . . ' He waved a dismissive hand.

'Look, I'll give you money. I'll pay you. Let me go and let my child go and I'll give you anything you want!'

If only another car would arrive or someone emerge from the distant buildings, then she might shout, grab Adam and try and make a run for it. But no car did; and the only movement was a flock of starlings that descended noisily onto the nearby trees.

Now the Mexican had come from the other car, which was a Renault, and gestured to the younger man to approach him so that, Lauren assumed, they could talk out of earshot of her. Well, good. It gave her a few yards start, though no more than that. *If only some other vehicle would appear . . . !*

She clutched Adam to her, ready to leap from the car and flee, wondering whether she was even now wasting what would turn out to be her best chance or whether she should wait till the sun was up and there would be people about to whom she could appeal for help.

The two men were talking in low tones. The Mexican seemed to be urging his colleague into some course of action that the younger man was resisting, shaking his head and raising his voice in what sounded like adamant denial.

467

So were they arguing? Was there a chance that this might give her her opportunity? It was a flicker of hope that kept her where she was for the moment, waiting to see what might develop.

Now both men were talking in raised voices but too quickly for her to follow what was being said. The Mexican was arguing furiously but the younger man was still shaking his head. And now he turned and began to walk towards Lauren, leaving the Mexican calling in vain after him.

He's going to let us go, thought Lauren in a sudden rush of hope. They can't agree on what to do with us and so he's going to let us go.

Then she saw – though scarcely able to believe it – that the Mexican was holding a gun. He had taken it from his jacket and was pointing it at the younger man as he walked away. She opened her mouth to call a warning but then there was a loud retort, like the bursting of a tyre. Then another one.

The young man grunted, his body arched and he collapsed to the ground in front of her.

Lauren screamed and pulled herself away from the window onto the floor of the car, holding Adam to her, trying to shield him with her body. For a long moment she could hear nothing beyond her own breathing, then she heard the car door being wrenched open.

'No, please,' she said, without looking round. 'Oh, please.' Still trying to keep Adam beneath her, and waiting for the shock of a bullet or a blow to her own back.

'Get out,' came the Mexican's voice. 'Out. Now!'

'Yes . . . yes.' She scrambled out backwards, with Adam in her arms, stood up and turned to face him.

He was no longer holding the gun. Whether it

468

was back inside his jacket or he had thrown it away she didn't know. She could only stare at him. It registered in her mind that this was what they meant when they used the phrase 'cold-blooded killer'. This man, not five yards from her – he was a cold-blooded killer.

And she – she was his only witness.

The body of the young man was still on the ground where she had seen him fall. Now she tried not to look at it, and held Adam's head so that he shouldn't see it either.

Around them no-one else seemed to have been alerted by the shots. Only the starlings had been sent shrieking from the trees, and they were now returning, their din lessening as they settled again.

'Please,' she said again.

'Get in the car,' he said, motioning towards the green Renault. He sounded weary, almost indifferent, no longer relishing the situation but wanting an end to it.

'Yes,' she gasped, and hurried around the fallen figure and got herself and Adam into the back seat of the Renault.

If he had been going to shoot her, wouldn't he have done so then out there on the tarmac? Or was he simply wanting to drive her to a more secluded spot before killing her?

She could only sit there, with Adam on her knee, not daring to look round. Though she could see him anyway. The wing-mirror was angled so that it offered her a reflection of him dragging the fallen body away – towards her own car? Yes, he had dragged it out of sight behind the Toyota. She saw the lid of the boot being lifted, caught sight of the body being raised and realized he was hauling it over the sill and into the boot.

469

Then he returned and got into the driver's seat in front of her. She saw the perspiration on the back of his neck, then he turned towards her, his face suddenly close, unshaven and smelling of tobacco, so that she flinched away.

'I'm not going to harm you,' he said.

She nodded dumbly.

'You just sit there, keep quiet, and no-one will harm you.'

'Thank you,' she said.

'We're just going for a little ride.'

He turned the ignition and the car began to move forward, across the still deserted car-park and onto the slip road. Lauren glanced behind them and saw her own car, now small and abandoned-looking. She didn't want to think of the body inside it.

The sky was suddenly streaked with orange and the trees around them became a deeper green. The day had begun then. A day that should have seen her reaching the coast and the prospect of freedom but which, instead, had plunged her into this nightmare of terror and sudden death and which was now taking her and her son she knew not where.

35

The sun climbing into the sky to their right meant they were heading north. Not back into Switzerland then but deeper into France. Where this might once have been a hopeful sign, the murder of the young man now only made Lauren fear for the worst.

She had already considered and re-considered every possibility. The only one that made any sense was that they were being kidnapped. That their captor was double-crossing Revachier and spiriting them away to some hide-out where he would demand a ransom for their return.

It was a cause for faint hope – that they might be worth more alive than dead – but she couldn't and would never forget the merciless gunning-down of the young man back there in the car-park.

She could only give thanks that she was still alive and Adam unharmed and pray that some miracle might come along to rescue them.

Her arms had become stiff from holding Adam to her, yet she didn't want to disturb him by moving and, anyway, she had nowhere to lay him in the moving car. They had left the N44, the major road, and the few signs that Lauren had glimpsed since had been directions to local villages, telling her nothing. The countryside around them had grown steadily wilder and less cultivated. There were still vineyards, some stretching for what seemed to be miles, but they were now topped by rocky peaks and interspersed with shrubland, where large, pale cattle grazed. With just the occasional sign of human life: a twist of smoke rising from a farmhouse; a sleepy-looking peasant riding a mule through a meadow of tall grasses, barely raising his head as they swept past.

She assumed they were still in France, though this was not the France she had been used to, with its poplar-lined roads and shrines to the Blessed Virgin. This was more like bandit country, private and inhospitable. Even when they had stopped, having to pull over to allow a lorry to squeeze past, Lauren had no thought of leaping from the car. Where would she go? Who could she find here that she might turn to for help?

Besides, she believed – not with any great confidence but even so – she believed they were safe for the time being. As safe as they could ever be when their driver had shown himself capable of such casual slaughter. But she no longer feared he might be taking them to some secluded spot where he might dispose of her as the only witness to his heinous crime. For one thing, there was a map clipped to his sun-visor, to which he constantly referred. He was a man driving with a particular destination in mind.

Adam began to whimper, though his eyes were still closed. Then they opened, his lip trembled and two large tears slid down his cheeks.

'Darling, oh no,' Lauren whispered. 'Whatever is the matter?'

Either he was hungry again or it was her own fear communicating itself to him. She tried to relax, forcing herself to smile. Now that he seemed to be properly awake, she jiggled him up and down on her knee, then lifted him up so that he could see out of the window.

'There we are, look. Cows. D'you see, over there? Yes! Of course you do.'

She heard the Mexican saying something, the first time he had spoken since they had begun their journey. 'Pardon?' she said, but got no reply. He was muttering to himself angrily.

Alarmed, she whispered to Adam, 'Now be quiet. Just be a good boy and be quiet for mummy,' and pulled him to her. She realized that the car had stopped: they had come to a cross-roads. The Mexican consulted his map, then they were off again and he fell silent.

Lauren began to breathe again. So his anger had been at the map or at the roads which weren't on the map but, anyway, not at her. She looked at her watch and saw it was approaching half-past-six. They had been driving for two hours. She had been sitting, terrified, in the back of the car for two hours, clutching a small baby, with neither drink nor food for either of them and not a word of explanation from the monster who was driving. The realisation of how vilely they were being treated, and how she had so far made no protest or even questioned what was going on made her annoyed with her own passivity.

Well, no more.

'Monsieur?' she said. 'Excuse me, monsieur?'

'What?'

'How long will our journey be? Only I would like to know for the sake of the child.'

'God knows. This map . . . ! We should have been there an hour ago.'

He sounded weary and at his wits' end. It encouraged her to be bolder still.

'I need to buy things for the child.'

He gave a hollow laugh. 'OK, so where would you like me to stop? I mean you see a shop, you tell me and I'll stop.'

She looked out at the hills around them. They were on a road that was little more than single-track, a road they had been on for some time. It wound upwards like a slow helter-skelter then plunged them down into deep and hidden valleys. The shrubland was almost everywhere now, with little sign of cultivation. No more vineyards. The farm buildings they passed might have been derelict but for the sound of dogs barking and the smoke rising from the chimneys.

She said: 'I'm very hungry and thirsty and so is my child.'

She heard herself sounding like the school-teacher she had once been. But never mind: she must make him pay attention to her. She must stop being the cowed and cooperative victim. Besides, wasn't it common knowledge that in hostage or kidnap situations those being held should try and establish a dialogue with their captors?

She tried again: 'I said I'm hungry and thirsty and – '

'Yes, yes, so you want a hotel? You want a cafe? Any of these you see you let me know, OK?'

He was beginning to sound impatient, but she risked a further question: 'Where are we going?'

'You'll find out when we get there. Now madame, please – just keep quiet, all right?'

She had begun to doze herself, her head lolling to the jolting of the car. But then was suddenly awake and on guard, without knowing why. She knew only that the car had slowed and that the Mexican was muttering to himself again, though this time not cursing but rather . . . well, it sounded as though he was congratulating himself.

She saw they were heading up a dusty lane towards a group of farm buildings. So was this their destination? She sat up and placed a protective arm around Adam. She had become accustomed to being in the car and had begun to feel safe there. The prospect of their journey ending filled her with alarm and brought the fears flooding back: that she had been the sole witness to a brutal murder, and had been brought here by the killer for reasons she could only guess at.

They stopped before the farmhouse, which was white with a roof of red tiles, though picturesque only from a distance. Up close, you could see it was ramshackle and neglected. The ground before it was ribbed with baked mud and there was a cluster of outbuildings in various stages of dilapidation. Pieces of rusty machinery lay about in front of the house and, as they approached and stopped, two large, black dogs appeared and began to bark and circle the car.

The Mexican, who had opened his door and been about to climb out of the car, pulled it smartly closed again, cursed and gave a series of short blasts on the horn. A woman in a white apron appeared in the doorway, observed the car, then shouted something back into the house.

The sight of the woman gave Lauren sudden grounds for hope, that here might be an ally, or at least someone of normal human sensibilities – female sensibilities. She now saw there were flowers around the door, geraniums standing in all manner of broken pots and tubs.

Now a man had emerged, pushing past the

woman. Like her, he had the stocky frame of someone accustomed to physical labour; he also seemed
only half-dressed, wearing a vest and trousers and
carrying a towel. He now flapped the towel at the
dogs, shooing them away from the house and into
the barn beside it, pushing closed the wooden door
with his foot.

The Mexican opened his car door again, got out
and closed it, without a word to Lauren. She saw
him cross to the farmer – as she supposed the man
with the towel to be – and they shook hands and
began to talk. Watching them, she had the impression that the car's arrival had been expected: there
was much nodding from both men, then they were
laughing and the farmer was gesturing to the Mexican that he should enter the farmhouse. The woman,
who was still in the doorway, had to stand aside to
let them pass, then she put up a hand to shield her
eyes and peered in Lauren's direction as though
trying to make out who might still be in the car,
before turning and going back into the house herself.

'Well, now they've all left us, haven't they,'
Lauren said to Adam, who was still awake but
silent.

She looked at the ignition but the Mexican had
taken the car-keys with him. Of course she could
open the door and get out of the car, but what then?
How far would she get, making a run for it with
Adam in her arms? No doubt they had been so
carelessly ignored and left alone like this precisely
because there was nowhere for them to go, no-one
for miles around from whom they might seek help.

Still, they were alive, and together. The death of
the young man made their survival seem like an
achievement in itself.

Lauren lowered the car window, then put Adam on her knee so that he might see the hens and geese that were scratching around. 'Look,' she said. 'Hens. Geese.' There would be no baby-talk for him; she had long ago vowed that he would learn the proper names of things from the outset.

Which had been how long ago? It seemed ages had passed, an uncountable span of years, since she had been at home busying herself with baby-grows and sterilizers. Even the word 'home' had an unreal ring to it: a detail from a fairy-tale one might tell to comfort a child.

The Mexican had emerged from the house, now with a cigarette in his mouth. He came striding across the mud towards the car and pulled open the door. 'Bring the child,' he said.

She struggled to obey, alarmed at having to leave the car which had become her sanctuary.

'Where are we?' she demanded, as she stumbled after him back towards the house, Adam in her arms. 'And what's going to happen – '

'No questions.'

She followed him inside, ducking after him under the low lintel of the doorway. She found herself in near-darkness and realized that the shutters were still pulled to across the windows. She felt a stone floor beneath her feet and could smell the aroma of strong coffee. She stood still, frightened to move until her eyes began to adjust and she saw that she was in a long, low room with a wooden table in the centre at which there were people sitting, the farmer and the woman she had seen earlier. She now saw they were both of short stature, probably in their forties and were gazing at her with undisguised curiosity.

'Good day,' she said, but got no reply.

'This way,' said the Mexican, gesturing her towards an open stone staircase at the far end of the room.

Lauren went towards it, picking her way carefully around what she took to be a pile of clothes but then realized was an ancient dog lying supine before an empty fireplace. Above the fireplace a large crucifix displayed the suffering figure of Christ. She gave a cry of alarm as she felt her hair catch on something and stepped back. But it was only a row of herbs and dried fruits suspended from a beam. She ducked beneath it and followed the Mexican onto the staircase.

It was only as she ascended and paused to cast what she hoped was an appealing glance back in the direction of the farmer's wife that she noticed there was another person in the room: a young girl, no more than eleven or twelve years old, with long, straight hair that fell to her waist. She was standing against the wall, her eyes fixed on Lauren.

'Come on,' ordered the Mexican.

She followed him onto a gloomy, narrow landing where one of the doors stood open. It was through this that he now led her, and she found herself in a bedroom which was dominated by a double-bed, with a wash-stand, a chest of drawers and a chair wedged into the spaces around it. He had remained by the door as she entered so that she was aware of his departure only when she heard the creak of it closing.

'No, wait – ,' she cried.

But too late. The door had been pushed to and there was the sound of a bolt being rammed home.

'We need some food,' she shouted, angry now. 'And something to drink!'

There was no response, save for the footsteps

going away. 'Bastard,' she said; then, for Adam's benefit: 'Sorry. Pretend you didn't hear that.' At least it was a relief to be left alone, and to feel she could at last put Adam down in the middle of the bed, which was covered by a heavy patchwork quilt. He lay there, arms wide, gazing up at the ceiling.

Oh, poor love, she thought. What have I brought you to? Out of one prison and into another.

She went to the window, which had a scroll-shaped latch in the centre and which pulled open towards her, then she pushed on the shutters with both hands. They swung open, crashing back against the wall, to reveal a breath-taking view of woods and valleys, over which a dazzling sun had already risen.

And now, too, she could see the room properly. The furniture was rough-hewn and the walls were of white plaster, with just the single devotional picture of The Last Supper tacked up above the bed. The chest of drawers held a few well-worn clothes; there was a willow-patterned bowl and jug on the wash stand but both were empty. In other circumstances she would have welcomed the room and called it simple and charming. Now she wasn't sure. Things had moved with such dizzying speed that she didn't yet know whether this was a place of safety or death-cell.

She returned to the window. The drop to the ground was about twelve feet, too much for her to jump, even without Adam. And then again, where would she go? The view offered her no hope of neighbours or nearby town or village. There was a track of sorts a couple of fields and a copse away but it was hardly the kind of well-used route on which she might hope to flag someone down or hitch a lift.

Adam began to cry. He's hungry again, she thought. Well, yes, it must be the best part of four hours since she had fed him at the service area and then he'd still been partly drugged, not taking as much as he normally would.

She went to him on the bed and began to shush him but then thought no, why am I doing this, the instinctive motherly thing of trying to keep the baby quiet so as not to disturb others? Christ, these were kidnappers and murderers she was trying not to disturb. Let him yell the house down and remind them they had two real, live human beings locked away up here.

'Yes, you tell them' she encouraged him. 'You tell them they can't do this to us!'

Then she heard the bolt on the other side of the door being tugged open. 'Shush, quiet . . . !' she said, in a sudden panic. She grabbed Adam and held him to her as the bolt was finally released and the door swung open.

Standing in the doorway was the young girl she had seen downstairs, holding a tray. The Mexican was behind her. It must have been he who had opened the door.

'Just take it in and put it down,' he instructed the girl.

She came forward to the bed and placed the tray carefully on it, as if she was proud to be given the task but anxious she should do it properly.

'I need a change of clothes for the child,' said Lauren, determined to make the demands before their captor could slip away again. 'And nappies and something to wash him with – '

'Yes, yes,' he said, holding up a hand to silence her. 'All this will come later.'

'Never mind later. I need them now.'

'And what, you think this is Paris?' He waved a derisory hand at the window. 'You think there are shops on every corner? Have a look out there. You can see the Eiffel Tower, eh?'

'There must be shops somewhere,' Lauren insisted.

'Yes, somewhere. But not here.'

She saw that the girl had put out a hand and was gingerly holding Adam's podgy fingers.

'Hello,' said Lauren, deciding to ignore the Mexican. 'And what's your name?'

But she only pulled her hand away as though the words had been a reprimand and stared dumbly at the bed.

'OK, let's go,' said the Mexican.

But Lauren leaned towards her and said quietly: 'My name's Lauren. Won't you tell me yours?'

'Matilde,' said the girl, still without looking at her, and giving a small bob, almost a curtsy, which made Lauren feel she might have been an honoured guest rather than a prisoner.

'Matilde. That's a pretty name. And this is Adam.'

'Adam ... ?' The girl tried the name shyly on her tongue.

'I said come on,' said the Mexican gruffly, but they were now in a small conspiracy to ignore him.

'And do you live here, Matilde?'

'Yes,' said the girl, and then said something else, to do with the bedroom, probably that it was usually hers, but Lauren found the accent unfamiliar and didn't follow.

'All right now, come on, out, out, out ... !' said the Mexican, clapping his hands at the girl as though she were a flock of geese till he had her retreating before him.

481

'Why don't you come back later?' called Lauren as the door was closed and the bolt pushed back into place.

She turned her attention to the tray, which had cold meats and cheese and bread on it, as well as a large cup of lukewarm coffee and a glass of milk. Well, she was grateful for it, of course; but how was she to feed Adam, who was already eyeing the milk with interest?

In the end she used the spoon that had come with the coffee. It was a tedious business, with half of each spoonful dribbling down his chin but a good deal better than nothing. She ate everything else herself, ravenously, and drank the coffee.

'Sorry we can't share,' she said. 'You'll have to wait till you get some teeth.'

When everything had been consumed, she placed the tray on the floor and, feeling weary, stretched out on the bed beside him. She stroked the soft, flat top of his head, talking to him, telling him over and over, 'This is mummy. You remember mummy, don't you. Well, I'm back and I'm never going to leave you again.'

It was a comfort for herself, never mind what he thought, and one she needed, to be able to cuddle up to him and shut out all thought of how they had come to be there and what might still lie ahead. If the rest of the world had receded and abandoned them, as it seemed to have, at least she was reunited with her son, lying with her head touching his and gazing into one another's eyes.

The opening of the door again caught her by surprise. Once more it was Matilde who appeared, but this time accompanied by her mother. Lauren sprang from the bed and began pleading again for the supplies she needed so that she might tend Adam.

'. . . Clothes and a towel, and some water so that I might wash him . . . '

But the woman merely stared stupidly, as though she didn't understand. Or perhaps it was her way of protecting herself, remaining uninvolved in whatever was going on here.

'. . . I'll give you money, look. Take this, please . . . '

But the money didn't seem to interest her either. When Matilde put out a hand to Adam, she gave it sharp rap, then gave her a push so that the child grabbed the tray and scurried from the room. The farmer's wife followed her and the door was closed again.

Lauren flopped back onto the bed and snuggled up to her son. But now she found it harder – impossible even – to forget the precariousness of their situation or to obliterate the memory of that morning's callous shooting and so could only lie there beside him, envying him his innocent sleep while her mind churned with questions, about Revachier, about the Mexican, about why they had been taken to the farmhouse, to which she had no answers.

Lunch was brought by Matilde, this time unescorted. It was a kind of cabbage hot-pot, with another glass of milk for Adam. Lauren ate sparingly with one hand while feeding Adam with the other.

'You know I love you,' she told him. 'So don't mind if I tell you the truth. You're beginning to stink a little bit. Oh, yes, you are. But then I don't suppose I'm all that wonderful to be near either.'

She had spent the morning either sleeping alongside Adam or standing by the window, looking out over the fields and wondering why they had been brought there. The only answer she could come up with was that the Mexican was demanding a ransom from Revachier for their return. So would he pay it? And, anyway, wouldn't it be a ransom for Adam alone? She was expendable. Worse than that, she was a liability, a witness to murder.

The thought frightened her but also struck her as faintly absurd. Her life couldn't just end like that, cut short in this foreign land with no-one around to pay much attention . . . could it?

When Matilde returned for the tray – still alone – Lauren asked if she could have some water and, if possible, some soap and towels please. The child seemed gentle-natured and eager to please. Perhaps it was rare that anyone took much notice of her in that taciturn household.

'Yes, madam,' she said, and lifted down the large water-jug.

Lauren moved to take it from her and said, 'Look, I can do that – '

But the child started back in alarm. 'No, no. I must – ' she said.

Evidently it had been impressed on her that Lauren was not to leave the room.

Well, so be it. So she was under some kind of benign house-arrest. She and Adam would be fed and not ill-treated so long as she remained where she was and didn't try to escape. For how long and what purpose she still didn't dare to contemplate.

There were heavy footsteps approaching along the landing. Lauren moved quickly to where Adam was lying on the bed and placed a proprietorial hand over his tiny one. The Mexican appeared in the doorway. He was carrying a cardboard box, which he placed on the chair. 'This is what you wanted, OK?' he said. And was gone again before she could speak.

She pulled back the flaps on the top of the box and peered inside. It was full of baby things: nappies and jars of food and an assortment of clothing. 'Oh, great,' she muttered. 'Marvellous.' There was even a feeding-bottle. 'Thank you!' she called after him.

Matilde returned and, gasping from the effort, hoisted the now brimming water-jug up onto the wash-stand. She had a towel over one shoulder and produced a lump of soap from her pocket. Lauren took them from her and gave her a hug of delight. Now at least she would be able to care properly for Adam, to make sure he was clean and properly fed.

Matilde seemed inclined to stay, so Lauren encouraged her, letting her hold Adam while she bathed him. The company was welcome but it also struck her that here might be an opportunity to discover something of what was going on.

'Your father – is he a farmer?' she asked, keeping her voice low. Matilde struck her as nervy, frightened even, and liable to bolt at a raised voice or, for that matter, a raised hand.

'Yes,' she said.

'And the lady – she is your mother?'

'Yes.'

'What about the other man, the man who brought me here? Do you know him?'

She hesitated, then said, 'I think he is called Térence.'

Térence. Well, she had learned something anyway and at least didn't have to think of him as 'the Mexican' anymore.

'But do you know why he has brought us here?'

'No.'

Lauren gave a smile to hide her disappointment. So perhaps it wasn't going to be so easy then. Or perhaps the child wasn't so ingenuous as she appeared. Lauren tried again. 'But you knew we were coming, did you?'

Matilde, now speaking with more confidence, said that she knew someone was coming. She had heard her parents talking about a baby. She added that she liked babies and wished they had one of their own.

'You help look after the baby animals on the farm?'

'Sometimes, yes. When I am allowed to.'

'Tell me, Matilde,' said Lauren. 'Do you like Adam?'

Yes, she liked Adam, she said. And stroked his cheek with her finger.

'Then can't you tell me – and tell Adam too – why we have been brought here?'

But once again she only shook her head and said no, she had no idea. Which Lauren, looking into her wide, blue eyes, had to believe.

Still, perhaps there were other things the child could tell her, if not that. Lauren cast around for further questions.

'Have there ever been other people come here and stayed with you?'

Sometimes, yes.

'And have they been locked up like we are?'

No. No, the other people had been visitors. Gentlemen, who would stay for a day or two, then go.

'Do you have a telephone here, Matilde?'

'No.'

'Well, then how did your parents know that we would be arriving – '

Oh, that would be the radio, she said. There was a radio transmitter in one of the barns, the one she wasn't allowed to go into.

She gave a sudden start and spun round guiltily

486

at the sound of the bedroom room being pushed open. Lauren also gasped, feeling that they had been caught in something, but it was only the farmer's wife, standing there and giving Matilde a hard stare.

'Your daughter has been very helpful, madame,' said Lauren quickly, wanting to save the girl from any chastisement that might be coming her way. 'She has been helping me with the child.' The woman gave a begrudging nod, then gestured to Matilde that she should leave. 'Perhaps she could come back later,' said Lauren, as Matilde scurried from the room. The farmer's wife said nothing to that, just gave a small nod that Lauren took to be more of recognition than assent, then stepped out onto the landing and closed the door.

It was as though she didn't want to become contaminated, thought Lauren. As though I'm diseased and so should be treated kindly but at a distance. What was the hospital term for it?

Barrier-nursed.

Though the bright side was that she now had everything she had been pleading and nagging for since they had arrived. (Had it only been that morning they had been driven there? She already felt to have been in the room for a significant portion of her life.) Matilde had brought the water, soap and towel for washing and the box that Terence had delivered contained everything she needed to care for Adam.

Checking that the door was bolted fast – though from the outside, but she could do nothing about that – she stripped off and indulged herself in the delicious luxury of washing herself slowly and carefully from tip to toe. Then she stood at the window to dry off. Outside there was no sound or sign of life. Even the hens and geese seemed to be taking a siesta in the afternoon sun.

She tried to make sense of her plight. Oh, she knew she was only tormenting herself and that a wiser course would be to accept that she could do nothing to influence their fate and so should simply accept it and wait to see what would turn up next. But she couldn't. She had never been one for drifting with the tide but had always needed to know the whys and wherefores of everything and to feel she had at least some kind of tenuous, finger-tip grasp on events. She couldn't change that and would continue to torment herself till she could make sense of everything.

Start from the obvious. Shortly after she had fled Geneva with Adam on the back seat, the alarm must have been raised – either by the nurse whom Bill had given the run-around or by someone discovering the empty nursery. Panic, alarums, despair. (Well, yes, she knew that side of things all too well and didn't wish to dwell on it.)

Then they must have remembered the novice English nurse who had left so precipitously with her cloak wrapped around her. After which, Revachier had sent his employees in hot pursuit and they had cornered her at the service station outside Chalon-sur-Marne because she had been stupid enough to stop and fall asleep.

Then Térence made a phone-call, argued with his companion and killed him.

More-or-less fact up to there, but now a certain amount of speculation had to be mixed in.

She had supposed the phone-call to have been to Revachier but it now seemed a fair bet that it had been to someone else. Perhaps to the farm here. Perhaps Térence and the farmer were accomplices, plotting to hold Adam until Revachier coughed up a hefty ransom. The young colleague of Térence had refused to go along with that and so had been shot in the back and stuffed in the boot of the Corolla.

OK but . . .

Térence had never been to the farm before. That much was clear from his desperate attempts at map-reading and his frequent curses at the remoteness of the place. She doubted he had even met the farmer. Certainly he was a stranger to Matilde.

Which made it unlikely that they had conspired together. More likely then that there was a third party involved here and that the phone-call had been to that third-party, seeking instructions.

Well, yes, possibly. Probably even. But where did that leave her and Adam?

It was a bitter irony to think they might both be dependent on Revachier for their salvation. That it was his money that was going to buy their freedom.

But what happened if he wouldn't pay? Suppose he refused and left the hostages to their fate, what were their chances then when Térence had already demonstrated his willingness to take life if it suited him and she was, whether a ransom were paid or not, the sole witness to that earlier murder?

It came to this: if Revachier paid the ransom, then he would be paying it for Adam and not for her. She was expendable, even someone he might be glad to hear would never trouble him again.

While, to Térence, she was not only expendable but a positive danger.

Twist it as she may – put the best gloss on it she could – it came out much the same and left her shaking and sick with fear. She was being allowed to live only because they needed someone to tend to

Adam. It was Adam to whom she owed her life. Once he was returned to Revachier, she would lose it.

The afternoon dragged by. Lauren, who had dressed herself again in the same clothes, prowled around the room, desperate and tearful, knowing she mustn't give way to self-pity but unable any longer to fool herself that this might be a halfway house to freedom. Adam lay on the bed and played with the discarded wrappings from his new clothes. Every so often, overcome by her fears, she would scoop him up and hug him to her, then he would become distressed and begin to whimper and she would force herself to put him down again and speak gently to him.

The sun moved slowly over the bleached fields. She heard the dogs barking and other squawks and crowings from outside while inside too there was a renewed sound of movement and conversation from downstairs.

At six o'clock the door opened again. This time it wasn't Matilde, as she had been hoping, but Térence who brought in a tray.

'How long are you going to keep us here?' she said, made defiant by her fears.

He shrugged. 'Be patient, madame – '

'No, I will not be patient! I want to know – '

But he had gone, slamming the door behind him. Lauren tried to pull it open but the bolt had already gone home and she couldn't move it. She went to the tray, which had been placed on the bed. There was a plate of liver and onions, a glass of red wine and, as before, a glass of milk for Adam. Well, she would give Adam the milk, of course; but she toyed with the idea of refusing the food as a gesture of protest. Then thought – but what purpose would that serve? Only that I would be helping to kill myself and so saving them the trouble. And, anyway, she was hungry, ravenously so.

Once she had Adam fixed up with his feeding-bottle, she tucked into the liver and onions with gusto and drank down the wine. Well, she might as well enjoy the good things of life while she had the chance.

Térence returned to collect the tray. He looked to be on his guard, watching her in case she should start her protests again, but all she said was, 'I need to use a toilet.'

This seemed a surprise to him, something he hadn't anticipated, then he took the tray and motioned her to follow him downstairs. Lauren went out onto the landing, then waited to hear whether there would be a reaction from Adam. When there wasn't, she followed Térence down the stone staircase into the living-room which now smelt overpoweringly of cooking and tobacco. There was a jug of wine on the table where the farmer was sitting. Of Matilde there was no sign.

The farmer's wife was delegated to take Lauren outside to where the toilet – the old, French type, a hole in the ground basically – was built to the side of the house. Lauren felt a sudden misgiving about coming outside like this, leaving Adam alone. But, of course, this was why her captors were so unconcerned, knowing she would never escape while he was still held by them.

Back in the room, she bathed and changed Adam once again, then lay on the bed beside him and played with him, reciting nursery rhymes over and over until he began to show signs of sleepiness. The fierce light of the day had retreated from the room,

491

leaving it in a shadowy twilight of its own. Lauren went and pulled the shutters closed in order to keep out the midges, then lay beside Adam.

For the moment, fed and weary and believing from the scene she had glimpsed downstairs that nothing more would happen tonight, she stretched herself on the bed beside him and drifted into a welcome sleep.

She awoke in darkness, not knowing where she was. There were voices – men shouting – and another sound, one that it took her a moment to place. The crackling and snapping of a fire . . . !

She gave a cry of alarm and sat bolt upright, looking around, staring against the darkness, and now beginning to see the outline of the room. She put out a hand and felt the warm bundle of Adam beside her, breathing steadily. The sounds were from outside, beyond the shutters, she realized.

She eased herself away from the sleeping child and crossed quickly to the window. One push and the shutters swung open, and now she could see the dancing flames in the field beyond and catch the smoke carried on the night air.

Her first impression was that the whole field was alight. Were they in danger then? Or was this an act of providence, under cover of which she might escape? But, even before she could begin to find answers to the questions, she saw that it wasn't the whole field on fire at all: there were four separate fires, one in each corner. She became aware, too, of figures standing between the columns of flame and smoke, four of them grouped together beneath her window.

Her fear and her hope subsided together. This was no chance outbreak but something deliberate and under control. She and Adam weren't in danger; but nor did it put them anywhere nearer freedom.

She had barely time to wonder what strange ritual she might be witnessing before her attention was wrenched away by the heavy drone of an engine which sounded to be descending fast, coming at them from the other side of the house. She looked up but could see nothing. The figures in the field had also turned and were pointing skywards.

It was descending on the house! The noise was directly above her, making her flinch away. She looked back at Adam, still sleeping, but couldn't bring herself to leave the window.

A helicopter swept into view above her, its underside a gleaming yellow and its blades beating the air so that the smoke from the fires was flattened and sent gusting sideways. She watched, mesmerized, as it circled the field, then began to settle in an ungainly, shuddering fashion, enveloping all of them in the roar from its engines and a blinding, choking swirl of smoke and hot air.

36

She understood now how the fires had been a signal, lit in the four corners of the field in order to help guide the helicopter to a safe landing. But bringing who? And for what purpose? Her assumption had to be that this was to do with herself and Adam, a thought that reawakened all her fears.

She heard a shrill cry from the bed and turned to see that Adam was awake and waving his arms and legs in protest against the noise or, more likely, against the smoky, swirling air that had invaded the room.

'It's all right,' she shouted over the booming of the helicopter. 'Come and see what's happening.' And she lifted him and carried him to the window. His wailing ceased as the leaping fires caught his attention. 'Yes,' said Lauren. 'Yes, I thought you'd like that.'

Though her own attention was on the helicopter, whose blades were now slowing so that the air ceased to surge against the side of the house and the engine noise began to die. Then a door opened in the side of the helicopter and metal steps were unfolded.

Lauren watched with bated breath as one . . . two . . . three . . . three men emerged. They were too far away and, anyway, it was too dark for her to know whether Revachier was among them.

494

They came together towards the house and Térence moved forward from the group of watchers to greet them. Lauren drew back into the room, not wanting to been seen. Adam gave a squawk of protest as being denied the sight of the fires. 'Sorry,' she said. 'You can have another look later.'

She felt she should prepare herself for the worst. Whoever they were, she must face the awful prospect that they might have come to take Adam away. She must be prepared to defend both of them. She clutched Adam to her and looked desperately round the room for some weapon or perhaps something she might use to jam the door closed from the inside but she could see nothing that offered itself as being of any use. Perhaps if she could move the bed . . .

She placed Adam on it, then tried to pull the bedhead from the wall so that she might get her shoulder behind it. Hopeless. For all her grunting and heaving, it wouldn't budge an inch. 'Oh, God,' she said, anguished. 'Oh, God, what? What can I do?' She rummaged in the box that Térence had brought but there was nothing in there more lethal than a wad of nappies.

Well, all right, so she had no weapon and she was one woman against four men at least but she would kill them or force them to kill her before she would allow them to take her son away.

Yet still there was no sound of anyone on the staircase or landing. They had had ample time to have entered the house and climbed the stairs . . . so why hadn't they?

She moved swiftly on tiptoe to the door and placed her ear against it. She could hear voices, male voices, coming from below, then a burst of laughter. Then, as she continued to listen, the voices settled into the steady rise and fall of conversation, in the midst of which she also heard the clink of glasses or crockery.

Had they not come for her at all then? Were they here for some other quite separate reason? She began to hope and pray that it might be so. Otherwise why hadn't they come upstairs to view their captives?

One thing it certainly suggested: Revachier was not among the three men who had arrived. He would certainly have been bounding up the stairs and into the room to reclaim the son he believed to be his own.

Her ear began to ache from being pressed against the door so she went and sat on the bed. Adam seemed to be falling asleep, making his little sounds of contentment as he did so. Well, she wasn't going to sleep. She would sit up the whole night if necessary, guarding her son in case the new arrivals should be waiting until the early hours before bursting into the room and making off with him.

She awoke to find it was morning and she was under the quilt with Adam beside her. She couldn't remember when she had abandoned her vigil and climbed into bed but never mind: at least they were both still here. There had been no midnight raid.

She pushed back the quilt, feeling hot and sticky in her clothes, and went to the window, wondering whether the events of last night had all been a dream but no, there was the helicopter sitting in the centre of the field, no longer the fearsome creature dropping from the skies but a smallish piece of machinery in colours of red and gold. There were four blackened circles where the fires had been.

She tested the door and found it still bolted. Well, all right. It suited her that it should stay that way. She listened and heard muffled voices from below. And let them stay there: that would suit her too.

496

She waited till Adam was awake, then cleaned him with baby-wipes and changed him, using the provision from the box, which were almost exhausted. 'We're going to escape,' she told him as she did so. 'Don't ask me how, but we are.'

She felt a revival of her old determination, the spirit that had carried her this far. It had also been the business of trying to move the bed and finding it so obstinately anchored. An idea had begun to grow: if she hadn't been able to use it to block the door, might she not turn it to a different use?

Her ears caught the scraping sound of the bolt being withdrawn. She moved quickly to place herself between Adam and the door but, when it opened, she saw to her enormous relief that it was only Matilde, piping out a good morning and bringing in the breakfast tray.

'Well, good morning,' said Lauren. 'And how are you?'

'Very well, thank you, madame,' she said with her little bow.

Lauren moved quickly to pull the door closed before she could leave. 'Those men who arrived last night – who are they?'

'I don't know, madame.'

'You've never seen them before?'

'No.'

'But what did they talk about? Did you hear anything of what they were saying?'

'Only that they have been travelling for a long time.'

'Are they French?'

'No, madame, not French. They talk in English.'

This was so unexpected she found it hard to believe. 'English? Are you sure?'

'I think so, madame, yes.'

She was still wondering what to make of this when she heard a heavier tread on the landing outside and, feeling herself caught unawares, turned to see Térence opening the door and entering the bedroom, which was suddenly crowded with not just Térence and Matilde but another man who had come in behind Térence and to whom Térence now turned as though in deference. This man was tall with receding, silvery hair and a hooked nose. He was wearing a suit and an open-necked white shirt. Lauren stared at him fearfully. He looked her up and down and then looked at Adam, who was lying on the bed.

'Ah, he said. 'The child.'

Lauren retreated and put out a hand to Adam. So they did speak English after all: Matilde had been right.

'Oui, monsieur,' said Térence, looking pleased with himself.

The silver-haired man addressed Lauren: 'This is the son of Marcus Revachier?'

'No, he's mine. My son,' said Lauren, and gathered him up in her arms.

The silver-haired man frowned and turned to Térence, who said quickly in French, 'She's lying. She took him from the house. I saw her there.'

He sounded not just anxious to be believed but frightened lest he shouldn't be. This is the man he is answerable to, thought Lauren, the man he telephoned before shooting the young man.

'Whose son is this?' demanded the silver-haired man.

'Mine,' said Lauren.

'Take no notice of her,' said Térence, glaring. 'The woman's stupid, out of her mind.'

The silver-haired man seemed to be controlling

himself with difficulty. Lauren had the impression
of a man not used to being crossed, whose temper
was on a short fuse.

'Revachier is the father!' shouted Térence, moving
threateningly towards Lauren so that she backed up
against the wall. 'Yes?'

'Is this so?' said the silver-haired man.

Lauren looked from one to the other and, with
no choice, muttered, 'Yes.'

'Yes, there!' said Térence, triumphant.

The silver-haired man nodded, apparently satisfied. Though he was still curious. 'And you are his
mother?' he asked Lauren.

'I . . . we . . . my husband and I, we adopted him.
So he's ours. We adopted him in England.'

'I see,' said the silver-haired man. 'Yes, I see.'

'It's Revachier's child,' urged Térence. 'He dotes
on him. I've seen him and, believe me, he'll do
anything to get him back. Anything.'

'Good,' said the silver-haired man. 'So now he is
like the rest of us. He is no longer impregnable.'

And he left the room. Térence gave Lauren a
warning look as though her answers had been some
kind of trick that had failed and that must not be
repeated, then hurried out after him.

Lauren found herself trembling from the encounter. Though the man had said little, she had found
his manner unnerving. In fact, perhaps it was because
he had said so little: making no approach to Adam
but viewing him calculatingly, weighing his value.

Matilde came forward from where she had shrunk
into a corner. 'I have to go now,' she said. 'But can
I come back later and play with Adam?'

'Of course,' said Lauren.

The child gave another of her little bobs and
skipped out of the room.

She had been right then in claiming that the newly-arrived party spoke English but it was only now, with time to reflect, that Lauren was able to identify the accent.

It had been that of the South African, the voice of the Afrikaner.

37

The night following Max's abduction, Marcus remained awake and pacing the house, going from room to room, willing the phone to ring, then cursing when it didn't, going into the nursery and back again to his study. It amazed him that he had once been happy to live alone in this mausoleum. Certainly he wouldn't be able to live in it again unless Max were returned and so its life could be restored. As the night progressed, he set himself hourly deadlines: if nothing had happened by three, then and only then would he go to bed. Then he postponed it to four . . . then to five, when the light began to break and so he decided to give bed a miss altogether and went and had a shave and shower instead.

When the phone did begin to ring, infuriatingly it was only the press wanting to question him. He would speak to none of them and told them so in ugly, insulting phrases. They remained polite and insistent until all he could do was slam down the receiver.

Jacques Martin-Achard had remained with him in the house, cancelling his day's appointments. Marcus had tried to persuade him otherwise but no. In truth, he was relieved, grateful for the other man's presence. They went over and over the circumstances of the abduction; Marcus vowed vengeance and Jacques counselled patience.

501

They reached the second afternoon: twenty-four hours had elapsed since Max's disappearance had been discovered.

'They must be in England,' said Marcus, with a gesture of despair. 'By now they must be.'

'Not necessarily. Remember the woman is travelling on her own, with a child to care for – '

'I shall hire detectives. I shall have her traced. I don't care where she goes or what she does. She can ring her house with steel but she will not keep my son!'

He knew he was ranting but couldn't stop himself. Anyway, he was entitled to this expression of his feelings. This sense of loss and grief was new to him. More so than on the day of the bombing or when he had lain in hospital kept alive by machines, he felt that his very life was in the balance.

'You are certain it is the English couple?' asked Jacques.

'Who else could it be?'

'Some kidnapper or – '

'So why haven't we heard anything? Why haven't they made their demands?'

'Perhaps that will come.'

This exchange, or some variant of it, took place almost hourly. Marcus was now certain that it was the English couple, and not Jarman, who had stolen Max from him. He also believed that Jacques, in his heart, agreed with him. It was his lawyer's mind that made him wary of conclusions that were jumped at and led him to spell out the constant reminder that they didn't yet know, they couldn't yet be sure, who was behind this.

But Marcus knew. It was the knowing that was all the more painful. The knowing without being able to do anything about it.

502

There was still a police-car at the gates, though what it was doing there he couldn't imagine. Closing the stable door. When he questioned those in charge of the investigation, Inspector Marti's minions, he was assured they were doing everything possible and were receiving every cooperation from their French neighbours.

'So why can't they find her?' he moaned to Jacques. 'How many women are there crossing France with babies in the backs of their cars for Christ's sake?'

'Probably quite a lot,' said Jacques prosaically. 'They'll catch her when she gets to the ports or wherever it is she's heading.'

And he offered another thought.

'Look at it this way. Suppose she does get past the police and the emigration people and manages to convey the child to England. Not that I think she will, but just suppose. She can hardly keep the child a secret, can she?'

Marcus hesitated. 'Why not?'

'Because the adoption hasn't been completed and she wants it to be. She needs it to be. So she has to go to the authorities and admit to what she has done. When that happens, I am sure that the Swiss courts will apply the maximum pressure for his return.'

'And the British courts will take not the slightest notice,' said Marcus sourly.

'They may have to. How can they give their seal of approval to an act of this kind?'

'Well, yes, possibly,' muttered Marcus, though far from convinced. His faith in British justice had been severely dented by his experience of the adoption hearing. Besides, he didn't want to have to rely on courts and their long-winded ways. He wanted

503

this crazy woman stopped and his son returned to him before it could come to that.

Yet it seemed more and more likely that the woman had, indeed, given them the slip, all of them, police, emigration, everybody, as they reached the second night and still there was no news of any sighting. Jacques insisted they ate what he called a proper dinner and encouraged Marcus to drink. 'Or take a sleeping-pill,' he urged. 'I'll be awake if anything happens.' Marcus opted for the drink, and got through a bottle of claret and then a couple of after-dinner cognacs. At midnight, with still no news, he shook hands with Jacques and, feeling as sober as a judge, went through the motions of going to bed. It was a surprise to find himself slipping into a fitful sleep, which carried him through the small hours and might have lasted into the morning but for the telephone at his bedside starting to ring.

'Yes?' he said, grabbing the receiver, even before he was properly awake.

'It's me, boss. Térence,' said the voice at the other end.

'Yes, what?' Unable to stop himself hoping: why else would Térence call at this hour if not with news that was too pressing to wait?

'We've found them.'

'You've found ... ?' The words overwhelmed him. It was what he had prayed for but could hardly believe.

'We've found them, yes. We've got your son.'

He offered up a short prayer: Thank you, O My Saviour, for redeeming me by Your death on the cross and now by this. Then asked Térence, needing to hear it again: 'You've found Max?'

'Yes. And he's OK. Being well looked after.'

Now Marcus was wide awake, pushing himself out of bed even as he spoke into the phone. 'And where? Where are you?'

'Well, quite a way out. Way off the beaten track I can tell you –'

'But in France?'

'Oh, sure. France.'

'And the woman? She's there, is she?'

'Yes, she's here. She's still looking after the child. But don't worry – she's not going anywhere. And listen, boss –'

'What?'

'Well, things aren't that simple. I mean we can't just bring her back, or bring the child back.'

Marcus froze. 'Why not?'

'The cops are here and they ... See, she's told them that the child is hers and of course we've told them how she's stole him from you and ... well, I don't think they know who to believe.'

'But they're not going to let her go?'

'No, I don't think there's much chance of that. Not till they've sorted the whole thing out.'

'Tell me where you are,' said Marcus. 'I'll come immediately.'

He could picture all too clearly how the crazy woman would have insisted that Max was hers, citing the cock-eyed judgement of the English court. No doubt she would urge them to consult the British legal authorities to have her story confirmed – which was why he had to be there to put the other side, to establish that he was the true father and she a common-or-garden kidnapper. The French police might well have looked askance at Térence and Beat and been inclined to favour the woman; but he didn't doubt that the truth would prevail once he were there in person to champion it.

505

He threw on his dressing-gown and ran to his study and, picking up the phone there, took down a page of directions from Térence.

Well, he'd been right in saying they were way off the beaten track: somewhere in the North-East, wedged between the Belgian and German borders so far as Marcus could judge. With more time he would have questioned Térence on why the woman had struck out in such an unlikely direction and, for that matter, how on earth he and Beat had managed to pursue and catch her, but such things could come later.

(Part of the answer occured to him as he flung himself into the shower: she would have been wary of the French ports and would have been planning on crossing into Belgium and taking the boat to England from there, trusting that the Belgian authorities would not have been alerted to stop her.)

He roused Eduardo and told him to prepare the car for a long journey. While that was being done, he went to the kitchen and grabbed a cup of coffee and some toast. Which was where Jacques found him. He had been awoken by the sudden activity about the house and was anxious to hear what had happened to cause it.

'They've found Max,' said Marcus, smiling.

'Yes?'

'Térence and Beat. They caught up with the woman in France.'

'Oh, wonderful,' said Jacques, taking his hand. 'Oh, that really is wonderful.'

'I know,' said Marcus, touched by Jacques' elation and pleased he had been able to give him the news himself. 'But I have to go. The police are making things difficult.' And he gave him a resumé of everything Térence had told him: how the French

506

police were being forced to decide between the two competing accounts.

Jacques' smile had faded during the telling. 'Could be tricky,' he mused. 'It re-opens the whole question of the authority of the British court and your claim that – '

'The woman kidnapped him!' protested Marcus. 'There can be no question of that surely!'

'Well, no but – '

'Anyway, that's why I've got to be there.'

And the sooner the better, before it became a matter for the lawyers to pontificate over – though he wasn't going to say that to Jacques. Something else he wasn't going to admit to Jacques was his hope that this might be settled by a quiet, ex gratia payment to the policemen on the spot.

Jacques poured himself a coffee. 'How long is it since they were found?'

'Well, I'm not sure. Not long ago by the sound of it. Perhaps sometimes during the night – '

'By Térence?'

'Well . . . yes.'

'And the French police were there already? Or did they arrive later?'

Marcus could only shake his head, admitting that he didn't know. There had been no time to ask – and what did it matter anyway?

'I'm just wondering why they haven't contacted the authorities here in Geneva.'

'They might have.'

'Then why haven't we heard?'

Marcus shrugged, not really seeing the point of this either. 'Middle of the night,' he hazarded. 'Most of these people work office hours, don't they?'

'Well, yes but . . . look, can you just give me five

507

minutes? I just want to make one or two calls. See if I can find who else knows about this.'

Marcus suppressed his feeling of irritation at the prospect of a delay, however brief, and said that yes, of course he would wait. How else could he response to a request from the friend who had stood by him through the last two dreadful days?

He went to find Eduardo and gave him the sheet of instructions he had taken down from Térence. The young man's eyebrows rose as he read them.

'Don't worry,' Marcus reassured him. 'We'll find the place. Only I want to be there fast.'

Eduardo shrugged. 'Sure.'

Marcus went back into the house and found Jacques replacing the telphone and shaking his head as though puzzled. 'I don't understand.'

'No?'

'No-one seems to have heard anything. I mean from the French police. There's been no communication, nothing.'

'Perhaps they don't want to admit they have Max until they can decide what to do with him, whose story to believe.'

It was a thought that made him all the more impatient to be away. There had been enough debate and speculation; the house had contained more of it over the last thirty-six hours than it had over the last ten years. Without being rude to Jacques, he needed to begin the journey to his son.

'But, anyway, whatever the reason ... I really must go.'

'Let me come with you,' said Jacques.

Marcus smiled and pretended to consider the offer, though knowing full well it was the last thing he wanted. Later perhaps he would need Jacques, his counsellor and lawyer, by his side; but, while

508

things remained in a state of flux – as they seemed to be, with the police not knowing which story to believe and the Swiss authorities not even having been informed of the child's whereabouts – well, he wanted a free hand to influence things as he saw best. It might mean playing the bully; more likely, it would mean greasing a few palms – the overjoyed father understandably wishing to reward those who had reunited him with his son. Whichever way he had to play it, Jacque's presence would be more hindrance than help.

'I know you would,' he said. 'And I'm grateful. Believe me, I am. But I need somebody here, somebody I can rely on.'

Jacques seemed inclined to argue. 'If the child has been taken into police custody – '

'We don't know,' said Marcus, cutting him short. 'We don't know anything. Which is why I must go. And why I would like to know you are here, holding the fort, yes?'

He was on his way through the door even as he spoke, leaving Jacques with little option but to agree. 'Well, I suppose there are one or two more people I could ring, see if they know what's going on . . .'

'Yes, do that. We'll keep in touch.' He threw himself into the back seat of the car. 'Go,' he said to Eduardo. 'As fast as you can.'

The idea of escape was now uppermost in Lauren's mind. The arrival of the helicopter and the visit of the distinctly sinister silver-haired man had transformed it from a vague notion to be attempted if and when opportunity presented itself into a matter of life-or-death urgency. She couldn't believe that she and Adam would be left undisturbed in the

509

bedroom for much longer; the farm-house was only a transit-camp, a rendezvous point for Térence to hand them over to the men who were now here and who were unlikely to be planning on a long stay.

She still had no idea of where she would go or how she and Adam would survive out there in the open countryside; even so it offered a better chance than meekly sitting and waiting for their fate to be decided for them. The silver-haired man had made it abundantly clear that he was interested only in Adam. Adam was the real hostage, the pawn in whatever game they were playing. She was being tolerated only as his nursemaid; once separated from him, she would become an embarrassment to be disposed of.

Her first thought had been to consider escape via the landing and stairs. It would be easy enough to get out of the bedroom, especially if Matilde continued to be entrusted with the job of serving their meals. The problem was that the stairs took her directly into the living-room, which she was unlikely to find deserted. What she had seen of it had suggested a room permanently occupied – except perhaps at night, but that was when their own door was closed and bolted.

Which left only the window.

It was the bed that had inspired her to think of this as a possible escape-route. The heavy, wooden double-bed which had proved impossible to move when she had had the desperate notion of using it to barricade the door. Useless as a barricade, it might though make the perfect anchor.

'We'll try it,' she said to Adam. 'Why not? What do you think.' He gazed up at her and gave a small hiccup. 'OK,' she said, 'but don't forget we're in this together.'

She took a sheet from the bed and began to gnaw at it with her teeth. It was a thin cotton, worn even thinner over the years, and split easily. She tore it into three roughly equal strips. At about six foot each, that gave her a comfortable length to each from the foot of the bedstead over the sill and to the ground outside. Though she would need more to tie Adam to her.

As plans went, she knew it was hardly devastatingly original – more Girls' Adventure Annual stuff – but it had always worked for those heroines of her childhood so she saw no reason why it shouldn't work for her now.

She was beginning on the second sheet, ripping at it with her teeth, when she heard a faint creak on the landing and then the sound of the bolt being withdrawn. She gave a start of fear – if she should prove to have delayed too long! – and stuffed both the whole sheet and the one she had already torn under the quilt. Then she stood over Adam, ready to take him into her arms, and faced the door.

It was Matilde, only Matilde. Lauren gave a gasp of relief. 'Well, hello,' she said. 'Come on in.'

The girl stepped forward cautiously, concentrating on the tray she was holding, fearful of spilling anything.

'Why, thank you,' said Lauren, taking it from her. She saw there was a thick mug full of steaming black coffee and a glass of milk. 'And would you like to give Adam the milk? Yes, I bet you would, wouldn't you.'

Matilde nodded and said, 'Yes, please,' so Lauren transferred the milk into the bottle and settled her on the edge of the bed with Adam on her lap. At the same time pushing the door closed. It would be her last opportunity to try and discover more about the new arrivals and what their own plans might be.

But this time Matilde needed no pumping. 'The men who came last night are planning to kill somebody,' she announced.

Lauren stared.

'Yes.' The girl nodded, proud of her information and the effect it had achieved. 'I know because I heard them talking. And they have guns. I've seen them.'

'And who . . . ' Lauren could scarcely form the words but it was a question she had to ask, ' . . . who is it they're going to kill, do you know?'

Matilde shook her head. 'Someone who is coming here.'

'What, coming to the house?' said Lauren, seizing on that. She had wondered whether it were her own execution the child might have been unwittingly announcing. But, if it were someone who hadn't yet arrived, then it couldn't be her . . . could it?

'Someone who is coming here,' repeated Matilde. And added, 'There's a man watching the road. And mama and I, we have to go away, to Uncle Gerard's.'

So it wasn't her; there was another intended victim, Lauren concluded, taking what crumbs of comfort she could. But when was all this to happen? How would it affect her own plans to escape?

'But when is this? When are you going to your Uncle Gerard's?'

'Soon.'

'This afternoon?'

'Yes.'

'And do you know who – listen, Matilde, this is important – do you know who is coming? Who it is they are waiting for?'

She shook her head. 'A man,' she said, and turned her attention to Adam, who was clutching at her

512

hair. All this talk of intended murder means nothing to her, realized Lauren; she was accustomed to being excluded from the world of grown-ups and paid as little attention to it as they paid to her.

Even so, Lauren took her information seriously. She had seen enough of Térence to believe that his associates were capable of anything. And now she wondered, this man they were waiting for – could it be Revachier?

She remembered what the silver-haired man had said: 'So now he is like the rest of us. He is no longer impregnable.'

Suppose she had been wrong in thinking that she and Adam were being held for ransom? Suppose, instead, they was there as bait, to entice Revachier out of his stronghold and into the trap that was being prepared for him? Amid her fears for herself, she felt an unexpected concern for the man who had for so long been her enemy, the man who had claimed Adam for his own. Set against the brigands now holding her, he struck her as less enemy than ally. She may have hated him and still feared him for his determination to wrest Adam from her, but that didn't extend to wanting to see him gunned down. If only there were some way she could warn him . . . ? But no, that was foolish and wistful thinking. She must concentrate only on getting herself and Adam out of the firing-line.

She saw that the bottle was now empty and took it from Mathilde. 'Thank you, Mathilde. And now I think you ought to go and get ready for your journey to your uncle's, don't you?'

Matilde said, 'Oh, there's no hurry. They said he won't be here yet.'

'Even so,' said Lauren, and took Adam from her.

Matilde took her cue and trotted to the door. 'Goodbye, Madame.'

'Goodbye.'

And God bless, thought Lauren. You're a kind child who deserves better than this. Then she had to smile as she heard the bolt shoved home. The kind child was very much one of their gaolers, perhaps even a double-agent, going downstairs now to report their conversation to her parents.

She pulled the sheets from beneath the quilt and renewed her attack on the second one, soon splitting it with her teeth into another three strips. Now she had more than enough both to allow her to reach the ground and to fasten Adam to her.

She stored them under the bed and wandered over to the window. The sun was remorseless, producing a heat haze over the distant hills. She tried to guess what might be her best route once she had hit the ground and was running. There was no alternative but to cross the open field, which still had the helicopter sitting in the centre of it. If only she could commandeer that and fly away to freedom . . . ! Now, that was strictly Girls' Adventure Annual. No, the best she could hope for was that she would make the trees at the far side of the field without being spotted.

Matilde had spoken as though Revachier – if, indeed, it were Revachier who was due to arrive – would not be there until later in the afternoon. Arguably that would be the best time for her to make a break for it, while her captors' attention would be elsewhere.

She thought suddenly of James, poor James, anxious and alone, wondering why she hadn't rung. And no doubt still worrying that she might earn a black mark in the eyes of the court. She gave a sad smile at the thought, the innocence of it. Well, she would ring him as soon as she could, ring and apologize.

Right now she had other things on her mind.

38

Sitting in the back of the Mercedes as they swooped past everything else on the motorway, Marcus had time to consider the call he had taken from Térence and the questions it raised, questions he had thrust aside since all that mattered then had been that Max had been found and how quickly could he get to him.

For one thing, how had Térence and his partner, Beat, managed to track this woman down to a farmhouse in the wilds of Picardie? Marcus' forlorn hope, when he had sent them out in pursuit, had been that they might come across the woman within a hundred kilometres or so inside France. Even that would have been a miraculous coincidence, but to have lighted on her after some four hundred kilometres and some thirty-six hours after the child had been taken . . . that suggested either the greatest of good fortune or brilliant detective-work. Neither of which he could quite believe. The thought began to haunt him that there had to be more to this than met the eye and that Jacques had been right to be suspicious.

What's more – according to the account given him by Térence, the French police seem to have been gifted with a similar omniscience, for they had managed to turn up at the same time and in the same place . . . !

No, he didn't believe it. He couldn't believe it, however desperately he wanted to.

So Térence was either telling him an outright lie or, anyway, a highly doctored version of the truth. The problem was that he couldn't believe that either. Térence had been one of the first guards to be assigned to the villa and so one of the longest-serving. Admittedly, he was something of a poser, with his belt of cartridges slung over his shoulder, but even he must know that Marcus would kill him if he were to attempt any kind of deception involving Max. Besides, he would be eager for the reward and would surely do nothing to jeopardize that.

So perhaps . . . perhaps this really was a chance in a million and this woman had been tracked by both Térence and the French police to a remote farmhouse in Picardie and every word of the account Térence had given him was true.

He would dearly like to think so. He would give anything to have it true. But, of course, he would find out only when he got there, when it might well be too late to do anything about it.

He rang Jacques on the car-phone. 'Any news?'

'Only that I've been speaking to Inspector Gaillard. You remember the one who – '

'I remember.' Gaillard was a big man with a soldier's bearing, whom Inspector Marti had placed in charge of the investigation. And who, as he had told Marcus, had five children of his own.

'I told him about the phone-call from Térence and that we were looking for confirmation. So he contacted his French opposite-number, then range me back.'

'And . . . ?'

'Well, nothing to report. His French opposite-number had heard not a dickey-bird.'

516

'And where is he based, this French opposite-number?'

'I'm not sure. Nancy, I think.'

So Nancy was a long way from Picardie and, if it had all happened in the middle of the night, then those involved might have been understandably reluctant to have roused their superiors from their beds. Particularly if the situation threatened to be embarrassing with the kidnapper claiming to be the child's mother and nobody knowing what to make of it.

'Marcus, I think you should be very careful.'

'I will be.'

'I'm not saying that Térence is lying but I do think – '

'I know. I know. But what can I do? The only way to find out the truth is to go there, and I'm halfway there already.'

He didn't want to tell Jacques of his misgivings in case they should turn out to be misplaced. It was still in his interest to keep this low-key, something he could handle on the ground when he arrived. Though a certain amount of insurance wouldn't go amiss.

He leaned forwards and said to Eduardo: 'I want to call at the warehouse.'

Calling at the warehouse involved a detour towards Dijon and the addition of perhaps half-an-hour to their journey. It was a windowless, brick building, indistinguishable from those on the industrial estate around it save for the encircling barbed-wire-topped fence and the security camera peering down inquisitively above the door. 'REVACHIER – EXPORT ET IMPORT,' said a discreet sign. It was here that the bulk of his arsenal was stored.

He knew that his unannounced arrival would cause his chief storeman, who was called Doncoeur, to run around like a headless chicken, whatever pains Marcus took to reassure him that his calling was of no importance, a brief stop on the way to somewhere else. And no, he had no time to discuss anything, even those matters which Doncoeur considered urgent; they would have to wait. He went to his own small office, which was kept locked, and collected a Smith and Wesson point forty-five automatic and a hundred rounds of ammunition, signing out for it in the correct fashion. Then he wrapped the lot in a plastic bag, said goodbye to Doncoeur, who was still in a condition of mild shock, wringing his hands and smiling nervously, and hurried back to the car. Seeing Eduardo standing by the open door, smoking a cigarette, he took a quick decision.

'I'll drive myself from here,' he said. 'You see Monsieur Doncoeur. He'll arrange transport for you back to Geneva.'

'You are sure, monsieur?' said Eduardo, surprised.

'I am sure, yes.' Whatever he would find in Picardie, he didn't want to have to be having to concern himself with the welfare of some callow Italian youth.

Eduardo shrugged and moved away towards the warehouse. Marcus threw the gun and bullets onto the front passenger seat and drove off, heading back to the auto-route.

The unease he had begun to feel earlier, the growing suspicion that the phone-call from Térence had been a hoax, had now resolved itself into a quiet fury. That his son had been taken had been bad enough, a blow which had left him reeling; but to have his hopes falsely raised, that would be a betrayal of the bitterest kind, an unforgivable act of treachery for which Térence would pay dearly.

Lauren had waited – this had been her plan – waited for the house to settle into the same siesta-like torpor that had descended upon it yesterday afternoon, believing that that would be the best moment for her escape attempt, but the sound of conversation and movement had continued below till she had begun to despair of its ever ceasing. She reminded herself that there were three new arrivals also present in the house; no doubt they were involved in whatever preparations had to be made to greet their luckless victim, this man they were going to kill, as Matilde had casually put it.

Some time in the middle of the afternoon Lauren heard a lorry or van start up and drive away; she supposed that it was Mathilde and her mother off to seek refuge at Uncle Gerard's.

And after that, finally, the murmur of conversation did at last die away.

Perhaps the men had gone outside: she had no way of knowing. Her view was limited to the back of the house and there she could see no-one. She took a deep breath and told herself it had to be now – now or never. Though her heart was thumping with fear and she delayed for more long minutes, listening and watching, half-hoping that something would happen to cause her to postpone the attempt further. But nothing did. The house had either fallen asleep or was alert and watching – anyway, there was a continuing silence. Outside the window all was stillness, the hills beyond hazy with the accumulated heat of the afternoon.

All right, she told herself, so what're you waiting for?

She had already knotted the lengths of torn sheet together and now, with clumsy, trembling fingers, she tied one end of the chain to the foot of the bed. Wanting to be sure that it would hold, she pulled on it as hard as she could: the knots tightened and the bed remained solidly immobile. Next – and perhaps the most difficult manoeuvre of the lot – she took the two spare strips of sheet and used them to tied Adam onto her back. She had thought about this and decided that the only way was to wrap the strips around him – with knots to stop them tightening – then to lie beside him on the bed and to pull and fasten them around herself. It required the skill of a contortionist but she finally managed it, and then gingerly got to her feet, with Adam riding her back like a papoose.

Her head was full of nightmares, competing visions of everything that could go wrong, the first and most terrible of which was that she would hoist herself out through the window and then find – too late! – that Adam had wriggled free and was plummeting to the ground while she screamed helplessly after him. She checked the knots again and took a few experimental jumps to make sure they would hold.

She could feel Adam's warm breath on her neck and would have even sworn she heard him chuckle as she bounced the two of them up and down.

She went to the window, stuck her head out and looked around. There was no-one to be seen and, just as important, no sign of the two dogs who had threatened them on their arrival. 'OK, Adam?' she said in a voice that trembled only slightly. 'We're going to slide down, so you just cling onto mummy.' The area on her back where he was pressed against her had already become hot and sweaty. 'Here goes,' she said, and threw the free end of the tied-together sheets out of the window, knowing as she did so that the die was now cast and she had to go through with it.

She gripped the material with both hands, heaved herself onto the window sill, then wriggled and pivoted until her legs were sticking out into the open air. She took a new, firmer grip on the sheet and eased herself backward into space.

The sheet strained but held. She stayed there, elbows on the sill, for a moment, teetering on the brink, then began to lower herself inch by inch, clinging to the material and taking small steps down the wall, its stones seen in sudden up-close looking pitted and pourous. Her shoulders ached as Adam's tiny weight pulled her earthwards. He gave a whimper but she tried to shut him out, to ignore him, and made herself concentrate instead on moving first a foot and then a hand, then the other foot and then the other hand. The sheet pulled painfully against her fingers. Her grip failed her for a moment and the material scorched her palms till she could seize it again and hang on, controlling her descent. It couldn't be more than a few feet now but she forced herself not to look down, not until she had taken another small step downwards, shifted her grip, taken another step and shifted it again, the effort becoming enormous on her arms to a point where she felt she couldn't continue.

Till she realized that she was almost there, the ground no more than a couple of feet below her. She swayed above it, not wanting to drop lest Adam should be dislodged, managed a further hand-over-hand descent, then let go - landing with a bump and reeling backwards but managing to keep her balance.

She heard herself groan aloud from the pain in her arms and shoulders but now there were other fears assailing her: that she might be seen – or even shot at. She pulled at the knotted sheet around her, which at first resisted her shaking fingers – the knots had pulled tight during her descent – then came free so that she had to crouch down to allow Adam to slide from her back. She saw the startled look on his face as she gathered him up, with no time to release the strips of sheet around him so that they too were gathered up in her embrace.

'Good boy,' she said. 'Oh, you good boy.' And she began to run, away from the house and across the field.

She saw only the ground in front of her and heard only the sound of her feet on it and her own harsh breathing, cocooned in the physical effort being demanded of her. Seventeen, eighteen, nineteen . . . she counted the steps as she ran, not knowing why but unable to stop the numbers going through her head. The helicopter loomed in front of her, no longer a distant toy but large and menacing, making her swerve around it, ducking under the blades though she knew they were many feet above her head. Then swerving back so that the line she was following would place it between her and the house and give her a few seconds' cover.

All the time being aware of the target she presented. The thought went through her mind that she would probably never even hear the shots that would hit her and so would have no warning.

The field seemed to stretch forever. She gulped in the hot air, fighting to keep her breathing regular. And now Adam was beginning to cry, protesting at the way he was being thrown about in her arms. She clutched him more tightly to her and fixed her sights on the trees that seemed to be receding ahead of her. If only she could reach them and get among them, then she would allow herself a pause, would grant herself the luxury of stopping and looking back. Until then she would keep going . . . seventy-five, seventy-six, seventy-seven . . .

She was twenty, then ten, yards from the trees when she saw – though she could scarcely believe it – the figure of a man. He was standing there. He was waiting for her.

She gave a cry of despair and stopped so abruptly that she almost toppled forward and had to take a few more steps to regain her balance.

'No,' she moaned. 'Oh, no, please.'

She didn't know what she meant: please let me go or please let this be an illusion, a mirage.

'So,' said the man, stepping towards her, 'we meet again.'

And she knew it was no illusion, no mirage, no trick of her fevered imagination but the flesh-and-blood man she had last confronted in Adam's nursery, her old enemy before these new enemies had arrived to supplant him – Revachier – there in front of her, cutting her off from the copse of trees and the safe haven towards which she had been heading.

39

She could only stare, still terrified by his appearance
before her and, anyway, she was gasping for breath,
incapable of speech. He gave a twisted sort of smile
and said, 'Once again you're trying to steal my son.
Well, this time – '

'No, no,' she protested weakly. She took a quick,
desperate glance back at the farmhouse: miraculously, there still seemed to be no sign of activity, no
alarm being raised; only the torn sheet hanging
from the window like a long, white flag, irrefutable
evidence of her escape. 'I'm trying to . . . trying to
save him . . . '

'It's fortunate I decided to approach the house in
this rather unconventional fashion,' he said and
stepped towards her. 'Otherwise I might have missed
you.'

She shrank away. What was she to make of
things now? Was he in cahoots with the men inside
the house or had she been right in her earlier guess
that Adam was being used – had now been successfully used – as bait to draw this man, Revachier,
into a trap? Not knowing, she heard herself blurt
out: 'They're going to kill you, the men in there,
they're – '

'Really, madame?' he said, seeming unmoved, not
believing her. 'And what men are these?'

524

'Three . . . I don't know who they are.' She gestured wildly. 'They came in the helicopter.'

For the first time she sensed her words had reached him. He looked past her at where the helicopter was standing, then back to her.

'Please,' she said. 'It's true.'

But her hopes she might convince him were dashed as he stepped towards her and raised his hands. 'Give me my son, madame.'

'No!' It was almost a shout. Suddenly she didn't care about alerting her captors. Let them come running with their dogs and guns. This was a worse threat – that she might lose Adam again to this man. 'No, he's not your son – he's mine!' And she hugged him to her, her body poised for combat or flight, daring Revachier to try and take him.

He stared, checked for a moment by her sudden fury. 'You are – '

'I'm his mother. I'm his mother and he's my son!'

He nodded, as if this answered a question for him. 'You think that because the English court – '

'I adopted him!'

'He is not for adoption. He is my son. Now give him to me – '

Lauren braced herself to resist, then heard a distant shout and turned. There, at the side of the farmhouse, one of the men had appeared. He shouted something again – she couldn't tell what; alerting his colleagues no doubt – then he ran back around the front of the house and disappeared from view.

She saw that this had also claimed Revachier's attention and said quickly, 'They're going to kill you. Please believe me. They're going to kill you and they're going to kill Adam as well!'

She saw him hesitate. 'Max,' he muttered.

525

'What?'

He gave a quick shake of his head and demanded, 'Who are these men? The police?'

'No!' How could he be so stupid? She was becoming frantic, wondering what she could say that would make him understand. 'I told you, they came in the helicopter!'

But he only shook his head. 'I think they are the police. And I think we shall go and meet them and get this whole thing sorted out, yes?'

He stepped forward and took her arm.

'No!' she screamed, wrenched her arm free from his grip and began to run, thrusting her body forward as though to a finishing-line so that she was at last into the covering shade of the trees. But then he had caught her again, gripping her more harshly this time, his fingers digging into her flesh, so that however she wriggled and pulled she couldn't get away.

With all the time Adam held between them and being thrown to and fro despite her efforts to shield him. Now he began to cry, a long, miserable wail that made both of them stop, frozen in mid-struggle.

'If you harm my son . . . ' Revachier said.

'He's not yours!'

There were more distant shouts, that made both of them turn. A line of three men . . . no, four . . . had spread itself across the field and was advancing towards them.

She searched for something, anything, she might say to save them. 'Listen. Please, listen. They're not the police. They're . . . well, I don't know who they are, but there was a girl in the house and she told me . . . ' She knew she was gabbling, not making much sense but what else could she say?

'One of them's a South African.'

She felt his grip slacken. 'South African?' said Revachier softly.

'Yes,' she said, staring at him and seeing his face go slack, wondering why those words should have had such an effect: it was as if she had stunned him with a blow. He had now let go of her altogether.

'South African, yes,' she said. 'Tall with grey . . . well, silvery hair and – '

But now he was looking at the figures moving towards them across the field. 'Quick, back here,' he said, his manner suddenly as urgent as her own as he pulled her into the deeper shadow of the trees. He believes me, she realized with surprise and an immense relief, then she gave a start of alarm as she saw him produce a gun, a heavy-looking pistol, from his pocket.

She hugged Adam to her. He had stopped crying now but was squirming to be free.

Revachier had moved a small distance, nine or ten yards, away from them and was peering out at the approaching figures, who had advanced as far as the helicopter. 'You're right,' he said and then: 'Thank you, madame. Thank you for saving my life.'

Lauren said nothing, wondering – if, indeed, that was what she had done, saved his life – what the cost would turn out to be. Besides, she was mesmerized by the gun he was holding and which he now raised to eye-level, gripping it with both hands. She felt herself flinching in expectation of the firing and placed her hands over Adam's ears. There was a loud crack and the gun jerked upwards. Revachier steadied himelf, then fired again. Another crack, like a branch or thick ice breaking.

There came a flurry of distant shots in delayed

527

reply, weak-sound after the close-up report of Revachier's gun. But with them came a whining and splintering in the trees around them, prompting her to crouch down, trying to shield Adam with her body.

'Here ... !' Revachier was shouting, and she looked up. 'Take these, quick!' He was holding out a bunch of keys. She rang forward, still bent double, and took them from him. 'Go straight ... ' He gestured with his arm into the trees beyond. 'When you come out of the wood, you'll see my car. Get into it and wait for me, yes?'

'Yes ... yes,' she assured him. They were allies now, in this together.

'Go on!'

And he turned away, gripping the gun again. Lauren began to run in the direction he had pointed, picking her way through the gloom of the trees. She heard him loose off another volley, then became too busy keeping her feet over the uneven ground, avoiding the treacherous roots that threatened to hook her feet and send her sprawling, to listen for any response. The shield of trees thickened behind her and she felt confident enough to straighten up and slow to a steady trot, her own laboured breathing now louder in her ears than the spluttering shots.

She came out of the trees into sunlight and stopped until her eyes adjusted. And there was the car, as Revachier had promised, a maroon-coloured Mercedes, pulled onto the grass from a road that was little more than cart-track. She jogged over to it, shifted Adam to her left arm and fumbled with the keys until she found the one that opened the door.

A voice in her head was urging her to hurry. She would get into the car and drive off. How foolish he had been to think she would obediently wait and so run the risk of losing the son she had regained from him! She must drive off before he could dispose of his enemies.

Though how to do so while keeping Adam safe was a problem. She must find some way of wedging him in the back seats of the car so that she would be free to drive.

And quickly, quickly before Revachier could catch up with her!

She lay Adam on the rear seat, then hurried round to the boot and heaved it open. There was a rug inside, thick and folded. 'Oh, yes,' she said, 'yes.' She lifted it out, pull the boot closed, then took it and made a sort of nest on the floor of the car between the back and front seats. 'Something else you haven't to tell the agency about,' she said, placing Adam inside it and rearranging the folds until she was satisfied he would be safe enough, at least till she could come up with something better.

She closed the door on him and moved towards the driver's seat. She was still shaking with fear and from the effort of her charge across the field and then through the trees. Her clothes were sweaty and stuck to her as she moved. She swept back the damp strands of hair from across her face and looked back into the wood, trying to envisage the battle taking place beyond it, wondering who was firing the shots that were now coming less frequently.

So go, the voice urged her. What are you waiting for? Get in the car and drive!

She sat in the driver's seat, found she had to stretch for the pedals and took a few precious moments to understand how to move it forward. Then had once again to find the correct key, this time for the ignition.

Now then. Go!

'Oh, God,' she said in despair, letting her hand drop from the key she had been about to turn.

How could she go? How could she drive away and perhaps sentence Revachier to death by doing so when he had allowed her to escape to safety – and to bring Adam with her – placing himself between them and their attackers? He must have seen the possibilities. He was no fool and must have known she might have been tempted to drive off and abandon him. By giving her the keys, he had placed himself in her power.

No-one will ever know this, screeched the voice inside her head. And you will have Adam with you for the rest of your life!

And, anyway – becoming cleverer, weighing the odds – it might not be Revachier who appears out of the trees but one or more of his enemies, and then what good will your stupid sacrifice have been? You owe it to Adam, if not to yourself, to drive away now!

Well, yes, she knew that, but even so . . .

She realized, with a fresh alarm, that the distant popping had stopped. She waited, hardly daring to breathe. A minute - she resolved she would wait no more than that, which was surely enough to give him time to get to her if he were able. She looked at her watch, then, when she looked up again, there was a flash of movement between the trees and, with a lurch of despair, the awful realization that her chance had gone, she saw Revachier emerging, now without the gun and coming towards her at a slow trot.

Go now! go now! the voice screamed.

But now it was too late. He was too near. The car was angled away from the track so that she would have to manoeuvre it before she could go forward.

She cursed herself for her weakness, her pathetic failure of nerve that, having come this far, she had allowed her resolve to soften and now faced a defeat that was of her own making.

He seemed to stumble but kept his balance, holding out his arms as though on a tight-rope. She watched, puzzled as he began to move, no longer towards her, but sideways. There was something wrong. He had been hurt perhaps . . . ?

Despite her feelings of dismay at herself and her renewed fear of him, she pushed open the car door and stepped out. She saw that he was falling and sprang forward, her own arms out to grab him, but too late – he collapsed to the ground even as she arrived beside him.

'What . . . ? Are you all right?' she said, bending over him.

It was then she saw the blood, pumping from the wound in the side of his chest, the side that had been turned away from her as he had approached. She gave a cry of dismay and looked around, as though there might have been help she could summon, but of course there was no-one.

So go now, said the merciless voice inside her head. See, how you've been given another chance!

She knelt beside him. 'It's all right,' she said. 'I'll help you. We'll get you to . . . ' Well, to somewhere, she didn't know.

She put an arm beneath him, trying not to look at the pumping blood or at his ashen face. She attempted to lift him but he was too heavy for her.

'Can you get to the car?' she appealed.

He shook his head.

'Yes!' she insisted. 'Come on. I'll help you!'

His lips were moving but, even when she bent

531

close over him, she couldn't hear the words. She heard a faint groan, then nothing. She forced herself to look at his wound and saw that the flow of blood had stopped.

'Oh, come on!' she cried. 'You must!'

But he lay still. She took his wrist and felt for a pulse, finding none.

So now will you go? asked the voice.

She left him lying there, scrambled back into the car and fired the engine. There was nothing to do but drive – in whatever direction. The car reared and bucked over the bumpy track and she winced, thinking of Adam in his cocoon on the floor of the car, though she could not stop: the important thing was to keep going forward without a backward glance, without even thinking of the slaughter she was fleeing.

After long minutes of this, the track joined a road. Lauren looked at the sun and chose the direction which she judged the more likely to be north. The first sign she came to confirmed her choice: carved in stone so she had to slow to read it, it said 'LA BELGIQUE 50 kms'.

An hour later she was crossing the border, being waved through by a youthful guard who barely bothered to glance at the car, much less check what it might contain. For the first time she allowed herself to think that the gods might at last be on her side, aiding and abetting her escape.

She stopped briefly in a small town called Gembloux, where she bought a change of clothes for Adam and drinks and some food for them both. It seemed to be market day. Anyway, no-one minded her, even when she found herself weeping though not knowing why. Was it for Revachier, who after

532

all had been Adam's father and was now dead, or simply a mechanical response of her own body, overwhelmed with relief that she had her child at last? Oh, things remained to be resolved, she knew that: there might well be legal wrangles and even official disapproval awaiting her and then, in time, there would be the consequences of all the bloodshed she had witnessed, that must surely one day reach her. Yet none of these challenges, however uncomfortable they might turn out, would be sufficient to wrench Adam from her.

She dried her tears and they had a small picnic in the car. (Another detail to be resolved: what to do with the car? Leave it on the quayside? Probably, yes – it wasn't really important.)

Adam was showing signs of sleepiness as she wedged him once again below the back seat. She drove on into the setting sun and found herself on a motorway that took her around Brussels and towards Ostend. She knew now that everything was in her favour and she would not be stopped.

She followed signs to the car ferry terminal and, taking Adam with her in her arms, went to enquire about tickets. Yes, there was a crossing that evening and, yes, they could certainly take her and her child. Only one thing remained. She went to a cluster of telephones and awkwardly, because she was still holding Adam, picked out the number of the home she had left so long ago and then waited for James to answer, picturing the hallway and him entering it with his long stride, so that she might arrange for him to meet her and tell him she was bringing home their son.